Snow slithered down Quinn's expensive, silk-lined boots, but she laughed, her heartbeat slowing. "Remember that fragile ego, Buster."

"That a challenge?"

The heat in Pierce's whisper promised a hint of what she could expect after he undressed her. Anticipation shook her. "I'd throw down my glove but my fingers would freeze."

"Warming fingers is my specialty."

"There you go. Being eager again."

Ahead, blue lights flashed, police radios crackled. Three whistle-blasts stopped her at a red light. Pierce's voice faded in the crunch of tires. She yelped and jumped sideways. Her bum ankle buckled, collapsed. She groaned. A savage grinding of gears released the metallic taste of adrenaline deep in her throat. She rolled onto her side, flailed to get to her feet, imagined a car fishtailing on the ice.

Blood roared in her ears. She scrabbled backwards, twisting her head toward the car she couldn't see.

Stand up. She had to stand. Had to...get...away.

Instinct warned trying to stand promised disaster. Ice demanded crawling. Crawling offered a small hope of survival. She flopped onto her stomach. Her wrists wobbled. On the second try, they supported her weight. Her heart beat too hard. Too fast. Unable to catch her breath, she tucked her head and crabbed across the icy sidewalk. Too late, panic shocked her like electricity.

Wrong way—she was going the wrong way.

Turn around. Turn...

A blur of black rolled toward her. Closer and closer. Headlights blinded her. She opened her mouth. Wind swallowed her scream.

Praise for Allie Hawkins

"Allie Hawkins has a deft touch with romantic suspense, drawing her characters so they become real to the reader and defining the conflict. The story comes alive, so much that the reader gets lost in the plot. Could not put it down once I started it."

~Desiree Holt

Enjoy figuring out the identity of the killer!

Unraveled

by

Allie Hawkins

Allie Hawkins

12/11/12

This is a work of fiction. Names, characters, places, and incidents are either the product of the author's imagination or are used fictitiously, and any resemblance to actual persons living or dead, business establishments, events, or locales, is entirely coincidental.

Unraveled

COPYRIGHT © 2012 by Allie Hawkins

All rights reserved. No part of this book may be used or reproduced in any manner whatsoever without written permission of the author or The Wild Rose Press, Inc. except in the case of brief quotations embodied in critical articles or reviews.
Contact Information: info@thewildrosepress.com

Cover Art by *Debbie Taylor*

The Wild Rose Press, Inc.
PO Box 708
Adams Basin, NY 14410-0708
Visit us at www.thewildrosepress.com

Publishing History
First Crimson Rose Edition, 2012
Print ISBN 978-1-61217-553-9
Digital ISBN 978-1-61217-554-6

Published in the United States of America

Dedication

As always, thank you, David,
for your patience and support and encouragement.

Other Titles by Allie Hawkins

Presumed Guilty

Chapter 1

The Country Club Plaza - Kansas City, Missouri
Monday Before Thanksgiving—6:15 A.M
25° Fahrenheit

Hissssss. A faint rustle whispered through the desolate underground garage like steam escaping through a crack in hell.

Quinn Alexander stopped. She tuned out the buzz from the overhead fluorescents, cocked her head, listened and heard...the lights.

Great. Six nights without sleep, waiting for the overdue birth of her first niece, and she was hearing things.

Or not.

Exhaling, she hitched the unwieldy box of doughnuts off her ribs and suddenly felt every one of her thirty-four years. Stale gas fumes overpowered her favorite aroma of sugar and grease. Talk about hell.

Warning—Brain is stressed. May overheat. May even hear bumps in the dark.

A red light on a surveillance camera stared at her like a peeping Tom. She jutted her chin at the electronic voyeur and shuffled onward.

Thank God Pierce never went over security tapes. But if he did, she doubted he'd notice the bags under her eyes or give a second glance to her loose coat.

1

Would he realize she'd lost five pounds?

Five pounds and your mind.

Quinn groaned and shifted the briefcase higher—a micro-inch away from calves abused from walking in skinny, three-inch heels.

Forget Pierce. He doesn't give a damn you're sleep-deprived. Or that you could pass for a recently exhumed corpse.

Actually, not that good. She grimaced and juggled the pastry box. Thinking about Pierce proved she needed more sleep. When her brain wasn't AWOL, she forgot he existed.

Uh-huh.

Hisssss.

Heart stampeding, Quinn teetered on the damn heels. The weight of her briefcase pitched her off balance. She yipped, danced sideways and managed to remain upright despite the pastry box. She stood unmoving. Held her breath. Death-gripped the briefcase. What better weapon against a mugger?

Silence eddied around her. Deep. Scary.

Scary, dammit, because she'd heard something. Not once, but twice. She might look like a corpse, but her ears worked fine. She'd heard...something, but what?

Her stomach clenched. For the first time, she noticed darkness shrouded the nearest corners and posts. She picked up her pace, confident she'd beat her staff into the office. She'd down a gallon of coffee and laugh at how easily six sleepless nights had derailed logic.

Hisssss. A masked figure, sporting a black cape, leaped out of the shadows like a Cirque du Soleil acrobat.

Quinn's throat closed. Her mind balked. Seeing is *not* believing.

"Yo! Hot mama!" The guy pirouetted and gave her a half bow. Coming upright, he threw out his chest and snapped one arm up over his head. The cape swirled away from his slim, hard body. Yards of shiny fabric hissed through the air like a giant bat wing unfolding.

"Oookay, these doughnuts are to die for, but this—" The grease oozing from the box proved she wasn't caught in a nightmare. "Wha-what do you want?"

"Whatever you want to share with me." His pale green irises were huge, his pupils overly bright, but Quinn detected no hint of booze or pot. Was he high? Sick? Dangerous? How dangerous?

"What's that mean?" She focused on his bushy orange moustache.

"Whatever you want to share with me," he repeated in a subtly mocking tone.

"You know we're being taped."

"What's to tape?" The guy caressed his moustache, leaned toward her and wiggled his long nose. "Me sniffing Lamar's?"

"Here! My compliments." Knees shaking, she pushed the box at his chest and realized her mistake. Damn, she should've set the goodies at his feet. Muscles in her arms quivered, but she lifted the box a millimeter closer to his nose. "Early Thanksgiving appetizers."

"Appetizers. Cute." He twirled the cape around his body.

"Cute is me screaming my head off." Quinn shuffled backwards. Her briefcase banged her knees.

She yelled and hopped from foot to foot like a rapper. *Drop the damn box.*

"Watch out!" A human torpedo, he raced toward her.

Splat! The box broke open and two dozen golden wheels rolled onto the grimy cement. Years of playing first base came back to Quinn. She dropped the briefcase, screamed an enamel-shattering screech, and scooped up four sticky doughnuts.

Wham. Wham. Wham. Wham. She fired her missiles at the bastard's head. His orange pigtail whipped across his chest like a mad rattlesnake. He tap-danced in place, dodging her first three pitches. The fourth one smacked him on the cheek.

"Stay back." She panted, her shoulders rising and falling faster than she could fill her lungs. "I'm—I'm—I'm bringing out the marshmallows next."

He laughed and vaulted over the golden line. "Let's talk," he whispered as if they were good friends about to share a secret. "Just you and me."

"How about you talk to security? I'm sure the guard's on his way. He watches the cameras 24/7."

"I'm thinking he went for chocolate-glazed sinkers. They'd hit the spot, doncha think?"

Her insides sloshed around like a washing machine foaming with too much detergent. She yanked her briefcase off the floor and held it in front of her, chest high. At five-ten and a hundred thirty pounds, she'd at least give him the mother of all headaches. "Stay back."

"Careful you don't drop your shield and break a toe." Crouched low, cape slung over his shoulders, he circled her, humming.

She rotated in a counter-clockwise parabola,

keeping him opposite her. Her biceps screamed. Her throat was so dry she couldn't feel her tongue. Sweat blurred her vision.

Wild-eyed, he swooped in on her. His cape billowed behind him. He cackled and came so close he blasted Quinn with cinnamon breath.

Dread propelled her thrusts. God, what if she brained this guy?

Riiight. He towered over her by a head. Aiming for his wrist, she lunged. He leaped straight up in the air, turned twice and landed with the precision of an aerialist on a high-wire.

"Hope those aren't your breakfast, Mama."

"You—" She sucked in air. "You should cut back on sugar."

"Heh, heh. Your mistake, Mama."

Her feet felt like frozen rib roasts as she planted them in a wider stance, hoping to offset the wobble of her high heels. Her arms trembled, but she shoved the briefcase in short, tight jabs. If she wasn't careful, he'd bash in her brains.

Behind her, a door crashed open. "Freeze! Police!"

The guy's shriek raised the short hairs on the back of Quinn's neck. She dropped to the filthy pavement like an extra in a low-budget horror flick. This guy was a nutcase.

He stared at her for an eternity, then tossed a silver canister over her head.

Smoke blinded her. Pride evaporated. She rolled over the doughnuts and hit the nearest wall.

****

Forty-five minutes later, bald, slim-waisted Detective Todd Miller stood in the middle of Quinn's inner office. His search had revealed no sign of the guy in the garage or an accomplice. "You ought to review that video ASAP, Miz Alexander."

Oh, goody. Exactly what she needed—a tape of her nosedive.

"Today's out." Quinn could imagine—meeting Detective Miller's steady blue gaze—a furious Pierce insisting they watch the tape. Together. At least twenty times. "I'm expecting a call any minute."

"Watch while everything's fresh in your mind. Pure luck the security system rebooted when it did and the guard caught sight of you with Cape Guy and called us. We need details."

Quinn shook her head emphatically. Her knees burned, her ribs ached, her lower back throbbed. Dirt and oil and sticky crumbs coated her skirt, but nothing mattered except that phone call. "We expect my brother's first baby any minute. In St. Louis. I can't hang around reviewing videos of kooks."

A V appeared between Detective Miller's thick brows. "How do we know he's a kook?"

"First, he didn't threaten me. It wouldn't surprise me if he swore I attacked him." She ignored the tingle under her fingernails. "He's a dim bulb. Creepy, not dangerous."

"And not your typical stalker."

Stalker? Quinn shivered. Why not dim bulb? Unnerved, she stared past the policeman to the phone. *Ring, dammit.*

"Gonna be there for the delivery?" Miller segued to the new subject with an easy, toothy grin inviting openness.

In my dreams. Quinn shook her head. "My sister-in-law's had a...difficult pregnancy. She wants no one but my brother present."

"Let me guess. Is he a cop? Or just a workaholic?"

"Investment banker." Quinn stopped edging the detective out the door. "Michael makes workaholics look like slugs. The less he sleeps, the bigger the deals he closes."

The smell of her smoky clothes hurt her head, and she was talking too much. But bragging helped ignore the flutters spreading to her chest. "How'd you know?"

"When my wife got pregnant, I racked up major comp time." Detective Miller smoothed his bald spot, shrugged. "Baaad decision. I should've stayed home more."

"My sister-in-law wants a Stay-At-Home-With-Pregnant-Wives Law." Quinn rolled her eyes. "She also wants nothing but the best for her firstborn. Think Harvard Law School."

Detective Miller whistled. "I'd have to work non-stop for the rest of my life."

"If anyone can balance work and fatherhood," Quinn boasted, "it's my baby brother. Lucky for me becoming an aunt's a no-brainer."

A sharp pinch twinged under her left breastbone. Another no-brainer?

Giving up fantasies of babies with a man she couldn't trust. She closed her eyes. Opening them, she caught Detective Miller studying her. She raised her chin, then blasted him with a full-voltage laser smile.

As a rule of safe business practices, Quinn saved full voltage for executives—decision makers—she courted to hire the computer-hotshots she represented. Full voltage never failed, and her executive search business had soared in the past four years despite the Great Recession. Nobody beat her at matching professional computer wonks with prestigious firms. Generous firms that respected their employees' skills, rewarding them—and her—handsomely.

In the outer office, Detective Miller reverted to cop mode, extracting Quinn's promise to lock the glass-paneled front door whenever she worked alone. "Incidents like this happen on The Plaza more often than you might think." His serious blue eyes never blinked. "You can't be too careful."

"No, you can't." Quinn bit her tongue, smiled, and shook his hand hard enough his eyes widened in surprise.

Did he assume she was dumb as a rock because she was blond? Did he think she'd stayed here late night after night, weekday and weekends, with her door unlocked?

Just doing his job, she soothed her cranky inner critic.

Right now, her job was damage control. Get cleaned up. Dig out new pantyhose. Change clothes. Then...spin the guy in the garage to her three savvy employees without scaring them to death.

****

Five minutes after Detective Miller's departure, Quinn gasped at her reflection in her tiny bathroom's mirror, then ignored her wild hair and glassy eyes. If makeup could make the dead presentable, there must be hope for her.

Of course she needed a miracle to get cleaned up before her associates showed up. Straining to hear their voices in the outer office—where she'd left every light blazing—she washed her scrapes and cuts. She ripped open a box of Band-Aids and peeled off a cover. And another. And another. Two strips turned back on themselves, wrapping around her fingers like mutant leeches.

Damn. Damn. Damn. She pried off the ruined adhesive strips, mashed them into a ball and tossed it into the trash. Her back spasmed, and air whooshed out of her lungs. She grabbed the sink, inhaling deeply. Slowly, the sharp needles in her back turned to dull stabs.

Dammit. She didn't have time for this. Not even if Michael didn't call.

The back pain receded. She stood, stiff all over, but thanks to half a dozen Band-Aids, she'd manage without a full body cast.

"Lame, Quinn," she muttered and reviewed her plan to order more doughnuts.

When the order arrived, she'd call Leah, Janelle, and Sami into the conference room. While the three primed their arteries for Thanksgiving, Quinn would ease into the incident in the garage. Her clothes stunk of oil, but she'd downplay the details, stoking her co-workers' excitement about the baby.

"Fluke," she mumbled. Not incident. Incident sounded too much like a near-mugging. As she inched the second leg of her spare pantyhose over the mosaic of Band-Aids, the phone in her office rang.

Thank you, God. She lurched to her feet, fighting the pantyhose and staggered out of the bathroom. A close encounter with a wing chair triggered a replay of her nosedive in the garage.

Nosedive, not concussion. She kicked free of her

chastity belt and raced for the phone. Who said women can't handle stress in the corporate world?

Caller ID confirmed her hunch. Michael. Excitement hummed in her veins.

"Yes! Yes! Yes! This is it, Baby Bro." She punched the speaker phone and yelled, "Boy or girl?"

"Pierce Jordan's a rat bastard."

"Whaaat?" Her brother's unexpected malice shattered Quinn's skin-tingling anticipation. His mention of Pierce sent her heart pounding.

Forget Pierce, think baby. Static crackled. Michael's voice faded, died. Two hundred and fifty miles away, the drone of St. Louis traffic came through loud and clear.

"Michael?" She fell into the leather chair behind her desk, jammed the receiver against her ear, and ignored a Call-Waiting beep.

A flashing red message light replaced the beep. Tough, but Michael came first.

"Earth to Michael. Earth to Michael. Godmother Quinn calling." She erased images of her younger brother in a car wreck and visualized him behind the wheel of his new Mercedes.

Not the car for a father-to-be, Mom had observed with no criticism in her tone. Still, Quinn had jumped to Michael's defense. He worked hard. Too hard. He earned the big bucks. Provided for his family. He deserved a reward. A Mercedes wasn't illegal, immoral or illicit, so where was the harm?

More static, a squawk, Michael's voice. "...fired...Rex."

"Whaaat?" Quinn pressed the phone harder against her ear and stared at the light. She and Detective Miller had talked to Pierce's security czar. He must've informed Pierce she was okay. Must've tattled about her refusal to review that damn tape.

He's calling about Rex. The logic-leap made sense. If Michael was so furious about his best friend he hadn't bothered asking about her, Pierce must be livid—about having a security problem and having to find a new computer wizard to replace Rex.

Her heart twisted. Unwelcome tears stung her eyes. She blinked, reminding herself Michael knew nothing about the fluke in the garage. Expecting him to ask about her was childish. As for Pierce calling to start the search for Rex's replacement, he could stand in line. Soon-to-be new dads needed to conserve their patience for wailing babies, anxious wives and sleepless nights. Any problem that interfered with Michael bonding with his newborn had to be resolved. Now, if not sooner.

Call Waiting beeped again. Pierce never had considered patience a virtue.

Michael boomed, "Jesus, Quinn! Did you hear a word I said?"

"Uh-huh." The beep in her ear stopped. She rubbed a spot on the desk, but saw frame after frame of her and Pierce finishing their business reviews with mind-bending sex on the shiny glass surface. Of course she'd thought they were making love and unspoken promises.

"Quinn!"

She swallowed, her throat so dry she inhaled twice. "Sorry. I spaced out for a sec."

"What the hell's wrong with you?"

"Nothing's. Wrong. With. Me." Four calls in ten seconds represented a record—even for Pierce.

"Someone should've knocked His Pierceness off

his hobby horse years ago."

She flinched, hating the flutter in her stomach, and tried to marshal a defense.

A snort from Michael wrecked that coping technique. "You're a wimp, Big Sis."

"Am I?" Show her a wimp who fought off caped crazies with—

"Let's say I put a gun to your head." Michael's offhand tone carried a shot of venom.

Her breath caught. She should tell him how she'd felt three years ago when he asked her to find the perfect job for Rex.

"Which would you choose, Quinn? Arguing, or appearing buck naked on Oprah?"

"Your point being? Oprah's left her daily sho—"

"Ten times out of ten, you'd go with Oprah." Gotcha rode his undertone of certainty.

"I see." He knew she loathed arguing, but he didn't have a clue how much she'd always disliked Rex, his bud since kindergarten. She massaged her temples. The sleet smacked her floor-to-ceiling window, cracking like bullets.

"You know I'm right." Aggression sharpened his words.

"I know I don't like arguing. That makes me a wimp." Stiffness crept from her bruised knees to her neck. "Pierce, on the other hand, lives to argue. In your eyes, that makes him a bastard."

"Go ahead, defend your prince." A long sigh. "I'm not like you. I don't pretend life's a fairy tale."

Eyes stinging, she crossed her fingers. *Don't let him go there. Please. Not today.*

"We both learned a long time ago shit happens," he

said.

In self-defense against his words—harsher because he whispered them—she tuned him out, but couldn't tune out another Call Waiting. Pit bulls showed less persistence than Pierce.

"Pierce fires Rex. Who cares?" The silkiness in Michael's tone telegraphed danger.

Quinn picked up the silver-framed picture of her and Mom seated in front of Michael in his Mizzou cap and gown. She knew she should care about Rex, but she didn't.

Not a truth her brother wanted to hear. She said, "Just tell me why Pierce fired him."

The question rang in her ears as Michael kept on ranting. He hurled new slurs at Pierce's character and lamented Rex's fate. She heaped Rex with silent curses. Selfish, demanding, whining jerk. Some friend—saddling an exhausted father-to-be with one more problem. She exhaled then interrupted.

"But why?" she insisted, willing her voice to remain neutral.

"Because he could, the SOB." Michael drove home the rest of his message by shouting, as if she were deaf and stupid. "Did the bastard ever look back after he pierced your heart?"

Shame caught in her throat. She whispered, "He never pierced my heart as you put it. We broke up—"

"Yeah, yeah, yeah. His Pierceness can screw over anyone he damn well pleases." Between the third or fourth regurgitation of this insult and the repeated beeps of Call Waiting, Quinn developed a splitting headache.

And it wasn't even eight o'clock.

Chapter 2

"Your call is being transferred to auto—"

"Goddammit, Quinn!" Pierce Jordan punched DISCONNECT, counted to five, and hit REDIAL for the umpteenth time and listened to the robotic intonation of Chatty Cathy.

Staring eight stories down, unable to see Brush Creek Park through the fog and sleet, Pierce knew his short fuse was lit. He wanted to kill Rex Walker. He should've known the little weasel would run straight to Michael Alexander.

Of course Michael lost no time putting the screws to his big sister.

Pierce swatted REDIAL, listened to a nanosecond of white noise, and slammed the receiver back in the hook. "Sonofa—"

The gold-framed picture of his parents skittered across the polished desktop. He fisted both hands. He wanted to punch Rex Walker, but Quinn...what did he want to do to her?

The question mocked him. He pivoted around and stared at his reflection in the dark, sleet-flecked window. The grimace spreading over his face belonged to a TV-tough guy—all that make-my-day rage. His teeth buzzed with cold fury.

Christ, how could he help Quinn when she'd rather kiss a snake than accept ice water from him in hell?

A sharp knock sent an iron fist into his gut. He'd barked no interruptions at his secretary when she arrived at 7:24.

"Better be good, Linda." He swung his chair around to face the door. "I'm sitting here butt-naked."

She pushed the door wide open, looked down her long, bronze nose like an Aztec princess, shrugged. "Steve needs a minute."

At six three, a hundred eighty pounds and at-attention posture, Steve Cutter looked like the retired U.S. Marine Colonel he was. He shook hands with Pierce firmly enough to crack a few dozen bones and got right to the point.

"We had an incident in the garage a little while ago."

Surprise, surprise. Pierce motioned his security chief toward a wing chair. "What'd the weasel do? Total my car on his way out?"

Steve snorted. "Walker left docile as Mary's little lamb."

"You mean he's smarter than we gave him credit for?" Pierce glanced at the phone. He didn't give a damn what happened in the garage, but trusting Steve, he said, "Go on."

Steve's black eyes flashed—the only signal he was flesh and blood, not stone. "Minutes after he drove away, some weirdo scared the bejesus out of Quinn Alexander."

Feeling sucker-punched, Pierce jumped to his feet. "She's okay?"

"Scraped up. Probably black and blue by now. Laughed in my face when I offered to take her to ER. Informed me her brother's baby is overdue, Made clear she had no intention of going to ER. I don't mind saying I shut up."

Dry-mouthed, Pierce chuckled and eased back into his chair, but couldn't stop the video unwinding in his head. *Before dawn a week ago. Quinn entering the elevator. Like two strangers, they chat for six and a half seconds about the weather. A pause. Awkward, stiff. He asks about Michael's baby a second before the doors open at her floor.*

"Due anytime." Waving, she hustles off, schlepping her hernia-inducing briefcase, never glancing back to make sure the door hasn't closed on Pierce's arm or he hasn't had a fatal coronary.

The mental video stopped. Pierce said, "She'd raise the dead for Michael."

The older man showed zero reaction to the hyperbole. He waited a beat before saying, "The security breach isn't Joe's fault. Some kind of virus took our system down. The hacker was damn sophisticated. I can't find zip. Since the buck stops with me, I'll resign now or—"

Pierced leaped up, planted his knuckles on the desk, leaned forward. "Find this guy."

A flush spread along Steve's jawline. He nodded, got to his feet. "That's the plan."

Pierce straightened from his orangutan-pose, but hot blood kept churning in his brain. "Any ideas where to begin?"

The former Marine looked Pierce straight in the eye. "Makes no sense, but the first thing I'm going for is a connection between our wannabe-mugger, the hacker, and Walker."

The door snicked shut behind Steve. From the

corner of his eye. Pierce watched sleet slam the windows. He exhaled through his mouth and hit REDIAL one more damn time.

One more damn time, he got Quinn's voice mail. Voice low and harsh, he left his seventh demand to call him ASAP. Christ, he'd love to hear the spin Michael was putting on this.

Poor Rex. We can't turn our backs on him, Quinn. He's like family, Quinn. You know Pierce hired him because you asked him, Quinn.

Pierce nodded in agreement with this last bit of the imaginary monologue. It didn't matter the personal relationship between them had ended in bitterness. It didn't matter the weasel was the only bad hire she'd ever recommended. Guilt after their break-up had made Pierce stupid enough he'd hoped somehow to regain her friendship.

Friendship, hell! He stared at the gloom swallowing the park. He'd wanted to crawl back in her bed. Figured if he hired the weasel, she'd give him a chance. He'd ignored every instinct, disregarded his better judgment, and hired the cocky little bastard.

He wasn't about to disappoint Quinn.

And she wasn't about to disappoint Michael. Then. Now. Or ever.

The realization stung. Pierce jerked open his top drawer. He removed the weasel's file. His fingertips buzzed as if he'd touched a live wire. An electrical current shot to his brain, and he saw how Quinn's brother would bring her to her knees.

He would, of course, play the A-card.

Jesus! As if being abandoned by his father thirty years ago explained why Rex Walker embezzled five million dollars from people who had never hurt him in any way.

"Five million bucks," Pierce whispered. Fuckingincredible Walker had pulled it off. More fuckingincredible how many people now knew.

Christ, what a fuck-up. The fallout was going to be ugly.

The ashes in his gut stirred, but he laughed at the irony. Would Michael trot out the ugly scapegoat argument?

Hell, let him. The weasel was a thief. Not up there with the talented Bernie Madoff, but would even tabloid readers feel sympathy for the bastard?

Pierce closed his eyes, reading imaginary headlines. Abandoned at Birth, Disfigured Computer Whiz Embezzles Five Million Bucks!

Pierce pinched his nose, studied the ceiling and edited his imaginary headlines: Disfigured Computer-Whiz-Turned-Embezzler Will Walk.

Without repaying a dime. Or spending a day in jail. Or losing a night's sleep.

"Sonofa—" Pierce pulled out the report that had knocked him for a loop. Let the shit hit the fan. He'd take care of Quinn.

First, though, he had to make sure he'd covered his own ass.

****

"What? No Lamar's?" Nineteen-year old Leah's yelp carried through Quinn's closed door and into her office. She covered the receiver. How much longer could Michael ventilate?

"Shhh. Quinn's on the phone." Officer Manager Extraordinaire, Sami ruled the outer kingdom. "It's not as if there's no Santa Claus."

Muffled laughter made Quinn smile. Horns honking and tires screeching stopped her cold. "Michael?"

She grabbed the receiver and jammed it against her ear. Please, let him be okay and she'd give up sarcasm forever.

She imagined pressing his head against her heart, holding him, protecting him, soothing him the way she'd done so many times when they were kids sharing her guilty secret.

"Michael," she whispered, her voice thick.

"Damned rubberneckers." He spoke in a quiet, amused tone, sounding more like himself than at any time during his tirade.

"You okay?"

"Peachy. One-celled organisms would outscore these rubberneckers on an effing driver's test." He sighed. Long. Loud. In the next breath he said, "You know that damn job is Rex's life. It means everything to him. If he does something stupid, it's on Pierce's head."

"Okay, okay. I realize Rex's computer-analyst identity hinges on thinking he's as intelligent, as interesting and as important as DAs and MDs." Two dozen white roses and a handwritten thank-you note had arrived from him for the past three years on his anniversary with Jordan Banking Consultants.

"Pierce does nothing related to business without a reason," she said. "Why'd he fire—?"

"He claims Rex embezzled five million dollars."

"Five mill—" Quinn's brain ran down like a broken toy.

"Rex swears he's innocent. I believe him."

The hard, flat pronouncement discouraged further questions, but dozens of them collided in Quinn's head. In this post-Madoff age, how could anyone embezzle five million dollars? How did Pierce determine Rex's guilt? What, or who, tipped him off? Were there other suspects? Was Pierce pressing criminal charges?

After her ears stopped ringing, she asked, "Where is Rex now?"

"Across the street. In the park. His Pierceness escorted him out of the building."

Weak knees and aching ribs reminded her of her fall an hour earlier, and now she'd fallen into this quagmire. Was it too late to back out?

And upset Michael?

Risk an argument that could end in a car accident?

Potentially rob her unborn niece of a father?

The hollow in her stomach contracted. She closed her eyes, unwilling to face the irony. Why couldn't she like Rex? Michael had always considered him his younger brother.

"I'm worried, Big Sis." Michael's compassion drew her unwillingly back to the present. "He sees his whole future going down the toilet."

Her guilt buttons started going off like fire alarms, but she inhaled and held her breath. No rushing toward inevitable capitulation. If she shared a bit about her morning... Seemed only fair her own brother should listen for a while to her problems.

Since he has none of his own at the moment.

Something inside her shrank, and shame made her voice small. "Is he going to call me?"

"Let me call him. He's afraid you won't believe him. How long before you can see him—ten, fifteen minutes?"

"Why wait?" She glanced at the clock, felt her stomach lurch, but lied anyway. "My first appointment's at nine-thirty. He can come over right—"

"Won't work." Her brother's impatience felt as if he'd shaken her, the way some adults shook children who dared to disagree.

Carefully neutral, she said, "Why not?"

"He doesn't want to risk a showdown with Pierce."

"But he wants me to go out in the cold?"

A blip of silence deepened. Her heart clanged in her ears. Kansas City's not Siberia, she thought, ready to surrender. Michael didn't need attitude from her.

As she opened her mouth, he whispered, "You—of all people—can't give Rex a break?"

****

The laughter died as soon as Quinn stepped into the outer office. Lounging against Sami's desk, twenty-year-old Janelle recovered first. "Whoa!"

Sami's dark eyes widened. "What happened?"

"You did take the other babe out, didn'tcha?" Janelle jabbed a right over Quinn's head like a prize fighter.

"Janelle!" Sami and Leah said in unison, their eyes bright with curiosity.

"Do those bruises have anything to do with no food?" Janelle punched an imaginary opponent.

Feeling naked under their scrutiny, Quinn nodded. So much for makeup camouflaging scratches and bruises. "When I get back, I'll tell all." Quinn tugged the collar of her wool coat, glad to postpone telling them about the fluke in the garage. "In the meantime, who needs a carb fix?"

Groans gave her the answer she expected. Afraid she'd never leave if she delayed longer, she told Sami to dispatch the cab, warned them to save her at least one glazed chocolate fat pill and slipped out the door before anyone fired off more questions.

Luck was with her for the first time that day. The elevator arrived empty and made no stops on its descent to the lobby. Joe had gone off duty, replaced by George, another senior citizen. He made noises of commiseration about her "troubles."

"Let Joe know I'm offering a reward if he loses that tape."

"Oops. Mr. Cutter already took it."

"Darn." Quinn snapped her fingers, gave George a glib wave and sailed outside into a blast of Arctic air that collapsed her lungs. Sleet pelted her face, snaked past her scarf and formed ice-clumps halfway down her back. An eerie, silvery fog reduced her visibility to the level of the legally blind.

Her heart banged her ribs. Worries about the security tape evaporated. Her major concern now was surviving a trip commonsense advised forgetting.

"Only for you, Michael," she muttered and stepped gingerly off the curb to cross Forty-Seventh to Brush Creek Park. Jaywalking was illegal, but her guardian angel, or maybe it was sheer dumb luck, guided her safely to the other side, which, illogical as she knew it was, felt a hundred times darker than the steps in front of The Jordan Building. She glanced over her shoulder. Nothing visible except her breath. Fog had engulfed the eight-story building she'd just left. Mist and shadows surrounded her. For a second, she was back in the parking garage.

Panic uncoiled in her stomach, rushed up to her chest and roared in her ears. "Nothing to fear but fear itself," she whispered, taking no comfort in the cliché.

Breathing hard, she stumbled toward the hazy glow from a street lamp. Why, in God's name, hadn't she let Michael offer her comfort? Like he always had?

An image of the masked marauder tried to surface, but she clamped down on her imagination and sucked in a deep breath. A rush of cold air seared her lungs, brought tears, and cleared the mental cobwebs.

"Breathe." Comforted by the drop in her pulse, she inhaled more deeply.

The masked marauder was a fluke. Plain and simple. Why tell Michael about a homeless guy who'd probably missed his meds?

Besides, it wasn't as if her kid brother had held a gun to her head. She'd volunteered to meet Rex. She was always volunteering. Another major character flaw. So, it was pay-up time.

Or, she could turn around, sneak back to the office and swear she couldn't find Rex.

How the heck could she find him in this gloom?

Listen for screams, she thought, immediately disgusted by her cynicism about Rex's face.

She took another step. God pity the unsuspecting jogger who met up with Rex. Catching sight of him in murk like this could send the fittest jock into cardiac arrest.

No sane runner's out this morning. Quinn kept her eyes on her feet, acknowledging this certainty, but seeing in her mind's eye the bumpy, livid port-wine stain that covered the entire right side of Rex Walker's face and body. He'd told her once, in a sad, sardonic wail, that his face was the prototype for Phantom of the Opera.

Wrapped up like an Eskimo, Quinn shivered. Okay. She knew she was being silly, letting the deserted park, the fog and her mixed-up feelings about Michael's boyhood chum give her the willies. In reality it was the encounter in the garage that had left her edgy. What she ought to feel was shame. Michael shouldn't have to worry about Rex. Not when she—

A feathery touch on her elbow jerked her heart up and down like a yo-yo. She whirled, salt filling her throat.

"Thank you for coming." The fog muffled Rex Walker's husky baritone, but his voice vibrated with an intimacy that prickled the hairs on her neck. "Did Michael browbeat you into meeting me?"

"Of course not." She stuffed her hands deeper into her pockets, fighting the urge to rip off his head, pressed her elbows into her sides and felt a stab of triumph when he let go. "Meeting you was my idea."

Her head ached—from the cold—she reasoned, not from lying.

His wide-brimmed felt hat, made popular in the Thirties and Forties, hid most of his face. But the anemic light from an imitation gas lamp caught the fever in his yellow eyes. Quinn's heart shifted into overdrive.

"Hey!" Rex chaffed his gloved hands together. "Let's get out of the cold. I think I can still afford a cup of coffee."

If Pierce's accusation was right, he could afford the whole damn coffee plantation.

Afraid the thought would bypass her brain and

become speech, Quinn said, "I shouldn't stay out of the office that long."

Rex rocked back on his heels as if she'd slugged him. "Right. Sure." He pushed the cuff up on his cashmere coat and squinted at his Rolex. "You've probably got a ton of paperwork before your first appointment."

Sarcasm? He had to realize clients with any sense would cancel. Those without sense simply wouldn't show up.

But his easy-out tempted Quinn, and she said, "I swear I leave two papers on my desk overnight, and there are ten the next morning."

He gave her a wan smile. "Ain't it the truth? That's why I went in at six this morning. Wanted a head start on the end-of-the month reports. Pierce is a stickler for detail, you know."

Beneath the bluster, he sounded scared and lonely and sad. Was he crying? Was Michael his only friend in the world?

Sleet was filling her chest cavity, shrinking her lungs, choking her. They walked toward the park entrance by unspoken agreement, their footsteps echoing on the brick path.

At least Quinn assumed they were walking toward the entrance. The fog disoriented her, made her extra cautious. Every step sent shivers up her legs and back. She was terrified he'd break the silence, force her to play act, pretend she wasn't shallow enough to let his face bother her.

The truth caught her off guard. She exhaled. Her breath exploded in little silver puffs, triggering memories of ice skating and sledding with Michael on sunless winter days after school. So long ago. Heart aching, she felt as if she were watching a movie starring other children in another dimension.

She glanced at Rex from under her lashes. What kind of childhood memories did he have? Did she really want to know?

He slowed, stopping under a street lamp, his birthmark hidden by the slant of his hat. He kept his hands jammed in his coat pockets. "You do know, don't you, Quinn, how indebted I'll always be...for your help in getting me the job with Pierce?"

She swallowed, stuffed her hands deeper into her pockets and fought down the temptation to wring her hands. Finally, they'd come to it. The reason she'd left her toasty office to freeze her butt off. She nodded. "I know."

"Remember," his voice vibrated with eagerness, "how you coached me?"

A favor to Michael.

"You counseled me on everything." He breathed excitement, wonder, even, in each syllable. "From what aftershave to wear to what phrases to avoid during that first interview."

"I remember." Would she ever forget the images of dark, primitive Amazonian forests his heavy aftershave conjured—making her stomach lurch, her head ache?

"Your coaching's why I got the job."

Her back stiffened. "You got the job because you know computer systems inside out."

Pierce had done neither of them any favors, of that she was positive.

"I didn't steal that money."

"Knowing Pierce, I can't imagine he doesn't have

evidence."

"Ssst." Rex stamped his foot.

A wire in her brain tripped. In her head, she heard the hiss of a cape. She flinched, her whole body tensing.

"Evidence, proof, whatever you want to call it, can be manufactured," Rex said as if speaking to an airhead. "People fall for lies and false documentation all the time."

"Pierce isn't people." Ticked by his tone, her own edginess and the biting cold, she snapped out the words, rushing on in a hard, impersonal voice. "You said it. He's a stickler—"

"Yes, but let him leap to one of his famous conclusions, and you can forget persuading him to see anyone else's viewpoint."

The bitterness—understandable—still grated Quinn's raw nerves. Damn, why couldn't she like this lonely, pathetic man?

"What viewpoint did you try to persuade him to see?" Her throat ached, so the question came out a croak.

"That someone else is guilty."

Quinn stifled a groan. Ask a stupid question... She bit her tongue. Asking "who" simply compounded her stupidity and fueled Rex's antagonism. Sometimes, she wondered how much Michael had told him over the years. On the other hand, did she want to know what her brother had told someone outside the family?

Her indecision didn't deter Rex. He made his point. "Pierce didn't even pretend to listen. It was like telling him the world really is flat."

"You mean it isn't?" God, was her brain locked in

stupid mode?

The approach of a city bus saved her from making a total fool of herself. Instead of pushing her under the wheels, Rex maneuvered her away from the curb. An island of diesel-infused warmth enveloped them. He held onto the brim of his hat, struggling against the bus's backdraft. The tail lights disappeared, and he extended his hand.

"Thank you for coming. I hope Michael tells you every day how you do him proud."

His sincerity stuck in Quinn's conscience like a bayonet. Oh yeah, no doubt about it. Michael was certainly going to be proud of his big sister.

About as proud as she was of herself.

"I'd walk you to your office, but Pierce advised me to stay away from the building. Doesn't want me upsetting people. Thinks he rules the universe because he owns the whole damn block."

Tears flooded Quinn's throat, stopping speech for the second time that day. How would she feel if she and Rex changed places, and he left her alone like Humpty Dumpty—to pick up the pieces of her life?

"Well." He dropped his hand. Nothing in his face or body language gave a hint he'd taken offense at her bad manners. "I'm sure I'll see you at Baby Quinn's baptism."

Whether it was the cold, congenital stupidity, or most likely guilt, Quinn blurted, "Since Pierce doesn't rule the universe yet, let's go back to my office. We'll strategize finding you a new job over coffee and a couple of Lamar's."

Chapter 3

Pierce tossed the weasel's file back in his top drawer, scrubbed his eyes and pushed away from his desk.

Strange how facts didn't change. Now for the fun part. He took out his cell phone, dialed Quinn's personal cell, caught Chatty Cathy, disconnected and immediately dialed the phone on her desk.

Her AVR picked up. He redialed her cell. She finally picked up on his third try to her desk phone.

"I'm in conference," she said in her Miz In-Control Voice. "I'll get back to you,"

"You know about Walker, don't you?" Pierce opened the top drawer of his desk and fingered the file that contained the seeds for their bankruptcy.

"Yes."

"Is he there now?" A red haze tinted Pierce's vision.

"Yes."

How could one word shrivel a man's balls faster than a laser?

"If I charge in there on my white stallion and sweep you away for coffee, will you be eternally grateful?" Pierce imagined Quinn's frosty tone turning him into an ice sculpture, crashing onto his solid mahogany desk.

"I'm in conference."

"Okay, scratch the eternally. I forgot you don't appreciate small talk." Or romantic gestures. "I expect too much."

"Is it 'conference' that confuses you?"

"I'm coming down there." He glanced at his watch. "Eleven minutes."

"No!"

Keep it simple, Stupid. "Ten minutes, fifty-nine seconds."

"I said—"

"If he's still there," Pierce slammed the drawer, "it will get ugly."

His bad imitation of a tough TV-detective disgusted him so much he hung up, choking on the stench of testosterone. The smell permeated his office. Hung in the corners like smog.

Wired, he whipped through a dozen chair push-ups.

Hell, maybe testosterone poisoning explained why he'd repressed how much Quinn hated ultimatums. From the first time he'd thrown one at her, she'd come back at him, both barrels blazing.

"You know," she hadn't cracked a smile, "why men are like copiers?"

Arrogant male that he was, he'd said, "No, why?"

"You need them for reproduction...that's about it."

His desk phone rang, but he ignored it and came out of his chair. The mutual need for control had long ago destroyed their personal relationship, but until now, their need had never impinged on their professional dealings.

"Way to go, Pierce." He stopped in front of a mirror in the bathroom. A face that would scare babies and pit bulls stared back at him. He leaned closer. Yep, sure enough. There was blood in his eye.

Taking the stairs down four floors boosted his adrenaline supply instead of depleting it. Random images of Quinn, superimposed by images of the weasel's shock this morning, tumbled through Pierce's head. Dammit, she had to see reason. Say no to Michael. Protect herself.

Walker ripped off little old ladies' savings accounts.

Firing the bastard was the right decision. The only decision.

Why couldn't Quinn see that?

Because, Pierce answered himself, per St. Michael, the weasel's practically an Alexander clansman. No way she'll ever see he's a snake.

Not as long as she thinks you're lower on the food chain than pond scum.

****

Pierce ignored the protests of Quinn's office manager and stalked through her door, ready to beat Walker to a pulp.

Quinn raised her chin, but remained behind her desk. "You're late."

"Guilty as charged." Luckily, there was no sign of Walker or he'd be guilty of murder.

The crown of her usually smooth, ash-blonde hair was frizzy. So she'd gone out of the building to meet the creep—despite the welt on her chin, the cut above her top lip, and the bruise around her left eye. Pierce clenched his hands at his sides. Had she told Michael about getting mugged?

Bet she doesn't trust me enough to admit what I already know. Guts churning, he asked, "What happened to your face?"

"I had a facelift."

"I figured it was something like that." Pierce leaned against the wall, going for the casual body language, taking in the red splotches on her elegantly sexy throat. "Did you tell the weasel about the guy in the garage?"

"Why would I do that?"

He snapped his fingers. "Sorry, I forgot. Nothing scares you. You're a modern, self-reliant, independent—"

"Who's not discussing the fluke in the garage." She jutted her chin higher, but blood stained her throat and cheeks a harsh crimson. He pretended not to notice. "So what do you want, Pierce?

"You know what I want." He wanted her to pretend his worry for her mattered. Pretend he'd find the guy who scared her in the garage. Pretend she knew he wanted her safe and happy.

This particular insight felt like a nail in his liver. Since it was nothing he intended sharing, he tried stalling. "I was late because my bum knee's acting up."

A lie. It was his heart acting up. Thumping too hard. Still aching, after four long years, for a kiss from Quinn.

Lips pursed, she locked eyes with him, her gray glare cold enough to freeze the lower regions of hell. "You don't have a bum knee."

"True. But speaking of bums—"

"Referring to yourself, are you?"

Another smooth segue shot down.

He moved closer to her desk. "Believe him or believe the evidence."

"Evidence?" She tapped a yellow pencil in the middle of her desk. Pierce enjoyed the power jolt that looming over her gave him.

The pencil-tapping stopped. She lifted one eyebrow. "Facts, proof, whatever you want to call it, can be manufactured. People fall for lies and false—"

"That's bull and you know it." He wanted to shake her but knew he was too close to her as it was.

Tension between them snapped, crackled and popped. They stared at each other, eyes locked, two predators in the wild, ready to pounce at the slightest provocation. Hell, he wanted to pounce on her without provocation. Long ago, they'd played a game. Whoever blinked first decided where they'd make love. Memories of them in this office, on this desk he'd given her, pulled him into the past. His eyes burned. Did she remember?

Remember was Quinn's middle name. He felt her stare boring past his skull, past nerves, deep into his brain. The game had changed. They were professional colleagues now. She'd ripped their emotional relationship from her mind like a page from a calendar.

He blinked.

She stared.

Defeat tempted him to wink, but the strain around her eyes and mouth pushed him to maturity. He eased into the nearest chair and broke the deafening silence with a sigh. The extra oxygen helped. He said, "One of my hotshots got suspicious a couple of weeks ago. He told two auditors."

The knot in Pierce's stomach hardened. Now came the tricky part.

The pre-dawn rehearsal in front of his bathroom

mirror faded. To hell with softening the statement as he'd originally planned. But he did cross his legs and swing his foot.

"The auditors confirmed—positively—last Thursday that Rex Walker's been manipulating accounts at Plaza Reserve Bank for the past eleven months. I assume he told you how much money's miss—"

"Last Thursday?" Quinn whispered the question, adding in the same lethal tone, "Why'd you wait until now to tell me? I thought we were—"

"Friends?" Pierce interrupted. "Exactly why I didn't tell you. My lawyers said wait until I reached a decision. Quinn," he leaned forward. "I only decided last night."

"Did you stand next to him while he packed?"

"Of course not. Security handled that. Stop being melodrama—" He changed his mind. "Stop biting my head off and think. The guy stole a cool five million bucks—a little more loose change than I usually carry in my pocket."

"Are you bringing charges?" She reverted to the whisper, her eyes huge, all pupil.

"Not if I can keep it quiet. I've already repaid the bank."

"But he swears—" She held Pierce's gaze, then looked away.

"He's lying. No one framed him. He did it." Pierce planted both feet on the carpet where they'd made love more times than he could remember. He tensed his leg muscles and started to stand, but a sharp pain pressed against his lungs, slowing his breathing and bringing his understanding into clear focus.

No use going to her. Touching her. Kissing her.

The way back to her had vanished long ago.

"I know about his father."

"Do you know why he believes his father abandoned him and his mother?" She twisted the small pearl earring in her left ear as if the question was rhetorical and not a trap.

The edge to her tone made Pierce think twice about expressing his theory of paternal abandonment. Big mistake, though, to say he didn't give a damn. If he was smart, he'd keep his mouth shut. His head felt like the blood in his brain had reached full boil.

"I know silence is the better part of valor, but I'll point this out anyway," he said. "Your father also deserted you and Michael and your mom." She flinched, but Pierce drove his point home. "Yet none of you—not a single one of you—has broken the trust people have placed in you."

He shifted his crossed legs and placed one hand over the other in a strategic position he hoped would deflect the lightning bolts blazing in her eyes and aimed right at his balls.

"That's...below the belt." Her chin quivered, and she bit her bottom lip.

"True." He passed her a white silk handkerchief and winced when she blew her nose into it with the gusto of an elephant with packed sinuses.

"I'm sorry." Hackneyed, but sincere considering she'd turned the big guilt guns on him with her smoky, hurt whispers and trembling chin and wet eyes.

The rules according to Quinn Alexander hadn't—apparently—changed in four years. Mention of her father bordered on pinching babies and kicking puppies.

She absolved Pierce of his breach with the barest of nods, touching a raw nerve that made him forget caution.

"Dammit, we're wasting time feeling sorry for this sociopath."

"He can't help being ugly, Pierce. Any more than you can help being handsome as a movie star."

"Yes, but I wasn't born handsome." Moving his head from side to side, he patted his hair. "Hair mousse turned my life around. Without it, I'd cry myself to sleep at night."

Laughter gurgled in the back of his throat. The day he used that gunk on his hair was the day they laid him out in a coffin.

"Admit it," she said, her jaw nearly locking. "You've got the empathy of a rock."

"Comes from having a heart of stone." Pierce deliberately narrowed his eyes, and once more morphed into Mr. Hard-Ass TV-Detective.

After a beat, she said, "Comes from having a head thick as cement."

"Uh-huh. Mr. Cement Head, that's me. And being thick-headed makes this easy for me to say. To you. To Rex. To Michael. I don't give a damn how awful Rex's birthmark is."

Her sharp intake of breath sliced Pierce's heart like a razor, but had no impact on his tongue. "I don't give a damn how awful it is his father abandoned him. I don't give a damn how awful having only two friends in the world is."

His breathing was shallow, ragged. He paused— out of necessity to catch his breath—not out of courtesy. But the pause gave her the chance to jump in and call him names, accuse him of arrogance and show him the errors of his pigheaded ways. She surprised him again by saying nothing.

Fine. He'd take her silence and have the last word, feeling somewhat ridiculous, but not ridiculous enough to sit there mute when their business and personal reputations could go down the tubes.

"None of those misfortunes, by themselves or together, gives Rex Walker an excuse for stealing someone else's money. Or for ruining our good names—and our businesses—if news about the embezzlement gets out."

"So the truth doesn't matter."

"The truth definitely matters. That's different than a happy ending. Tell the truth to our insurance companies, and we'll have a very unhappy ending."

She laid down the pencil. "He told me the happiest day of his life was getting hired by you."

Pierce snorted, fast losing his battle with temptation. The glass slab that functioned as her desktop provided a great opportunity to ogle her long legs. "My happiest day in a long time is today."

This admission said all he wanted to say about the weasel, but he recognized the point Quinn's silence screamed. You are an idiot. You are the village idiot. You are an idiot's idiot.

Gut burning, Pierce summoned his in-control-CEO voice. "If I'd trusted my gut, I'd've let him go three months after I hired him. Today, I'd be ecstatic."

Maybe not ecstatic. Because, then, he wouldn't be sitting in Quinn's office admiring her legs. An insight Pierce kept to himself. She'd cut him off at the knees if she suspected he wasn't really mesmerized by the spray of white orchids on the credenza behind her.

Crrr-aaa-ck. The pencil she'd been turning over and over between her fingers broke into two pieces. She laid them in the middle of the glass slab as if they were holy relics.

Pierce focused on the orchids, remembering the first one he'd bought her. He'd special ordered it from a place on the Big Island, selecting the nineteenth-century Japanese Imari bowl that now sat empty in a corner behind her. Slow, random images unwound in his mind of Quinn gasping at the white orchid, stroking the bowl, then kissing him on the mouth.

"What cause did you have for firing him that long ago?" Her voice came from far away. "You've always said he's brilliant."

"Brilliant." Pierce blinked away the memories and felt a fleeting rush of regret at the same time he said, "Not to mention paranoid, temperamental and egotistical. He's a loner who constantly wants to bend the rules. He also likes taking shortcuts and expects constant praise. Someday you'll have to tell me what you and Michael see in him."

"He's Michael's friend." She said this so fast Pierce almost missed her baffled tone.

'Oh, well,' lacked the ring of empathy, so Pierce settled on nodding. You*'ve always known what she'd do for Michael has no limits.*

The muscles in Pierce's shoulders burned as if colonies of fire ants were marching across his back in lock-step. He slammed the Michael-door shut. The water under the bridge had risen and washed the bridge away. Relaxing his jaw felt like torture, but he put on his best listening face.

"Right now," Quinn said in a hushed, earnest tone, "Michael doesn't need any more on his plate. After all the problems with the pregnancy, the baby's overdue. He hasn't slept in weeks. I don't think he's eating. There's a glitch in announcing his new—"

She blew out a breath, looking ready to cry. Except Quinn never cried.

For the first time since storming into her office, Pierce felt bad for dumping on her. She was caught in the middle between Mr. Cement Head and St. Michael. That realization turned on a light in Pierce's brain and turned his guilt to fresh lava. "Tell me you're not helping Walker find a new job."

"Why wouldn't I help him?" The lift of her chin belonged to a queen.

"Are you nuts?" Pierce clamped his mouth shut. Way to show concern, idiot.

"I like to think I'm humane. Whether I like him or not isn't the issue. The point is—"

"The point is he stole—"

"The point is he has an aged mother."

"You're positive about that?" He didn't flinch though the look she shot him could set an iceberg on fire. "All right, let's say he has a mother. Let's say he adores his mother. Stealing money to care for a consumptive mother went out with Dickens."

Quinn shot out of her chair. She whipped around her desk and came at him like a feral cat protecting her new litter.

Instinct got him on his feet. The heels on her sexy, leather boots put the top of her head even with his chin.

Two spots on her cheeks flamed as she got right in his face. "And your point is?"

"Believe me, I have a point. One you should listen to." His heart fired rapidly, but he knew better than to tell her to calm down. Especially with the spooky gray light blazing in her eyes. Not to mention the smoke coming out her ears.

"Please. Take your time." Her top lip twisted into a sneer that went with arms crossed over her chest. "I have nothing better to do than listen to the great Pierce Jordan pontificate."

His mouth twitched. Quinn Alexander had an attitude, and she knew how to use it. After the incident in the garage, she was probably a breath away from throwing him out of her office. He tapped an index finger in his palm. "My point is—someone who thinks logically provides a nice contrast to the real world."

Shoulda told her to calm down.

Hindsight came a fraction of a second too late. Quinn flexed her long fingers, digging her nails into her palms. Pierce didn't consider himself a candidate for natural deselection so he drew back a little.

Just in case she became physical.

"God save us," she hissed, "if you're someone who thinks logically."

She stepped back from him, watching him like a shark coming closer to baby dolphins, and ripped open the door into the reception area.

"I'll have a cashier's check to you for two point five million dollars by end of day tomorrow." Disdain blazed in her narrowed eyes. "I'll include your handkerchief."

Chapter 4

"Dammit!" Quinn sat in her deserted office at the end of a fourteen-hour work day. She wanted to blame the ringing phone for the garbage she'd keyed into the Excel spreadsheet. Hitting the wrong key for the third consecutive time forced an admission of the truth.

Juggling her finances to pay Pierce had left her brain dead.

Proof positive the human brain requires more than coffee and carbs as a day's sustenance. She punched the speaker phone and chirped in her brightest voice, "Hey, Mom, you're ahead of me. When'd you get home? Don't you have rush-hour traffic in St. Louis?"

Talk fast enough and maybe, just maybe, she'd fool Sarah Alexander. "I planned to call you."

"So I've saved you some trouble?"

"You're never trouble." Quinn closed her eyes and saw her mother at fifty-seven, face unlined, hair ash-blonde, and figure trim enough strangers often mistook her and Quinn for sisters.

"You're feeling weepy, aren't you?" The omniscient-mom tone made the question rhetorical.

"I'm taking the Fifth." Quinn cocked her stiff neck from side to side, stared out the frosted window and shivered. "Michael called you, didn't he? He knows me too well."

"Michael's a topic for later." The U.S. Navy could

learn from Sarah Alexander about radar.

"Have I ever told you how proud I feel every year you throw your Thanksgiving Bash?" Mom also put heat-seeking missiles to shame.

Quinn's neck and ears stung. All thumbs, she saved her useless file and started shutting down her PC. The bruise on her cheek ached. Pulsated, as if warning her against lying to a woman whose emotional crystal ball never failed. Was probably at that moment detecting the throb in Quinn's left hip. The throb was the nastiest reminder of the morning's garage-adventure.

Hard-wired for stamina, her mother kept going and going and going—like those old Energizer-bunny commercials. She expressed awe at the number of people invited, the menu, the location, Quinn's generosity. The words of comfort pushed Quinn dangerously closer to self-pity. Despite all the money she'd spent, the plans she'd made, she'd miss the "Bash"—probably her last one—if Baby Quinn entered the world on Thanksgiving Day.

She swallowed, fighting a rush of anger. Dammit, she deserved to wallow a little after her bizarro day. She wanted someone to understand about her scare in the garage.

Recognizing the slippery slope, she stood. Her bare feet sank into the Aubusson carpet. She padded into the empty outer office and turned off the lights she'd requested Sami to leave on as she left. By next year, she'd be lucky if she could afford space in the parking garage after she paid Pierce her share of Rex's debt. Paying that debt meant the end to the Thanksgiving Bash she'd hosted for four years, providing great food, fun company and fabulous views of The Plaza lighting ceremony that officially kicked off the holiday season in Kansas City.

Her mother continued talking as Quinn returned to her office. She swallowed a groan. Her hips and legs and ribs weren't letting her forget the garage. Determination to think about anything but the garage set in, and she made small talk, crossing her fingers she could fool her mother. Her gaze followed the downward spiral of several fat snowflakes stuck together, and her neck muscles relaxed, letting her appreciate the dreamy quality of the scene.

"It's snowing here," she murmured.

Mercifully, Sarah Alexander took the cue and went with a riff on the weather she hoped for in San Francisco, her every-other-year-vacation destination. Scheduled to leave the next morning, she wanted lots of sunshine. Quinn listened with half an ear and repressed another shiver. Twelve hours ago, she was buttoning her coat to meet Rex in the fog.

"We had fog like London this morning in St. Louis."

After a double take, Quinn assured herself her mother didn't read minds.

"Luce was frantic. She called Michael. His cell was busy. He didn't hear Call Waiting or see her text messages." Sarah sighed. "They had a burst water pipe in their brand-new house and she wanted Michael to handle it. She called me in tears. He told me yesterday he had this important meeting so I asked my plumber to go by."

Careful. Careful. Careful. Quinn pinched her lips together and dozens of invisible hot needles stabbed her bruised cheek. She knew better than to lie outright to her mother. Inhaling silently, she eased into the wing chair opposite where Pierce had sat. "I assume she reached him."

"Not until noon." Her mother sighed. "She's terrified about the baby, of course...what'll happen if she goes into labor and can't reach him."

"Our Michael's got a full plate, doesn't he?" Sweat slicked Quinn's hands. She picked up the front page of the *Kansas City Star*, crumpled it and pitched the wad at the waste basket. The ball bounced off the metal rim and toppled onto the carpet.

"How about overflowing?" Mom sighed louder. "Luce complains he leaves before dawn. Comes home later and later. Doesn't eat. Doesn't sleep. She's worried he'll never have time for the baby."

"That should all change once he starts at the Fed."

Too bad Quinn couldn't find a job for Rex at the Federal Reserve Bank.

Not in St. Louis.

Definitely not in St. Louis.

Michael didn't need the hassle of having Rex so near after Baby Quinn's arrival. The sooner she found Rex a new job, the sooner one more worry fell off her brother's plate.

Frustration percolated in her stomach. Lolling on her desk, a green-eyed monster winked at her. She crumpled more paper. Resentment flared and she shook her head. Whatever her feelings, she wasn't jealous of Rex. Absolutely not. Why would she be jealous?

Nervous the mom-radar would pick up on the mental war, Quinn smoothed out the paper and let the conversation run down. Five more minutes, and she'd confess about the nutcase.

Or about Rex.

About Michael being on the phone with her talking about Rex instead of on the phone with his wife talking about their baby.

And as a result of that conversation, she had cashed out her savings, mortgaged her future, and was hoping for the best—keeping it all bottled in so Mom wouldn't worry.

Quinn wiped her sweaty hands on her greasy skirt. She'd never gone home at lunch to change clothes. Which didn't matter. What mattered was sending her mother on vacation thinking about her first grandchild instead of worrying about Michael's stressed marriage. Mom definitely didn't need the additional anxiety about what happened in the garage.

Because what happened was a fluke.

And finding a job for Michael's best friend was a favor.

A favor Quinn would fulfill, so why spread the worry?

Silence echoed across the miles. She asked her mother to repeat her last comment. Her mother insisted she'd said goodbye. Doubt flickered in the back of Quinn's mind. What had she missed? Something important?

Then, Mom did say goodbye, adding, "Whatever's bothering you—"

"Just tired..." Not to mention feeling damned annoyed about the troubles that came with Rex Walker. No matter what Pierce said, she wasn't losing her business because of Rex.

"And still weepy."

"A little," Quinn lied, her pulse skipping. "But I've

got a great book waiting at home."

"Call if you can't sleep."

Quinn hung up, before Sarah Alexander, librarian extraordinaire, asked the title.

****

Quinn turned off the lights in her office and stood transfixed by a distant hazy glow. The snow and fog reduced her visibility, but behind the haze, the illuminated replica of the Giralda tower rose. The Plaza landmark always improved her mood. The red-tiled, Moorish architecture provided a constant reminder of her unforgettable summer in Sevilla, Kansas City's sister city. She'd met Pierce in front of La Giralda.

"Why not slice and dice your heart?" she whispered and switched her mental TV channel.

Images of her with Mom came into focus. Strolling The Country Club Plaza's blocks and blocks and blocks of boutique shopping. Lobby-hopping the ritzy hotels. Eating at gourmet restaurants. Critiquing the architecture of new buildings and comparing them with the old ones. Throwing coins in Nichols Memorial Fountain.

Without warning the masked face exploded in memory, wiping out the fairy tale she'd woven. Her heart revved up, but she pushed the masked image deeper into the basement of her brain. Think homeless guy. Think nutcase. Try hard to forget this morning. Don't let a fluke make her afraid to roam The Plaza—or anywhere else. She massaged her arms and her pulse slowed. Putting him behind her made sense...tomorrow.

Tonight, after beating off her own personal fluke, common sense dictated requesting an escort to the car. So what if it was a nuisance for George? She didn't intend to make a habit of asking him to accompany her to the garage. But the septuagenarian liked her. He wouldn't mind her request.

Of course not. Give him the choice of leaving the over-heated lobby or trekking into the chilly garage. Naturally, he'd walk her to the car, grinning like a kid with an ice-cream cone.

Quinn swallowed, tasting disgust at her idiocy. Forget George. She was a big girl. A big girl didn't need someone twice her age as a babysitter.

Especially since she wasn't carrying a box of greasy goodies.

An anemic rectangle of light trickled from the hall, through the frosted window in the front door, and spilled onto the carpet in the reception area. Too whacked to turn on the closet light, Quinn jerked her coat off the hanger. After paying Pierce two and a half million bucks tomorrow, she'd be lucky if she could afford electricity.

Everything I've worked for...She fumbled with her coat, buttoned it in semi-darkness, rummaged in her purse for her cell phone. Probably another luxury after tomorrow.

The taunt sucked out her last drop of energy. Fatigue settled in her aching muscles. She'd feel even stiffer tomorrow. Too bad she'd promised Pierce his check in the morning. Otherwise, she'd stay in bed. All day. Sleep. Forget today. Go into denial-hibernation.

Let Michael and Rex take care of their own lives.

She snorted and straightened her shoulders. Her mother hadn't raised her to whine. Left alone with two kids under the age of eight, Sarah Alexander had raised her and Michael and never whined.

Quinn took a deep breath, exhaled and dug deeper.

"Dammit!" She never left her cell phone in her car, but this morning...

Wearily, she dragged her butt the dozen steps to Sami's desk. She didn't dare sit down or she'd fall asleep. As it was, she could sleep on her feet.

George's voice came on immediately. "This is George Brown. I'm either on the phone or..."

"Yada, yada, yada, yada, blah, blah." Quinn hung up, feeling frustrated and silly and defensive for changing her mind about not calling the old guard. She massaged her aching head.

Let another nut come after her. She'd show him. She'd studied Tai'chi and knew karate. Skills she'd forgotten this morning, but now they bolstered her.

The return trip to the closet *felt* shorter. Her coat, on the other hand, weighed a ton. Or maybe her purse weighed a ton.

"Dammit!" She leaned her head against the closet door. She'd left her briefcase in her office on top of the credenza.

Well, too damn bad. Since this morning, briefcases had slipped from her first choice as weapons of self-defense.

The front doorknob rattled, shocking her heart into orbit. She whirled around and slammed into the open closet door. Stars danced. Fingers sweaty, she gripped the knob and eased her head beyond the edge of the door.

Someone—face scrunched against the frosted glass and shielded between skillet-sized hands—peered into the reception area.

Damn, and she was fresh out of Lamar's.

Her legs wobbled. *No hysterics.* She bit her bottom lip.

The knob turned. Her heart slammed against her ribcage. *It's locked*, her mind whispered. Definitely locked. She'd locked it...after Sami left. Around six.

Fingers tapped the glass. She clamped down on her bottom lip and jammed the tip of the car key between her thumb and forefinger.

The knob jiggled once, twice. Then nothing. Slowly, the shadow turned away. Quinn strained to hear footsteps in the carpeted hall. She heard only silence.

Adrenaline popped along her stretched nerve endings. Logic evaporated. She reverted to instinct. She dropped to all fours. Her office had magically relocated to the next county. She stopped crawling every few inches and turned to stare over her shoulder.

The light in the hall threw off about three watts. How much could someone on the other side actually see in reception? What if he came back before she reached the phone?

Air whooshed out of her lungs, and the floor tilted.

Get a grip. She tucked her head and kept crawling. Security procedures required a badge after hours for entering the building. But if someone left a door open...which happened. Too often. The trembling in Quinn's arms snaked down her backbone. She paused and glanced over her shoulder.

The hall light again. Her heart jammed her throat— exactly the way it had when she'd been afraid, as a little girl, to check for monsters under the bed.

A shadow materialized at the door.

Quinn fell on her stomach. She inhaled a snootful of dust from the runner. Too late, she covered her mouth and nose. Her ears exploded from the pressure of stifling the sneeze. Tears stung her bruised cheek.

The door handle rattled. "Quinn? You in there?"

"Pierce?" She scrambled to her feet, banging the side table and knocking off a pile of magazines.

Her feet slipped on one of the slick covers. Surprised, she yipped and hydroplaned several feet before kicking the magazine out of the way.

"Wait, Pierce! I'm coming."

****

Quinn threw open the door hard enough to shake the glass and Pierce's gut. He stared at her. "Is it my hair or what?"

"Did you come by here a few minutes ago?"

It took him a nanosecond before he realized she was shaking with terror instead of outrage at seeing him. He shook his head. "Saw your car in the garage and—"

"You didn't come by here two, three minutes ago?" Her voice cut like a new razor.

"Are we in parallel universes here?" Pierce crossed the threshold, flipped on the lights and sidestepped an open magazine on the floor. "What the hell spooked you?"

Quinn stood frozen near the doorway, glancing toward the hall. "I was in the closet."

She stopped fumbling with the buttons on her coat and pointed to the closet.

"Putting your coat on, I bet," Pierce coached her, careful to keep his distance. She was already too close, too vulnerable.

Eau de terror oozed from her, shaking him. "I-I-I was in the closet."

"Uh-huh." What could he say? Genius that he was, he recognized a closet when he saw one, and he sure as hell knew better than to touch her. "I can go check the hall."

Blood drained from her face. "No! Don't leave. He's long gone...I'm sure."

"What happened?" Pierce plopped on the arm of a sofa and let his foot dangle like he was Cary Grant. His heart was racing a hundred miles a beat. He relaxed his jaw. No way he'd give her Clue One how much he wanted to hold her. Just hold her.

"Someone...came by...tapped on the window." Shock hummed below her rage.

"Hey, that'd raise my pulse." Pierce went for teasing so she wouldn't guess he'd decided to kill the little weasel.

"He tried the door knob. Two or three times."

"He?" The bitter taste of too much coffee and too much rage bubbled in the back of Pierce's throat. He planted both feet on the floor. Let the weasel crawl back under a rock. Let him hide there until he felt safe. Let him rot in hell. Pierce would find him and make him pay for scaring Quinn.

"He looked inside." Quinn framed her face with her hands. A bead of sweat lined her upper lip. "He didn't say anything. Just looked inside."

"Creep." Pierce glanced at the open door, flashing on Brittany, the interior designer who'd persuaded him frosted windows were elegant. Inviting. Very "in" as doors went.

Absolutely not a security problem in a modern building like this, she'd assured him.

"He tried the door twice." Quinn's voice, steady

now, almost matter-of-fact, brought Pierce back to her office. "He left a few minutes before you showed up."

"Must've used the stairs." Pierce picked his words carefully, worried he'd push her to the edge of hysteria. "I was using one elevator. George was probably using another one. The other four—"

"I know. They're shut down at seven. I called George. He wasn't at his desk. Maybe he came up—checking on me."

"George wouldn't rattle the door. And he'd identify himself immediately."

"Okay, okay. I see your point." She wrapped and unwrapped the long purple scarf around her neck. "It probably wasn't George. No probably," she amended.

Pierce opened his mouth, but she waved at him and retied her scarf. The desire to kiss her, hold her, reassure her, made him look away. He stared at the frosted door.

"I told you frosted doors were a bad choice."

Her tone stung like a slap in the face, but to hell with giving her any satisfaction. He swiveled his gaze to meet the accusation in her stare. "I remember."

Face stiff, she fingered her damn coat buttons. "See, there really is more to me than my pretty face."

The bitterness didn't surprise him, but he waited a beat before answering. He didn't want her to see how much her crack had caught him off guard. His tongue felt bigger than a tree trunk, but he said, "There was more to Brittany than her pretty face."

"Uh-huh." A muscle under Quinn's eye jumped. "Like her hot, sexy bod?"

"Like her sense of humor," Pierce countered, his jaw cracking.

"Oh, yes. It was hilarious when I found the two of you stark naked in my office."

Stark naked bounced and skidded and caromed around in Pierce's brain, fueling him with a crazy, intense desire to lean forward and kiss Quinn until she got stark naked.

Her curled lip brought him back to his senses. He said, "Not the way it was."

Quinn shrugged with the least movement possible. "So I exaggerate. Sue me. But you better hurry. This time tomorrow, I won't have enough left to make it worth your while."

This second, meteoric change of subject set his head swimming. Sudden subject changes typified the ploy she'd used from the beginning, every time he'd tried explaining about Brittany.

So, like any red-blooded male accused of being a goat for a sheep, he finally gave up. Brittany welcomed him with open arms. She didn't give a damn he was on the rebound.

Stuck in the same rut he and Quinn had churned so many times, Pierce hesitated, his mouth clamped shut. Her scent of roses, mixed with violets, undermined his determination to get them back on track.

Anger uncoiled in his stomach. She had to think Walker was her boogeyman. Push her on that hunch and she'd shut up like she'd contracted lock jaw.

Why mention the weasel when she could throw Brittany in my face?

"You want to know what I saw in Brittany?"

"Do I look as if I watch Oprah?"

He shrugged, ignoring the barb. "I saw her good sense. She never demanded an affidavit signed in blood

53

that I wouldn't abandon her."

A sense of pride surged into his gut. He hadn't said *leave*. He'd used the *A-word*. He'd said abandon.

One look at Quinn's pinched, startled face and his stomach lurched. Damn, what a prince. Disregarding concern for his safety, he reached for her. She flinched. A hormone-attack hijacked his brain. He clasped his hands under his chin and fell on one knee.

"Go ahead," he said. "Kick me. Hurt me. Put me out of my misery. Please."

For a fraction of a second, he'd swear her mouth twitched. Once. Then she pressed her lips together and tossed her head—a gesture he'd never seen her use.

"I don't think so. Get up. I'd rather see you really squirm."

Common sense told him to take his time. "You're going to enjoy this, aren't you?"

"After the day I've had, I deserve a little enjoyment. Stand up. Look me in the eye."

"Do I get a blindfold?"

"No blindfold. No cigarette. No mercy." She took off her coat and tossed it across the nearest chair.

On his feet, Pierce tensed, half expecting she'd roll up her sleeves and deck him.

"Repeat after me." She met and held his gaze. "I, Pierce Jordan..."

The words had a familiar ring. She snapped her fingers, and he repeated them in his most confident tone.

"...do solemnly swear..."

Oh-oh. He had to clear his throat twice, but finally said the phrase, asking quickly, "You sure you wouldn't rather kick me to the curb?"

Narrowing her eyes, she continued. "...I am incapable of commitment to Quinn Alexander or to any other woman in the galaxy."

Ouch. His tongue flopped like a dying fish. He swallowed three times before croaking the lie. He watched her closely because, God save him, she was smiling... and enjoying every second of this game.

"Is that it?" Bad move—an insight that came with hindsight.

"Not quite." She arched a brow. "Ready?"

"Sure. I like being flayed alive."

"That's a little kinky, don't you think?"

His heart missed a couple of beats, and he mentally tripped when he focused on the deep, sexy purr from the back of her throat. God, she was...flirting.

"I'm into kinky." His tone was as cool as if he channeled Cary Grant.

"Good. Then say, 'I lied about Quinn's demand for a signed-in-blood affidavit.'"

"In my own defense—"

"Say it."

"Okay." He spit the words out faster than bullets from an Uzi. "Satisfied?"

She sighed, long and deeply. "Best orgasm I've ever had."

Chapter 5

No facial or body tics gave away Pierce's thoughts or feelings as he and Quinn marched to the elevator in silence. She, on the other hand, was having a hard time keeping a straight face. She wanted to skip down the hall like a kid recently visited by Santa.

What fool said revenge wasn't sweet?

A fool who knew zip about broken hearts. Quinn smiled to herself. Hard to believe she'd extracted the revenge she'd dreamed about for four years. Her pulse hip-hopped. Laughing at Pierce in her office, she'd almost certainly guaranteed the end of their professional dealings. The thought sobered her, but she felt so jazzed, so indomitable, she didn't care.

Maybe, just maybe, he finally had an inkling of what humiliation tasted like.

A clue his nerves were stretched tighter than a matron's Botoxed forehead came from his clenched jaw. It was a wonder bones and teeth didn't tumble out of his mouth. He gripped his black leather briefcase at the ready—as if to beat her off.

Quinn swallowed a giggle. She could tell him a thing or two about his briefcase-strategy.

At the elevator, he slapped the DOWN button a little harder than necessary. Thank God she'd nixed any discussion about the shadow outside her office or the nutcase or Rex. Pierce had tried to protest, but she insisted.

Talk would detract from the honeyed taste of revenge.

The elevator door glided open, and he stood silently aside. She stepped into the wood-paneled space, faced the control panels and jutted her elbows out at her sides. Pierce entered on the clean scent of lemons. Her nose twitched, but she didn't recognize his aftershave.

Definitely not the lavender fragrance of Canoë he'd used when they were together. Kissing him had always left her wanting more. Heat stung her cheeks, but she kept her eyes on the controls and she punched GARAGE. She'd forgotten until this moment how much she missed his scent. How much she associated it with his supremely natural self-confidence.

Neither spoke. Her neck and back muscles could serve as elevator cables if they had to make a quick escape. Impossible to relax with him so close. Dressed in a forest green crew-neck sweater pulled over a green and burgundy-plaid shirt, Pierce had changed clothes since morning. He was leaner, trimmer than when he wore pin-striped, double-breasted suits. The soft recessed light added a brilliant sheen to his ebony hair, free of spray or gel.

The nerves in Quinn's fingers jumped. They still carried the memory of caressing his naturally bronze face, his shiny hair and other places she refused to think about. She stared at the doors, acutely aware of his hip-hugging jeans.

There should be a law against such flagrant baiting of one's former sex-starved lover.

Dry-mouthed, she pressed her lips together like a pissy, born-again virgin. He didn't know she was sex-starved. He might suspect after the theatrics in her office, but he'd been coming on to her. And he must've known she viewed his come-on as one more assault in a day when she'd had enough. Too bad he just happened to stray into her fallout zone.

Cold, stale air in the garage took Quinn's breath away. She shivered, felt her bravado slip a notch and forced herself to step into the desolation. "You don't have to walk me—"

"Like hell. You think I want to face another kangaroo court like that one in your office?"

"Kangaroo court?" Quinn hooted, realizing they'd passed the spot where she'd dropped the pastry box and confronted the nutcase. Her self-assurance surged. She faced Pierce.

"Since I'm now absolved of my one grievous offense—"

"You'll walk the straight and narrow forevermore?" Quinn pressed her new Avalon's remote, but missed a couple of keys in the combination.

"You probably have to take off your gloves," Pierce offered.

"You probably have no idea why I'm letting you live." She jerked off her glove and stuffed it in her pocket.

He opened both his palms. "What'd I say?"

"I said I'm letting you live." His suggestion had carried no trace of smugness or condescension. His suggestion made sense. And he'd kept his word and said zip about the bizarre day, but damned if she'd let him off the hook.

The taillights remained off after repeated jabs on the remote. "I. Am. Dreaming."

Smart man that he was, Pierce saved his life again. He refrained from suggesting he try the remote. He said, "I bet your battery's dead."

"No way. I bought this car two months ago. Off the showroom floor."

"Curiouser and curiouser." His frown did nothing to mar his good looks—but what did? "It's not cold enough for a new battery to go dead."

"No, but it is the Monday from hell." She spoke in a bantering tone that mocked her, jammed the key in the lock, slid behind the steering wheel and slipped the key into the ignition. "Ever had that feeling a black cloud's hanging over you?"

"Your cloud's black? Mine's puce."

"Goes well with your hair." Live by the acid tongue, die by the acid tongue.

The honey-sweetness of her earlier Pyrrhic victory tasted bitter as old coffee grounds. Because he was standing there, she'd go through the motions. She turned the key. Her gut already told her that her battery was deader than their once hot romance.

"Deader than old e-mail," Pierce intoned and shook his head.

She locked her jaw and managed to repress another sigh. No use getting in the habit of sighing, because, mercifully, there was only one Monday per week. "I'll call Triple A."

Pierce snorted. "Expect Santa Claus before they show up. I'll take you home."

Ride in his car with the ghosts of that kangaroo court riding with them? Quinn's stomach dropped. Not in this lifetime. She shook her head.

"Thanks, but if I stay, they're more likely to come

and fix the battery." She stepped out of the car, cell phone in hand. "Otherwise, I have to deal with no car tomorrow morning."

"I'll swing by and pick you up."

Several dozen neurons in her brain misfired. Repeatedly. So fast, she couldn't think. Her heart banged her ribs. They'd have about ten inches separating them in the car.

"Don't think so." Playing with matches raised the likelihood of getting burned. "You'll want to rehash the whole day. I'm not up for that."

"No rehashing." He held up his right hand and nailed her with an unblinking stare. "The guy in the garage? Erased from my memory. The one outside your office? Out of sight, out of mind. I swear, no mention of the weas—of Rex. No more cracks about kangaroo courts. I'll even drive like a choir boy."

His declaration rang with sincerity, but he was grinning like an executioner.

****

The 'Vette's engine turned over the first time. Pierce felt like crowing, but caught himself just in time. No use bragging a new Avalon couldn't hold a candle to his classic wheels. Knowing Quinn, she'd think she'd gotten under his skin with that stupid oath.

I...incapable...commitment to Quinn Alexander or—

"Nice toy." She clutched the seatbelt. "Like a certain comic-book character's wheels."

"Bought it three years ago..." He stopped before he inserted his foot in his mouth and told her it hadn't healed the cracks in his heart. "I bought red instead of black because red tights are flashier."

"Smart."

Snow hit the windshield as soon as they cleared the underground garage, but the 'Vette's wipers flicked it off with quiet precision. The precision failed to impress Quinn, Pierce noticed.

Wipers...a guy thing.

They whipped onto Southwest Trafficway and made a right at the foot of the Forty-Seventh Street hill, accelerating through the light and up over the top despite the slush. Quinn gasped and he swallowed the impulse to yell, Eeeeeha! A few feet below the crest of the hill, two SUVs, abandoned, covered with snow, straddled the curb under the EMERGENCY SNOW ROUTE sign.

"Hot dogs." Pierce tapped the brakes and shifted again going down the long, treacherous street. The 'Vette held as steady as if they rode on the streets of Miami.

He watched Quinn in his peripheral vision. She released her death-hold on the handle, dialed her cell phone, listened and grimaced, reminding him of his futile efforts to reach her this morning.

"Isn't technology a marvel?" She threw him a glance and snapped the cell cover shut.

"When it doesn't turn on you."

"That happened this morning. Luce called Michael repeatedly on his way to work. No signal..." Quinn punched REDIAL, sighed, hung up.

"Find some music," Pierce invited, hoping to distract her for two minutes from saving the world. "You should find at least one CD that's not Country."

He crossed his fingers. She hated Country.

She shook her head. "Ten minutes to my house. I

like the quiet."

In other words, remember your promise to drive and say nothing. Keep your mouth shut and don't disturb her by yakking.

"I didn't mean that the way it sounded." Her tone sounded genuine, but she stared out her window as if she'd never seen snow.

"Hey! I'm tough. Did I cry once during your kangaroo inquisition?"

"Your bravery was commendable."

Her failure to remind him the inquisition was off-limits surprised him.

Before he could tell her he was pulling her chain, she said, "I know I sound as if I should cut back on caffeine, but I don't think I can manage choosing a CD. My mind's flying off in a dozen different directions."

"Your car." He flipped on the high beams and searched for a rip in the snow-curtain alerting him to other idiots driving in a storm straight out of the movies.

"That's the least of it." Her tone was flat, barely audible.

"The guy in the garage?" Mounds of snow, recently shoveled and piled on the shoulder, narrowed the curving stretch of Highway 50.

"Forgot all about him."

"Uh-huh." Pierce took his eyes off the road.

"A fluke." She wiggled her fingers dismissively. "Nothing."

"According to Steve Cutter—"

"Ah-ah-ah. You swore." The glow from the dash softened her scrapes and bruises, but even in the poor light, she looked so tired and so vulnerable, Pierce wanted to pull over, take her in his arms and make more promises he couldn't keep.

"Sorry." He slowed crossing Brush Creek, mentally cursed his stupidity, figured what the hell, and decided he could always come back to Michael. "Gotta be Rex Walker."

"Bingo." She wagged a finger. "Off limits, remember?"

"You can't save the world, Quinn." He rolled the taste of her name in his mouth like fine wine.

"I know. I know. But I feel sor—" She exhaled, then whispered, "OooomyGod.".

He tromped the brakes. The 'Vette's rear end fishtailed, then straightened. His heart tripped over his vocal cords, choking him. He croaked, "What's wrong?"

A smile lit her face, and her gloved fingertip grazed his nose. "Look!"

The snow seemed to slack off enough for him to take in a shimmering white blanket stretching over the fifteenth green of the Kansas City Country Club. A thin winter moon hung like a mirage, filtered through the falling snow. Pierce stopped the 'Vette and let the powerful engine idle. He'd never seen Quinn lovelier or more desirable.

She pressed her nose against the window like a child. His heart ached. Quinn was like a child in some ways—filled with wonder and convinced most people had hearts as soft as hers. How had he ever been such a fool...

"You dressed for a short walk?" He didn't trust himself any longer in their magical igloo. "It's pretty nippy." God, he couldn't believe he was yammering about the cold when what he really wanted was to get her blood boiling.

"I can trudge across the tundra in this coat." She was already scrambling out the door.

Pierce had to hustle, but he made it around to her side of the car without falling on his ass. He took her elbow. They stepped into an ankle-deep drift. She yipped but plowed forward. They were panting and laughing and shushing each other by the time they reached the hedge bordering the golf course. He spread a couple of low pyracantha branches, and she slipped between them like a princess passing through golden doors. Lights from The Plaza—over a mile away—reflected an aurora borealis of hazy pinks and subdued purples. The kaleidoscope of colors and patterns bounced off the fresh whiteness. Snow muffled the silence.

Quinn exhaled, blowing out a circle of silvered air. "Michael and I used to go sledding on nights like this."

"I bet you pulled him most of the time." Pierce hooked a damp curl behind her ear.

Her eyes widened, alight with memories. "Pulling was the most fun."

The blood in his veins was scalding. Like the lone survivors on earth, they reached for each other. He had no idea who made the next move. What's more, he didn't give a damn. All that mattered was that Quinn lifted her face at the same time he lowered his head—first to brush her parted lips, then to kiss them hard when she didn't pull away or slug him.

Desire sucked him into a mindless vortex of falling snowflakes.

"God—" Something whizzed over his head.

Instinctively, he shoved Quinn away from him.

She squawked and flapped her arms like a wild goose separated from the rest of the flock. "What the heck happened?" She tilted her face up at him.

"Beats me." Enjoying her closeness, Pierce planted his feet and peered over her head.

A high, whistling sound grabbed his attention. He tackled Quinn instinctively, then scrambled to his feet. The second potshot connected squarely with the side of his head. Stars cha-chaaed between snowflakes. He grunted. His legs gave way. He hit the ground hard enough his back teeth clacked.

"That was loaded," Quinn called.

"With titanium boulders." Pierce sat up, touched his temple and examined the tip of his glove. "No blood."

Quinn crabbed toward him and swiped snow out of his eyes. Having her so close made his head spin. Or maybe it was having his dinosaur brain on the fritz. Whichever, he knew his mission. Get on his feet. Go after his assailant. Take out the bastard.

The pep talk failed to solve his major problem. He couldn't stand. His boots kept slipping on the ice-crusted snow. Quinn whispering his name, patting his shoulder, nursemaiding him further stymied his good intentions.

A surge of disgust at his wimpiness drove him to lurch upright. He wobbled. His chest heaved as if a rhinoceros had gored him, but he fantasized receiving a medal for bravery.

While he grinned goofily, Quinn clipped him behind the knees, yelling, "Duck!"

He bellowed and nosedived into the snow. He

bucked her off him and came up sputtering for air. Two feet away, a snowball dropped short of his aching head. Arms and feet flailing, they scuffled and grunted, each intent on winning. A barrage of snowballs fell around them like showers of meteors. They huddled together and lay absolutely still.

Zing. Zing. Zzzing. Three more snowballs cut through the cold air, whizzing over them.

"Stay down." Pierce raised his head and swiveled it from side to side.

"What's he doing?" Quinn raised her head even with his.

Near where they'd slipped through the fence, their attacker, dressed in white ski pants and parka, head and face covered by a white ski mask, packed another handful of snow.

Pierce narrowed his eyes and brought The Abominable Snowman into focus. The bastard fired three speed balls with uncanny precision. Swearing, Pierce ducked, shielding Quinn from the next volley. A pause in the action gave him the perfect offense. He leaped up with such a blood curdling shriek he imagined himself a blue-painted Celtic warrior. He slowed for a fraction of a second halfway across the golf course.

Why hadn't the neighbors called the cops? This was not a neighborhood tolerant of racket on the golf course. One of Fairway's finest should appear any minute and nab Ole Abominable. Until then, Pierce would play hero.

Huffing and puffing, he changed course—intuitively heading for the stand of trees on the opposite side of the greenway. If the bastard made the trees...Pierce ignored his heart roaring in his ears and ran as if he could see. He lost momentum as he stooped and grabbed a handful of snow. The cold burned through his leather gloves, but he packed the missile on the run, zigzagging toward where he expected the phantom.

It was hard to tell, but Pierce thought he was gaining. Or maybe the phantom was slowing. Pierce pumped his arms and followed the ragged breathing of his unseen attacker. Was it his imagination, or was the snow letting up? How much longer could the race continue?

Abommie pivoted, lobbed a pitch, disappeared. Testosterone fumes spurred Pierce. A copse of trees rose from the whiteness like black ghosts. He sprinted toward the total blackness yawning past the trees. Without warning, his ankle turned. He grunted, stopped, and leaned over his knees. He kneaded the stitch in his side and gasped for breath. An impulse to touch the blood running from his head wound took hold, but Quinn's shriek overrode everything else.

He raised his head, and the pressure squashing his brains exploded. His whole skull throbbed. He tried to draw air into his lungs, but they burned too much to expand. His feet felt like snowshoes. He watched—in stunned fascination—as Quinn hurtled toward him.

"You should've..." She skidded to a stop. "...tried out for the majors."

"Bas-bastard got away." Pierce groaned.

"He had a big start." She threw Pierce's arm over her shoulder like an Amazon helping a pygmy. She staggered under his hundred and ninety-seven pounds.

His pulse shot up. "Take it easy, okay?"

"Give me any trouble, and I'll sling you across my back and carry you to the car."

He pressed a knuckle against his bottom lip, then said, "That I'd pay to see."

"Tsk, tsk. You'd force me into such an unladylike activity?" She jostled him a little, and he cursed.

Macho Celt, he jerked off his gloves and touched the back of his head, then jumped as black dots tap-danced in front of his eyes.

"Stop that." She grabbed his sticky fingers and gently brushed at the spot where his brains were undoubtedly seeping out. "You've got a goose egg bigger than Rhode Island."

For a second, he stupidly fought with her. His whole body twitched with the urge to examine the knot again. "I beg your pardon." He swayed against her, figuring she wouldn't hit an injured man and went for pathetic. "It's twice as big as Rhode Island. And it'd feel a hundred percent better if you kissed it."

Her guffaw lacked any essence of elegance. "I'm freezing. I can barely move my lips."

He traced his thumb across her bottom lip. "Kiss me and get lips hotter than matches."

She slipped out of his embrace so fast he thought he'd imagined her arms around him. "Sounds dangerous. Like I could set us on fire."

"That's the general idea."

"How about if I drive you to my house and examine the holes in your head instead?"

****

The snow fell faster and harder leaving Quinn breathless as she half-carried, half-dragged Pierce toward the hedge. Constant checks over her shoulder slowed their progress and wasted time. Their attacker couldn't see them any better than they could see him, but they'd never survive another sneak assault.

"You're not the first person who's wanted to examine my head,"

"Uh-huh. I suppose scientists are lining up from around the world."

"Damn right."

His almost inaudible slur scared her, but when he handed over his car keys without a murmur, her stomach contracted. Did he have a concussion? Should she take him to the ER?

Heart fluttering, she maneuvered him into the passenger's seat. He complied so easily with her order to lie still and close his eyes that she kept sneaking looks at the rise and fall of his chest. She held her own breath during the drive to her cul-de-sac.

The Corvette's headlights swept past the Neighborhood Watch sign and picked up the black Jeep parked at her end of the cul-de-sac. Damn. Why did teenagers neck in cars when most parents allowed kids to listen to music or do homework or play video games in their own bedrooms?

Pierce groaned and Quinn forgot everything but getting him inside. Automatically, she dragged her fingers across the soft leather of his visor without finding her garage door opener.

Dammit. She bit back a scream. The minute he'd suggested driving her home, she stopped using her brain. She'd left it—along with the stupid remote—in her car.

Clumps of snowflakes clung to the windshield like fine lace. God, she soooo did not want to move. "Stay put," she said. "I left the garage opener in my car."

"What?" He sounded groggy and unfocused.

Impatience sliced through her fleeting good intentions, but guilt won out. The man had a head injury for God's sake. She softened her tone. "I have to open the door with the keypad."

"Huhhh?"

Quinn doubted he understood how her mind was plodding along. "We'll go inside."

"Hmmmm."

Was he laughing? God save him if he was faking his head injury. Anger knotted her stomach. She shot him a death glare. He didn't move a muscle.

Which in itself was suspicious. Suspicious enough she wanted to wring his neck.

"Okay," she snapped. "So I don't want my neighbors to notice how late you leave."

Or, if he didn't leave.

****

Quinn peered at the white layer covering her driveway and tried to work up courage to step outside. Pierce's eyes remained closed, his body stiff, his breathing shallow. The blood had congealed on his left temple in an ugly, wet blob. She cracked the car door and pretzeled out. Her feet slid in opposite directions. Like a whale on ice skates, she grabbed the edge of the open door. Her ankle twisted as she fought to avoid falling on her butt. She took a tentative step. Her ankle wobbled, but she held onto the side mirror and inched forward, head down against the driving wind. She imagined backtracking, getting in the car, taking Pierce to the hospital.

The man was the poster boy for hardheaded, but

the snowballs had done definite damage. He was hurt—maybe seriously hurt. He could require professional help.

But on a night like this with the first big storm of the season, normally careful people forgot how to drive. They plowed into everything from stalled cars to telephone poles and ended up filling the ERs. St. Luke's was on The Plaza, but it could take hours before a nurse or doctor or intern even looked at Pierce.

What if Michael calls?

Shivering, fingers numb, she removed her gloves and stared at the keypad—her mind blank as a TV turned off. Dammit, what was wrong with her? She knew the code. She knew the damn code. She knew... She swallowed, tried a combination, cancelled it and felt dumb, dumb, dumb. Closing her eyes, she let her fingers work the keypad.

The smooth, nearly imperceptible hum of a motor shot through her like electricity. Her eyes snapped open. She laughed too loudly. The overhead lights brought the chaos in her pottery studio into stark relief, but for one fleeting moment, Quinn saw the underground garage in Pierce's building, heard the hiss of a cape, smelled cinnamon breath. Her own breath caught.

She blinked. The unfired pots remained static. Her pulse slowed. Reason resurfaced.

Feeling ridiculous, she returned to the car on trembling legs. When she whispered Pierce's name, his eyelids fluttered, but his eyes remained closed. He lay so still she worried he'd lost consciousness. Her pulse stuttered. In that instant, she reconsidered backing into the street and heading straight for St. Luke's.

Later. She drove the Corvette into the garage. *If he needs to go.*

Which he won't. She fought her dread, reassuring Pierce he was fine, urging him to open his eyes and talk to her. She turned off the ignition, then went behind the car to open his door. His breathing was ragged, and his eyelids trembled as she eased him out of the front seat—careful to avoid bumping her kiln. Between starts and stops, quiet moans from him and coaxing from her, they inched away from the car. She punched the interior keypad, automatically checking over her shoulder.

Headlights off, the black Jeep rolled past her drive.

"Yessss," she said under her breath. The teenage driver must've realized she'd seen him and figured she'd call the police if he hung around much longer.

Pierce's dead weight made her forget everything. Her ankle ached from supporting him and from waiting for what felt like hours before he managed to lurch up onto the step separating the garage from the mud room. The trip of a few feet felt like a marathon. They shambled into the kitchen. Despite her zigs and zags around knobs and handles, Pierce banged his hip on the table. He yelped and fell into a chair, dragging her down with him.

His pupils had shrunk to glassy pinpoints. His fingers grazed his head. "Oww..."

Chest contracting, Quinn caught his fingers, squeezed them, stroked his cheek. "I'll make it feel better."

"Feel better." He sounded so much like a bewildered little boy, she felt like crying. She'd never seen Pierce vulnerable. The man she knew was too cool. Too cocky. Too in-control to show a side of himself that was anything but tough and hard-edged.

Repeated reassurances convinced him to let go of her hand. Even so, she continued talking to him as she found a flashlight, then pulled a can of OJ from the freezer. Having nursed dozens of Michael's boo-boos, she knew from experience that food and drink often distracted wounded male warriors.

"Talk to me," she called.

"...tired."

"I know." She dumped the flashlight, first-aid kit, several clean towels, and a can of orange juice on the table. "Fresh coffee later. For now, how about juice?"

"'Kay."

His terse, flat answers bothered her. The Pierce she knew delivered sharp, off-the-wall comebacks. At least, she soothed herself, he seemed to understand everything she said to him. She mixed water and juice. The full glass baffled him. He stared at it as if seeing a rare artifact for the first time. He pushed the glass away like a tired child, sloshing juice on the table.

Quinn pulled the glass toward him, raising it to his mouth. "C'mon. One sip. Just one."

"Uh." He tilted his head back to swallow and flinched when she parted his matted hair away from the wound.

"It's deep." She worked quickly, using eyebrow tweezers to separate clumps of his bloody hair. "The good news is, I don't think you need a stitch."

"Mr. Cement Head."

The tension in Quinn's shoulders let go, and she exhaled loudly. He was lucid again. "You might need a tetanus shot."

"No way."

73

Disappointed he reverted so quickly to monosyllables, she said, "A tetanus shot—in case there was metal in those snowballs."

He started to shake his head, but stopped. "No way."

Inflexibility was a positive sign. She squeezed excess peroxide from several cotton balls, glanced at the wall clock and decided he couldn't speak so clearly if he'd suffered a concussion. "No way there was something metal or no way you need a booster?"

He didn't answer so she gently tipped his head forward.

He inhaled loudly, through his mouth. "Damn."

"Sorry." She patted his arm and felt her throat close. "I said it was deep."

"Forgot." He didn't move while she tried to figure out how to bandage his scalp.

"You've got too much hair. It's too curly."

"Always liked...my hair."

Her heart banged. She hadn't liked his hair, she'd loved it. He'd worn it longer four years ago, but it always smelled clean and shone like ebony. She routinely ran her fingers through his hair during foreplay.

"Can I move?" he asked, his voice thin as an old man's quaver.

"Yes, I'm sorry. Yes." She offered him her arm and came close to knocking him off his chair when her ankle suddenly gave way. "You'll be more comfortable in the family room."

Muscles tensed, she stayed by his side as he shuffled across the tiled kitchen floor.

"Feel like a-a geeze-a geezer."

"Our little secret," she said, aware that even an insipid secret with Pierce sent goose bumps hopscotching on her arms.

He grabbed her hand, and heat shot through her fingers to between her legs. "Golf course guy...garage guy..."

An image from the garage collided with the figure in white. Could they be one and the same person? Quinn shook her head. Pierce had the head injury, but she was the one not thinking straight. She draped her favorite throw over his knees. "Shhhh. You need to rest."

"Need a kiss." The corners of his mouth twitched.

The phone rang, killing the mischievous grin she expected.

"Take a little nap." She bent, pressed her cheek against his and limped to the kitchen.

What would she do about Pierce if Luce had gone into labor?

Chapter 6

"It's me, Quinn." Rex Walker, the last person on earth she expected, identified himself before she finished saying hello. "Is this a bad time? I hope I'm not bothering you..."

She didn't wait for him to launch an apology. "How'd you get my home number?"

"Michael—"

"When?" She hoped Rex understood she didn't believe him. Tough unemployment times brought lots of computer whizzes to Alexander and Associates. Most qualified applicants were men. Michael would guard her personal info as carefully as movie stars guarded the name of their plastic surgeon.

"I-I don't remember. A while ago. Not recently."

"Okay. Why?" No use mincing words.

"That I remember." He rushed on, his voice eager. "In case there was a problem with Luce, and he couldn't reach you."

"Why wouldn't he be able to reach me?" Mind spinning, she pivoted toward the kitchen slider, the phone pressed against her ear, listening to him breathe as if in cardiac distress.

"I-I don't-I don't know. I'm sure he had a reason...at the time. I don't remember...what—what it was." His voice grew higher, shriller, then faded to a whisper.

Pockets of hazy light glowed through the clean blanket of snow, tempering Quinn's impatience. But Rex started talking again in his whiny, defensive tone, and she resorted to biting sarcasm. "Do you remember why you called me?"

"Of course. But do you mind telling me why you're pissed? Did I wake you? Get you out of a hot bath?" He spoke in the stacatto cadence of a used-car salesman not letting the customer get in a word, rushing on as if he figured she'd hang up on him.

The skin on Quinn's entire body shriveled and tried to crawl off her skeleton. The idea that Rex Walker might think about her naked, anytime, anywhere, turned her stomach upside down, flooding her throat with a metallic taste.

"Sorry," he said. "My mother taught me better manners." Maybe afraid Quinn might contradict this statement, he spoke faster. "Michael left a message on my machine at 9:30—"

"Is Luce in labor?" Quinn bit her tongue. She'd choke before she asked why Michael called Rex instead of her. "Did she have the baby?"

"No, Michael sounded—"

"Is he all right? Why didn't he call me?"

"If you'll let me talk—" Rex shifted the receiver so clumsily Quinn jumped, feeling dizzy and disoriented. He said, "Sorry, I have another call."Hang up. Calm down. Check on Pierce. "Take it. I'm pretty busy right now."

"Probably Michael again."

"Why call you again? Why not call me?"

"I can only guess." Self-importance deepened Rex's tenor and deepened Quinn's doubts.

Whether the caller was Michael or not, she now wanted details. "Check Caller ID."

"I don't recognize the number. Maybe it's a telemarketer. Or Michael's at the hospital. I'll call you back."

Heat stung Quinn's cheeks, and her palms felt slick on the receiver. She swallowed her pride. "I'll hold."

"I'll get back to you as soon as I know anything."

White noise crackled on the line. Covering the mouthpiece, Quinn walked to the threshold of the family room. Pierce lay with his eyes closed, his mouth slack. Asleep—or in a coma? His breath came out in shallow, ragged spurts. The knot in her stomach contracted. What if Michael needed her? What if she had to leave Pierce alone? What if...

"Shut. Up. Quinn." She counted to ten, turned her back on Pierce and stared outside.

Diamonds sparkled on the snow. The wind had stopped gusting. She stared at the loveliness. Serenity seeped into her bones. If she had to drive to St. Louis tonight, she could do it and expect to live. I-70 rarely shut down because of weather conditions. State snow blowers kept the East-West artery cleared for trucks running the route day and night.

Imagining the four-hour trip, Quinn glanced at her watch, tapped her foot, rechecked the time. Rex had kept her on hold for less than a minute, but her pulse was accelerating by the microsecond. She felt as strung out as the hundreds of tiny bee lights wrapped around the trunks of the old oaks bordering the creek.

Paradise. This was where she should have stayed this morning. Safe from masked creeps in tight pants or ski suits.

A mental snapshot exploded. She saw the snowball knocking Pierce down. The white noise on the phone roared in her ears, and her heart pumped harder and harder and harder. She threw her hand out, placing it on the icy pane of glass, exhaling, steadying herself, wishing she didn't feel so alone.

****

"A dollar for your thoughts." Pierce lay in the recliner, drowsy and relaxed.

"You lucked out," Quinn said. "I'm on hold. You won't have to pay one dime."

"Anyone I know?" The way she stiffened clued him in.

Fury burned the back of his throat, and he barked, "Forget it. None of my business."

He kicked off the crocheted cover she'd thrown over him but decided against standing until the room stopped spinning. He rubbed the back of his neck. His skull throbbed as if someone had driven a dull nail through hair and bones and brains.

Common sense told him to shut up, but he said, "Know anybody else besides the weasel who'd wear a ski mask off the ski run?"

Quinn's lovely, luscious lips thinned like a frozen green bean. "He told me you didn't like him, but—"

"But I'm being ridiculous, right?"

"Ridiculous sounds too bland. Personally, I think you're being unfair."

"Oh-oh. This conversation leads only to the same dead end you and I have reached too many times." Pierce examined his cuticles. "I'm going to shut up while I'm ahead."

"Promises, promises."

Pierce bit his tongue and shifted in the chair.

An elephant stomped on his brain. Momentarily stunned, he sat there mute and considered the virtues of silence. The air between him and Quinn hung heavy, became awkward.

The awkwardness deepened. He wasn't up to reckoning with her stubborn pride.

An eon or two later, she said, "Better spill what's on your mind before your head explodes."

"Nothing's on my mind."

"Riiight." She gave him an eye-roll, then slapped the phone in her palm.

Pierce shrugged and allowed a big, innocent smile to stretch his lips. Let her have the last word. But don't tell him the phone wasn't a substitute for his head.

A muscle ticked under her left eye, and her jaw cracked. She gave no indication she noticed either involuntary reaction.

The yearning to take her in his arm swelled, but he shut down the fantasy. Why keep banging his head against that particular brick wall?

The brick wall always won, and his aching head needed a time-out.

Nothing between them had really changed. Quinn wanted more from him than he could give. Which meant he had no right to tell her who to help and who to turn her back on.

"I haven't exploded yet," he said, forcing his voice into neutral, "but my bones are weary. I'd better fire up the Gomobile and mosey—"

"Shhh." She wagged a finger, gave him her back and hugged the phone like a lover.

No matter how hard he strained to hear, Pierce

picked up none of Quinn's words. Irrationally, her attitude got under his skin. He saw her talking to the weasel, and he wanted to punch out the lying little creep. Quinn couldn't see her brother's best bud as Abommie, but Pierce didn't buy the out-of-the-blue appearance of their attacker.

"Michael and Luce had a big argument." Quinn materialized next to Pierce's chair. She sounded—looked—ready to bawl, her eyes dull, her jaw slack. "He called Rex instead of me."

"I'm sorry." Mine fields lay hidden on all sides, but Pierce risked patting the leather arm of his chair. "There's nothing wrong with the baby, is there?"

"Not yet." Quinn watched his fingers caress the armchair with the intensity of a mongoose. "Luce and her obstetrician want to induce labor tomorrow."

Patting the chair began to feel obsessive-compulsive. His inability to stop, to say something comforting made Pierce feel stupid. He fumbled for the lever on the recliner. A tough TV-PI would be on his feet by now, holding the distressed babe in his arms.

"Big decision. I mean, inducing labor...doing it tomorrow."

Brilliant conversation beat tough every time.

"That's why they argued." Quinn looked past him into deep space.

The recliner's back slid forward, jolting the top of Pierce's skull. A fleeting thought imagined Luce's pain. Her risks. Her panic. "Luce must be scared." He paused, added, "Michael too."

"I think he's terrified." Quinn hugged her waist. "He refuses—absolutely—to agree to the procedure tomorrow."

Why? The thump of Pierce's feet on the thick carpet set off an explosion in the back of his head. Despite the fallout in his brain, he remembered Michael could say nothing dumb, make no bad choices, do no wrong in Quinn's eyes.

Pierce pitched his voice to neutral, "What about a second opinion?"

"Michael got a second opinion."

Her words came at Pierce from outside his fantasy as the tough PI. His clammy skin and wobbly legs also weakened the image. Standing and taking her in his arms wasn't going to work. He asked, "Do both doctors agree?"

"He didn't consult a second doctor."

Pierce leaned forward, frowning, unsure he'd heard. "He didn't—"

"He consultled Rex."

"Has he lost his mind?" A stab of pain honed the dullness of Pierce's comeback. She'd clam up if he didn't sound more supportive. He swallowed and summoned a tone he hoped wouldn't sound sarcastic. "Any idea why?"

She pressed her elbows into her ribs so hard Pierce winced. She whispered, "Mrs. Walker delivered Rex after-after...her doctor induced labor..."

****

By 10:30 Pierce looked ready to keel over. So Quinn swallowed her tears. Time for bawling her eyes out later. After she fed him.

Contrary to culinary myth, she knew that making scrambled eggs wasn't child's play. Outstanding scrambled eggs required a chef's full attention. So no thoughts about Michael.

Or the golf-course creep.

Or the garage nutcase.

Or even Pierce, who kept trying to make her feel better by asking questions for which she had no answers. She banished him back to the recliner. The clink of eggs cracking against the metal bowl brought back memories of late-night summer snacks she'd whipped up for her and Michael. More often than not, they ate their eggs and pretended Daddy was on an extended business trip.

Thirty years later, English muffins popped up in the toaster and brought her back to dishing up the eggs. Barely moist, their fatty fragrance of butter and cheese mingled with the yeasty scent of bread—which triggered a memory of Lamar's.

"Yo! Mama!" The off-the-wall greeting bounced around in her mind.

SPLAT! The first spoonful of eggs hit the tiled floor.

She snatched a paper towel off its roller and mopped up the glop.

No crying over spilt eggs. She grimaced and inhaled a long whiff of her creation. Her stomach growled. Deftly, she filled their plates. She'd made enough for six people so they wouldn't starve. They ate off TV trays—a habit Quinn hated admitting she'd acquired, but justified because the trees and creek and wildlife in the backyard always soothed her after a long day. Pierce inhaled his eggs—convincing her she could've set his plate on the floor.

He kissed his fingertips, then threw the gesture to her. "I'll clean up."

"Don't think so." She swallowed before speaking

again. "I think you should go to bed."

"After I do the dishes."

No question about where he should go to bed she noticed, but said, "While I do the dishes. You look like hell, Podner."

"I told you I needed a bandage and a kiss."

The eggs in her stomach rolled. "You were delusional."

"I'm not now." He pushed his TV tray aside.

Alarmed by the heat rising off her, Quinn got to her feet first. "The downstairs guest room's quite sexy."

Oxygen evaporated around her. She heard her gasp and felt ridiculous as heat ignited in the pit of her stomach and went straight south.

"Sexy sounds good," Pierce drawled.

"Comfy," she whispered. "I-I-I meant comfy."

"As in, how you feel after you come?" He took a step away from the recliner.

Quinn's heart hit the inside of her skull. She stepped backwards. "Did you say that?"

"You started it." He took another step.

"I'm ending it." God, her legs wouldn't move. "Right now."

"Why? Why not give each other a little...comfort?"

"Stop that." She couldn't breathe. "My views on sex haven't changed in four years."

He cocked an eyebrow. "Tell me you've been celibate."

"Don't question my celibacy."

Pierce tugged his earlobe. "I saw you with Justin Carpenter—"

"Justin's a teddy bear." She threw up her hands, warning Pierce to keep the arm's length between them.

"After he broke up with Stephie Stone, he needed a friend."

"So since you and I had gone our separate ways, you and Justin helped each other. That about it?"

"It—whatever it is—doesn't remotely fall in the same category as Brittany."

"Okay." A shrug. "But didn't you go skiing with Bob Matthews a couple of times?"

"What is this?" Even as Quinn pretended outrage, heat flared between her legs.

Disgusted by her hormones' betrayal, she picked up his plate, laying it on top of her own. "How could you live with Brittany and keep tabs on me?"

He spread his hands wide in the universal gesture of openness and friendship. "We lived together for three months. Then, she met someone and married him a week later."

"A week later?" Quinn stumbled on a chair leg, rattling plates. Red-faced, she motioned Pierce to sit down. Dammit, she passed that chair a dozen times a day without mishap.

He grinned. "Brittany and I were sorta like Julia Roberts and Lyle Whatshisname."

Quinn laughed. "And look how that went."

"Well, Julia and Brittany are with someone who makes them happy now, and you've avoided my question about Bob Matthews."

Quinn jutted her jaw. Her glare yelled, *Don't mess with me, bud.* Instead of falling off his high horse, he returned a smile so sexy she felt her toes curl.

"Bob and I have known each other since grade school." Each word crackled like icicles breaking. "He's like a member of our family. He moved here and—" Her chin came up another inch. "And I can't believe you sucked me into this conversation."

"Naked curiosity. And speaking of naked—"

"Do not even go there." She stomped toward the kitchen.

"I hate that phrase."

She turned in the doorway. "Because you hear it a lot?"

"Believe it or not, I had a devious, underhanded reason for starting this conversation. Giving or receiving insults is not the reason." He wiggled fingers on both hands at her, then at his chest. "This is where you say, 'So what was your reason, Pierce?'"

A gun to the head couldn't have moved Quinn to repeat this question. How, on the other hand, to deal with it? Four options flashed in her head.

Kill him.

Protest exhaustion.

Hear him out.

Laugh it off.

Her ankle ached and the dishes felt like led ingots so she pitched her voice waspish. "Better not tick me off. I'm on estrogen overload, running out of places to hide the bodies."

He exhaled. "For the record. Brittany and I never pretended we loved each other. We made no promises—and we broke no hearts."

When Quinn thought she could speak without her voice cracking, she opened her mouth and the phone rang.

"Let voice mail pick it up," Pierce said in his CEO-voice. "If it's Michael, you can call him right back."

Torn by her fantasy of setting him straight and her

habit of caring for her brother, she wanted to take thirty seconds to explain why she wanted a man she could trust. But the phone rang again. She raced for it, ignoring the hot needles stabbing her ankle, and didn't look back.

****

For two cents, he'd rip the damn phone out of the jack.

Temptation beckoned, but Pierce carefully turned and inhaled. Miraculously, his head didn't explode. The scene in front of him, on the other hand, wiped out any vague idea of calling the Fairway police about their attack.

Thinning snow drifted downward—with open space between the flakes. Light from the crescent moon spiraled through the crack, lighting the backyard with the diamond brilliance of high noon. Two deer, heads touching, tails wagging, munched on a snow-covered juniper bush.

"Quinn! Come here. Quick," Pierce whispered, looking over his shoulder

The room spun, and he clamped his mouth shut and turned his head back to the scene like an old man. She was on the phone. Busy with her real life. He could rage or he could figure out how to become a part of that life or he could go back to getting through each day kicking his ass for his stupidity.

The smaller deer continued eating, but the larger one lifted her head. She flicked her ears and seemed to gaze right at Pierce—on alert for any sudden movements. Her watchfulness reminded him of Quinn's super-vigilance for Michael—a guy who wasn't on Pierce's Favorite-Hundred-Thousand-People List. The doe continued staring toward Pierce as she ambled closer to her companion.

Obviously a pair—like Quinn and Michael.

The doe arched her neck, giving some kind of silent signal. The pair glided past the window and into the bushes as silently as ghosts. Pierce stayed absolutely still and thought about his next move. Quinn needed to take care of Michael. She didn't need any grief. So, he'd can the wise-cracks, swallow his opinions and morph into Mr. Supportive if it killed him.

Luckily, she returned before he broke his arm patting himself on the back for his newly discovered maturity.

"Can I help?" He held out his hand and shuffled toward her.

She met him halfway. Her fingers laced with his. Lord, she was fine boned.

"It was Rex."

"Ahhh." Pierce's guts rolled, but the frown between Quinn's eyebrows reminded him he aspired to maturity.

"He's going to St. Louis tomorrow, talking to Michael face-to-face. He wanted to be sure I hadn't set up any job interviews yet."

"Two days before Thanksgiving?" Pierce couldn't believe the weasel's nerve.

"Why not? I don't have much time before the rumor mill starts up."

"It won't start up on my patch."

"I hope not." Her voice caught.

Pierce held his ground. "Trust me."

Her bleak eyes held his, but there was a tiny quirk at the corners of her mouth. "I hate to break it to you,

Pierce. But...you're not God."

His jaw dropped. He slapped his chest in mock disbelief. "You're sure ?"

The cost to his pride was worth the half-smile she flashed him. She said, "I should go to bed." Something in her tone nixed all double entendres. "I may go with Rex tomorrow."

"I see."

"I can set up appointments while he drives."

"Sounds like a plan." For disaster, but Pierce still longed for maturity.

"If I go, there is one problem." She let go of his hand and withdrew a step.

With the tom-toms in his head pounding double-time, Pierce couldn't duck—even if he'd seen what came next.

"I won't be back in time to give you your check."

****

Sleep eluded Quinn like a cat burglar.

Counting sheep set her teeth on edge.

Reading required too much concentration.

Watching the light snow revved up her pulse.

Pokes and punches to her pillow zapped her but didn't bring sleep.

A second shower—cold—at midnight, cooled the heat rising off her but also woke up all her little gray cells. Snowflakes gliding down her windowpane slowed her pulse as she applied Band-Aids to her jewel-like bruises.

Every moan and creak—in the rafters, on the stairs, in the hall—raised visions of Pierce stealing into her room, ripping off her nightgown, smothering her with kisses. Eyes wide open, she held her breath, shivered in anticipation and waited. And waited. And waited.

Pale moonlight bounced off her door handle—which turned slowly. A sixteenth of an inch. Then another sixteenth. The air in her bedroom became so quiet she could hear atoms bump into each other. The down comforter felt as if it was lined with asbestos and aggravated her numerous abrasions. Her nerves screamed.

Here he comes. Here he comes. Here. He. Comes. Her stampeding heart all but lifted her out of bed. She knew he couldn't hold out. She tiptoed toward the door, unsteady on her swollen ankle. A cold draft snaked across her feet, up her knees, higher.

Oh, hell. She'd crawled into bed without underwear.

What an oversight.

A memory-flash dragged her into the past—the first time she and Pierce made love. She'd lit a match to their mutual desire and worn white cutoffs. Shamelessly, without panties.

The microscopic turn of the door handle yanked her back from the past. She pressed a hot cheek against the frame. Disbelieving her ears, she pressed harder. With the same results.

Nothing.

No heavy breathing.

No heartbeat except her own.

The day's events—confronting Dim Bulb, arguing with Michael, meeting Rex, facing off with Pierce, coming under attack on the golf course, twisting her ankle, nursing Pierce—swept over Quinn like a tsunami. Wiped out, she climbed back in bed, pulled the covers over her head and curled into a ball.

Pierce was not Rhett Butler. Pierce had received a head injury that would fell an ox. Pierce undoubtedly slept like a baby.

While he slept, she'd lost her mind.

****

The strong, enticing smell of mocha amaretto at 5:45 penetrated Quinn's sleep-deprived brain. Her nose twitched. She opened one eye and stuck her head out from under the covers. Total darkness filled the sky. Pierce should be sleeping, knocked out by the rock to his head.

Groaning, Quinn fell back on the pillows. The early bird shouldn't get the worm. The early bird should get shot.

The squeak of the fifth step brought her bolt upright in bed. Her mouth went dry. She licked her lips and ran a hand through her hair, imagining the ends wild with static electricity, her face battered as a prizefighter's. She must look like a zombie.

A soft tap on her door. "Room service."

Her heart dropped like a rock into her quivering belly. "I'm not dressed."

"Your point being?"

She was going to kill him. "Go away."

"Sure you don't need a backrub in the shower?"

"Sure you don't need a brain transplant?"

He laughed. "Oh, you sweet talker."

The fifth step squeaked under his weight, but Quinn counted to a hundred, then limped out of bed and listened at the door.

Was her life caught in some kind of perpetual soap-opera loop?

Impossible to contemplate such spiritual matters so

early. She jerked open the door and snatched up the tray. The aromas of coffee, strawberry jam and butter on the English muffin made her mouth water. She pushed the door shut with her toe and managed to carry the tray to her bed. Still standing, she knocked back a full cup of coffee, then dialed the bedside phone.

Too bad for Rex if he'd planned on sleeping in.

Voice mail came on after the first ring. Maybe he was in the shower. Unless he'd already gone to St. Louis.

Without calling her?

Had Michael nixed the idea of her going?

Her pulse stuttered. She inhaled, exhaled, inhaled again and hung up. Simply thinking about Michael talking to Rex infuriated her. Was her brother losing it? Was he really afraid Baby Quinn would be born with a port wine stain? Quinn shivered. Needing light to think clearly, she switched on the lamp and massaged the goose bumps hopscotching on her arms.

Dammit, Michael should be talking to her. To her, not to Rex. She redialed, left a terse message, drained her coffee cup and swept half a dozen Band-Aids out of her bed. She pulled the bottom sheet snug as the cover on a trampoline. The Band-Aids symbolized a terrible, horrible, very bad day that caught her off guard.

Today, bring it on. She switched on the closet light, pulled out a hanger and stroked the front of the high-powered raspberry-colored pantsuit she saved for tough days.

Chapter 7

Pierce met Quinn at the foot of the stairs and came close to biting through his tongue.

"Not a word about how I look." She held the tray in front of her like a damn shield.

"Not even that I can't see the bruises?" he lied.

"Not another word or I'll describe how you look. In vivid detail." She held the tray high, pushing past him, calling over her shoulder, "Where's your bandage?"

"Came off in the middle of the night. I thought about coming upstairs and asking you to replace it, but—"

Raspberry splotches, bright as her pantsuit, covered her neck.

"But," he continued, staying far enough behind her that her icy stare didn't freeze his balls, "but my head felt so good I tossed the bandage in the trash."

She whipped around and the china rattled. "You may have a concussion, dammit!"

"I don't. Not Mr. Cement Head." God save him, if she guessed he'd actually tiptoed up the stairs like a moron. Why the hell he hadn't knocked on her door escaped him. That must've been one helluva head blow, but he intended to make up for his stupidity.

Until the time was right, he'd keep his distance.

"Mister, not doctor," she said—reminding him of

his shortcomings with a touch of scorn.

"Point taken." He lounged against the doorjamb while she rinsed dishes and loaded the dishwasher. "I know going to work this early drives you crazy—"

Smooth opening, Pierce.

"Half the people in the U.S. suffer from sleep deprivation," she shot back. "Scientists think lack of sleep actually shrinks the brain, weakens short-term memory."

"No kidding?"

God knew, he didn't clearly remember why he'd started down this path to hell. Maybe he needed that bandage after all.

The phone interrupted his mental lapse. Mr. Helpful, he asked, "Want me to get it?"

Tell the creep to soak his head?

Water sluiced down Quinn's wrists. She grabbed the phone. Pierce poured himself another cup of coffee and sat down to eavesdrop. The first words out of Quinn's mouth made him want to shake her.

"I intended to go with you." A frown knit her brows together. "I don't care what time he called, you should've called me." She stared right through Pierce. "I was awake all night."

Quack, quack. Quack, quack. Pierce mentally whacked himself upside the head. God, he was dumb as a duck. The coffee tasted bitter and did nothing for his black mood. The conversation with Rex didn't seem to improve Quinn's mood much, either.

"I'm not shooting the messenger, Rex." Icicles tinkled.

She tapped her foot fast enough to lift off into space, listened longer than Pierce expected, then spit out shards of ice faster than Uzis spit out bullets. "I know Michael's upset. But not so upset he can't talk to you. Please tell him I expect a call from him later today."

Yessss. Pierce quickly got the smile twitching his mouth under control, glad he wasn't on the receiving end of her tongue, but disappointed the weasel got off easy.

****

Talking with Rex before seven in the morning had vaporized the part of Quinn's brain that managed speaking in complete sentences.

She also had hand-eye coordination problems putting her arms through the sleeves of the coat Pierce held for her. Accepting his small courtesy made arguing with him seem petty so she agreed to stop by his house before going to the office. Ostensibly, he needed clean clothes.

"And going to my place, you'll get to see my new house."

"I didn't know you had a new house."

"All the more reason to go along for the ride."

"You should just drop me off at the office, then go to a doctor."

"Showing you my house is better medicine."

Fatigue checked Quinn's impulse to snort. She yawned, instead, and rubbed her eyes. She should call Triple A about her car, but an image of Pierce eavesdropping clobbered the idea. She'd call from the office. How long could a stop at his place take?

The street workers must've spent all night cleaning the streets, she realized, huddling against the car door. Please, please, please, let Pierce shut up.

Which he did. Until he started swearing, then stopped so fast she jerked awake. Even in her dazed, half-comatose state, Quinn recognized the KCPD squad car parked in front of ornate iron gates. Damn, she should've realized he'd report last night's attack to the police.

"Where are we?" She felt dull, more asleep than awake in the white world surrounding them.

"My house." Pierce rolled down his window as a young policeman with a neat, dark moustache approached the Corvette. "I'm Pierce Jordan. This is my house. What's wrong?"

"Sir, your housekeeper called us at six fifteen and reported a break-in." The policeman leaned into Pierce's car. "We responded immediately. Found blood all over the family room."

"Blood?" Quinn squeaked, like a bird waking up in the dark.

"Is Mrs. Taylor okay?" Pierce demanded.

"She's scared. We took her to the Greens'." Verified by checking a three by five notebook. "Says she tried calling you after she notified us."

Quinn thought the cop's blue eyes were harder than they should be for someone so young. His eyes said he understood—Pierce and Quinn coming home after a night of partying, not interested in picking up voice mail after such a fun time.

Apparently, he didn't see the gash in Pierce's head. Or remember the snowstorm.

"Mrs. Taylor tried your cell twice." Officer Blue Eyes leaned in—up close and personal.

Checking if we're drunk. Or maybe he thinks we're high. Stunned, Quinn listened to Blue Eyes finish his spiel about their unavailability.

Pierce, his hands loose on the wheel, his body relaxed, must have seemed cool and collected under the circumstances. He returned the officer's gaze without blinking. This equated to an unspoken challenge in Quinn's opinion.

The young cop shifted his weight, pulled up his gun belt, patted his sides and leaned deeper into Pierce's space. "Mrs. Taylor said she didn't get an answer at work either."

"That's right." Pierce held the cop's gaze. "But, as you can see, I'm right here."

The knot in Quinn's stomach contracted, and she wanted to smack Pierce on the nose like a naughty puppy. Why show courtesy when he showed contempt so well?

"If you'd move your car a few feet," he said in a tone that made Quinn cringe, "I can park in my driveway."

Once Blue Eyes was out of earshot, her stomach flip-flopped. "He's just doing his job."

"He could take some lessons."

Adrenaline pumped into Quinn, bringing her wide awake, but she bit her tongue. The crack of Pierce's clenched jaw sliced through her raw nerves. Though not as deeply as the thought of blood in his family room. Her mind veered away. They parked in the middle of a snow-cleared circular, brick driveway in front of six white marble steps.

"You'd better come in," Pierce said.

Quinn pulled her coat collar higher and followed him up the clean, dry steps. A gust of cold wind slammed into her back, taking her breath away. The wind ruffled his hair, revealing the gash and triggering Officer Blue Eyes' bombshell. Blood...all over the family room...

She blinked rapidly, opened her mouth to announce she'd wait in the car, but Pierce said, "I figured you wanted to forget calling the cops about The Snowman, but here I have half the KCPD department in my house. I'm sorry about this, Quinn."

She took his arm. "It's not your fault."

Inside, pale apricot walls soared two full stories. Above the double doors, three tiers of windows faced Southeast. Sparkling globes in a brass chandelier threw off pools of lemony light onto dark hardwood floors.

Quinn's mouth dropped. The place was straight out of *Architectural Digest*. She caught their reflection in an oversized gold-framed mirror hanging above a Queen Anne table and blurted, "It's so...so neat."

Pierce's laugh was strained. "Thanks to Mrs. Taylor. She comes early—so she can stay on top of my clutter."

"Clutter? You? The hopeless, unrepentant junk collector?"

Hoping to distract him for a second or two longer, Quinn, who could not abide messy, kept chattering. "The bungalow always looked like the aftermath of an earthquake."

Not dirty—just messy.

He pointed to a living room—spacious and impeccable. "I don't think you want to see the family room."

She managed to hold back a sigh of relief. "Let me know if I can help."

"Having you here helps a lot." He turned away

before her relief turned into guilt.

In the living room, Quinn picked up a coffee-table book about Maui. A gift from Pierce's parents, inscribed on the front-page. Mrs. Jordan was Hawaiian, dark and exotic like her son. She never tired of trying to lure him back to Hana, where she and Pierce's retired Navy father lived.

Quinn turned the pages, remembering her first visit to paradise—long before she knew Pierce. She'd gone twice with him. Each time she returned home, determined to ignore his mother's unspoken—but unmistakable—disapproval. Three months after their last trip, she'd discovered Pierce with Brittany and kicked him out of her bed, making his mother very happy she was sure. Rumors were she liked Brittany.

Pictures of romantic beaches and blazing sunsets blurred, and Quinn mentally kicked herself for letting the past suck her downward. She sat up straighter and tried to imagine Pierce in his family room staring at blood. She flipped past several more pictures without seeing them, without feeling the paper. Images of her opening her arms to him distorted the photos. Footsteps sent her heart racing and short-circuited the familiar ache of longing. She whipped around, expecting Pierce.

The book slipped through her fingers, but she caught the spine before it hit the floor. She lurched out of her chair. Her legs felt like stilts—too stiff and wobbly to carry her across the room. Pierce came toward her. The short, red-haired man beside him studied her thoughtfully. Grim-faced, shoulders sagging, Pierce shook his head.

Her heart twisted high in her chest, but she bit down on her bottom lip, holding back a whoosh of sympathy. Careful. She had to be careful. Very careful. Too much had happened for her and Pierce to go back. She'd offer sympathy, but measured sympathy. Sympathy from one old friend to another. Nothing too personal. Nothing he could misconstrue.

"When will you know for sure?" he asked, his voice hoarse. He never took his eyes off the policeman, but reached for Quinn and tucked her under his arm,

"Couple of hours. Sooner if the M.E. isn't swamped." Penetrating eyes stared openly at her bruises. Her throat closed, but she returned the stare.

"In the meantime, search the house again. Just because we can't see anything missing doesn't mean there's not. And, you may find other evidence." The policeman hesitated, looked at Quinn and exhaled. "Or the body."

Sheer willpower kept her from parroting, *the body*? But willpower didn't keep the hair on the back of her neck from standing up or her heart from slamming against her rib cage like a freight train.

Pierce steadied her and agreed he'd follow up. A nod, then the policeman snapped his fingers. "For the record, Miz Alexander, did Mr. Jordan spend last night with you?"

His implication put her on the defensive. Face burning, momentarily mute, she felt like a teenager caught necking at a funeral. She stared at him without speaking, letting her silence slam into his self-satisfaction, letting her silence make him shift his weight from one foot to the other before she moved her head downward in a curt, defiant nod.

"Can you swear, ma'am, that he never left at any time?"

"If I had to." She primped her lips, holding the elf's gaze, feeling like a phony for sounding like an outraged Victorian maiden, but enjoying his frown.

The silence expanded, contracted, scraped her nerves, making her feel guilty and edgy—aftermath of two near attacks in one day, she assumed. Unsure what was happening in Pierce's house, she wasn't about to bring up yesterday's attacks. Whatever the cop read on her face raised his busy brows, but he tipped his head in her general direction and strutted back to the family room.

"What body?" Quinn forced herself to speak normally.

Her ankle hurt and her knees felt so weak that she wanted to scream the question. Better, she wanted to forget it. She didn't know people who got themselves murdered. Dead bodies belonged in books or in movies or on TV...along with nutcases and ski-masked attackers.

"We think—" Pierce looked toward the family room and cleared his throat. "We think someone...someone came in the house and...killed...my...my cat."

"Your cat? You don't have a cat."

Good thing Pierce knew she was intelligent, or based on her response, he might conclude she was mentally impaired.

"Yeah, I do." He swallowed and kept his gaze on the family room. "An old orange and white guy. Fat Floyd."

Silence. Charged silence. Skin-twitching silence. The silence swelled, threatening to take over and shut her out.

Determination coiled into a knot in her stomach. She squared her shoulders and took Pierce's hand. He looked like a little boy who'd dropped his ice cream cone in the dirt.

"I-I'm surprised. You've never had a pet. I never even knew you liked cats."

"Floyd adopted me a couple of years ago—after Brittany left. He treats me just fine." Pierce released Quinn's hand and scrubbed his eyes so viciously she winced.

"Why?" he demanded. "Why come in and kill a harmless old tomcat?"

He looked at Quinn as if she must know the answer.

****

Depressed and confused, Quinn left Pierce's for work, driving his Corvette. Mercifully, he didn't ask her to stay while he continued searching for Fat Floyd. She promised to return for lunch. Just to make sure he ate something.

Maybe she'd talk him into going to the office.

Unless they found the cat's body.

Pushing the thought aside, she concentrated on negotiating the morning traffic. The powerful car demanded her full attention. Street crews had salted the streets, but extra-cautious drivers posed more danger than ice.

Cars crept bumper to bumper along Ward Parkway, the major North-South traffic artery from The Plaza. East-West traffic from nearby Kansas suburbs like Fairway, where she lived, vied for the same lanes. Gridlock reigned on the bridge spanning frozen Brush Creek. Fears spurred by the recession were bringing people to work despite the weather,

Quinn checked her rearview mirror. She needed to call Michael. Remind him the recession, the weather, and the time of year added up to the worst conditions ever for finding Rex a job. Factor in no references from Pierce...

Her mind veered back to Pierce's troubles. They all assumed the blood belonged to Fat Floyd, but what if it belonged to a human? The senselessness knotted in her stomach. She rechecked the mirror.

Three cars behind her, a black Jeep changed into her lane. She couldn't see the driver's face, but her heart fluttered. She switched her gaze to the side mirror, but a blue Lexus SUV blocked her line of sight.

You're being ridiculous. She craned her neck, saw only the SUV and tried thinking logically.

Jeeps weren't common vehicles on The Plaza. Thinking this one was the same vehicle on her cul-de-sac the night before screamed coincidence.

The car riding her bumper moved into the far right lane. The SUV moved up, but not before the Jeep also switched into the right lane.

Her heart pounded and her mind leaped to a new coincidence. The Jeep was black. Her wannabe mugger had worn all black. Pierce's assailant wore all white. What if...her mugger drove his Jeep to her cul-de-sac and morphed into Mr. Ski Mask?

The driver to her left took advantage of her momentary lunacy and cut in front of her. A Mercedes behind the lane-changer moved up next to Quinn. Instead of moving forward, the Jeep stalled. Horns blared. The light turned green. Quinn hit the gas and tailgated the lane-changer through the intersection.

Adrenaline buzzed in her fingertips, and she whipped up the incline on Southwest Trafficway without a hitch. Cold deliberation spurred her past the entrance to the underground garage. Forty-Sixth Terrace was only half a block long before it intersected with Wornall Court doubling back the direction she'd just come.

If the Jeep took the same convoluted route into this area of outrageously priced high-rise condos, she'd know she wasn't dealing with a coincidence. She'd know the driver was stalking her.

She kept her foot on the brake and inched down ice toward Wornall. Fighting for calm, she parked illegally under an EMERGENCY SNOW ROUTE sign. Her fists clenched reflexively, and her stomach knotted as she checked and rechecked the rearview mirror every five seconds.

Ten minutes passed before she turned the key in the ignition. She felt ridiculous for succumbing to paranoia. A traffic cop came toward her, ticket book in his hand. She wet her lips, swallowed and rolled down her window—resigned to accept her punishment.

****

Quinn's headache evaporated the instant she drove into the garage behind Janelle. On the one hand, she had no intention of letting the Dim-Bulb incident make her afraid for the rest of her life. On the other hand, she didn't mind a companion on the day after the encounter.

"Hey, Quinn." Janelle circled the Corvette. "Where'd you get the wheels?"

"Where'd you get the wings on your feet?" Quinn countered, focusing on walking without limping. "How'd you get out of your car and over here so fast?"

"Are you avoiding answering my question by asking two more?"

"Now why would I do that?" The chatter helped Quinn ignore the dull ache in her ankle.

Janelle tossed her head, and her long black hair flew out like a black cape. "I think I see where this is going."

"Where?" Quinn clenched her jaw. Stop obsessing about Dim Bulb.

"Nowhere." Janelle punched the UP button on the elevator.

Laughing felt good until they walked in the office and Sami cried, "Thank God, you're here. Rex Walker's called every ten minutes since I opened the door at eight. Triple A called twice. Want me to pick up your private line? It's on the second ring."

"Thanks, I'll get it." Stomach churning, Quinn jogged awkwardly past the closet door. She didn't know if her stomach hurt because of residual stress from last night's scares or because of this morning's parking ticket or because of new stress from not knowing who was on the other end of the phone. Her breath sounded ragged as she grabbed the receiver.

"Glad you made it safely," Pierce said.

Her stomach dropped. She'd never heard him so down. "Did you find Fat—"

"Nothing yet. I'm taking a sanity break."

"Uh-huh. I used to be schizophrenic, but we're okay now."

Silence boomed in her ear.

"God, Pierce. That was stupid. Insensitive. Off the wall. I'm sorry." She wished she could see him, look him in the eye, prove her sincerity. "Hold on. Next mood swing in six minutes."

He surprised her and actually chuckled. "I should do the apologizing. With everything on your plate, you don't need me whining and wringing my hands."

"You're not. Honestly. What can I do? Come back?" She stopped unbuttoning her coat.

"No. Isn't this where I'm supposed to say just hearing your voice is enough?"

"Hard—after my dumb-ass jokes."

"Blessed are they who can laugh at themselves, for they shall never cease to be amused."

Caught off guard, Quinn blurted, "Did you just make a joke?"

"You know I'm humor impaired. Ask Detective Olsen."

She balanced the receiver between ear and shoulder and lowered her backside into the chair behind her desk. "The elf?"

"None other. He can't believe I can't give him a dozen names of people who'd do something this vicious." Pierce exhaled. "Rex is the only name I came up with since I don't know our golf-course nut."

Quinn bit her tongue, then said, "Maybe the break-in's a fluke—a random act."

"No way. Whoever broke in has to know computers damn well. Besides, you know what they say about coincidences."

A sudden spurt of fire burned through the lining of Quinn's stomach. "You mean, isn't it a coincidence Rex knows computers damn well?"

"He had means and motive and opportunity." Pierce's calm recitation shook Quinn.

"Opportunity?"

"That attack on the golf course wasn't a random coincidence—excuse the redundancy—or whatever it is."

Vocabulary didn't interest her. Thank God she hadn't mentioned the black Jeep. Pierce would, she was certain, declare Rex was the driver. She held back a sigh and said, "When did Rex have opportunity?"

"Last night. On the golf course. The little creep followed us, put me out of commission, then came here for more fun."

"You make him sound like a monster."

"Monster pretty much does it for me."

The harsh judgment knocked the breath out of Quinn. Her throat ached from holding back tears. The problem was, she could almost buy Pierce's scenario. Almost.

"It's snowing again." She rolled her chair closer to the window behind her desk. "Traffic's standing still on Southwest Trafficway."

Without missing a beat, he said, "Is your next line, 'the traffic's a monster'?"

"Close." Below her, a distant red light flashed behind the gridlock. "I'm wondering why a monster would drive five hundred miles in this kind of weather to help a friend."

A snort. "Easy. There's a payoff."

"What payoff?"

"You won't like it, so you go first. Change my mind."

"I accept that challenge." The red light wove through three lanes of traffic, past the intersection to an accident Quinn couldn't see from her vantage point. Traffic below her inched forward.

She took a deep breath and said quietly, "Rex already has his payoff. I promised him yesterday I'd help him find a new job."

"And you wonder why he goes off like a Donner Party explorer to help Michael?"

Consciously, she chose to ignore this trap and made her point. "Being with Michael actually hurts Rex. Some of the people stranded in their cars on Southwest Trafficway, work in banks. Some of them will—unlike the Donner Party—turn back..."

"I hope he turns back. I hope he finds out every VP in town stayed home."

Quinn closed her eyes and said brightly, "Guilty until proven innocent, right?"

"Will you come to lunch if I say yes?"

She waited a beat, hoping he'd worry about her answer, then said, "What time?"

"About one. Does that give you enough time to work a few miracles?"

"Absolutely." She paused, dialing back the aggression in her voice and softening her tone. "And if there's bad news about Fat Floyd, I'll come sooner."

****

Miracle workers multiplex. At nine on the dot, Quinn booted up her PC, dialed Rex, and punched the speaker phone.

"Are you just getting into the office?" he asked, his tone low and ugly.

Not a good beginning, but she didn't give a damn. Except he was meeting Michael. She kept her voice businesslike. "The weather's screwing up phone service."

"You should've kept trying. I expected a callback

no later than seven."

Tough. At seven, she'd been at Pierce's trying not to throw up. She rocked her foot back and forth, hoping to loosen the stiffness in her ankle. "Traffic's a circus."

"Tell me about it. A big rig jackknifed outside Blue Springs."

"Damn, I can't believe it." Where the heck was her screen saver?

"Believe it. The Highway Patrol estimates another half an hour. I've talked to Michael twice. He suggested meeting me in Mexico."

"In good weather, that's at least an hour from St. Louis." Quinn slipped out of her chair, stuck her head under the computer desk and rummaged for the damn power strip.

Her ankle screamed with a million pinpricks of stabbing pain. "How would he get home if Luce goes into labor?" she shouted.

"Why are you yelling?"

"The better to hear me." Quinn withdrew her head and forced a normal voice through clenched lips. "I'm checking to make sure my PC's plugged in."

"Why the hell wouldn't your PC be plugged in?"

"Because two asteroids collided last night?" She took a deep breath and dove back under the desk. "I don't know why, but it wasn't. Okay?"

"Wellll, excuuuse me."

A thousand smart-ass comebacks flooded her brain. Jamming the plug back in the power strip took the edge off her throbbing ankle.

"Can we go back to Michael?" Her hostility was winding down, but she didn't soften her voice. Rex wasn't getting the upper hand—no matter what she owed him. "Is he meeting you in Mexico?"

"Of course not." Surly. "I talked him out of it. Swore I'd meet him by one."

By then she'd be at Pierce's. Guilt ate into her. "You'll never make it."

"Luckily, I have a bladder like a camel. There's not much traffic and no snow east of Columbia. I'll make it."

"Bless you," she said softly, meaning it.

"You know how I feel about Mich—oh-oh. Believe it or not, a State trooper's waving me on. Gotta hang up. Don't want a ticket for driving and talking on my cell."

Chapter 8

Quinn couldn't decide if it was disgust with Triple A or worry about Michael or frustration with Kansas City bankers or exhaustion or hunger. But she felt like a zombie.

Her ankle throbbed and her neck hurt from pressing the phone against her ear and her fingers ached from dialing half the banks in town. Most banking execs had taken off for the holidays. Stomach growling, she made a last call before lunch. Calling a banker at noon was like E.T. calling home. Iffy at best, a waste of time at worst. When Edward Roslyn's secretary put her through to him, Quinn stumbled for a minute before hitting her stride.

Once she did, the bank prez didn't stand a chance.

Rex's computer skills rolled off her tongue like perfect-cut diamonds. Hard-working, self-motivated, brilliant—virtues that made him sound like a candidate for sainthood.

His reason for leaving his present job?

Her mind didn't miss a beat. Not enough challenge. He was bored. Money couldn't keep this amazing employee in an environment without challenge. At this point, she held her breath—amazed her tongue didn't stick to the roof of her mouth.

Worries about honesty and integrity evaporated as Edward Roslyn made noises of interest. "Any reason we can't set up an appointment with him tomorrow, Edward? I mean, the weather won't keep you at home..."

"That's right. We'd call this a spring day in Kalispell."

Quinn waited thirty seconds after hanging up before she let out a whoop. "Afternoon snacks on me," she yelled, then left Rex a voice mail. "Call me. Immediately."

****

Pierce heard the garage door and literally raced out of the house. Quinn had called from the foot of the hill, and he'd opened the front gate again. He'd left it open most of the morning, closing it when the police finally left at eleven-thirty. A century ago now.

The fragrance of Mrs. Taylor's freshly-baked bread followed him into the garage. No way he'd eat, but he knew Quinn would be famished. Normally, she ate enough for two professional full-backs. Under stress, she could eat the entire Kansas City Chiefs under the table. She eased out of the car, bright-eyed and heart-knockingly gorgeous. Wired, too, though she was trying her damnedest to cut back on the electricity she generated.

"An early visit from Santa?" he asked, his neck muscles twanging, his tone pissy. "Or an interview all wrapped up for Rex?"

"We don't have to talk about it." She tipped her head back and sniffed.

"Garlic and cumin."

"Smells like perfume." She unbuttoned her coat and her stomach rumbled.

A signal, Pierce figured—that she was both

starving and close to exploding from suppressed excitement.

"Who is the idiot?"

"Edward Roslyn." One thing about Quinn. She didn't play games.

The door into the house hit Pierce in the ass. "Is this what you call poetic justice?"

"Do we have to talk about it?" She turned and her coat slipped off her shoulders.

Fury slammed into his chest, but Pierce caught the coat by the collar. "Talk about feeling like you pulled the rug out from under me? Hell, no. Let's talk about the weather. That's a safe subject. How long do you think the snow will last?"

"Can't we talk about...Fat Floyd?"

"Sure, but the conversation won't last long. I haven't found him." She looked over her shoulder as he led her past the family room. No sign of blood stains.

"The carpet cleaners did a great job." Belligerence rode the comment as he hung her coat in the closet. He shut the door—hard, like a spoiled little boy.

She jumped—as if he'd caught her doing something unnatural.

"An appointment two days before Thanksgiving...Guess I'm not the only one who can charm birds out of the trees." He pulled a wing chair closer to the living room fire and reached for the poker. God, he'd seen too many old movies.

Quinn ignored his stupid cliché. Apparently, she hadn't seen the same movies. The wounded lead sitting by the fire brooding. She stayed on her feet instead of kneeling at his feet and crying her eyes out.

Her lovely, kissable mouth twisted. "I didn't charm

Edward."

Pierce heard the edge and didn't give a damn. She'd crossed a line and she could bat her baby grays at him all day, but she knew she'd crossed the damn line.

Red splotches flashed on her cheeks. "It's possible Edward won't hire Rex."

"I'd say you can take that idea to the bank—once I talk to Edward." Since he was holding the poker, Pierce opened the glass screen and jabbed at the logs.

"Stop that."

On the defensive, he arched a brow. "Mrs. Taylor said lunch won't be ready until one."

"Stop avoiding me. Stop patronizing me and stop threatening me. You're the idiot." The bruise under her eye stood out purple and ugly against her crimson cheeks.

"Don't hold back, Quinn. It's a myth guys have feelings too."

Disgust flashed in her eyes. "If you've got such a strong case against Rex, have him arrested. Don't attack his character behind his back. That's not fair."

A neuron—or something basic—snapped in Pierce's head like a nuclear rubber band. He slammed the glass doors. "But I suppose it is fair that you set up an interview for an embezzler with my mentor."

"Edward has a brain. So do you. What better place for a man you think is an embezzler than working for Edward Roslyn?"

"It's like giving the bank robbers the combination to the safe."

A heartbeat of silence, then she said, "I don't want to fight. Can we agree to disagree?"

A simple yes or no would've done nicely, but

Pierce couldn't let go that easily. "About his guilt? Or about his interview with Edward?"

"About whether he's a Leo or a Taurus. About whether he's a misfit or misunderstood. About—"

"Okay, okay." Her rumbling stomach sounded like thunder before a summer storm. Pierce said, "I agree to disagree."

At that moment, Mrs. Taylor called from the hall that soup was on. He and Quinn started—like kids caught arguing by parents who had ordered them not to argue or else.

"We're eating in the kitchen," he said. "Unless you—"

"The kitchen's fine." Now—when it didn't matter—she was Ms. Congeniality.

"My gosh." She stopped in the door and snickered. "Your refrigerator's bigger than your entire kitchen in the bungalow."

A smile tugged at Pierce's lips. "It's Mrs. Taylor's domain, but I still like to cook."

"Isn't she eating with us?" Quinn pointed at the table set for two.

"She's a little upset. She and Floyd share the domain since I'm gone so much."

"Am I naive, thinking—since you haven't found him—that's good news?"

Pierce swiveled his gaze away from her. "I wish I knew."

****

"I bet you don't have problems with vampires in this neighborhood." Quinn's mouth watered as she leaned over her bowl of steaming soup.

Pierce gave her a passable smile. "Lots of garlic in

Mrs. Taylor's herb garden."

In Quinn's mind, the soup, the garden, the plate of yeasty rolls now offered three safe topics for lunch-time conversation. Rex and Fat Floyd were not safe topics. Pierce showed zero inclination to reveal any feeling except anger.

Or, maybe she didn't feel inclined to delve into his vulnerability—as readable as newspaper headlines on his bewildered face. Certain he'd hate her insight, she resisted pointing out he needed more than two spoonsful of the wonderful chicken soup to keep up his strength.

Did he think she was as sensitive as a pig at a trough?

Did he remember that tension always made her ravenous?

If Floyd was her cat, there wouldn't be enough room in Pierce's wall-to-wall fridge to stock fuel to feed her. Fortified by a second helping of soup, she decided which safe topic to pursue and opened her mouth. Just like on the TV soaps, the phone rang.

The bronze tones of Pierce's face paled. He pushed his chair away from the table. "Detective Olsen...with results...blood test."

Quinn waited until she heard Pierce acknowledge it was the red-haired detective. Despite her stomach's protest, she pushed away from the table, grabbed a roll and limped into the pantry.

Pierce motioned her to stand next to him and tilted the receiver toward her.

Detective Olsen spoke fast. "The blood in your family room was not your cat's."

"Christ. You mean it was human?"

"No, it wasn't human."

"You're sure?" Pierce swiped his sweat-beaded forehead.

"Positive. The lab confirmed it's chicken blood."

Quinn grabbed Pierce's elbow and yelled softly, "Yesss."

He frowned. "So where the hell's my cat?"

A loud crash, followed by a blood-curdling yowl, drowned out the response.

Pierce punched SPEAKER, shoved the phone at Quinn and sprinted toward the kitchen. Ignoring Detective Olsen's questions, Quinn dropped the phone and dogged Pierce. In the middle of the table, tail whipping back and forth like an angry orange and white cobra, Fat Floyd disregarded the broken blue bowls on the floor. He was too busy scavenging tidbits of chicken in the broth dripping over the side.

"FF, you devil," Pierce yelled. "Mrs. Taylor?" His grin spread from his mouth and lit up his black eyes. He grabbed the cat, scratched him behind the ears and held him under Quinn's nose. "Mrs. Taylor!"

Floyd growled like a starved tiger. He struggled to jump back on the table. He dug his toes into Pierce's side and lunged at several chicken pieces he'd missed vacuuming up.

Quinn held out her arms. "Finish your call. I'll corral his royalship." She followed Pierce, petting and talking to the complaining feline.

"What is it? What's wrong?" The housekeeper hustled into the kitchen, her eyes wide. She took one look at Floyd and cried, "Fat Boy."

The cat backflipped like a contortionist out of Quinn's arms and landed at Mrs. Taylor's feet. He bumped her ankles, and she knelt, crooning his name, promising him a treat.

Pierce's boyish grin reminded Quinn of a young Cary Grant. "Sorry, Detective," he yelled like a kid discovering treasure, "but the great cat caper is now solved."

"Glad to hear it, Mr. Jordan." Quinn winced at the detective's booming voice. "Just a couple more loose ends before I hang up."

"Okay." Pierce circled Quinn's waist, hugging her, pointing at his ravenous cat.

"I'm sure you want to know who got in your house and painted your family room with chicken blood."

Pierce's arm circled Quinn's waist, but she couldn't repress a shiver. He asked, "Any chance the bastard got the wrong house? I maintain I don't have a lot of enemies."

A long, loud sigh. "Yes, sir. I know, I know. I rarely meet anyone—normal folks like yourself, that is—who can think of someone vicious enough to vandalize their property."

Detective Olsen let this sink in before adding, "Have you found any valuables missing?"

"Nothing." Pierce stretched the phone's cord to its limit and strained to watch his cat devour a plate of cooked chicken. "I don't keep anything of value in the house."

Detective Olsen frowned. "No electronics? Smart phones? PCs? TVs?"

"The three TVs are attached to the wall. My computer's in my office." Pierce patted his pockets and produced his phone. "I carry my Droid everywhere. No need for a PDA."

A sigh preceded the detective's flat response. "That leaves us at a dead end. Hold on."

A mumble of voices buzzed in the background. Pierce grinned at Quinn. "Ever seen such a spoiled cat?"

"No, and I've never seen a human so besotted, either."

"Moi?" Pierce laughed. "Did you hear that, Mrs. Taylor?"

"Heard it and couldn't agree more." She winked at Quinn.

Detective Olsen came back on the line. "We checked with your neighbors, by the way. None of them saw or heard anything. And none of them has reported any incidents."

"Not surprising, is it?"

"No. It sorta leaves us with three ways to look at what happened. The vandalism to your house was a random act. Or it was it a mistake. Or...it was planned."

"I'm guessing we'll never find out, Detective. Let me know what I can do to help."

When Pierce hung up, the housekeeper shooed Quinn and Pierce out of the kitchen while she cleaned up Floyd's mess. "Five minutes until dessert," she said.

In the foyer, Pierce grabbed Quinn and twirled her around until she felt like a kid on a merry-go-round. His kiss added to her delirium, but didn't vaporize the nagging in the back of her mind. She held onto his neck and said, "You didn't mention your suspicions about Rex. This morning you told me he was your prime suspect. What changed your mind?"

Pierce dragged a fingertip across her bottom lip. "Gut reaction's all I have, Quinn. If he did manage to get in and pour chicken blood in the family room, I'll live with it. In his shoes, I might even do worse."

****

"Over the river and through the woods..." Pierce chanted, fighting the urge to grab Quinn in a hug that would make her weak in the knees. Instead, he flipped on the 'Vette's wipers.

She stuck her head out the window. "My kind of weather."

"Hooky weather. Let's do it. Play hooky."

She laughed and caught a mouthful of snow. "Are you insane?"

"Nope. You nailed an interview for Rex tomorrow. I've found my cat. Steve and Tony think they have a lead on the security system crash yesterday." He spoke fast, piling on every argument he could marshal. "Why not celebrate? Those kids have the right idea."

Three ruddy-cheeked kids, bundled up like Eskimos, trudged up the hill pulling their sleds. They waved at him and Quinn.

"Uh-huh." Quinn pulled her head inside, rolled up her window, and waved until the kids disappeared over the summit.

Ruddy-cheeked herself, she shook her head, spraying Pierce with snow. "Those kids don't have forty people coming for Thanksgiving. They don't have a brother who's having some kind of meltdown. They don't have a car with a dead battery."

Silenced, Pierce considered saying, *"No, they've got a life."* He tapped the brake, feeling stupid for inviting Quinn to play. Play was a four-letter word in her dictionary. "What's wrong with your battery?"

"Who knows? Triple A called and said it wouldn't

120

hold a charge. They promised to change it out today, but they're swamped. Maybe I'll just ski into work mañana."

"What about getting home tonight if they don't get to you?"

"I'll put a call in for a taxi right now." She pulled her cell phone out of her coat pocket.

Mr.Cool said, "I can take you home."

"I thought you were going to play hooky."

"Not by myself." Then, because he sounded so pathetic, he said, "Skiing's fine by myself. Ditto, snorkeling. Deep-sea diving, fine. Playing hooky definitely requires a playmate."

"Get thee behind me, Satan. Or, I'll breathe on you." She stared out her window.

He laughed. "I should've offered you a toothbrush. Mrs. Taylor keeps new ones in the guest room for Mom and Dad."

After a decade, she finally turned to face him. "How are they? Are they flying in tonight?"

Now it was his turn to stare through the windshield like a geek. "They're probably landing in Sydney about now. It's Sandi's turn to have them. She invited me, but I opted out. I'm staying home."

"You're not skiing?" Quinn jammed the phone back in her pocket and pulled her gloves out at the intersection of Brush Creek and Forty-Seventh.

"Not this year." Smart decision since paying out two and a half million dollars put a crimp in his play money, though Quinn didn't need to know that.

"What are you doing about Thanksgiving Dinner?"

"You saw my kitchen. I'm cooking."

"How big a turkey?"

"Cornish hens—though Floyd prefers turkey." He could see where this was going.

"You can't celebrate Thanksgiving alone." Quinn's need to mold the world into a Norman Rockwell painting punched Pierce in the gut.

"I won't be alone. Floyd loves strutting his holiday finery."

"You're kidding, right?"

"There's a painting of a forty-pound wild turkey on his Thanksgiving kerchief. Mrs. Taylor will press it—"

"You've gotta be kidding." Quinn shook her head. "You, the banker born doing everything by the book. I don't believe it."

A rush of heat filled his stomach. He deliberately missed taking the yellow light. Damn, it was fun catching Quinn off balance. He wiggled his eyebrows and gave her his best wolfish grin. "I've changed a little in the past four years."

"A little? I'm thinking I'm sitting next to an alien."

The light turned green. The driver behind them laid on his horn. Pierce shot him the bird.

"Pierce!"

"Quinn?" He drove through the intersection like a sane man. Mr. Impatient rode his tail.

"What are you doing?"

"Jerking that guy's chain."

"You're scaring me to death."

Good. Scared to death meant she might just forget about inviting him to her annual Thanksgiving Bash.

"Don't worry," he said, "I've got a tire iron in the trunk."

"Who are you?" She grabbed the door handle as he peeled into the parking garage. He slowed immediately to 5 MPH.

"Relax. The jerk went on."

"So what? What if he wrote down your license? What if uses it and finds out where you live? What if—"

"What if the sky falls, Chicken Little?" Pierce pulled into his reserved spot, killed the engine and took her gloved hand. "I'm sorry if I scared you. Hard to believe my IQ's higher than an eggplant's, isn't it?"

"Right at this moment, I think I'd need some hard proof."

Right at this moment, the hard proof he had made him look like a fool. She unhooked her seatbelt, and he silently groaned. He couldn't move his legs, let alone walk.

"I'm sorry." Stalling, praying she didn't jump out of the car, he slunk to the level of a snake and went for her soft spot. "Remember, I suffered a severe brain injury last night."

Her mouth twisted. "Stop that...before I hurt you."

"Promises, promises." He was already hurting— hurting bad. He'd never suffered like this in adolescence. This must be what hell was like.

Her laugh sounded like an angel's solo. Idiot that he was, heart galloping, Pierce leaned across the ten inches separating them and traced the line of her jaw— from under her ear to the tip of her chin. The smoky gray of her eyes changed to black—like the sky before a storm. She lifted her mouth to his.

She pulled away too soon, tugging her coat collar higher. "That was a mistake."

"Huh-uh."

"Let's agree to disagree." She cracked the door.

"I don't want to agree to disagree." Another minute and he'd be crying for his mommy. "I already agreed to disagree. Now, I want to kiss you again."

She shook her head. "Been here, done this. Dèjá vu."

"Dèjá vu. You said that last night. On the golf course." He had no idea how his brain derailed so fast.

"I did?" She swung her feet onto the pavement, turned in her seat and gave him two raised eyebrows.

Way to go, Pierce. Keep her hanging on your every word. He said, "Exhaust fumes? They make my head hurt. That's why I changed subjects so fast."

Her mouth twitched, and she shook her head. "I have no idea what you're talking about."

"Me either. I just want to kiss you again."

An expression he took as regret darkened her eyes. She slid out the door, wiggled her fingers at him and called over her shoulder, "Work calls."

****

Quinn's legs wobbled like a toddler's. Pierce trotted behind her. On her heels. He'd catch up with her in five, six seconds at the most. He was right about the fumes. They made her head hurt too. She glanced at the security monitors, and her cheeks burned. Just what she needed. Joe watching her and Pierce steam up the car windows.

"Going to a fire?" Pierce fell into step beside her.

"As a matter of fact, I have about four to put out. I need to call Rex. I should've called him from the car."

"If you had, we'd have missed that Hallmark moment."

"Don't go there. Monitors or not, I could still kill you. Plead insanity."

Pierce's laugh bounced off the cement walls. "Better find a better defense. No one will ever buy you've gone 'round the bend."

If you only knew. Stiff, nervous he'd pick up on her raging feelings, she kept her distance as he punched the UP button on the elevator.

The door snicked open. Pierce stood back. She entered first. He smacked LOBBY and she made a noise.

"This will take thirty seconds," he said. "I have questions for Joe about yesterday."

"Oh, goody!" She felt like smacking him. "Since I don't have any questions, I'll go—"

"Thirty seconds." The door opened and Pierce depressed the STOP button.

Hot blood rushed up Quinn's neck to her face, but she resisted the urge to slap his hand away. He wanted to forget a nut vandalizing his house, she wanted to forget a nut jumping at her in the garage.

A smile jiggled Joe's wrinkles. He came from around his desk, hobbling a little and greeted them. Heat from the lobby rolled into the elevator. After the cool air in the garage, the building felt too hot to Quinn.

Probably can't be too warm for Joe's arthritis. She ignored Pierce and spoke to the older man.

He massaged his gnarled fingers, barely waiting until she finished asking about his new treatment before he said, "That was quite a scare you had yesterday, Miz Alexander."

"I'm fine, Joe." She avoided eye contact with Pierce and noted the other five elevators remained at the top floor.

Joe edged a little closer and lowered his voice.

"The police came by a little while ago—one-thirty to be exact—but I couldn't tell them anything more."

Quinn resisted the urge to push Pierce's index finger off the STOP button. She said brightly, "Not much to tell, is there?"

"Not much," Joe agreed. To Pierce, he said, "Steve Cutter and Tony Franklin are right on top of it. Tony took the tape."

The whole garage scene flashed in Quinn's mind, and her heart hammered in her ears. She stepped around Pierce and chirped, "Why don't I take the stairs? I need the exercise."

"Here's another elevator," Joe said.

Pierce caught her arm. "Thanks, Joe. Catch you later."

The doors slid shut. Quinn stumbled backwards, fell against Pierce and wished time-travel was a fact of twenty-first century life.

Smoke was seeping out of his ears, but his face resembled a block of ice. When he spoke, she couldn't see his lips move. "Wanna bet Joe's as confused as I am?"

Invisible pulleys carried them upward, but her stomach dropped. "Nothing happened. You already know that." Damned if she intended to explain.

"I know we should've discussed your mugging incident earlier." Pierce turned the little key on the panel, and the elevator glided to a stop. The doors didn't open.

"You're being melodramatic." She leaned back against the mahogany wall and pulled out her cell phone.

"Wrong. I'm being pissed."

The icicles in his voice froze her ESP. A fraction of a second too late, she saw his hand shoot out. Her phone disappeared into the inside pocket of his suit jacket.

"You can't make me talk."

"Nooo?" His drawl sent shivers slaloming down her back.

"Stop acting like your knuckles drag the ground."

"My knuckles do drag the ground. What the hell went down with you yesterday?"

Her nostrils flared. Dammit, he knew she hated ultimatums. Worse, she hated men throwing their weight around. "I don't need your protection for your freaking information."

"Uh-huh. You know tai-chi, right? Yet you got mugged in my building." He touched the bruise under her eye so gently she barely felt it.

"I didn't get mugged." Her cheeks felt like a snow grader had scraped to the bone.

"You should get a refund on your facelift then." He tucked a chunk of hair behind her ear. "Can we stop acting like idiots for half a second?"

Her throat closed, and she blinked quickly. It'd been so long since she'd loved and trusted him, she'd forgotten how wonderful tenderness felt.

"If anything happened to you..." His deep, throaty voice cracked.

Her own throat ached with repressed tears. Swallowing brought no relief.

"We may never have a future together, Quinn, but we have a past I'll always treasure."

"I know." She kicked herself for being so weak but told him anyway about the craziness in the garage. She finished by saying, "I honestly think it was a fluke. At one point, I thought the guy was more surprised at seeing me than I was at seeing him."

"I'd probably agree if I didn't have a goose egg from our walk on the golf course."

When Quinn didn't answer, couldn't answer because she couldn't explain the snowball attack, Pierce turned the key, and the elevator hummed. "But fluke or joke or attempted mugging, I'm sure as hell not letting what happened go without finding out why."

Chapter 9

Head down, Quinn whirled into her office and started putting out fires.

Both afternoon appointments had cancelled. No surprise in the toughest job market since the 1930s. Lousy weather beat out a depressing meeting to develop a job-search strategy.

The wonderful, efficient Sami offered to work with the caterer on last-minute details for the Thanksgiving Bash. She left Quinn dialing Triple A, massaging her pounding head and silently fuming.

What planet did Rex inhabit—ignoring her voice mail? Don't tell her he and Michael were talking. About what, for so long?

Triple A's canned music scraped her nerves, but it quickly provided the kind of mindless background noise accompanying her own private movie. Luce went into labor naturally, alleviating the need for Michael to change his mind about inducing birth. Rex was chauffeuring them to the hospital—which explained why he hadn't called.

He couldn't call and drive safely.

Her pulse raced and she allowed herself hope. Michael's fine. She doodled fine on the blank piece of paper in front of her, underlining each letter and adding four fat exclamation points. He's just tired. Tired and stressed, but fine...

He knew you'd find Rex a job. She gnawed her bottom lip. Good ole Michael. She folded the paper into a crude airplane and pitched it into the air. Gravity jerked it down to the floor. Someday, someday soon, she had to set her baby brother straight. Tell him—except for this one time with Rex—she only worked miracles on Wednesdays and Thursdays.

Sami stuck her head in the office. Janelle had the caterer's checklist in front of her. Leah was busy updating their computer files. Sami volunteered to sit on hold with Triple A.

"Thank you, thank you," Quinn mouthed, handed over her insurance card, then made the follow-up call she'd avoided making since her return from Pierce's.

Unlike at Triple A and the caterer's, a warm body answered at First Plaza Bank. Yes, her cashier's check was ready. She should bring a picture-ID with her.

Before four. "We're closing early because of the weather."

Surrpise, surprise. Snow now fell from leaden skies in fat, wet clumps, gusting like little tornadoes on the ground. Traffic once again stood at a standstill on Southwest Trafficway. Quinn grimaced. Snow covering tiled roofs, fountains, and streets made The Plaza as ethereal as a fairy tale, but Janelle drove an ancient, unreliable Beetle without snow tires. Leah lived north of the river, and Sami had two school kids dismissed early. If the three left right now, they might arrive home for Thanksgiving.

Humming *Over the River,* Quinn went into the outer office. The quiet chatter stopped. She said, "An announcement, ladies."

Leah blew an invisible trumpet.

Quinn bowed and grinned. "Thanksgiving begins today. See everyone Monday."

After the cheering died, Sami said, "We're on hold with the caterer and Triple A."

"Hang up. The caterer swears she'll be here on Thursday at three—even if she has to hire sled dogs. If Triple A doesn't fix my battery, I can haul out my cross country skis."

"Whoa. Start a trend." Janelle squealed. "Cross country skis with a little black dress."

Five minutes later, the three other women left together, repeating their thanks and wishing each other Happy Thanksgiving. When they entered the elevator, Quinn locked the door. One more call to Rex before she hiked down to First Plaza...as close as she was likely to get today to playing hooky.

Her call to Rex switched immediately to voice mail. Damn. She exhaled through her mouth, left another message, locked her desk and headed for the coat closet. When her land line rang, she hesitated, let the phone ring two more times and lost the debate about answering.

"Do you know what's wrong with me?"

The teasing in Pierce's tone sent heat surging into Quinn as she buttoned her coat. "You mean," she said, voice breathy, nerves jittery, "besides being stubborn, cocky, and mouthy?"

"Dumb. You forgot dumb," he said in a tone inviting her to play.

"I'll give you dumb. What else?"

"The same thing that's wrong with you."

He has to be laughing, she thought and imagined the skin around his eyes crinkle.

"Funny, I didn't think we had that much in common."

"You won't deny we're both incorrigible workaholics."

A statement, but Quinn fanned her face before replying. "Nooooo. I won't deny it. So?"

"So, here's your second chance. Let's play hooky. I just sent my whole staff home—"

"Me too." She laughed as if they'd shared a huge secret. "Small minds run in the same creeks, I guess."

It wasn't that funny, but they both laughed like maniacs. No, fools, she thought. Fools for forgetting the divide between them.

"Well, let's go. I'll be down in three minutes."

He hung up before she could tell him she had to go to the bank. Damn, another contest of wills. But she was not caving on this point.

Coming through the door two minutes and fifty seconds later, he grinned, his black eyes flashing. "And to think I thought you'd change your mind."

"No play until after I run an errand." If he didn't like it, he could play hooky by himself.

"No problem." He bussed her cheek. "I've never seen you so eager."

"How many changes of clothes do you keep in your office?" She hoped the question deflected questions about her errand.

"You're eager. I'm prepared." He wore old cowboy boots, a red crew-neck sweater, and a flannel-lined jean jacket. He gripped the seams of his jeans midway between hip and knee and turned slowly like a model.

She pushed him into the elevator, following at a distance.

"See?" He nudged her toward a corner. "Can't keep your hands off me."

"Only because you don't wear a baseball cap backwards or jeans low enough to display a piece of anatomy better covered."

Without warning, he dropped a long, sweet kiss on her lips. Her head felt heavier than a bowling ball as she turned her face away. What was wrong with her—making that crack about his ass?

Suddenly all business, she said, "Remind me to get my garage door opener from the car."

"At your service."

"You're drooling." She poked him in the ribs. He leaped at her, pinning her against the wall and giving her a quick pinch on the butt as she squirmed away, giggling.

"Keep your distance." A clump of hair fell onto her forehead. Pierce took a step toward her. She waved him away. "I'm serious. Stop hitting on me."

"Your hair looks...disheveled. Sexy, but disheveled."

Hormones, she thought and tugged at her hair. Her estrogen overload, his testosterone fumes. Hers she could get under control.

Patting her hair, she said, "You should put mirrors in these elevators."

"In the ceiling?" He wiggled his eyebrows and stroked an imaginary moustache.

"In your dreams."

The temperature in the elevator hovered around five hundred degrees Centigrade. Heat rose off Pierce in waves and rolled over her like fresh lava. Damn, damn, damn. She must've had some kind of mental breakdown to get in an elevator with him.

They stopped two floors below her office. Before the doors opened, she managed to push him away and snag her hair back in a knot. She went to the opposite corner, refusing to look at him. Her face felt as if she'd had dermabrasion with a floor sander.

A young, twentysomething brunette with lots of long black curls, heavy eye makeup and fat crimson lips got on, nodded to Quinn and looked at Pierce with a wide, open smile, asking him what he thought of the weather and if he had a long drive home.

Quinn covered her mouth and stared at the ceiling. Her ears felt ready to explode from swallowing the laughter bubbling in her throat. When Pierce followed her off at the garage level, the brunette looked so disappointed she rode back up to another level.

"Good thing I was in there with you." Quinn smirked. "You never know who may get excited just being in the same space with you."

"You exaggerate. Besides, I only have eyes for you." He hummed a few bars of the old torch song.

She laughed. "Ahh, ever the platinum-tongued devil, aren't you? That babe's attention wandered a little lower than your eyes."

"Careful. You'll turn my head." Unless she was mistaken, he did have the decency to appear flushed. "I'm sure she noticed I did, in fact, only have eyes for you."

"The quarters were a little too close for her to notice me."

"Right. You're so petite, it's real easy to overlook you."

Flushing, she stopped at her car. "Enough with the

pick-up lines. Remember, our outing starts after my errand."

"Why wouldn't I remember?" He looked at her like a puppy who couldn't get paper training right. "Just don't tell me you want to go by Rex's place."

"I want to go to First Plaza. Your check's ready."

"Forget it." He waved his hands in front of his belt buckle like a baseball umpire.

Her whole body stiffened. "We've danced this dance before. I'm not asking you to take me. I'd planned on walking."

"You'll freeze. You're limping like a stunned goose."

"Toodle." She wiggled her fingers, pivoted around, hoping her ankle was reliable, and started for the the lobby, knowing without a doubt he'd follow.

"Toodle?" He leaped in front of her and walked backwards as easily as if he had eyes in the back of his head. "Do you have to have your Goddamn way on every single issue?"

"Why not?" She lengthened her stride.

He stumbled once.

"See how women feel dancing backwards? You just need a pair of three-inch heels."

"I'll pass on the heels." He now matched her lead, step for step. "I don't want your money."

"Catch me after I go to the bank. Maybe then I can pretend I'm interested."

"Huh-uh. Let's talk. Now." Without warning, he jumped in front of her and she ran right into his chest.

Her heart jitterbugged, but she walked around him, head high.

Still walking backwards, he stayed in front of her.

Behind him, a man got off the elevator, watched them with naked curiosity, then dodged through the cars parked to their left.

"I don't get it," Pierce said. "I don't need the money."

"But I need to pay you the money." She stopped and pointed over his shoulder. "We're six or seven feet from the lobby door. The pavement slopes up. I don't want you falling on your butt after your head injury."

"Considerate of you to warn me."

"That's me. Miz Considerate."

Somewhere in the garage, a motor roared, then quieted. Any minute the car would come past them.

Quinn tasted the oil and gas fumes. "I am going to the bank."

"All right. All right." Pierce threw his hands in the air. "Do you have to walk? Or can I at least drive you?"

"As long as you can get me there by four—"

"Yessss!" He leaped in the air and clicked his heels together.

****

"This is me eating crow." Pierce held the steering wheel with his left hand, pretended to scoop food into his mouth with his right hand and hoped for a smile from Quinn.

Her laugh—a sound he'd always loved—rang with fun. "How are the feathers?"

"Tough." She laughed again, and he glanced at her out of the corner of his eye. "Aren't you going to say you told me snails move faster than the traffic?"

"Finish your crow first. I don't want you to have indigestion."

"Indigestion is a natural state after your near-mugging experience."

She groaned and rolled her eyes. Exactly the response he'd expected. Still, he enjoyed the feeling he'd caught her off guard and pressed ahead while he could.

"Indigestion is what I had after my conversation with Steve Cutter. Who, by the way, can't explain why the security cameras didn't work yesterday morning but do now." Confident the gridlock wouldn't inch forward any time soon, Pierce stopped peering past his windshield wipers and locked eyes with Quinn. "Tony's coming up blank too. He's on The Plaza grilling the security company."

"Well, if I emitted less electricity early in the morning, I'm sure the cameras would've operated fine."

Pierce risked electrocution and took her hand. "You should sleep in late—so the world doesn't short out."

She squeezed his fingers and threw him a thousand-watt-smile and sent his heart into defibrillation. "Right now, my brain's about to short out from over-thinking that garage soap opera. Rehashing it isn't my idea of playing hooky."

"I suppose the same goes for discussing our ski-mask friend."

"Oh, my gosh!" Quinn widened her eyes. "You are teachable."

"We always come back to who's in control, don't we?" He wiggled his eyebrows, hoping to take the sting out his question.

"Always. So here we are. Two control freaks stopped in their tracks by gridlock."

The pressure in his chest eased. "Do we have a

Plan B?"

Frankly, he didn't think much of Plan B, but for once he kept his opinions to himself. Limping probably would get her the four blocks to the bank faster than idling in the Gomobile. No doubt she'd arrive frozen stiff. No doubt she'd then veto a romantic ride in a horse-drawn carriage and they'd forget the hooky idea altogether. Unless he thought of something else.

At a momentary loss for other hooky-options, he remained adamant on one point. "No jay walking. This weather requires x-ray vision."

"We agree. I'll get out at the next light."

His jaw dropped. Had she ever acquiesced to one of his suggestions so quickly? "Are you pulling my leg?"

"I'm being flexible. See how flexible I am?"

"Flexible enough to give me a kiss before you get out?"

The logical part of him expected a rebuff—a sigh. A head-toss. A look. So, when she brushed his cheek with her warm lips, he damned near rear ended the Lexus in front of them.

She whispered, "I'm looking forward to playing hooky with you."

****

Snow crashed down around Quinn like an avalanche. She trudged the last two blocks to the bank, praying she didn't trip over an invisible trash can or collide with another fool when Rex called and started speaking as soon as she said hello.

"Are you eating? You sound like you've got a mouthful of mush."

"Bingo." Edgy about snow-blind drivers jumping

the buried curb, she had zero tolerance for wisecracks. She pulled the wool scarf away from her mouth and asked, "How's Michael? Did Luce go to the hospital?"

"You've got questions, I've got answers." A buzzing undercurrent of power rode his attempt at humor. "Thanks for the interview mañana. Give me facts about Edward Roslyn."

"Give me facts about Michael, and I'll tell you everything you should know about Edward." Inhaling snow with each word she uttered, Quinn wasn't sure if she sounded hard-nosed or stuffy-nosed.

Too bad for Rex if he expected her to have Michael's soft heart.

"Okay, okay. Oooookay. I suppose your concern for your baby brother trumps my concern about eating next month."

His whine grated her nerves like a dentist's drill. Hang up. She bit her lip and let the fantasy slip away. He had answers she needed. "What about inducing labor?"

"I talked Michael out of it. For now. Luce's too terrified."

A sudden wind slammed Quinn in the face. She gasped, wiped her eyes and plodded forward. The bank closed in nine minutes. No one would wait a pico-second for a no-show in this storm. "Maybe I should call Luce."

"Why? You've never had labor induced. You've never even had a kid."

Quinn flinched. She tried to imagine speaking so bluntly to Rex, pointing out he'd never had people look at him without recoiling. Never known a woman—except maybe his mother—who told him he was handsome. Never looked in a mirror and smiled at his reflection. Biting her bottom lip, she shook so hard she dropped the damn cell phone.

It sank like a rock sucked into quicksand. Millions of snowflakes swirled around the nearest street lamp, reducing its incandescence to a weak, whitish-blue halo. She stood stunned, muscles locked, mind frozen.

"Here you go." A man dressed in black emerged from the shadows, scooped up the phone and pressed it into her hand.

She reeled backwards. Fought for balance. Struggled to see the man's face, saw the masked face in the underground garage. Her heart kicked a couple of ribs. Her lungs deflated like punctured balloons, but she lunged at a black sleeve. She caught a handful of snow.

The Samaritan was gone, lost behind the solid white curtain.

In the middle of her anxiety attack, the faint scent of spicy cologne made her freezing nose twitch. Her lungs shrank, making her breathing ragged. She took a small, hesitant step toward the smell, shielding her eyes against the thick flakes. Snow had already filled his footprints. The high beams on several cars crawling toward her cast ghostly streams of light through the white veil, but it was too late. He was gone.

Gone. The word relooped through her brain as she pivoted, mumbling incoherently.

"What?" Rex yelled. "I can't understand you. Speak up."

"I'll. Call. You. Back."

The marble bank building rose out of the murk like an ancient monolith—ablaze with lights. The heavy glass doors weighed a ton and her feet slipped in knee-deep drifts. She entered the lobby, shivering, rubbing her gloved hands together, cutting her eyes past the guard to the large wall clock. Four minutes before four.

For a second, she swayed with relief and her skin crackled. She'd made it. Despite Mother Nature. Despite Rex. Despite her jumpy nerves.

The husky guard said something and she laughed. The sound echoed in the lobby—empty except for her and him. He narrowed his beady eyes, focused on space behind her, and frowned. Her heart lurched. A glance over her shoulder confirmed no one had followed her inside. By the time she finished informing the guard she had an appointment, Douglas Prescott, 2nd VP for Customer Services was bustling toward her, his pale brows knotted together, his chicken lips set in a thin line as snow dripped off her, onto the marble floor.

Douglas made no small talk about the weather or about her well-being or about the upcoming holiday. He led her to his glass-enclosed office. He went behind his desk, opened a drawer and handed her a plain white envelope.

"This is a rather large check, Quinn." He pushed his rimless glasses higher on his long, straight nose as if he'd stated a profundity instead of the obvious.

Stating the obvious wasn't illegal. She flicked her eyes toward his desk clock, a pricy reproduction of an astrolabium timepiece with a miniature globe of the earth rotating around a brass sun. "Large for what, Douglas?"

"You've never made a withdrawal this large. Or a deposit."

"I've been saving up." She pressed her knees together and mentally talked herself out of biting off his head. She didn't need Douglas recounting her meltdown to his Thanksgiving high-society dinner guests.

Hyper-aware he was leaning toward her like the brass sun, trying to pull her into his orbit, she slipped the envelope into her coat pocket. "You're closing early so I won't keep you."

"Did you park downstairs?" He pulled his coat off a brass rack.

"No, I figured it was full." She reached for the doorknob and smiled at her illogical lie.

"Do you need a ride to your car?" His tone held all the enthusiasm of a mortician greeting attendees at a funeral.

"I'm meeting someone." She couldn't bring herself to say thank you.

"It's brutal out there." Apparently unaware of his hollow observation, he followed her into the desolate lobby.

"I love snow. I dressed for the Arctic." She spared a second to consider changing her mind, throwing herself on the pompous jerk's mercy and asking if she could wait in the lobby.

The guard straightened as they approached and unlocked the front door at Douglas's signal. Too late now to do anything but leave.

She raised her coat collar to her ears, wished both men Happy Thanksgiving and stepped into the storm, feeling light headed. How easily she'd wiped out a million dollars from her ROTH account and closed all savings accounts and borrowed every penny of equity in her house.

For Michael, I'd do it again, she thought.

****

Quinn stood in the bank's doorway, stamped her numb feet, hugged her waist and pressed her cell against her stinging ear. Her breath came out in silver puffs. C'mon, Pierce. C'mon.

The phone rang and rang and rang. Why didn't he answer? Had he been in an accident? Her heart stuttered. Pacing a few steps away from the doorway, she scanned the blurry, oncoming headlights. Bullets of snow fanned out horizontally, blinding her.

Dammit. She'd never recognize her own car in this weather. Would she recognize the Corvette? On the fifth ring, she hung up, unwilling to leave a message. She wasn't sure she could talk without her voice cracking like a damsel in distress.

Pierce was fine. She was just edgy because she'd retraced her steps and found the guard had moved away from the bank's front windows. His absence, the empty sidewalk, and near zero-visibility left her feeling like the last planetary survivor. Lights aglow in the lobby reinforced the fact she was standing out in the cold looking in. She fought the impulse to press her nose against the icy glass. Forget the guard showing pity and letting her back inside.

The sensation someone was watching her skittered down her spine like icicles. She turned warily—nose alert to the scent of cinnamon, neck muscles twanging, heart ringing in her ears. She clutched her cell phone and saw, again, the man in black coming toward her. She took a step backward, bumping against the bank's front door. She opened her mouth, ready to scream. Snow gusted upward, but no one stepped through it. Disgust froze the bleat stuck in her raw throat.

Stop acting like a Gothic heroine, the voice of reason whispered over the BA-bum, BA-bum of her heart. Millions of men wore black. This one hadn't even smelled like cinnamon. Walking in snow on The Plaza wasn't like climbing stairs to the haunted attic or tiptoeing down to the spooky basement. Shivering, she flipped open her cell and debated calling Pierce again. She really needed to hear a voice besides the one babbling in her head.

The first notes of "Moonlight Sonata" made her smile. "ESP."

The idea that she and Pierce communicated via a mystical connection felt so good she almost picked up the call without checking the LED. When she saw Rex's number, she indulged in kicking snow over her head twice before she answered, trying to sound gracious.

Gracious was hard to do with her frozen tongue. She asked, "Can you hear me better?"

"I heard you fine before." So he felt no need to sound gracious.

"You were telling me about Michael." She returned to the bank's doorway and stared at the lighted lobby.

"Cut right to the chase, don't you, Quinn? For all you know I'm in a ditch right now. While you're snug as a bug."

The vision of him in a ditch didn't come, and she couldn't help it, she laughed. "Nooo."

"Snug enough you can laugh at me. A laugh's my thanks for doing you a favor."

"Stop right there!" Her scalp tingled. "I asked you not to meet Michael."

"Michael's my best friend. We're like brothers. I

thought helping him—the way you're helping me—was the right thing to do."

His whine ticked her off almost as much as his attempt at guilting her. "Thanks."

"Brrrr," he said. "I'd get more heat from an Alaska ice floe than from that thank-you."

"Newsflash. Forget heartfelt after poking me with a guilt stick. I'll call Michael—"

"Not smart."

His arrogance pushed her over the edge. "Not smart to call my own brother, but smart to listen to you whine? Don't think so. Drive safely."

She hung up and kicked up more snow and the memory of last night's snowball ambush unfolded in slow mo. "Thanks, Rex," she muttered, refusing to admit she—not he—had triggered the memory.

Chapter 10

Stomping and humming in front of the bank did zip to keep Quinn warm. A couple of smart-ass comebacks raised her blood to a boil.

Fuck off hummed in her head. She'd never used the phrase in her life.

Ever the slow learner. She wrapped the scarf across her mouth, walked two steps—smacking the cell phone in one gloved palm then in the other—pivoted and shuffled back to the bank's door.

Calm down. Calm down. She had to calm down. Talking to Michael in such a snit would only ratchet up the pressure he'd lived under for too long. His phone call yesterday morning attested to how close he walked on the edge. He had her number. He'd call.

When he was ready. When he finished dealing with Luce's hysterics—especially if she suspected he'd met with Rex.

Quinn massaged the invisible wire slicing her lungs and struggled to breathe normally, to focus on Michael instead of on Luce. She exhaled through her mouth. Poor Michael. His drop-dead gorgeous wife had a tongue like a razor—and she rarely hesitated to sharpen it on anyone who came within striking distance.

Anyone was usually Michael. Not that he was a saint...

A howling wind came at her and for a moment she

felt swept up in a sea of whiteness. Her lungs shrank to the size of peanuts. She sucked in the icy air, clearing her head. Rex was right. Definitely not smart to call Michael. Not when her own tongue was shredding the roof of her mouth into slivers sharper than poisoned spears.

Exhaling, she refused to peer into the deep shadows. "Stalkers don't stalk in blizzards."

She pushed up her coat sleeve. How many decades had she stood talking to herself and teetering on the edge of hysteria? Mist shrouded the face of her watch, but her cell lit up.

"Where are you?" she yelled, so eager to hear Pierce's voice she forgot to say hello.

"In a left-turn queue going straight to hell..." A blast of horns drowned out the rest.

"Where, exactly? I'll hike over." She moved from under the bank's overhang to the mound of snow she assumed was the curb and peered toward the opposite end of The Plaza. "I'm freezing," she yelled. "Where are you?"

"Are you outside? What the hell's wrong with Dougie Prescott?" The pitch of Pierce's voice rose, vibrating hard and fast. "That guy has the brain of of an eggplant—you see why I don't want him—or any banker—to find out about their missing money?"

Between shivers, Quinn said, "He offered me a ride. I refused. Said I have anti-freeze in my veins...hinted I'm burning up."

"Hold that thought. Forget walking. I'm across from Pinstripes."

Quinn hunched her shoulders and jammed her dead fingers in her pockets. She stayed as close to the buildings as possible. "Pinstripes isn't that far for a former Girl Scout."

Head down, Quinn plodded through the drifting snow, blinded by the whiteout. Dim Bulb could be slaloming two blocks ahead of her. Or two feet. Or two inches.

Pierce interrupted the unbidden image. "If I'd suggested an IOU until after Thanksgiving, would you have felt compelled to repay me today?"

"In hindsight, I think so. Probably." Her lungs, as inflexible as frozen turkeys, shrank.

Forget Dim Bulb. He was a fluke. A fluke. A homeless guy off his meds.

"Thanks for the probably. If you'd said absolutely—well, let's just say you salved my fragile male ego."

Remembering Rex's hurt feelings, she said, "Your ego's not fragile."

"Repeat that over supper tonight, okay?"

"Maybe," she said lamely. If she survived to eat supper.

"I'm stuck here till—an ambulance arrives. Want me to whisper X-rated suggestions in your ear? Turn the air so hot you'll rip off your clothes and run naked through the snow?"

Snow slithered down her expensive, silk-lined boots, but Quinn laughed, her heartbeat slowing, images of Dim Bulb fading. "Remember that fragile ego, Buster."

"That a challenge?"

The heat in his whisper promised a hint of what she could expect after he undressed her. Anticipation shook her. "I'd throw down my glove but my fingers would freeze."

"Imagine them tripping down my spine a few times. They'll feel like—"

"There you go. Being eager again."

Ahead, blue lights flashed, police radios crackled. Three whistle-blasts stopped her at a red light. Pierce's voice faded in the crunch of tires. She yelped and jumped sideways. Her bum ankle buckled, collapsed. Flat on her back, dazed, she groaned. A savage grinding of gears released the metallic taste of adrenaline deep in her throat. She rolled onto her side, flailed to get to her feet, put distance between her and the car she imagined fishtailing on the ice.

Her hands slipped. Her feet slid. Blood roared in her ears. She scrabbled backwards, twisting her head toward the street, toward the car she couldn't see.

Stand up. She had to stand. Had to...get...away.

Instinct warned trying to stand promised disaster. Ice demanded crawling. Crawling offered a small hope of survival. She flopped onto her stomach. Her wrists wobbled. On the second try, they supported her weight. Her heart beat too hard. Too fast. Unable to catch her breath, she tucked her head and crabbed across the icy sidewalk. Too late, panic shocked her like electricity. The wrong way. She—

Turn around. Turn...

A blur of black rolled toward her.

Wind swallowed her scream.

The blur collided with the post supporting the stoplight.

****

"What the hell was that?" Muffled voices offered Pierce no explanation. Frustration grabbed him. "What the hell's going on?"

No one replied and he really let loose. Forgetting he was an adult, he changed into a three-year-old in the middle of a major meltdown, yelling repeatedly, "Answer, dammit."

A clear, distinct male voice came on the line. "Mr. Jordan, KCPD Officer Tim Rourke here. Think of the next two minutes as a character-building exercise."

"Screw character building." The top of Pierce's skull retracted as bits and pieces of his brain exploded. Screw waiting. He slammed open the car door and stepped into an avalanche.

Christ, he should've skipped flirting. He should've insisted Quinn stay at the bank.

Insisted, oh right. That would've proved interesting.

Taunted by logic, he held onto the door and looked over the roof of the Gomobile. Lights on The Giralda's bell tower flickered in the distance, but offered no visibility west on Forty-Eighth Street. Drivers on all sides of Pierce opened their doors and piled out.

Gridlock blocked every exit off Pennsylvania. Headlights from six patrol cars lit up the space between a crumpled Prius and an ambulance. Four EMTs carried a gurney into the wind.

God, what if Quinn needed an ambulance? Pierce swept his forearm across the 'Vett's roof spraying snow like buckshot. Rage hammered his pulse. "What the hell's the holdup?" the driver behind him yelled.

"A picnic in the park." Pierce growled. Did the fool have a valid driver's license? His cell rang and he forgot the other driver.

"Mr. Jordan? Officer Rourke letting you know Miz

Alexander appears fine, but I'm requesting an EMT check her out."

Pierce's heart stopped. Missed two beats before he croaked, "Check her out?"

"She had a fall. A vehicle went out of control—"

"Sonuva—Was she hit?"

"The vehicle swerved at the last minute. Would you like to talk to her?"

Why would I want to talk to her? Pierce locked his jaw and spit out his reply. "I do definitely want to talk to her."

The sound of the phone being passed grated Pierce's nerves. It took forever before Quinn said, "I'm fine. Honestly. Snow's a softer cushion than garage floors."

Despite her attempt at levity, a quiver knotted in his chest. "What happened?"

Her account spilled out in short, fast fragments stripped of melodrama, devoid of images or phrases or specifics that could set him off. She might as well be reading the phone book. His breathing grew harsh, his eyes hot, his nerves taut enough to pop through his clammy skin.

"You said you couldn't see. How sure—I mean, are sure you saw a Jeep?" Pierce's brain felt punctured by shards of glass.

"A black Jeep. Like Tony's. Black contrasts nicely with the white powdery stuff."

"I called Tony right after you got out of the car. He was here on The Plaza. The cops kept traffic moving. No stopping. No waiting. I drove on—right into this zoo. I wanted Tony as backup—in case I got stuck. Or in case someone plowed into me."

And? Quinn's unasked question magnified the silence.

"Never heard back from him since...my phone's crapped out twice." Pierce pinched the bridge of his nose and worked the knot of tension growing bigger and harder between his eyes. His mind raced, sorting and resorting Quinn's info. "Lots of black Jeeps in the metro area..." Uncertainty flattened his monotone. The words stuck in his throat. On the defensive, he swallowed and tried again. "Tony would never leave the scene of an accident."

"Officer Rourke wants to speak with you."

"In a minute—"

"Mr. Jordan, I need the full name and home address of the guy who owns that Jeep."

And I want a hot bath and my fur-lined slippers. Pierce opted for silence as the better part of intelligence. Or maybe obstruction of justice.

"Officer Rourke? Helllllooo?" He dragged his thumbnail across the mouthpiece on his phone. "I'm having trouble hearing you."

"Funny. I hear you fine." Irritation tinged Rourke's tone.

It occurred to Pierce he wasn't doing Tony any good by stonewalling. Unsure why he was acting like such a dumbass, Pierce covered the mouthpiece with three fingers, held the phone at arm's length and spoke without moving his lips. "Can you speak louder?"

"Don't trouble yourself anymore, Mr. Jordan. Miz Alexander can give me a last name."

The click of the DISCONNECT caught Pierce by surprise, and he called himself a few names. They failed to capture his stupidity. He drummed his fingers on the cell's cover and jumped straight up several times—like a kangaroo on a pogo stick—trying to catch a glimpse of Quinn, though that was so stupid he thought he might be in the first stages of hypothermia.

He opened, closed, opened, closed, opened, closed the cell's cover. Snow dusted the keypad. He snapped the cover closed for the last time. If he called her, Rourke would know for certain Pierce was pulling his chain. Riiiight.

A swift, vicious kick to the Gomobile's back wheel reinforced the certainty he needed another outlet for his stupidity. He flipped open his cell and hit SPEED DIAL. Tony's voice mail picked up on the first ring. Pierce left a terse call-back message and hung up. A call to Tony's office phone met his same expectations—more voice mail. His next call to the company attorney yielded the same results, and Pierce tasted defeat scalding the back of his throat.

Dammit, he hated feeling powerless. Could he control the fallout if Tony had left Quinn in that snowbank? *If Tony left Quinn in that snowbank, I'm dumb as a day-old snowman.*

Ready to eat crow for screwing up with the cop, Pierce dialed Quinn and got voice mail.

"Sonuva—" Pierce slammed the phone on the Gomobile's hood and growled. Michael or Rex? Rex or Michael? She had to be talking to one of them. Why?

A siren's wail jerked his attention to the ambulance—moving at the rate of a hibernating bear. Three or four drivers stood in front of the emergency vehicle as if ready to hijack it and ride it out of the gridlock. Several cops, backlit by the headlights on their squad cars, approached the drivers, waving them out of the way, shoving one guy who refused to move.

The other drivers stiffened like a phalanx. They threw off a sullen, defiant 'tude that dared the cops to assert their authority. Pierce's gut flipped. He sympathized with the pissed drivers. They wanted to get home—before one of them ended up like the Prius passenger. Normally, they'd cooperate with the police, but their patience had unraveled. They were tired of waiting, feeling like prisoners in their own cars, tired of seeing how easily life fell apart under emergency circumstances.

Edginess receding, he slid behind the steering wheel and slammed his door. Let the cops do their job. The sooner they did, the sooner he'd see Quinn. He hit REDIAL.

"How's your reception, Mr. Jordan?"

"Perfect, Officer Rourke. I'm sure Quinn gave you Tony's last name. He lives five miles outside Tonganoxie. No street or house address, but here's his phone numbers."

During the pause that followed, Pierce imagined the cop writing. The head-movie helped distract him from thinking about Quinn, wanting to talk to her, wanting to take her in his arms.

"Miz Alexander and I can see your car. Expect us in five minutes." Rourke hung up.

Listening to dead air, Pierce clamped his teeth together, locking his jaw against his impulse to snarl at Rourke's casual dismissal. But images of Quinn lying hurt and scared after her near-miss with a hit-and-run driver looped through his fury, fueling his guilt as he saw a faceless cop offering her his hand.

****

Quinn and Rourke covered the last yards of their trek so fast she stopped looking over her shoulder for black Jeeps. She had zero doubt the cop could stop a Jeep. He could stop a freight train, and he'd go after Pierce with very little provocation.

When they came within shouting distance, she phoned Pierce. The howling wind curtailed prolonged conversation. He rounded the car and dragged her into a hug she worried would crack a rib. Her police rescuer showed remarkable patience during the hugfest, but finally tapped her shoulder.

Pierce released her, kept one arm around her shoulders and extended his free hand. "Tony would never leave the scene of an accident. Especially if he caused it." A chill crept into Pierce's tone, and Quinn put a little weight into leaning against him. He squeezed her waist and spoke quietly, "No way he caused an accident. He grew up driving in Colorado."

"Hope you're right. We're on the lookout for him in Kansas City, but the storm's messing up everyone. FYI, I'll alert the Johnson and Leavenworth County Sheriffs' Departments. I'd appreciate your cooperation by not contacting Mr. Franklin tonight. If he's done nothing wrong, he has nothing to fear."

"Understand." Pierce shifted his weight, keeping Quinn close yet leaning toward the policeman, telegraphing his intent to protect the man he considered his kid brother. "Tony's a key person in my business. One of my most trusted associates. Our office is closed tomorrow. Good business judgment dictates sticking to our nightly check-in."

A sharp wind blew over them, tearing a seam in the snow-curtain. Each man stood with the jutted jaws and hard faces of adversaries. A mound of white covered the top of Pierce's bare head. A higher mound topped Rourke's hat. The bill looked like a beak on some prehistoric creature. Quinn imagined mountain goats butting heads and scattering snow everywhere.

Bones aching from the cold, she moved out from the warmth and security of Pierce's embrace. "What if we ask Tony to go to the nearest sheriff's department?"

Rourke said, "He should show up in his Jeep. Hitting that light pole left a dent."

"Tony will cooperate," Pierce said with the confidence of a man accustomed to having his statements accepted without discussion. "I guarantee his Jeep won't have a scratch."

Rourke pulled two business cards from an inside pocket and gave one to each of them. "The storm's gonna keep me busy most of the night, but I will follow up if I don't hear from you or Mr. Franklin."

He made no effort to soften the threat in his tone.

"You won't have to follow up." A note of finality overrode the hum of rage in Pierce's clipped statement.

The cop nodded at Quinn, but said to Pierce, "Drive carefully."

She grabbed Pierce's arm. "Brrrrr. Pissing contest officially over."

"What's a blizzard to male egos? Besides, Tony's innocent." Pierce threw open the car door and guided Quinn into a cocoon of warmth that left her lightheaded.

"Oooooooo!" She stripped off her gloves and rubbed her numb hands, massaging each fingertip, trying unsuccessfully to snap her fingers.

Pierce slid behind the steering wheel and reached

for her in one fluid movement. He mashed his hot mouth against her icy ear, whispering, "Let's get your blood moving."

Heat shot into her, melting bones, boiling blood, searing her brain, pushing Tony to the back of her mushy mind. She felt like purring, but managed to say, "Best offer I've had all day."

His slow, easy grin promised another kiss. "I bet you say that to all the guys."

"Only to the ones who defrost my feet." A shiver shot up her legs and spine. At some deep level her mind made a connection with promises broken, dreams abandoned, and hurts unhealed. She was skating on ice too thin for flirting.

Pierce hesitated, his forehead wrinkled, his eyes looking somewhere else, someplace that caused his jaw to crack and his face to stiffen. Then, he exhaled and wiggled his eyebrows—a gesture that always made her laugh. "There's a challenge I can't resist."

The magic of his strong fingers slurred her response and total brain paralysis set in. Concerns about protecting herself against him evaporated as soon as he rested her ankle on the console and unzipped her boot. She closed her eyes. The hum of heat flowing through the vents calmed her. She sighed. Her eyelids crashed downward. Sleep teased her, reached for her, pulled her under once, twice...

A feather danced on her instep. "Forget Tony. Forget Rex. Forget Michael."

****

Michael's name jerked Quinn upright—like a child in the middle of a nightmare. Heart thumping, eyes staring, mouth dry, she screamed silently, *Where am I?*

"You're okay, Quinn." Fingers stroked her cheek, moved to the back of her neck.

She stared blindly at a blurred face and made a noise. Shapes she didn't recognize loomed in the distant shadows.

"You had a nightmare." The low, comforting baritone throbbed with male assurance. "You're safe. We're in the car. You're safe."

Recognizing Pierce's voice, Quinn felt the rawness of her fear recede. Slowly, she nodded. The snow-covered shapes took on the forms of cops and firemen. She turned her head, saw a few hazy lights, began to make out more ghostly shapes, felt her unease grow.

"Wh—what time is it?"

"Four fifty-five. In the afternoon."

"Did Michael call? Did Luce have the baby?" Unsure if her rapid, garbled questions made sense, she caught and held Pierce's hand.

"Your cell hasn't rung." Pierce stroked her thumb, infusing warmth into her entire body. "I'd say Luce hasn't had the baby yet, but why don't you call Michael?"

"Call Mi—?" Quinn frowned and resisted the impulse to tap the side of her head. "You mean call my brother—the one you've never liked?"

Pierce lifted one shoulder. The elegant gesture typified his reputation for arrogance. His smile was soft, accommodating, confusing in the hushed womb of leather and warmth.

"Go on," he said. "I enjoy counting snowflakes."

She stared at him. The erratic rhythm of his Adam's apple revealed the crack in his steely composure. "And now you're a diplomat?"

"Not a diplomat. But I am teachable."

Her stomach dropped. The yearning to be believed in his voice set her heart thudding and her mind racing. She looked away from the hope in his dilated pupils, wet her lips and said in a neutral tone, "I'll call Mom first. See if her plane's leaving at seven."

"Then call Michael. I'll be here when you're finished."

That sounded so scary, Quinn hit SPEED DIAL without a comeback. Was he saying she could depend on him? A part of her longed to tell him about the Samaritan in black.

Except she wanted to forget the man in black and the black Jeep.

So when did she plan to confess she'd seen the Jeep twice before tonight?

Her mother picked up, unruffled by an additional four-hour delay of her plane. "I may stay in St. Louis. I know Luce doesn't want us at the hospital, but once they go home, maybe she'll give us a reprieve about seeing the baby."

"Maybe." Quinn hoped she sounded non-committal. Luce had declared the baby off limits for one full month.

"I can go to San Francisco anytime." Her mother made life sound so easy. She already had a plan for getting home using a friend's limo service. "Michael called half an hour ago. Said he and Luce were about to lie down. Poor things, they're both frazzled."

Big surprise. Hearing Michael had picked up their mother at six that morning—ahead of the storm—Quinn felt a new chill and focused on the green dash light. What time had her brother called Rex? Did her mother know about their rendezvous?

"Maybe this nap is practice for when Baby Quinn comes," Mom said, upbeat as always.

"We can hope." Quinn tried to muster some enthusiasm so she didn't spill a word about Michael meeting Rex. "And we can hope he'll slow down."

Between trying to please Luce, driving their mother to the airport and hooking up with Rex, her brother must've burned several days' worth of adrenaline. No wonder he felt frazzled. She'd spent half his level of energy—yet she felt whacked. She kept up her end of the conversation for a few more minutes, hyper-aware of Pierce's methodical swipes at the windshield.

Whacked or not, if she was smart, she'd remember that trusting this man with all her heart belonged to the past. Logic belonged to the present.

Throat dry, she sensed Pierce watching her and refocused, taking in her mother's suggestion of a nap. Wouldn't Pierce love that suggestion?

Ridiculously, a rush of heat rose off Quinn's skin and she fought the urge to stare at him. Nervous her mother's famous ESP would kick in, she said goodbye, disconnected and faced Pierce. "Long delay out of St. Louis tonight," she reported.

"What about calling Michael?"

"Rex, first." She spoke hard and fast, a touch of steel in her voice, telegraphing readiness to defend her decision. Her stomach clenched, but she met Pierce's gaze head on.

"Not much light in here," he drawled, "except your eyes shooting fireballs."

"You always were astute."

"And you always were soft-hearted."

She flipped open the cell's cover. "What if Tony did hit that light pole? What if he asks you for help?"

Pierce's jaw cracked in the pulsating silence before he spoke in a flat, clipped voice. "Moot question since he didn't. He wouldn't hit and run. Wouldn't leave the scene of an accident. Wouldn't drag me into that kind of mess."

"Okay, okay, okay." Quinn held up her hand. "I'm calling Rex."

The lines around Pierce's mouth deepened. He crossed his arms and stared out the windshield as if counting every snowflake.

She sat up straighter, dialed and faked a warmth so phony she felt him flinch.

"God, I'm sorry," Rex said immediately. "Me and my big mouth. I don't know why I went off on you like that."

His sad, ugly face flashed in her mind's eye. Was he always the first to apologize? In this case, he owed her an apology, but he didn't have to eat dirt.

"Thanks." Pierce's snort short-circuited her playacting.

"You should've hung up. I was out of line. Michael's foul mood was contagious."

The muscles in her neck froze. Consequences of her own foul mood? She said, "I was feeling a little stressed earlier."

"That would explain your total lack of appreciation."

Total? That seemed a tad harsh. She pressed her tongue against the roof of her mouth. Dammit, Pierce didn't get the satisfaction of witnessing her destroy

Rex. She unfolded her legs, flexed her toes under the heater, and willed herself to say, "I know driving to St. Louis was tough."

"Let me tell you," Rex said in a high, nasal pitch that warned Quinn a whine was coming. "The weather was such a bitch when I left home. I never even got coffee."

"Lucky for me, Pierce fixed mine—" Ahhh, nooo. She administered a mental head-slap.

Pierce smiled as if totally unaware of his sexy grin. Quinn twisted toward the side window and pressed the phone harder against her ear. Stupidity merited some discomfort.

"Pierce was at your house at six-fifteen? What'd he do? Spend the night?"

"You were telling me about your meeting when we spoke earlier." Quinn spit out the words. Pierce must be choking on suppressed laughter.

"Earlier when?" Yah, yah, yah, yah, yah. His unspoken taunt mocked her. "This morning or when you hung up on me an hour ago?"

My, my how time flies when you're contemplating murder. Quinn swallowed her impatience, speaking slowly, "An hour ago."

A single beat of silence before he said, "I was saying I don't want to scare you."

Quinn's stomach buckled. Like hell, she thought and seized the opportunity to disabuse Rex of his power fantasies. "What could you say...about Michael...that would scare me?"

Rex sighed. "Remember, you asked me."

A man deeply torn. Contempt twisted her stomach. "Several times."

Another sigh. "Frankly, I think our Michael's a little...on edge."

A part of her tried breaking away from the rest of her body, but she wouldn't let it go. Not in front of Pierce. Losing control was scarier than anything Rex might say.

"He's tired and scared about the baby." She shook off the hand Pierce laid between her shoulders. "Wouldn't you be a little...on edge?"

"Sure, but—"

"If he was a little...on edge, would he have pled your case so forcefully yesterday?" She'd see if Rex could keep up with the twists and turns and contradictions of her fuzzy logic.

"Things change in twenty-four hours." He sounded like a lecturer enlightening the class dummy. "Countries go to war. Babies are born. People die..."

"People don't get enough sleep and get edgy. I think I understand your profundity." She wanted to wring his melodramatic neck.

"Is that why you're being sarcastic? You didn't get enough sleep last night?"

She considered telling him the sarcasm stemmed from wiping out her savings account to save his butt. Except that was a lie.

The lie didn't matter, but she sure didn't intend to tell him the truth. Admit his take on Michael had scared her senseless. Not in front of Pierce.

"I never get enough sleep," she said, alert enough to change the subject yet again. "What did Michael say about inducing labor? Don't tell me you talked him out of it. What did he say?"

"No way in hell. His exact words. But I knew what

he meant. He was terrified if his kid was induced, she'd turn out like me."

Quinn's stomach dropped. God, how had Michael sat during their meeting, looking at his best friend's burgundy, bumpy face, without recoiling?

"The best medical minds in the world can't tell you why nevus flammeus occurs at birth. I told him there's not a shred of evidence that inducing labor causes it."

Quinn's heart fired rapidly, but her mind blanked. Why did humans always want to know why? Pierce shifted in his seat, and the whisper of the leather sounded like sandpaper against cement. She bit her bottom lip and listened as Rex droned on and on and on.

"No one knows why the discoloration runs from barely visible to reddish-purple. Like mine," he added, his tone less strident.

Would knowing why make his life easier?

"What'd Michael say?" She pinched the skin inside her elbow.

"No way in hell. No way in hell." Rex's voice dropped to a whisper and she shuddered.

"Have you and Michael talked about this before?" The thought came out of nowhere.

"From the day we met. We don't have any secrets, Quinn."

Her breath caught. God, let him be wrong about that.

Chapter 11

"I told Mrs. Taylor to cut back on the garlic." Pierce fought the urge to drop a kiss on Quinn's nose as she sniffed the aroma of browned onions and garlic drifting into his garage.

"Vivaldi balances everything." Her voice sounded perfectly normal after they'd ridden—at her request—to his house in maddening silence.

"I figured." Drunk on her nearness, he stuffed the frustration over her call to Rex and opened the door into the kitchen. He mentally thanked his housekeeper for her classical music selection. Coming home to Roy Acuff would not impress Quinn or motivate her to open up about the weasel.

"I'll take your coat." To hell with the weasel. He'd been patient long enough. Any excuse to put his hands on her. On all of her.

As if reading his mind, she extended her arms. "Can never get too much help."

"I aim to please." He slipped off her heavy coat and bit back a growl of disappointment.

Her red pantsuit—despite its eye-blinking color—could pass for a nun's habit. Had she worn the outfit this morning? He tried to remember, but his mind stalled.

"Why do women wear pantsuits?"

She arched a brow at his eye-roll. "They're

professional."

"Sexless, you mean." He studied the buttons on her double-breasted jacket. They had a bar or clip that held them in place and required safe-cracking expertise to open.

"Professional," she maintained and threw him a non-professional smile that teased, taunted, and tempted him. "Men know nothing about women's professional attire."

"Is there professional underwear too?"

She lifted her chin at least two feet. "Ever hear of pantyhose? They're throwbacks to chastity belts."

"Women's fashion." He let his gaze travel slowly, very slowly, from her head to her bellybutton, lower, to her toes. Pantyhose underneath and a jacket on the outside that went past her hips. What was a red-blooded male to do?

"There's a fire in the dining room," he said. Not to mention between his legs. Hands sweaty, shoulders tense, betting it took an engineer to manage those damn buttons, he asked as casually as a man in severe pain could manage, "Want to take off your jacket?"

"I did notice global warming's hit here." She flipped the buttons open faster than he could take in a deep breath.

Under the jacket she wore a long-sleeved, high-necked sweater. It stopped at the tip of her chin. He exhaled. Hell, in some countries he'd see nothing but her eyes and half an inch of forehead.

"What's wrong?" She tucked a chunk of hair behind her ear.

"Not a damn thing."

Her coat and jacket filled his arms, but he leaned

into her and kissed her exposed ear. "Ears make my blood boil."

"You are weird." She arched her neck.

"MEEE-ooowww." Floyd bumped Quinn's calf with his head.

"Laundry room, Big Guy." Pierce hitched the clothes under one arm and reached down.

The cat rolled his ears back, growled, bared yellowed fangs.

"Whoops, His Highness has other ideas." Pierce ignored the growls and loaded the complaining beast on top of Quinn's coat and jacket. "He's shameless. He demands being the center of attention."

"That is shameless." Quinn cooed and tickled Floyd's head. "Let him stay."

Jealousy corkscrewed into Pierce's heart. "You've charmed him."

She patted Floyd with one hand and skimmed a fingernail on her other hand down Pierce's cheek. He couldn't decide which male purred louder.

"My charms work best in front of a fire." Her tone carried a low, dangerous throb.

The charm started working on Pierce before he shuffled another step. Without warning, he was hard. His feet froze. The coats and cat tumbled from his arms. Despite the soft landing, Floyd yowled and stalked off—his tail an orange exclamation point.

"I know where there's a fire." Pierce avoided mention of the flame building in his gut.

With his hair threatening to combust, he pulled her close. He'd waited four years for this moment. Her eyes widened, then softened. He linked her arm through his and sidestepped the clothes on the floor. He'd swear his feet didn't touch terra firma.

He threw open the double doors to the dining room. "Does this work for you?"

She gasped. Her eyes outshone the flames leaping behind the glass screen in front of the fireplace. Lights from The Plaza a hundred feet below broke the curtain of snow and spilled through the floor-to-ceiling windows in a gauzy rainbow. Silverware and china glowed. Crystal sparkled.

"Mrs. Taylor outdid herself," Pierce said, surprised he wanted to impress Quinn.

"You could charge admission," she whispered.

"Not to you." Pierce, Medieval Knight Besotted, scooped his lady fair into his arms. His back protested, and he made an unknightly noise.

"Put me down, you fool. You'll get a hernia."

"Is that what that is?"

More awkward than the most bumbling knight, he managed to sink down in front of the fireplace without dropping her. The death-hold she locked around his neck threatened his delicate equilibrium and forced him to breathe through his mouth.

She blew on his chin. "How romantic."

He laughed and fell backwards on the carpet, pulling her on top of him.

"Bowled you over, didn't I?" she teased.

In answer, he ran his hands down her back, enjoying the muscles under her sweater. The pantsuit hid her fitness. Did she work out? Weights might explain her round, firm butt. A perfect handful.

He drank in her scent of violets and roses and adjusted her long, curved body on top of his. "We still fit together just fine."

"Except for this instrument of torture." She slid off him, uncinching his belt buckle.

His heart thundered as he lifted his hips. Wordlessly, she pulled the belt through the loops. When she finished, she stood on her knees. A wisp of blonde hair fell across her cheek. She raised the belt over her head, cracked it once, then tossed it behind them.

"You're not going to handcuff me, are you?" he imitated the voice of a scared adolescent.

"Depends." She tucked her chin and went to work on his shoelaces.

He strained to stroke her hair, and her breast brushed his thigh. His breath caught. For a second, he thought he'd brushed against the fire screen.

"Depends on what?" He unzipped one of her boots.

"Now who's eager?" She pulled off one of his shoes.

"Not me. Not after that massage you begged for."

"Ha. Ha."

"Short memory." God, his dick begged for more than a massage, but as proof he was in total control, he removed both her boots before she finished tugging off his second shoe.

"Dah winner!" Pierce massaged her icy feet. "Does this mean your heart's on fire?"

"That's hands, you knave." Gently, Quinn cuffed him on the side of the head. "Cold hands, warm heart. Not feet. Cold feet are normal."

"Maybe." He wiggled his eyebrows, swirled an imaginary moustache, and rubbed his hands together like the villain in a melodrama. "But I remember how to make your feet feel like you walked across hot coals."

"Never. You must have me confused with—"

For an endless second, Pierce was sure they'd screwed up. Broken the magic spell. His chest tightened. An ache for wounding her squeezed his heart. He cursed himself for Brittany, for causing Quinn pain. He stayed absolutely still, suspended in a bubble of regret, letting her make up her own mind.

She wiggled her foot in his hand. "I'm from Missouri," she scoffed. "Show me."

So he did. In sync with Vivaldi's Winter movement, Pierce feathered the high arch of each foot.

Her feet twitched, but she pressed them against his fingers. "That's a start."

"There you go. Being eager, again."

Next, he circled her thin, narrow ankles between his thumb and forefinger and rubbed the heel of first one foot, then the other against his palm. Her moans made him smile, and he increased or decreased the pressure and friction with quiet glee.

"Okay, okay, I'm convinced." Her gray eyes darkened with pleasure.

"Thank God. These little piggies are almost too hot to handle." He tweaked her toes, one by one.

****

Quinn lost track of time and forgot everything but the electricity humming off Pierce. When she felt sure she couldn't hold back longer, she pushed his heavy boots to the side.

"What about your socks?" Desire seared her throat. "Should I just knock them off?"

His grin invited murder. The triangle of curls on his chest invited caresses. She licked her bottom lip, unzipped his jeans and tugged them down—down past his waist, past his hips, past his erection. The corners of his mouth twitched as she looked, and he took his time pulling her sweater over her head.

God, why was he so slow? Heat rolled off her. She bit back a groan. Couldn't he see she was ready? Had been ready since she got in the car?

His pupils dilated, his breath caught. He had the sweater bunched under her neck. His swallow was an audible gulp as he stared at her lacy, transparent bra. The one she'd changed after Rex talked her out of going to St. Louis.

"In my book," he drawled, his Adam's apple working, "a black lace bra definitely falls into the category of professional underwear."

"I should tell you right now I'm not impressed with boxer shorts."

"You're kidding, right?" He grabbed the waist of his jeans.

"Shhhh." Quinn dragged her tongue down his jaw, along his collarbone, into the hollow of his throat. Her tongue tasted and teased while his fingers drew exquisite, electrifying patterns on the insides of her thighs.

Then he found her softest part of all.

Her whole body arced backwards and she cried out.

He kept his eyes wide open, whispering her name in a raw, husky voice that flowed over her like water over the desert.

Quinn soaked up his desire, tucking away his moans and growls and whispers. Careful to guard the spell, she spoke nothing about love. This was sexual release. Love wasn't involved. Her heart hammered her chest. She took a deep breath, raised her hips, wrapped her legs around his waist and pulled him into her.

A kaleidoscope of colors danced around them. Taut nerves relaxed. The undulating rhythm of their bodies kept beat with their pounding pulses. Their primitive moans and groans sounded to Quinn like songs of celebration. His constant concerns about her pleasure swelled her heart. Jolt after jolt after jolt of desire left her lightheaded, deaf and blind to everything but his body.

They lay exhausted in each other's arms, patting, touching, healing. Their earthy, natural smells of lovemaking conjured up for her the image of a cocoon. Safety. Security.

The ear-shattering crack of a dying log crashed through her altered consciousness. She jumped, hand on her chest and blurted, "Oooomygod."

Pierce reined in his ragged breathing and winked. "I'm going to avoid any smart remarks about ending with a bang."

"What a wise man you are." Quinn twisted a couple of his chest hairs into a mini-braid.

"Remember when you used to braid my hair? I always looked like someone who'd just rolled out of bed after a bad nightmare."

"I'm surprised you remember." In fact, she was shocked. She shifted her head to his chest and listened to the erratic, hard beat of his heart.

"You'd be surprised what I remember." He laughed and Quinn's bones melted, her mind went blank. He snuggled her closer, stroking her damp hair, sighing from time to time for no apparent reason. "A dollar for your thoughts," he said.

"Sorry, but my thoughts don't come cheap. I

expect stock options and bonuses."

"Lord, give women an inch—"

Quinn pinched his hip. "Your chauvinism's showing."

"Again?" He raised his head and sighted between his legs.

"You are so-so—" She smacked his hand. "Impossible," she said lamely.

"But would you pay a dollar to hear my impossible thoughts?" His solemn gaze raised goose bumps on her bare arms.

"Will you take an IOU?"

"In a heartbeat." His voice deepened solemnly like an actor about to deliver his big lines.

She tensed, dreading a post-coital declaration. She poked his chest, then released the braids she'd just created. "Okay," she said with zero enthusiasm. "I'm all ears."

He propped himself up on one elbow, caught her hand and held it against his chest. His body hummed. "I don't know your intentions, Quinn, but I'm telling you mine right now. I don't intend to be a one-night stand."

****

D-U-M. The word looped in Quinn's head like a mantra.

D-U-M. Like people who drove and talked on cell phones.

D-U-M. Like women who jogged in parks at midnight.

So D-U-M, aliens would refuse to kidnap her.

Miserable and naked, Quinn lay on her side in Pierce's over-sized king bed. Her misery didn't stem from the twenty-pound, orange and white bowling ball lodged between her and him, making it impossible to pull the comforter up over her bare shoulder.

Her misery was worse. It was self-inflicted. She'd vowed to lie back and enjoy raw sex, and what happened?

She blissed out.

Blissed out. That's what she and Pierce used to call their post-lovemaking state. After the fireworks, the earth tilting, the planets colliding—came bliss. And she'd blissed out tonight—both times after going for raw sex. She'd blissed out so far, she'd capitulated—after a second thought—to sleep over at his house.

"Why are you awake?" The throb in Pierce's voice raised goose bumps, but she pinched the inside of her elbow.

"Why are you awake?" she countered. Damn, why hadn't she pretended she was asleep?

"I heard you beating yourself up."

"I'm not—" He reached across the chasm separating them and touched her chilled shoulder.

Floyd growled.

A slight increase in the pressure of Pierce's fingers, and Quinn turned on her back. A deeper growl and Floyd made known his disgust by using her stomach as a launching pad.

Air whooshed out of her. "Ummmf."

"He's miffed, but he'll get over it." Pierce arranged the comforter under her chin, then he pulled her into the curve of his arm as naturally as if they snuggled up together every night for the past four years.

Her skin prickled, and a shiver came from the deepest part of her. She blinked back tears. Her throat ached too much to trust her voice.

"Are you worried about Michael?"

"No." Of course she was, but D-U-M as she was, she'd forgotten her brother the moment she entered Pierce's house.

"Having second thoughts about Rex?"

"No." She'd erased all thoughts of Rex once she walked into Pierce's house.

"You think I'm a bastard? That I took advantage of you?"

"No." The truth? She'd wanted him, he complied.

Contrary to his no-one-night-stand declaration, Quinn knew better than to play in a bonfire. She said, "We're moving too fast. The sex was great, but—"

"You want the big *C*, right?" His throat sounded jammed with sticks of dynamite. Might explain why he rushed on. "What if I asked you to marry me?"

Luckily, she lay on her back. Even so, her heart lurched, making her dizzy. God, what if she was having a heart attack?

"Take your time," Pierce said.

A hole opened in her chest as he rolled away, propped his weight on one elbow and flipped on the bedside lamp. She squeezed her eyes shut.

The mattress shifted with his weight. She opened her eyes. He looked down at her. "Let me know if the light's too bright."

Distrustful of her voice, Quinn shook her head. The lamp threw off a soft, diffused lemony circle. Bright enough she could see the black hairs on his chest. Clumped together, they begged for her attention. She dug her fingers into her palms.

She absolutely wasn't D-U-M enough to braid the wiry black hairs. Or, for that matter, to touch him.

She licked her lips and began. "Don't take this the wrong way—"

"Oh-oh. Not a good sign." He barely raised the comforter, sliding under it at warp speed. On his side, with about a foot between them, he said, "Drafts make Floyd edgy."

Astonished, she whipped her head around so that she was staring into his eyes. "You let your cat sleep under the covers?"

Silently, she groaned. Astonishment didn't excuse such a D-U-M, irrelevant, off-the-track question.

"Huh-uh. Floyd lets *me* sleep under the covers." Pierce threw her a wink, and her skin incinerated.

Dammit, she recognized this trick. Back him into a corner, and watch him change the subject. Or, crack a joke. Or, distract his opponent.

"See how I've grown," Pierce said. "Grown—that is the PC-term, right?"

"The PC-term is professional relationship. You and I have one—I assume?"

"After you paid me more than two million bucks, I think that's a safe assumption."

Given a straight path to making her point, Quinn took it. "You see the situation with Rex strains that professional relationship."

His lips disappeared, and his eyes became slits.

"To the breaking point." Quinn couldn't decide if he was mad, disappointed or both.

"That's giving the creep a lot of power."

Scratch disappointment. She threw fuel on the fire. "Sex would be the straw that snaps our professional relationship."

One of his arms snaked out from under the cover,

and Quinn stiffened. He laid his arm on top of the comforter. "I didn't propose sex, by the way. I proposed marriage."

Not really, she almost said, saw the trick and said instead, "I'm juggling too many balls to think about marriage."

"That's a no, then?"

Without hesitating, she said, "That's a no."

****

"I'll take the guest room," Pierce insisted when Quinn announced at two o'clock she wanted to go home.

"I'd rather go home...if it's not too much trouble."

"No trouble at all." Mr. Accommodating, he shrugged, still under the covers because he figured hopping out of bed naked as a jaybird might stress their professional relationship.

In the past, whenever Quinn had worried her professional mask was slipping, Pierce noticed she talked to an invisible person over his left shoulder.

This time, since she lay flat on her back, also naked as a jaybird, she stared at the ceiling. "I know it's trouble."

Apparently, staring at the ceiling brought small comfort. She sighed, but kept her gaze there anyway. "I said, 'If it's not too much trouble.'"

"Nothing's too much trouble for you, Quinn."

After a minute, she said, "Then I'd appreciate it if you put a sock in the sarcasm."

"That'll be har-difficult. My socks are downstairs." He chuckled.

Her head whipped around and her eyes flashed. "Not funny."

The chuckle, halfway to a laugh, died in his throat. "Seriously? Sorry, I thought it was."

She narrowed her eyes, but he said, "I swear I thought...it was funny."

Did he get any credit for spontaneously correcting hard to difficult?

"I can call a cab. Hector Ramirez gave me his direct number years ago."

Uh-huh. And where was Hector's card? Pierce knew for damned sure Quinn didn't have it on her. Temptation baited him.

Tell her to call Hector.

Watch her kick off the comforter.

No peeking as she fumbled the top sheet off the bed.

Offer assistance wrapping the sheet around her.

No peeking at her naked bod while they tucked in the ends.

Warn her about Floyd's habit of hiding on the landing.

"I'll call Hector," she said to the ceiling.

"Forget it." Pierce kicked back the bedclothes.

Cool air chilled his hot head, but he forced his feet onto the carpet. "Get a grip," he said. "Don't peek."

Her laugh chilled the draft on his bare ass.

"Let me remind you. He who laughs last..." He strutted his stuff straight into the bathroom and slammed the door.

As far as he could tell, nothing fell off the wall in the bedroom.

****

Pierce figured they must've set some kind of world-class record for dressing. He took five minutes in the bathroom. After which, he cracked the door, found the bed empty and started grabbing clothes right and left from the closet. By the time he got downstairs, Quinn had her coat on. Floyd yowled, resentful she put him off her lap. The cat stalked off. Quinn stood, averting eye-contact with Pierce.

He yawned. His eyes felt like burned toast. He shrugged into his coat, told Floyd he'd return and followed Quinn into the garage.

The heat in there cycled off at ten, and the 'Vette felt like a meat locker. "It'll only take a few minutes to warm up," he said, his breath silver puffs.

"I'm fine."

No doubt. Icebergs didn't notice the cold he supposed.

The garage door slid up. Pierce shifted the 'Vette and his brain. Quinn wasn't an iceberg. Tonight had proven that fact. She tried his patience. She was stubborn, hard-working, loyal, and honorable.

She was no iceberg.

The front gate opened. He slid through and waited a minute at the top of the hill. Since The Plaza lightscape was no more awesome from the hill than from his dining room, he didn't mention the glow.

"Any idea how we derailed so fast?" he asked.

"Karma, I think." Since she couldn't stare at the bedroom ceiling, she stared out her side window and missed the panorama in front of her nose.

Ignored, he said, "Sure, why didn't I think of karma?"

The silence made the fifteen-minute trip feel like a trek across the North Pole. A part of Pierce welcomed the silence. It had stopped snowing. There was no traffic. The quiet gave his jangled nerves a rest and reinforced his determination.

Tomorrow, come rain, snow, sleet or an attack of locusts, he'd hammer out the ground rules for their personal relationship. Right now, he'd try not to open his mouth and self-destruct.

They passed the Kansas City Country Club. All signs of the skirmish on the golf course with Abommie lay hidden under shimmering whiteness. Wanting to share the scene with Quinn, Pierce said, "What time do I pick you up for work?"

Mesmerized by her neighbors' houses—which she saw every damn day—she didn't bother glancing his way. "I'll call Hector."

That popped his cork. Choking the steering wheel helped with his anger management. He said evenly, "You'll either call me or I'll sleep in your driveway. My, my, what will the neighbors think?"

"That you're insane?"

Before he could give tit for tat, she said, "I'll be ready at eight. Bring the evidence against Rex. I'll read it while you drive."

Chapter 12

Quinn's doorbell rang—long and loud and insistent. She slammed the drawer in the bathroom vanity. *Not a good beginning, Pierce.*

Not after their post-coital bliss derailed into post-coital angst reminiscent of Woody Allen. She leaned into the mirror. Dèjá vu. Soft light did absolutely zip to soften her puffy face. She stuck out her tongue.

No amount of makeup was going to hide the trunks under her eyes or disguise her resemblance to a corpse. Looking like a corpse had now become her new norm.

The doorbell pealed again and cut short her deep philosophical observations.

She flipped off the bathroom light and jerked her coat off the bannister, calling, "Ready."

Ready was a lie, but it delayed opening the door and inviting Pierce inside. She buttoned her coat. Call her rude, but she wanted to spend as little time with him as possible—not because he was obviously a bear this morning, but because of their three-A.M. ride home. Their electrified silence—with its unspoken accusations—had barely qualified as civil.

Working her gloves on finger by finger ate up two more seconds as the memory unwound of Pierce fuming in silence. Why his head hadn't exploded remained a mystery. They reached Quinn's cul-de-sac, giving her the false hope of safety. Of course Pierce didn't leave well enough alone. He pulled into her drive and went on the defensive.

She had, he pointed out in a mean-schoolgirl voice, jumped into his bed willingly.

Maybe he expected a denial. Or wanted a reaction from her. Or maybe he fantasized her agreeing. Whatever, his logic short-circuited her first impulse to lie. He was right—without saying another word. It wasn't like she'd lost her virginity. They'd—*she'd*—crossed a line or opened a door or one of those millions of other damn clichés about life. Mocked by the truth, she'd ordered him to remain in the car while she limped to the front door alone.

"What's the hold-up?" He pounded the door as if he intended to bash the wood to splinters.

"Coming." What fun riding with Grumpy. She threw a scarf around her neck and straightened her shoulders. She'd dragged into the shower at six, but she should've called, wakened him, and told him not to pick her up.

Instead, she stood under the cold water too long trying to kickstart her brain and had to crawl back in bed to stop shivering. A call at 7:10 from her mother taxed Quinn's brain so much she kept interrupting for understanding.

I almost wish I didn't know she's stranded at the airport. Quinn flung open the door and glared at Pierce, ready to take out her frustration, fatigue and sense of failure on him. Mentally, she dared him to utter a word about the bags under her eyes.

An anemic sun bubble surrounded him in morning softness, but his eyes—usually bright and dancing—belonged on a Basset Hound. Quinn's mouth dropped.

His cafe-au-lait skin resembled ashes more than coffee and milk. Her heart missed a beat. After one sleepless night, he hadn't turned into Quasimodo, but he'd probably place second in a Mr. America contest.

Her breath caught. "Don't tell me you slept in your car." She tried to remember what time she'd last checked the empty driveway.

"Can we go inside? I need to talk to someone besides myself."

A blast of wind gusted snow on the ground and ruffled his hair. Instead of looking boyish, he looked so worn out Quinn momentarily forgot her anger. What had it cost him to ask her for help?

Heart flip-flopping, she opened the door, but stepped back from the stiff wind blasting across the golf course. "What's wrong?"

"Detective Olsen dropped by the house before dawn." Pierce shook his head. "He claims he has evidence who vandalized my house."

Not Rex. She closed her mouth and exhaled. Rex wouldn't merit such remorse.

"Uh-huh." Pierce handed her his coat. "I know there's a screw up."

"What is the evidence?" She held his coat, making no move toward the closet.

"A Droid. The cops found it yesterday. Wedged in the family room sofa."

"Whose is it?" She could see it cost him to tell her.

"Tony's." Frustration resonated in his clipped reply and narrowed eyes.

Relieved, but puzzled, she shifted the weight of his coat. "What's the big deal? He must've left it the last time you two played pool."

"Makes sense, doesn't it?" Pierce nodded, but Quinn was hyperaware of his stiff, unyielding posture. He was like one of the old backyard oaks stretched to breaking under the accumulated snow.

As if picking up on her scrutiny, he jerked his gaze from somewhere over her shoulder and stared her straight in the eye. "How long would it take you to miss your phone?"

"Two minutes. It's like a second brain." A burn crept into Quinn's upper arms. His coat felt heavier than cement.

"Same for Tony. Who, according to my calendar, hasn't played pool or dropped by my place for a week." The accusatory note in his tone chilled her more than the erratic rise and fall of his chest. "He hasn't returned any of my calls from last night. His phone in my sofa? Makes no sense."

Someone should've knocked Pierce off his hobby horse the first time he stepped out of line. Michael's outburst echoed in Quinn's ears.

"Let's have a cup of coffee." Her voice sounded tinny and too loud to her ears.

"Shoot mine in a vein." Pierce stayed in the hall while she hung up both their coats, then dogged her into the kitchen. "Tony's never asked me if I found his phone."

"What'd he say when the police asked him?" She motioned toward the kitchen.

"They haven't asked him." Pierce collapsed in the same chair where she'd tended his head wound a hundred years ago. "They can't find him."

"Olsen must've called him yesterday at work?" She grabbed a sack of coffee beans from the freezer and dumped them into the grinder.

"Sure did. Never got a callback. So Olsen ran another routine computer check. Found Rourke's notification to the sheriffs' departments. They're up to their eyelids helping KHP, but the Tonganoxie cops went to Tony's. No tire tracks. And he didn't answer the door."

At six-six, built like a Viking, tow-headed Tony Franklin didn't exactly fade into the woodwork. Quinn thought for a moment, then said, "You said he was on The Plaza last night. Maybe he took off from there for Thanksgiving."

"Not without calling me. I think he went to The Plaza searching for evidence."

Quinn whipped around to face Pierce. "Tony blew the whistle on Rex, didn't he?"

The sullen expression he gave her confirmed the truth. "We're discussing his phone in my sofa. Next topic? Soaking my family room in chicken blood."

"Rex swears Tony loathes him." Linear thought eluded her. "Detests and hates him."

"Listen to Rex and you'll conclude Santa Claus hates him." Pierce scrubbed his face so hard she winced. "Tell me what their love-hate relationship adds to the phone in my sofa."

Caffeine might help him see, Quinn thought, but hesitated turning on the grinder. It sounded like a buzz saw. Not a sound conducive to priming logic. Taking advantage of the quiet in the kitchen, she said, "All the snow...maybe Tony's stranded."

Or hurt. A more likely scenario for why he hadn't called?

"He's too good a driver. I don't care what Rourke

thinks. Tony never drove that Jeep last night." Pierce shook his head—gingerly, as if trying to rescramble his thoughts. "Tony grew up in Denver—it usually snows there more in April than we get in February."

"So? Drivers go off the road in Colorado." She smiled and flipped on the grinder, and let it rip without giving Pierce a warning.

"Jesus, Quinn!" He yelped.

A sense of power invaded her. When she finished slicing and dicing their nerves, she measured out coffee like a mature person and spoke with what she considered restraint. "We know Tony went to The Plaza last night. Maybe he found zilch. You asked him to check on me. He couldn't bring himself to disappoint you about Rex. Didn't even realize he almost mowed me down and took off for Toganoxie. Hit a snowdrift or another light—"

"Christomighty, Quinn!" Pierce lurched in his chair, as unsteady as a geriatric patient, rocking forward, trying to propel himself to his feet. "Tony would call me if he hit that light pole. He would. He knows I'd help him."

Pierce's raw confusion and fear felt like a vise squeezing air from Quinn's lungs, cutting off oxygen, hijacking reason. She longed to throw her arms around him, cry for him, ease his pain. Pain she understood. Let anyone imply Michael lacked good judgment, and she'd lash out with the same venom.

Head averted, Pierce was already sinking back into his chair. She hesitated, measuring the distance between them. It would be so easy to take the first step...

"Tony hasn't done a damn thing wrong." Pierce's jaw cracked and she jumped.

"Okay." Any question of touching him instead of protecting herself evaporated. She opened the fridge, removed a carton of milk and held it against her chest.

"Sorry I took your head off," he mumbled. "I confused you with Olsen."

"Oh, geez. Thanks." The humor in her laugh sounded forced. Pathetic. Lame.

"The confusion of an idiot." Pierce jumped out of his chair and charged at her like a rabid rhino, invading her space. "I wouldn't blame you if you tossed me out on my ass."

His nearness brought a flash of the earth rotating around the sun on Douglas Prescott's gold clock, and she had to curl her toes under to maintain her balance. Pierce looked at her in silence. She caught his flinch as she spoke in the gentlest tone she could manage, "Reporting Rex must've put Tony under a lot of stress."

Pierce's head barely moved in agreement, but his jaw muscles clenched. The clench failed to stop the tic under his eye. *Your point being?* rang his unasked question.

Wanting to move closer, wanting to take his hand, squeeze his fingers, silently promise him Tony was fine, she squeezed the milk carton. "What if...what if it was too much stress?"

The tension around his mouth and eyes gave way to blatant disbelief and pity. The dismissal he made in the back of his throat—a grunt or snort or primitive noise proclaiming *you've gotta be crazy*—said it all, but he made sure she got the message. "No way."

"I understand—"

"Tony loved nailing Rex. He thought I should make sure the bastard got twenty years to think about stealing from people who never hurt him. Tony had his priorities straight." Affection and pride swelled Pierce's baritone and pinched Quinn's heart.

Small tremors twitched in her arms. "Is there any chance someone stole his Jeep?"

"Why?" The single word rang with suspicion, matching Pierce's frown.

"Monday night—after the attack on the golf course—I saw a black Jeep—"

"What? You never mentioned that. Did you see the driver? Was it Tony? What about the license?"

On the defensive, Quinn fired back. "I thought it was kids. Necking. I didn't see the driver, and I didn't check the license plate."

Easier said than done when helping a full-grown man into her house. Quinn kept her thoughts to herself.

Pierce exhaled, then laughed. "Tony would never ambush me."

What about hanging around your house? she asked mentally. Frames of the black Jeep following the Corvette across Brush Creek unwound in slo-mo. A coincidence, she'd wanted to think at the time—yet she'd played cat-and-mouse games that seemed silly after the Jeep failed to follow her off Southwest Trafficway. She set the milk on the counter, seeing the Jeep weave in and out of traffic.

"He might lay a trap for me," Pierce said in a voice proclaiming boys will be boys. After a beat, he shook his head. "But Tony would never deliberately hurt me. That wasn't Tony on the golf course."

"I can't remember how tall—"

"The bastard was a dwarf." Pierce's eyes flashed, daring her to contradict the statement.

Nodding, Quinn waited, sure he hadn't finished.

He hadn't. "There's a logical reason for Olsen finding Tony's phone."

"I agree. Mrs. Taylor is Martha's Stewart's clone. There's no way that phone's been in that sofa a week."

"See?" Triumph sent Pierce's voice soaring. "Logic rules."

"Okay." Quinn repressed a sigh. How did she bring the conversation back to the Jeep?

"Whoever vandalized the house obviously stole Tony's phone." A glare. "My bet's on you-know-who. Who else had a better opportunity to waltz off with Tony's phone?"

Quinn groaned. "Ever hear of a double standard? Tony's innocent until proven guilty, but Rex is guilty until proven innocent."

"I know Tony." Pierce got right in Quinn's face.

His breath tickled her nose, but she focused on making one point. "Michael knows Rex."

"Not the way I know Tony."

"Michael and Rex have known each other since kindergarten."

Unwilling to admit defeat, Pierce curled his lip.

Quinn leaned forward, shocked by the red threads in his eyes. "We agree losing our phones amounts to suffering a major stroke. Why didn't Tony report missing his second brain?"

"Easy." Pierce snapped his fingers. "He probably has two, maybe three phones. One for work. One for women. One for whatever."

"Ahhh." Quinn nodded, dizzy from their convoluted argument. "Back to logic."

"He's probably holed up somewhere with the light

of his life." Pierce stared out the window as if seeing Tony, shook his head and brought his gaze back to the kitchen. "You don't buy the idea he's holed-up somewhere, do you?"

"No more than you do," she whispered.

The bittersweet fragrance of mocha amaretto filled the room. Pierce exhaled. "Black coffee's my only hope."

"In a minute." The tremors in her arms had moved to her chest and legs.

Miz Melodrama Queen pulled out a chair, remembering the basics of Psych 101. Avoid looming over someone when delivering bad news. Establish eye contact. Touch the one about to receive the bad news.

Sitting, Quinn decided, was about what she could manage.

"You're finally going to tell me what's on your mind," Pierce said.

"You always told me I should never play poker." Her heart skipped hard.

"I promise I won't kill the messenger." He took her icy hand in his icier one.

Dry-mouthed, she said, "Remember, I drove your 'Vette to work yesterday morning."

He nodded—the gesture impatient and abrupt. *Get on with it.*

"A black Jeep followed me most of the way—all the way across Southwest Trafficway." She paused and hoped he'd missed the tiny quiver undercutting her confidence.

Pierce flashed her a look that yelled, *Stop pulling my chain.* "Sounds like there's a black jeep around every corner."

Quinn flushed, let the temptation to walk away fade, said, "You think two black Jeeps in twenty-four hours are a coincidence? One on my cul-de-sac, the other one outside your house?"

Pierce opened his mouth, but she talked over him. "I can't remember the last time I saw a black Jeep before Monday night."

"Guess you've missed Tony's at work. His parking space is next to mine." Pierce's smooth, seductive voice of reason brought blood rushing to her ears.

"When I come to work at oh-dark-thirty, I have other things on my mind than male toys." She dialed back the volume, speaking more slowly. "It took four years and a dead battery for me to notice your 'Vette. As phallic symbols go, cars don't turn me on."

"My point exactly. Two black Jeeps do not an invasion make."

She tapped her top lip, waited, said, "I might agree if the Ward Parkway driver had driven behind me. He didn't. He dodged all over the place. He didn't want me to see his face."

Pierce started to roll his eyes, caught himself, stopped. "Tony can save us this entire going-nowhere conversation. I'll drop you at work, find him and take him to the cops. Once they clear him, will you believe more than one black Jeep exists in the universe?"

****

The phone rang and Quinn all but levitated across the kitchen. Faced with Pierce's direct question, he suspected she'd rather dance in hell than deal with his barely repressed fury. He loved Tony. She loved Michael. How could she accuse Tony of stalking her without proof?

She looked at Pierce over her shoulder and collided with a kitchen chair. She yelped, but caught a back leg. A regal wave commanded him to stay put. She slammed the chair upright. The glow of righteousness shimmered around her. She grabbed the receiver as if grabbing the gold ring on a carousel.

Perfect timing, Michael. Pierce forced the rim of the coffee mug against his lips and swallowed the thought. The cold brew tasted as bitter as old coffee grounds.

Quinn surprised him by staring at the LED. Her face shut down. The skin tightened across the bones on her face. The circles under her eyes resembled prunes. She pressed her lips together and held the receiver at arm's length as if the phone leaked radioactivity.

Sour coffee flooded Pierce's mouth. Not Prince Michael, but his faithful minion Rex.

Damn, just thinking about the weasel spilled enough acid into Pierce's touchy stomach to grow an ulcer. He stared into the empty mug and massaged the burn under his left breastbone. His stomach calmed down. A little. His gut still churned, convincing him Rex Walker—somehow, someway—masterminded the convenient appearance of Tony's phone.

Uh-huh. And that hunch, plus three bucks, would buy a small latte. Pierce stood and sauntered toward the coffee pot. He held his mug in front of him, but eavesdropped shamelessly. Word-fragments pulsated in Quinn's agitated whispers. Her corpse-like stiffness telegraphed the need for a caffeine jolt.

Pierce filled another mug and carried it to her. Too bad she can't inhale it. He set the mug on the countertop and raised an eyebrow.

She turned her back and shouted, "Why would Michael stay home today?"

"Don't worry about me," Pierce whispered. "I'll entertain myself."

Frowning, she faced him, slicing her finger through the air an inch from his nose, saying into the receiver, "I'll call him later—"

Pierce tapped the face on his watch. No more time to soothe poor Rexie. Snow was falling again—not the blizzard of last night—but he needed to take off for Tony's. Now. Some deep part of him had hoped she'd offer to go along, but that hope belonged in a kid's daydream.

She stared at his watch and stopped talking, her eyes bleak, her thumb pressed hard against her bottom lip. She nodded as if Walker could see the gesture, shifted her gaze downward, nodded again, then said, "I understand, Rex. I'll wait for Michael to call me."

Pierce squeezed the handle on his mug and took a step backwards. The temptation to kiss the hurt taking over her face was beginning to feel reasonable—even after last night's disastrous ending. God, getting out of bed, driving without speaking, hoping—

"Let's review the strategy," she said, her professional voice giving no clue to her vulnerability. "Arrive ten minutes early. Expect to wait. Edward Roslyn's notorious for short first interviews. I'll call him this afternoon—"

The line between her eyebrows came back. Pierce imagined erasing the scowl. Not because it ruined her looks. But because the little creep shouldn't hold that kind of power.

Her frown deepened. She shook her head. "This

afternoon. Calling earlier makes you look over-eager."

"Hang up." Pierce leaned toward her and spoke in a normal voice. So what if the weasel heard him?

Quinn threw him a look that screamed, *Leave*. Her unspoken challenge cha-chaaed in Pierce's head. Why leave now? Pushing back offered too much fun. Took his mind off her certainty Tony—had Pierce wrapped around his finger. Curious, he played stupid. Not picking-his-nose stupid, just dumb-ass, smiley-face stupid. Courting death, he ignored a second ball-freezing glare and slugged back coffee.

"Listen to me," she said.

Reflexively, Pierce set down his mug and stood up straighter. How many times, in six years of elementary school, had he heard that tone from the nuns at St. Joseph's?

Quinn's tone hardened. "Talking salary at this juncture isn't wise."

Yessss. Pierce made a fist and shot it in the air.

No visible sign she'd noticed. If anything, her tone was more clipped, definitely curt. "Expecting a ten-K increase without a glowing recommendation from Pierce is dreaming."

Creepo apparently didn't get it. Quinn waited a heartbeat before saying, "Fine. Talk salary. Shoot yourself in the head."

She hung up. Within seconds the phone rang.

Pierce made a low sucking noise.

"Shut. Up." Quinn pressed a knuckle against her bottom lip but picked up the receiver on the second ring. "Stop wasting my time, Rex. You don't want to listen to my advice, don't."

Her face and ears turned scarlet, but her eyes

flashed. "Call Michael," she said in a tone Pierce remembered from his own evisceration. "I promised I'd help you before I realized you need a new brain."

Pierce laughed and gave her two thumbs up. Finally, some backbone. Once she read the weasel's file, she'd wonder how she'd risked so much for such a creep.

She closed her eyes and rubbed her forehead. "I am not abandoning you."

Adrenaline launched Pierce forward. Fists at his side, he roared, "Creep!"

A vein bulged in Quinn's temple and her fingers curled around the phone, draining the blood from her knuckles. Pierce tensed, half expecting her to throw the receiver at him.

Instead, she stomped to the sliding glass door, her voice rising with each step. "That's not fair. I said I'd help you. I can't if you sabotage me."

Snow fell faster, blanketing her backyard in the loveliness of a Hallmark card. Pierce watched her back as she stared at the scene, listening to Creepo.

"I'll call you before noon." The fire in her voice had evaporated. "Before I call Edward."

She ended the call not by pressing the OFF button, but by holding it down with her thumb as if squashing a mutant cockroach.

Touching her now, Pierce realized, would be like touching a match to dynamite. So he hung back, amazed she could stand with her shoulders and back as brittle as icicles hanging from the rafters. He said, "You are the world's best sister."

"That should keep me warm tonight." She stared at the snow another heartbeat before turning with the slow, jerky movements of an old woman. Her face was as frozen as the landscape. "I have some questions for Tony. I can be ready in five minutes."

****

It was 9:09 but Pierce reined in his impatience and let Quinn take charge of fixing hot chocolate. Just in case, she'd said, making a vague reference to the Donner Party.

God, being stranded with Quinn would make his day. He scraped snow from the car windows, feeling the first twinge of weather nerves. He estimated Tony's place in the middle of nowhere was about thirty miles from Quinn's driveway. New layers of white meant more black ice, lower visibility and a drifted, unsalted, two-mile county road to Tony's house.

With a little luck, the dumb-ass drivers will stay home.

Quinn climbed in, buckled her seatbelt and aimed her remote at the garage door. "I wish Michael would call. I don't want to be in the boonies when Luce goes into labor."

"We can always turn back if he calls." Pierce flipped on the wipers and eased into the deserted cul-de-sac, careful to avoid brushing Quinn's hair as he anchored one arm across the back of her seat. "I bet we find Tony in bed with the flu. The flu explains why he didn't call. Being sick provides the perfect alibi—"

"Did you bring Rex's file?"

"You asked me to bring it, I brought it." His tone was borderline curt.

"Good." Quinn pointed at the Neighborhood Watch sign. "The black Jeep parked there Monday night. It's a jog from the hole in the hedge, but it's not that far."

"If we weren't pressed for time, I'd show off here. Get out, check for tire tracks in a foot of new snow." He made his tone light, hoping she'd forget he'd snapped at her. "You know, like on CSI?"

"Never watch it, but go ahead. I'll act impressed."

"Next time." He wanted to say something that would kick her mood up a notch. Maybe show some enthusiasm about being alone with him. Maybe...his mind shifted gears. Dammit, her baggage weighed heavy enough without adding his ego. Coddling Michael and covering for Rex would throw Miss Mary Sunshine into a blue funk.

Pierce eased off the gas, feeling the wheels spin, then steady on the slick snow-packed street. "Rex's folder's in the glove compartment. It's your copy. Make notes if you want."

Snow mixed with sleet hit the windshield, but they rode in silence. He concentrated on the ice-covered Kaw River Bridge bisecting Johnson and Wynadotte counties. He doubted she noticed the frozen water below them. The weasel's file apparently mesmerized her.

He coughed. She continued reading—as if alone in the car. An occasional truck reassured him they were traveling in the New Millennium and not exploring in the eighteenth century with the French, the first European mapmakers of the Indian territory. After Quinn had kicked him out of her life, Pierce spent many long summer weekends kayaking and canoeing on the Kaw. Usually with Tony, his ski and tobogganing bud.

He's okay. He's fine. Scanning beyond his headlights, Pierce willed the knots in his shoulders to shrink. Tony joked about being The Hulk's cousin—

with better hair. Next to him the weasel was just that—a weasel that sneaked around looking for easy prey. Tony was anything but easy prey. Even if felled by the flu, he'd hold his own against the weasel.

Images of Tony in bed, weak, dehydrated, coughing and sneezing, unwound in Pierce's head. Realizing his imagination had derailed, he counted to ten, slowed as oncoming high beams ripped through the thick white curtain.

In need of hearing a real voice, he interrupted Quinn. "See why Rex is guilty?"

The second she hesitated raising her head and locking eyes with him telegraphed her answer. Adrenaline jolted through him, clenching his jaw, washing her face in a red haze.

"What?" The humiliation of his voice cracking stopped him. He clamped his mouth shut and slowed his breathing.

"I'm not an auditor." She opened the file and stared at one of the pages. "From a layman's perspective, Tony could be the embezzler."

"Bull!" Pierce flipped the wipers on high. She jumped, and pure pleasure jolted into him. He bit the inside of his lip. The smug smile threatening to spread died.

The silence in the car wrecked Pierce's willpower. "What about me?" He slowed as at the end of the bridge. "Why couldn't I be the embezzler?"

"Tony had access to the same files as Rex. Tony knew all the passwords. Tony should've reported the discrepancies earlier. Tony's missing two days after accusing Rex."

"Tony's not missing. He has the flu." Pierce

projected an inarguable finality.

"If Rex were guilty, why wouldn't he be halfway to Mexico by now?"

Her calm, quiet tone grated Pierce's throat like sandpaper, but he shrugged and swallowed before taking charge. "I refuse to speculate why Rex Walker does anything."

"Why would you? It's easier presuming he's guilty."

A muscle jerked under his right eye. "Easier? Easier is finding someone else with motive, opportunity and means."

"Tony—"

"Three forensic auditors and two corporate lawyers think that document is enough for an indictment. Against Rex. Not against Tony. Not against a phantom. Against. Rex."

"Paying two and a half million bucks doesn't entitle me to an opinion, huh?" Quinn cocked her head at him, and the angle of her throat made him want to stop the car and kiss her.

Since they drove on ice, he kept driving. "You didn't have to pay a dime to have an opinion. Everyone's entitled to an opinion. Even the jokers who think the world's flat. Or lightning never strikes twice. Or climate change is a conspiracy."

Her laugh, as always, sounded like music. God, she actually sounded amused. "Okay. I think I understand your argument, Pierce. But since I am so dense, let me re-read the file, and maybe I'll even accept your opinion."

Sure, when they're serving ice cream in hell. Figuring this thought guaranteed an incendiary reaction,

Pierce savored a brief fantasy of arguing with Quinn until she capitulated, accepting Rex's guilt as truth.

And that will happen when she can say Brittany without her heart splintering.

"I didn't say you were dense."

"How much longer?"

The detachment in her voice told him to answer the question, then shut up. Which he did, dropping his shoulders, loosening his fingers on the wheel and feeling his stomach unclench.

If pressed for the truth, he realized, he wanted another round of verbal ping-pong.

Chapter 13

Quinn's mind went numb re-reading the pages of legalese. Sensing Pierce's eyes on her, she pressed her forehead against her car window and expelled a breath. The file he thought was damning, she thought was inconclusive. Was that why he vetoed bringing legal charges?

In another lifetime, she'd loved debating him on any topic. They'd held back nothing, gone for the jugular, hurled zingers, then laughed and made love.

Different life, she reminded herself, studied the frozen fields, then said, "Edward will want an explanation for why Rex is leaving."

"Why would Edward—why would any banker—want to hire him?" Pierce shouted. "The creep's a thief. Let him find his own job—if he can."

"I promised Mic..." That sounded so whiny, so illogical, she started over. "Everyone deserves a second chance. Rex has a sick mother—"

"Rex Walker's had more than a second chance." The smile that flitted across Pierce's perfect face was the kind of smile Hannibal Lector must've bestowed on fava beans.

She rubbed the goose bumps jockeying up and down her arms. "Rex wants you to forward his last performance evaluation to Edward—along with a cover letter saying he was a satisfactory employee."

"Uh-huh. And I want world peace and a cure for cancer and an end to hunger." Pierce snorted. "I'm not paying two and a half million bucks out of my pocket, then telling my mentor Rex was a stellar employee. He's an embezzler."

Her tongue stuck to the roof of her mouth.

After a deep breath, Pierce looked at her like a parent about to break bad news to a child. "The guy flat out lies. I'd bet you my twenty bucks pocket change he doesn't have a mother—"

"Whoa." Quinn snapped her fingers. "Run that by me again."

"I can't prove it, but I think his mother's dead. Have you ever met her?"

Quinn nodded and swallowed her shock. "Years ago. At our house one Thanksgiving."

"How long since Michael saw her, talked to her?"

"No idea. Why would he mention it? What makes you suspicious?"

"You mean besides the fact I'm cynical? Skeptical? Suspicious by nature?"

The knot in Quinn's jaw made speaking impossible.

"I called the number he gave personnel for his mother." Pierce shot Quinn a glance she couldn't read.

"He told me today his mother's in Florida for the winter."

"Guess what? I called the Florida number in July. Called again in August, September, and October. Each time, the same message—confirmed by a phone company supervisor."

"Disconnected," Quinn said, her insides shaking as if she'd stepped onto thin ice.

"Uh-huh." Pierce met and held her gaze. "But there's more."

"What?" Quinn licked her lips. In the pit of her stomach, the cream and morning coffee curdled. Her heart sped up, and she had the sensation of falling. Faster and faster and faster.

"The phone in Florida was disconnected six months ago." The expression on Pierce's face was impassive, but Quinn thought she detected a flicker of sadness.

Or maybe she was confusing him with Michael. Sad wouldn't begin to describe Michael's feelings once he learned his best friend lied and kept devastating secrets.

How could Michael be so wrong?

****

Pierce checked the rear and side mirrors, shooting glances at Quinn. Sneaky glances, he hoped. The arm across her waist supported her other elbow, and her chin rested on her fist. His announcement about the disconnected phone didn't leave her speechless, but the news shut down the conversation. She stated she needed to think and withdrew into herself like a turtle.

Hands steady on the wheel, he plowed through the snow and his brain plowed through the recurring questions.

How much did Quinn personally know about Rex?

Why would he lie about his financial responsibility to his mother if she was dead?

Did Michael know if/when she died?

How much did her death strengthen Michael's loyalty to his chum?

Blood pumped into Pierce's veins and the

questions pounded in his ears. He tapped the steering wheel in sync with the questions' rhythm and tasted metal in his throat. Lies and deception didn't prove Walker's guilt, but Quinn must see they added to the big picture of an asshole thumbing his nose at the rest of them. She had to see...

He cocked his head from side to side, working out a kink in his neck. He stopped tapping the wheel and flexed his fingers. The tremor in his arms faded, but not the problem. Quinn didn't have to see a damn thing from his perspective. If Michael told her Rex was innocent, she'd see nothing but the weasel's innocence—no matter how damning the evidence, how convincing anyone's suspicions. Attempts by Pierce to persuade her to his view would cause her to dig in her heels. The interview with Edward proved her allegiance to Michael.

If Michael's so perfect, why's his best friend a sociopath? The question hit Pierce between the eyes like a fist. Had Quinn ever asked it? By her own admission, she didn't like Walker. What was the glue that bonded St. Michael to Rex?

A gust of wind slammed into the 'Vette, rocking the car. The back wheels slipped. The rear end fishtailed, kicked up snow, spun around like a top. Air whooshed out of Pierce's mouth.

Quinn made a noise he barely heard. Heart stuttering, he corralled the impulse to hit the brakes. He eased his foot off the gas. A light tap to the brakes slowed the car. He held the steering wheel steady, careful not to overcorrect. Inch by inch, the tail end straightened.

"We're okay. The wind—" He swiveled his head

toward Quinn.

"How much farther?" The Walker file lay open on her lap. A white-gold wing of hair cascaded past her cheek, shielding her face and eyes. "You said we'd be home if Michael calls."

Not exactly. "I think we're five, ten minutes—"

An idiot driving too fast, passed them, throwing clumps of snow onto the windshield. Cussing, Pierce eased up on the accelerator.

Quinn pressed her thumb knuckle against her bottom lip.

Pull over. For a split second, Pierce gave the idea a passing thought. The wipers whipped off the extra snow and he pointed at a side road buried in at least a foot of snow.

"That's Tony's turnoff." The unplowed road forced Pierce to slow to a crawl. Despite the 'Vette's great handling, staying in the ruts required plenty of arm muscles.

"Is that a light?" Quinn swiped the windshield, jabbing the glass. "Is it coming from Tony's house?"

Snow swirled around them like goosedown, but Pierce nodded. "It's his yard light. He's the first house on this road."

"How many people live out here?"

"Five families total." The 'Vette's front wheels hit a snowdrift, jarring Pierce's molars. "Sorry. Doesn't look as if the neighbors came through here today with the snowplow."

"My, my. Imagine a little snow stopping the pioneers."

"This place belonged to Tony's great grandfather." Pierce turned into a long, narrow drive, packed with hard snow and surrounded by roof-high drifts. When was it last cleaned?

"I thought Tony was a Colorado boy."

"His parents moved there thirty years ago. His great grandfather settled here after the Civil War. Became a U.S. Marshal in the 70s. Served in Congress two years. Became a state supreme court judge on his sixty-ninth birthday." Pierce realized he was blithering, but he wanted to keep his mind off the accumulation of snow ahead of them. No footprints.

"Is the real message here that being honest and law-abiding is encoded in Tony's DNA?"

"No, but good point." Pierce's coffee ulcer burned. No footprints. The new snow had covered the deputies' footprints. What time had they come by?

"No lights except the one in the yard," Quinn said. "No tire tracks."

"If he is sick, the Jeep's probably in the garage. We'll go in the back door." Pierce killed the engine, reached across Quinn and removed a key ring from the glove compartment.

On the off chance she missed the point, he said, "He has a key to my house too. That's why I know he didn't decorate my family room with chicken blood."

****

They opened Tony's back door and Pierce charged inside. To hell with how much snow he dragged across the shiny kitchen floor. Shouting, he jogged to the rear of the house. Not good. Not good. Quinn dogged his heels, adding her voice.

No response.

Ollie, ollie oxen free. Tension unspooled in Pierce's stomach as he ran down the narrow hallway.

He zipped past two open doors on either side of the hall. A glance revealed an office straight out of a magazine article on de-cluttering and a guest bedroom straight out of a home decorating 'zine. The spacious master bedroom reflected the same neatness and order. Bed made. Clothes put away. Curtains cracked. A dry terrycloth robe hung on an antique brass knob in the bathroom. Four towels dangled at the same level from a brass bar. Sink, mirror and fixtures gleamed, the shower door sparkled.

"What time did he get to the office on Monday?" Quinn moved aside as Pierce returned to the bedroom. No chance he'd accidentally touch her.

His insides burned. "He beat me. I got there at six. We wanted to review the evidence against Rex one last time."

"What time did he go home?" Quinn started for the door.

"Don't know. Around 6:30. We'd gone over every single fact until we wanted to puke. I was sick of the mess. So was he. It was snowing. I suggested he spend the night at my place, but I think he figured we'd keep going round and round like a couple of gerbils. So I sent him home."

"And two hours later, you showed up at my office..."

Wind howled, rattling windows, rattling Pierce, making the temptation to lie seem reasonable. Reasonable to him, totally unacceptable to Quinn. He said, "The nut in the garage—I didn't like you staying alone so late."

Her jaw dropped and she stared at him as if he were an alien.

Bracing for a tongue lashing, he planted his feet further apart and held up his palms. "I know, I know. You're an independent woman. You brought a mugger to his knees. You don't need, want or—"

"Will you shut up?" She lunged at him, threw her arms around his neck in a choke-hold and smashed her soft, hot mouth against his.

Her lips felt like a branding iron, and he imagined steam escaping from his sizzling brain. Her wide open eyes were bottomless pools of light and warmth. He'd seen the same intensity the first time they'd made love, revealing her vulnerability. His mind veered away from the past and he stayed in the moment, aware he was getting harder by the nanosecond, aware she was hyper-aware of the power she wielded over him, aware she tasted sweet and familiar and hot.

As if choreographed, they broke away at the same time. Both were grinning like idiots.

"My God, Quinn." He touched her cheek and electricity shot through his fingertips.

Her eyes softened. "Thank you for worrying about me."

"I like worrying about you. I'd like to worry more about you—I mean—you know what I mean." He felt like a seventh-grade geek on his first date with the most beautiful girl in school.

"I think I do." Her sly smile revived his defibrillating heart. "Which is really scary."

"Scary?" His right eye twitched. Damn, there went his Mr. Cool image.

"Scary that I understand what you mean after all this time."

"Wasted time." He pulled her toward him and

locked eyes with her. The directness of her gaze left no doubts about what she wanted. The same thing he wanted. He pulled her to him again, whispering in her ear, "Time we should make up for."

She took a step backwards. "We have to find Tony."

The longing in her low, sultry voice kept her words from feeling like ice cubes. He said, "Let's go into a more neutral room."

"Works for me."

The regret he heard made it easier to accept acting like an adult, but he was careful not to touch her. By unspoken agreement, they went into the kitchen. Nose in the air, she sniffed, and Pierce had to concentrate on water pinging into the stainless steel sink so he wouldn't grab her and kiss her.

"There's a sure sign he intends to come back." Pierce gestured at the dripping faucet. "He didn't want the pipes bursting."

"Clean. Neat. Prepared for emergencies. Some woman will definitely appreciate Tony." Quinn opened the fridge, calling out the contents of milk, cheese, sour cream, butter, a plastic bag of spinach and a large rib-eye steak. "The milk carton's full. Expires early next week."

"All signs he intends to come home." An invisible knife hacked through Pierce's vocal cords. "I'm guessing he planned on eating steak last night."

A nod from Quinn confirmed he hadn't lost his mind. He led the way to the living room at the front of the house without speaking. Like the kitchen, it was neat and spotless. Magazines in an orderly pile. CDs and books in perfect rows. No dust bunnies or cobwebs.

"Tony keeps a shipshape house," Quinn said.

"Wait until you see the garage." The knot in Pierce's stomach contracted.

The wind made conversation impossible as they trudged the hundred yards in ankle-deep snow to the detached garage. With each step, he cursed his sorry ass for not warning her before they left the house. The truth was, he wasn't sure he was prepared for what they might find.

Ice froze the lock. He chipped away, cursing under his breath, keeping his imagination in check. Once the key went in, he waved Quinn behind him. She didn't argue. The wind worked against him. He dug in his heels, huffed and puffed and finally got his weight behind the door.

Chest rising, eyes watering, he scanned the interior.

"No Jeep," Quinn announced the obvious with such relief Pierce wanted to kiss her.

No Tony, thank God. Pierce didn't know if he felt relieved or ticked off. He wiped his eyes and stepped inside the garage.

After opening and closing several closets where Tony had organized his tools, paint, garden equipment and recycling bins, they slogged back to the house. Pierce called the Wyandotte County Sheriff's Department. Quinn meandered from room to room, waved at Pierce and went out the back door again. On hold for a deputy, he watched her slip and slide down the long, drifted drive to the mailbox.

She returned, nose scarlet, eyes watery, and laid the mail on the kitchen table. Planting the receiver between his neck and shoulder, Pierce sorted through copies of *P. C. Week*, several flyers for computer games, and two legal-sized envelopes, both from a law firm in Kansas City. But it was the ornately, handwritten, pale lavender envelope reeking of heavy, overly sweet lilacs that told Pierce Tony hadn't come home last night.

"Was Tony involved with someone?" Quinn handed Pierce a lavender envelope.

He held the letter at arm's length, smiled a smile that hurt his jaws, felt his heart miss one, then another beat. He exhaled the building tension and said, "Molly MacIntyre's his fifteen-year-old cousin in Endicott, New York. Tony says she has a real crush on him—writes him every week. Apparently, she's a computer jockette."

The ice in Pierce's chest had spread to his throat. He swallowed, remembering Tony's delight with his young 'cuz. Turning the envelopes over and over, Pierce said, "Molly thinks Tony's wonderful. Here he is—an old man of twenty-nine—"

The back of Pierce's throat burned the way it had after his tonsillectomy at age ten. Tony was twenty-nine. He should have a whole lifetime ahead of him...

"Think about being fifteen." Quinn stepped into the silence and saved Pierce from his imagination. "I bet Tony's taught Molly a few computer tricks, right? Ergo, he's wonderful."

Swallowing didn't work, but Pierce said, "Better than that. He can beat her at all the computer games. She calls him 'Wonder Geek.'"

The sweet, soft smile Quinn threw him cut like a razor. Pierce winced. Waiting on the damn phone was driving him into the trough of self-pity. There had to be a clue here somewhere. Pierce knew he could find it if he looked hard enough.

"I'm surprised they don't e-mail each other." Quinn threw him another chance to come out of his fugue.

"I'm sure they do." He switched the phone to his other ear. "Tony uses his computer for everything—from making ski reservations to checking out recipes with butter."

Quinn fingered the envelopes, then laid them on the table. She came to Pierce and wrapped her arm around his waist. Having her so close was a gift—unexpected and that much sweeter.

"He must've had an accident, Quinn. He wouldn't take off. He'd leave me a message."

"Let's not go there yet." The gentleness in her voice almost undid him.

Impossible to force his head to move in agreement. In that same gentle tone, she said, "Why don't I woman the phone? You check your voice mail again. Maybe look around here some more?"

"I only look ready to tear the phone out of the wall." He shoved the receiver at her, hugged her and remembered his manners. "Thanks. You saved my sanity."

Ever the jokester.

On the off-chance they'd arrive—unannounced—and find Tony in an awkward situation with a girlfriend, Pierce had checked messages twice at work and twice on his cell even though he knew Quinn's views on driving and using a cell phone.

Third time's the charm. The cliché ran through his brain like water through a sieve as he dialed work. Eight messages, two from Edward. Zip from Tony. To hell with Rex.

Pierce rummaged through the mail, withdrew the law firm's envelope and held it up to the window. Naturally, he couldn't see a damn thing. Why the hell would Tony have business with Leonard and Yaeger— big-time Kansas City defense attorneys?

Maybe Tony's home office held some answers. Pierce gave Quinn the high sign he was going into the other room. She looked beat. Her patience amazed him. How'd she do it? Two minutes of waiting on the phone drove him nuts. A better man would give her a break.

"Want me to take over?" he asked with the enthusiasm of an eggplant.

She shook her head vigorously and waved him on his way.

Ethically and legally, Pierce knew breaking into Tony's PC was a lot like opening his personal mail. Ethically, Pierce felt almost no compunction about trying. At least not as long as Quinn didn't witness his shenanigans.

Not that there was much to witness. Unlike Tony, Pierce fell in the category of computer dimwit even after a good night's sleep. Stumped by the PC's hostility, he moved on to opening and closing drawers in the desk. Neat and tidy. Everything in its place. He flipped through letters filed in separate slots on top of the desk. Another envelope from Leonard and Yaeger. Postmarked a week ago and still sealed.

Curiouser and curiouser.

Quinn stuck her head around the corner. "A deputy's on his way. They asked us not to touch anything."

Pierce nodded, his whole body instantly rigid, his heart stone cold. He felt like a robot—mimicking the unnatural movements of a human being.

****

Tinted aviators hid the young deputy's eyes and left Quinn with the feeling she was talking to herself. For his part, the deputy nodded his buzzed blond head so often Quinn felt dizzy. She assumed he made the gesture to reflect his understanding. He expressed all the right words in a quiet, neutral tone.

His tone might convey empathy, Quinn thought, if we were aliens. But his body language was all wrong—rubbing his face too often, crossing his arms, tapping his toe.

Pierce, too, was throwing off megawatts of impatience, his jaw locked, his eyes narrowed, a vein bulging in his forehead as the deputy spoke more right-sounding words and nodded a few times without offering any concrete ideas.

Maybe he picked up on Pierce's pissy mood, because he abruptly moved off his script, speaking in a condescending tone that left Quinn's fingertips tingling.

"Mr. Franklin's a grown man. Being gone from home for a couple of days and nights isn't that unusual for a young, single guy."

"What about returning my calls?" Pierce demanded. "Tony never misses our nightly conference calls."

"Uh-huh. A little more unusual," Deputy Zack Wright drawled. "Doesn't prove he's missing. Based on my experience," the deputy assured them, looking from Pierce to Quinn with a bland, open face, "even though he didn't call you, I'd say there's no real cause for alarm. SOP requires us to wait seventy-two hours before filing a missing person report."

Pierce made a rude noise in the back of his throat which the deputy ignored. He spoke to Quinn. "We'll keep an eye out. Check the local hospitals. Review accident reports."

Worried because Deputy Zack was apparently blind to Pierce's scowl Quinn said, "Can you come by his house from time to time?"

"Sure. We can do that. We can also call his parents."

The remark was like a match to dynamite. Pierce's dark eyes flashed, his face turned stroke-red, and the pulse in his temple banged like a hammer. "Are you craz—?"

Quinn stepped between the two men, put her hands behind her and signaled Pierce to say nothing. Throat dry, she spoke to the deputy. "Crazy as it sounds, let's hold off on that. We don't want to alarm them without reason."

Deputy Zack shrugged. "Up to you. But he might be right there with them, you know."

"That's a possibility." Before Pierce exploded, Quinn led the deputy to the kitchen door. The wind knocked the breath out of her, but she walked outside with the guy.

"If Mr. Franklin doesn't show up or get in touch with his family or call Mr. Jordan after Thanksgiving, we'll take formal steps at that time," the deputy called, sprinting for his car.

How reassuring. Quinn turned and jogged inside. "It's okay," she announced. "He's gone now."

"You want to hazard a guess which end of the gene pool he swam in?" Pierce slapped a clenched fist against his open hand.

"I'd rather figure out if we should be worried. What about calling Tony's parents?"

Pierce tugged his right ear, inhaled, exhaled. "Don't think so. He's their only child. What if he's not there? We'd scare them silly."

"I could call them," Quinn volunteered. "Make up a story."

"Such as?"

Always the skeptic. She blew on her hands, rubbed them together, let the ideas come. "I can say he and I were going skiing together over Thanksgiving. I got phone mail from him—garbled. So garbled I couldn't understand it."

Out of the corner of her eye, Quinn sneaked a look at Pierce. His open mouth confirmed he was hooked.

"I'm calling them to see if he's meeting me at their house the way we discussed or if I should go on to Vail. Meet him there."

Pierce shook his head. "You just now made this up, right?"

Nervousness cramped Quinn's stomach, but her voice was harsh. "If you don't like it, we can come up with something diff—"

"I like it. Hell, I like it a lot." Black eyes glowing, he grabbed both her hands and squeezed as if they were made of glass. "Nothing like it would ever occur to me."

"I'm sure there's a compliment in there somewhere." Quinn arched a brow. She knew from personal and professional experience that Pierce didn't lack for imagination.

For the first time that day, he looked like his old self. Confident. Take-charge. Optimistic. He said,

"Let's try it. As we say in banking, what's the worst-case scenario?"

****

A woman Quinn assumed was Tony's mother answered the Franklins' phone. After Quinn confirmed this and identified herself, she forgot her thudding heart, turned up the smile-o-meter and smiled into the phone. "Tony introduced us a couple of years ago."

"We're so appreciative for your helping him get his job with Pierce. What can I do for you, Miz Alexander?"

Surprised at how easily Mrs. Franklin gave her the opening she needed, Quinn gave Pierce two thumbs up, hoping the details of her story came back to her.

"Is Tony there? I'd like his opinion on the weather between Kansas City and the Colorado border. They say the skiing's great in Vail, but I'm worried about the drive."

Quinn took a breath and stopped talking. Let the woman answer the question.

"Ohhh. He's not here. His dad and I are trying to accept he won't spend Thanksgiving with us this year."

Why not? Quinn's mind screamed. A glance at Pierce's frown told her he knew something was wrong.

"I'm sure you're disappointed," she said. "Is he headed for the ski slopes?"

Nothing like being downright nosy. But Mrs. Franklin had said they were appreciative about Tony's job. Maybe she wouldn't mind Quinn's sudden interest in her son's skiing plans—five years after his successful interview with Pierce.

"No, if he was going to ski, we'd see him for sure. Unless he flew directly into Denver. Which he almost

217

never does. He said he had too much work to do."

Quinn's heart stuttered. Thank God, she'd modified her story about meeting Tony at his parents' house.

Lied, she amended. But why would Tony lie to his parents?

The lack of response from Quinn didn't slow Mrs. Franklin, who kept chatting as if she and Quinn were old friends. "Tony said he and Pierce plan to work all weekend. Said maybe they'd have a turkey sandwich to celebrate Thanksgiving."

The older woman chuckled, a warm, open sound that reminded Quinn of her own mother.

...stuck at a hotel while you're out playing detective with Pierce. Quinn's heart thudded. How had she gotten sucked so deeply into Pierce's worry about Tony that she forgot her own mother? She swallowed, avoided Pierce's raised eyebrows and forced herself to laugh and listen as Mrs. Franklin went on to tell her how bad the driving conditions were from Kansas City to Junction City, the closest town to their ranch.

"You're more than welcome to stop by here for Thanksgiving dinner, Miz Alexander. We'd love to see you again."

Wiggle out of this one, fast-talker. Quinn moved the receiver to her other ear before saying, "Thanks, Mrs. Franklin. But I don't know if I'll get away."

"You young people. Work, work, work. I'm always telling Tony he needs more fun in his life."

Quinn mumbled some reply and they hung up. Heart aching, she took a deep breath, raised her face to Pierce and knew the ending of her story was written there.

Chapter 14

"Why did Tony lie to his parents?" Something in Pierce's tone sounded like blame.

Quinn bristled, but kept her tone neutral. "I should've asked Mrs. Franklin when Tony told her he was working the weekend."

"We never discussed it." Pierce jabbed his finger into the kitchen table. "What the hell am I missing? Nothing makes sense."

"I should've asked different questions," Quinn said. "I can call her back—"

"Hey!" Pierce grabbed her in a bear hug, lifting her off her feet. "You were awesome. Forget the what-ifs. You did great."

It was too little, too late, and the words didn't make up for forgetting her own mother stranded in St. Louis, but Quinn said, "Maybe we'll all laugh about this one day."

"Always the optimist." Pierce's tone said he'd rather listen to the snow fall than listen to more optimism.

"I need to get back to the office." She didn't have the energy for Pierce's disdain about Rex, and she lacked the self-discipline to withstand his lack of empathy for her mother.

Since he wanted five minutes in the john before leaving, Quinn punched SPEED DIAL. Her mother was still at the airport hotel expecting her flight to depart by two that afternoon.

"How's Luce?" Quinn sat in the spotless kitchen listening for a flush in the master bath.

"Michael thinks she's calmer. He's staying home today. Asked me to tell you he's taking the phone off the hook."

"Smart." Now Rex couldn't reach Michael after the interview with Edward Roslyn.

"I think he and Luce need a little alone-time. I said I'd text him after I land at SFO."

"Well, call me. I don't care what time, okay?" The sound of muffled water came too soon. Quinn disconnected and lurched to her feet. Lack of sleep made her lightheaded.

Not the best condition for a long ride with Pierce, but she'd fake falling asleep.

****

In the 'Vette, the moment with Quinn in Tony's bedroom felt as remote as a week-old dream. Obviously she wanted no reminders of how close they'd come to salving their old wounds. Knowing her, Pierce was surprised she'd failed to ask how he felt. Discussions about feelings were a big deal for Quinn. Pierce considered these discussions warm-up exercises for poking sticks in his eye. For once though, he was "in touch with his feelings," but the lines etched around her mouth and eyes curbed his tongue.

Give her a break. Tony wasn't her problem and Michael shouldn't be the pain in the ass he was. And life should be good fairies and rainbows after warm rains.

Pierce smacked the CD player and let John

Coltrane's haunting sax melt the smaller rocks in his neck. Thoughts about Tony, ping-ponging in his head, slowed. He dropped into Deppity Zack's ruts and drove in silence. Ridiculously, he worried that speaking his thoughts gave them power—to reveal the gut-gnawing fear and power to hurt Tony.

Quinn sat with her head back, her eyes closed. The snow had turned to flurries so they reached the state highway in good shape. Mile after mile flew by with Pierce gripping the wheel, hardly conscious when the snow stopped. The black clouds hanging over the barren, white fields diverted his attention for a while. When was the last time they'd seen the sun?

On The Plaza, acres of buildings and trees buffered the bitter Canadian air sweeping across the desolate plains. In the country, the damp and cold settled around Pierce's heart.

****

The bridge across the Kaw River gave Quinn the willies. Summer, spring, winter and fall, it had a notorious reputation for a high number of car wrecks. Too many of them fatalities. Commuters, leaving early, caught in the snow and slush, honked horns, hit their brakes, and generally drove like native Floridians, who had never driven north of Tampa.

Her right foot rode an imaginary brake as she kept one eye on the traffic and checked her voice mail. A dozen messages at work. None from Michael, one from Edward Roslyn. Later.

No signs from Pierce that he even realized she sat next to him. No inquiries about Luce. Or her mother. Dammit, how much more of his self-absorbed angst could he emit? Her fingertips tingled. She wanted to smack him. Commonsense took hold. His angst meant no rehashing that moment in Tony's bedroom. As long as he kept quiet, she didn't have to listen to him brood about Tony. Something was wrong there, but raising question after question after question felt wrong, too. Apparently making love didn't include opening up to her.

One-night stands rarely end in happy-ever-after reality, her Demon Fear whispered. Her breath caught and her heart boomed in her ears.

Reality meant calling Michael—despite his demands for privacy. She needed to hear him tell her what was going on. Was he really worried about nevus flammeus or was that Rex's take on reality?

Reality meant getting back with Edward Roslyn. She needed to come straight with him about Rex. The file Pierce insisted she read made some sense, but she wasn't a lawyer.

Reality meant dealing with Rex. She needed to report Edward's reaction. If he didn't cancel the appointment, she'd send him a dozen red roses. Dream on.

Reality meant avoiding a traffic tie-up at the light. "The back way's faster." she said, running her words together.

Pierce made the turn at the next block. "You're coming back to my house for the night, aren't you?"

Don't get excited. You already know the answer. Mouth dry, heart racing, she said, "I'm busy tonight."

A muscle ticked under Pierce's eye as he pulled to the curb, unbuckled his seat belt and reached for Quinn. "Come home with me."

The huskiness in his throat sent adrenaline

zooming into her chest. She closed her eyes, inhaled the comforting scent of his wool shirt and tried to sort out the feelings driving the jackhammer in her head.

"I asked Mrs. Taylor to fix us supper."

"Now you've pulled all the stops." The little girl in her chest, the one she almost never let out, fought against hyperventilating. "I'll probably open a can of chicken noodle soup. If I feel really creative, I'll throw in a little frozen broccoli."

"It's been a long day." He spoke in the solemn cadence Quinn remembered from the last time they argued about Brittany. "We'll kick back. Relax."

Good sex is always a release for men. Demon Fear's snicker released a snake in her tiny garden of ever-blooming fantasies.

"I've got a million things to do. Call Rex, Michael..."

The light in Pierce's eyes went out. He shrugged and said reasonably, "I know what that's like—to set priorities."

Hands on the steering wheel, he checked the rearview mirror, and pulled away from the curb. "Ya gotta do what ya gotta do."

"Typical," Quinn muttered to herself.

"Damn straight," he muttered back. "Men bare their souls and women clean the grout."

"Huh. Women don't leap with joy and men get their wittle noses out of joint."

"Funny, Quinn. Very, very funny."

If her own wittle nose wasn't out of joint, Quinn thought miserably, she'd apologize.

They topped a hill. A gust of wind shook the car. Instinctively, she pulled her coat closer. A picture of

Tony Franklin, hurt on some lonely back road in his Jeep, flashed in front of her. She sent a silent appeal for his safety.

Exhausted, she clamped down on her mind. A bone-deep depression nagged at her. Calling Rex was inescapable. But she wouldn't let him get her down any more than she'd let what happened between her and Pierce get her down.

A block from the golf course, she started gathering her things. No delays at her house made it harder to capitulate on Pierce's supper invitation. Glad some part of her brain still worked, she glanced in the side mirror

"Pierce!" She jiggled his forearm. "Check the rearview mirror."

He did, swore, and whipped a Uee. "Hold on!"

The black Jeep continued toward them. With about forty feet separating the two vehicles, the Jeep spurted forward.

"Jesus!" Pierce threw a protective arm in front of her, but her neck cracked.

Tires squealing, the Jeep made a U-turn, grazing their front bumper.

"That's Tony's Jeep." Pierce burned rubber. "We designed those purple stripes."

"We'll never catch him if he gets on any of the streets West," Quinn warned.

"I know, I know." Pierce floored the accelerator. Snow spewed around the headlights and hood. They leaped forward like a hungry lion sighting a flock of lazy gazelles. "He's got just enough lead..."

The traffic light at the end of her street and adjacent to the country club blinked red at the three-way intersection. The Jeep jumped the curb to the golf-cart path and plowed onto the snow-covered greenway.

"Holy shit, the guy's nuts." Pierce tromped the brake.

"Certifiable." Quinn swiped her window and strained to peer through the mist.

Pierce switched the wipers to high. "Imagine the groundskeeper seeing those tracks."

"My imagination's not that vivid," Quinn said. "It's only vivid enough to imagine that's the same black Jeep I saw the other night."

"Tony would never pull a stunt like this. Not unless someone kidnaped him and brainwashed him,"

A shiver tangoed down Quinn's spine. "Rex swears Tony embezzled—"

"And I swear Rex is a psycho." Jaw clenched, Pierce stared at the disappearing Jeep. "Two independent auditors confirmed the evidence."

Thinking out loud, Quinn continued. "We know the police found his Droid at your house. I know I saw a black Jeep the night of the golf-course attack."

"There are other Jeeps in the metro area, dammit."

"Don't forget he lied about working Thanksgiving weekend," Quinn said, refusing to point out what Pierce must have seen.

"I noticed the dent under his right front headlight." Saying the words added a thousand pound weight to Pierce's burning neck muscles. His need to hold Quinn made him feel like a fool. He stared at the tracks left by the black Jeep and felt hope drain out of him.

"I'll take you home, then report this," he said in a flat, take-charge tone. "No reason for you to hang around."

"Like an albatross around your neck?" She arched

a brow.

"I was thinking more like an anchor."

To his surprise, she laughed, then said, "Good comeback."

"Huh. Is this where you break my balls?"

"Strong women don't break men's balls."

"Just our hearts," he said before he could stop himself.

A red flush—almost as dark as Rex Walker's birthmark—flooded her face. Bastard that he was, Pierce felt a momentary triumph before regret set in. "Why would you want to spend time with me?"

"I never said I didn't want to spend time with you." She looked at him for what felt like a long hour. "I said I wasn't spending the night with you."

"Because you think I only want sex with you, right?"

"Bingo."

"What if I said I didn't want sex? What if I said I want to be near you, to laugh with you, to smell you?"

"To smell me?" Her voice rose a couple of notes.

He nodded. "To smell you. You always smell clean. Fresh—like rose soap—like a healthy and sane person."

"Are you pulling my leg?" Her cheeks looked like radishes.

"No. That'd constitute foreplay, wouldn't it?"

"Oh, God." She covered her face with her hands and peeked through her fingers at him. "I've lost my mind. Had some kind of mental breakdown. Lost too much sleep . . ."

A snigger got away from her and swelled. She clapped her hand over her mouth, inhaled, said, "If I start laughing, I'll never stop."

"Let's do it. Laugh together. My house. We'll watch Abbott and Costello movies..."

Whether Pierce piqued her imagination or simply wore her down, Quinn conceded. His surprise and elation exploded. With a whoop, he jumped out of the car. Snow slapped him in the face and slid down his neck. He didn't care. He yipped and ran around the car five or six times. Laughing and panting, tingling all over, he collapsed in his seat and declared, "Some drink from the fountain of knowledge. I only gargle."

****

Sucked into the fun of laughing at Pierce, Quinn didn't care if she'd lost her mind. If she told the truth, she didn't want to be alone any more than he did. He'd said no sex, and she'd hold him to that statement. Too bad if he thought she'd changed her views on love and sex.

Alan Ramsey, Security Czar at the Mission Hills Country Club, flashed his lights as he pulled alongside them. Pierce rolled down his window. Snow gusted into the Corvette, clung to Pierce's coat and jeans and gave Quinn a major case of the shivers.

"The SOB got through there, huh?" Alan pulled on his coarse, snow-speckled beard. "Bastard damned near ran over Ken Marshall. Ken said the guy was driving a black Jeep?"

"He was parked in front of my house Monday night." Quinn leaned past Pierce, took a blast of snow in the face and introduced herself.

"Kansas tags with purple stripes on the doors and a dented right headlight," Pierce said. "I suspect you're going to find someone stole it from a good friend of mine, Tony Franklin."

It took several questions for Alan to understand Pierce's reasoning, reduced to one terse sentence. "Tony's missed some important calls at work and we didn't find him at his house."

Quinn bit her lip. Pierce was never going to believe anyone but Rex embezzled the money. Not even if Tony confessed.

Alan tapped the paper where he'd written Tony's vanity license plate against his green-plaid beret and wished them Happy Thanksgiving.

"I'll be in touch," he promised, his eyes grim.

****

True to his promise, Pierce gave Quinn complete privacy in his office while he dug out his Abbott and Costello movies in the family room. Edward Roslyn had left her his home number, but she tried him at the office first. Of course he didn't pick up.

The bank was closed for the holiday, but calling Edward at home violated her sense of propriety. More to the point she wasn't in the mood for more bad news. By unspoken agreement, she and Pierce were tiptoeing around Tony's absence like a landmine.

The fragrance of Mrs. Taylor's freshly baked bread provided a small distraction. So did Floyd's pitiful moans and scratches at the door. Quinn moved toward the phone. Did she really think fresh bread, garlic chicken, and Abbott and Costello would make her laugh after she gave Rex the banker's decision?

Floyd yowled. She opened the door and spent five minutes procrastinating, cooing and baby talking to an animal who must've been a divine king in another life. Aware Floyd would never grow weary of her adoration, she mentally shook herself and returned to Pierce's desk.

The cat trotted ahead of her and hopped onto the desk. She sat and reached for the handset. Floyd bumped her hand with his orange and white head. This routine apparently soon bored him. He rolled on his back, legs in the air, and shamelessly invited ear rubs and tickles on his ample belly.

"Hey," she whispered. "You are a bad influence." She lifted the receiver, and he kicked it with the force of a small kangaroo. The entire mobile phone set crashed to the floor.

She risked mortal wounds from the cat's bared fangs and censure from the Humane Society. She picked up His Divineness and set him in the hall. "Get thee behind me, Satan."

Edward picked up on the second ring. He and Quinn chatted about the snowstorm for a minute, then, not wanting to waste his time, she got to the point and asked his opinion of Rex.

"His resume is impressive. He interviews very well."

Her heart wanted to leap up, but Quinn didn't let the comments go to her head.

"I should tell you," Edward was saying in his clipped, formal banker's tone, "that I am disturbed—by a source I can't divulge, you understand—that Rex left Pierce under unusual circumstances. You know I'll expect a current letter of recommendation."

Damn. A zillion tiny red dots danced in front of Quinn's eyes. So much for Pierce's promise there'd be no leaks from his people.

Out in the hall, Floyd lunged against the door like a

tyrannosaurus. Quinn made herself concentrate on Edward Roslyn. "Did your source give you any details I can check out?"

"Well..." He let the phrase hang.

Stall. She said nothing, waited, wary when he barked a little laugh, but was caught completely off guard when he said, "My source said you'd have details. Said you could tell me everything I needed to know and at the same time clear up my reservations."

Her heart thudded. She choked the phone. "I don't know everything."

But he could put money on her killing Pierce.

"I'm sorry to hear that. I want to fill that position ASAP." Yada, yada, yada.

Quinn tuned out his praises of the very strong candidate coming in Monday for a second interview and concentrated on Edward's final point.

Get the information he needed about why Rex left Pierce. Give him a day or two to evaluate the information. And get a letter from Pierce—said in a tone of reproach.

"Then," Edward said melodramatically, "I may ask Rex in for another interview. But the sooner I know there are no major problems, the faster we'll be able to move."

****

"The sooner I know there are no major problems, the faster we'll be able to move." Quinn held the dead phone to her mouth, primped her lips and tried to catch Edward's prissy tone but didn't come close.

Damn, damn, damn. Now, more fun lay ahead. What could be more fun than a chat with Rex?

A chat with Pierce, her inner demon offered. And

don't forget checking in with Michael.

"Can't have too much fun in one day," she muttered. Where to begin?

A yowl echoed in the hall, then repeated thumps shook the door. Grimly amused, Quinn stood. Floyd streaked through the open door just as Pierce rounded the corner.

He grinned. "Someone's in love. I'll feed him—"

"No." She wrapped her arms around her waist. "It's his house. I'm the interloper."

"You're not an inter— What's wrong? There a problem?"

"You're the problem." Her heart dropped too fast, making her dizzy, but she rushed on before he could regroup. "You talked to Edward."

His eyes flashed. "Not since I fired Rex. Edward's left me three, four messages. Do I need an affidavit I didn't return his calls?"

The invisible rubber-band in Quinn's neck contracted. "You like that word. You said I wanted a signed-in-blood affidavit you'd never abandon me."

"I recanted that...comment. On my knees, if you recall."

"Diversion won't work," she said, hardening her tone. "Not this time. Edward didn't identify his source, but I'm pretty confident I can eliminate me, Michael and Rex. So maybe I do need an affidavit."

"You don't. You can eliminate me too."

His eyes locked with hers. Breathing evenly, he showed no signs she could read of the quiet fury he'd unleashed when she accused him of sleeping with Brittany. She waited now, for him to proclaim his innocence. Prove he'd kept his word. Floyd growled and strutted away from her ankles, bumping against Pierce.

"Arguing makes him nervous," he said.

"Lying makes me more nervous." Why was she goading him?

"I'm not going there, Quinn."

"Who then?" she demanded, her voice rough because she was afraid it would crack. "You didn't tell Edward why you fired Rex. I didn't, Michael didn't. Who's left?"

"Tony." The hurt in his eyes told her what this cost him.

"Oh, Pierce." Her own fury died like a storm blowing out to sea. She wanted to bury her face in his shoulder but couldn't lift her feet. She should comfort him. "I...I jumped to a conclusion. I assumed Edward meant you were his source."

The hollow in her stomach burned with regret. "Can you for—"

"Yes." He pulled her into his arms and tucked her head under his chin. "Now stop beating yourself up, okay?"

She blinked tears, nodded. He tilted her head back, and she was sure he was going to kiss her. Instead, he said, "I fixed your favorite salad. Dinner's ready whenever you are."

"Let me call Rex," she whispered, vowing she'd give Pierce a real apology.

"Take your time. I'll call the police. See if there are any leads on Tony's Jeep—or his whereabouts. Don't tell me crime stops because it's Thanksgiving." The sadness in his tone brought tears.

She turned away. Pierce Jordan appreciated no

one's pity.

****

The phone at Rex's apartment rang three times. Hang-up time.

In conscience, Quinn knew she had to leave a message. She'd promised to touch base with him. She started mentally composing.

Hey, Rex. Life today was just one damn thing after another.

Let that gem sparkle for a minute, then reinforce it with solid examples.

Talked with Edward. He's digging around like a dog on the scent of a bone. She exhaled and massaged her temples. Mañana, she'd climb up on her white steed and fight the good fight. At the moment, she didn't have energy to climb out of her chair.

I wouldn't count on working for him, if I were you.

Her heart sank. If Edward said no, she was right back where she'd started on Monday—in the lowest level of hell. Expecting Rex's voice mail, his live voice surprised her. She jumped, but said, "You sound out of breath."

"It got late. You didn't call." He audibly sucked in air. "I gave up. Went for a run."

"In this weather? You're really dedicated."

"There's not much I can do about my face. So I work with what I've got." His pause seemed to invite admiring comments.

Quinn felt herself flushing. Rex had a bod all right—apparent even in his business clothes. But if he expected her to ooh and ah over his muscles like a teen-ager, he'd better start smoking something stronger.

Flattering him was not her agenda.

"I've talked with Pierce. He refuses to write the letter you want—"

"That bastard. That royal SOB."

She held the receiver away from her ear. Something that sounded like falling plaster came across the line loud and clear. Had he put his fist through a wall? His labored snorting and gasping sounded like an enraged ape about to fend off a wannabe alpha. Had he lost all control?

"I know you're upset." Quinn Alexander, mistress of the understatement.

"I know you're upset," he mimicked her accent and intonation perfectly.

"Stop that," she yelled.

"Stop that," he yelled back at her—in her own voice.

Taking a deep breath, she exhaled. She willed her voice to neutral. "Would you like to hear what Edward Roslyn said? Or would you like me to hang up, call Michael and tell him I don't owe you another damn thing?"

"Call Michael."

She didn't gasp, but her heart flipped over. That was the problem with being a bully. There was always someone eager to take your challenge.

"Go ahead," Rex said. "Make his day. Put the monkey on his back."

Patience. She stared up at the ceiling. "Let's talk Monday about your interview."

"Sure, why not? Let's put my life on hold for five days."

She winced. Caught between the cross-hairs of guilt and shame, she saw a way out. "How about talking tomorrow—after a good night's sleep?"

"Why not?" He sighed. "I won't ask you when since tomorrow's your bash."

Floyd was now slamming into the door—the way Quinn's heart was slamming into her chest. She felt sick. Maybe she'd had a stroke.

"Michael asked me to come there, but no way I'll go...not with Luce so miserable."

The meteor in Quinn's throat didn't give an inch. "I thought you'd go to Florida."

"No. My mother's in a nursing home. She asked me not to come, but I'll see her at Christmas. At least that was the plan."

So, contrary to Pierce's logical conclusion, Mrs. Walker wasn't dead. The knife in Quinn's heart cut something vital. She held her breath.

Rex gave the knife another twist. "That's why I've got to start a new job right away. I can't afford taking care of my mother on less than a hundred twenty-five K a year."

One hun—? Her mind stuttered. Before his interview with Edward, he'd said ninety-five. He must feel pretty cocky about how well the meeting had gone.

"Speaking of mothers," Rex was saying, "I was surprised Sarah headed to San Francisco. I figured she'd stick around this Thanksgiving—even if this is the year you and Michael do your own thing."

Damn. He'd managed to bring the subject back to Thanksgiving. Quinn heard the trap snap shut.

In a bright voice—reminiscent of TV commercials for Alzheimer's meds—she said, "Mom thinks life's simpler for Michael if he and Luce don't have to juggle Thanksgiving with two different families."

"Someday I hope I've got that problem." Rex adopted the same TV-commercial perkiness.

She squeezed her eyes shut. "Well, this year, why don't you come to my bash?"

"Gosh, Quinn, I can't tell you how much this means to me." He spoke fast—afraid, maybe, she'd recant the invitation. "I wasn't looking forward to Thanksgiving alone."

Stomach rolling, instantly regretful, Quinn held onto the desk. Watch out, Alice, I'm right behind you, she thought, seeing herself falling down the rabbit's hole.

"What time?" Rex asked, the upbeat note in his voice more pronounced.

"The caterer arrives around two. Most people show up between four thirty and five."

"You've made my day, Quinn."

Did she have to tell him again not to come before four thirty?

"The lighting ceremony begins at seven, so come at five and you'll have plenty of time to eat before it starts."

"Can I pick you up—since your car's in the garage?"

"Thanks, but I'll come early, check with the caterer on last-minute details."

"Computer geeks love details."

"Trust me," she said, feeling goose bumps chase each other down her spine. "You'd be bored out of your mind."

"I doubt it, but see you tomorrow. With bells on. Whoops, that's Christmas, isn't it? Whatever. I'll be there. Can't wait."

Face hot, Quinn hung up. His intense gratitude hung in Pierce's study like little pops of electricity. Thank God she'd wiggled out of riding with him. She'd walk first. She'd done her duty. She'd asked him to her bash.

The gesture came close enough to making her a martyr.

Chapter 15

Floyd threw himself against the office door with the fury of a caged tiger. When Pierce caught him before his second assault, the wannabe tiger hissed and pawed the air.

"Quinn could take this personally, okay?" Pierce sat on the floor and scratched his feline's head. "Give her a little time to see a few of your more mature qualities."

Feline disdain greeted attempts at appeasement. The old Tom squirmed and yowled like a cat on the rack.

"A smart man would shut you in the laundry room," Pierce said, piling on more hypocrisy. Secretly he hoped the racket would end Quinn's damn phone call. Couldn't be going well or she'd be in the family room sipping wine.

More caterwauls finally triggered a stab of guilt. Guilt for wishing he could break his promise to her about not making love tonight. Guilt for hoping Edward would take the first bus to hell before hiring the weasel. Guilt for wanting her to help figure out what was going on with Tony. Tony deserved her help. Rex did not.

Midway through another cat shriek, the office door opened. Quinn stepped around them like a queen stepping around debris. Floyd lunged at her like she was the biggest piece of chicken he'd ever seen.

Her back stiffened. She ignored her attacker and stared at Pierce. "Edward knows something's wrong with Rex's situation."

"It doesn't take an Einstein to figure out there's something wrong with Rex." Keeping an eye on Floyd, now bumping her ankles, Pierce stood, facing her. "Edward's a smart cookie."

"He said a source informed him Rex left you under unusual circumstances."

Anger flared in Pierce's stomach and spilled off his tongue. "Didn't we have this discussion?"

"We did. Why so crabby since you're not the source? Are you touchy because we can eliminate Rex and Michael, leaving Tony—"

A little love nip from Floyd made her jump back, giving Pierce time to come to her rescue. He scooped up his cat, dumped him in the office and closed the door.

"Sorry about that. I can administer first aid—"

"You can get back on the subject. Which is, who's Edward's whistle blower if we eliminate you, Rex and Michael?"

"Who says we can eliminate them?" Pierce spit out the question, his throat fever-dry, burning with hostility.

"Logic?" Quinn tapped her temple and spoke to him in a tone of complete control. "Why would Rex or Michael do something that could derail getting this job?"

A shrug, accompanied by a smirk gave Pierce a minute for a comeback. "My mind doesn't work like a sociopath's."

"You think Michael's a sociopath?" Amazingly, her voice remained modulated.

"I didn't say that." His reply came too quickly, and he shifted his gaze to the floor. Now he'd crossed the line.

"But you don't like him." Her voice vibrated with accusation.

"Do I have to like him to be in your life?" He pinched the bridge of his nose, then brought his gaze up to meet hers.

Her face was paler than snow, her lips bloodless. Lines furrowed her forehead, and thin red strings in her bloodshot eyes reminded him she was running on adrenaline fumes.

She let the silence hang for a decade, but not long enough for him to regroup.

"My personal life includes Michael." Disappointment punctuated each word, but her voice was strong, defiant. "Just as yours includes your mother."

His gut dropped. Leave it to Quinn to knock him off balance with her penetrating, disagreeable, on-the-money insight. On the defensive, he repeated, "My mother?"

"Disapproves of me as much as you disapprove of Michael." Drawing herself up until Pierce imagined her hitting the twenty-foot ceiling, she held up one hand. "And before you say something I'll regret, I vote for eating. I'm starving. We can talk later. After we get a few nights' sleep. Which can start tonight since we're not having sex."

"Sure, let's eat. The chicken passes the Floyd taste-test." Didn't he get any credit for the decision to forgo sex?

Sometimes the better part of valor was, in Pierce's

opinion, taking the option of least resistance. Having his own shaky intentions thrown back in his face felt like one of those times. Taking the option of least resistance also meant playing the role of good sport. It was a role he'd played with Quinn for four years. What was one more night repressing his views of Michael? Or cementing his mouth about the weasel? Or saying zip about Quinn's misplaced loyalty?

She was right...they teetered on the cusp of saying the unforgiveable.

Not a good place to teeter, Pierce reasoned, releasing Floyd from imprisonment and leading them to the kitchen.

They passed the closed dining-room doors, and Pierce saw a re-run of their slow strip-tease the night before. He saw them unable to get to a bed, making love on the floor. His dick tingled, and he missed a step. He pretended he'd stumbled over Floyd. Christ, he was hard just remembering. Quinn was as serene a Tibetan nun.

The kitchen blazed with enough electricity to land a 767 on the granite island. Quinn ooohed and ahhed over The Plaza lights, but they blurred for Pierce. After feeding Floyd enough roast chicken for a large mountain lion, he managed to pull her chair out without touching her, served her wine without touching her, passed her bread without touching her. The chicken was wonderful—he assumed. He didn't taste anything but desire. The conversation was mundane—he assumed. He didn't hear a word. Lust and excitement jitterbugged in his head and pushed worries about Tony, Rex, Michael, their mothers—and everyone but Quinn—out of his mind.

How much longer could he keep his hands off her?

They were behaving like Victorian lovers—reserved and socially correct—but he was shooting smoldering glances at her, willing her to take pity on him. Disregard his promise. Forget watching Abbott and Costello. Drag him under the kitchen table. Rip his clothes off...

How could looking at a woman's ears make him hard? How could she sit there as if he was contemplating world peace instead of ogling her body, luscious curve by luscious curve?

Midway through his exercise in masochism, the phone rang. Pierce heard it from another galaxy.

Quinn glanced at the kitchen clock. "Pretty late for telemarketers on a holiday, don't you think?"

He followed her gaze and felt the cream sauce in his gut curdle. "Telemarketers never take a holiday," he said like a child waking up in the middle of the night.

Something in his tone or his body language must have alerted her. She frowned. "Let's forget the movies tonight. I'll load the dishwasher. You go to bed—"

"What about dessert?"

Her mouth twitched. "Is that a double entendre?"

"For your enlightenment, I do think about other topics besides sex." Like the phone ringing at 7:18 at night.

She shrugged. "Sorry. I've confused you with the Pierce Jordan I used to know."

The phone stopped. Abruptly. A ring before going to voice mail. Pierce went absolutely still. Hyper-focused on the phone. Breathing steady. Muscles tense. Thinking of nothing but getting to the phone. Mentally, he counted to twenty.

The ringing started again. He leaped out of his chair. It hit the floor, knocking off a plate and silverware. Heart thudding, he spun into Quinn's shoulder, made no apology and lunged for the wall phone.

Confusion and surprise flashed across her face. "What's wrong?"

He yelled into the receiver, "I'm here, Tony!"

Her eyes widened. In slo-mo, she pushed away from the table and picked up Floyd, cowering near his empty dish. She whispered, "Is he okay?"

Pierce held up a hand, listened, nodded, listened, said, "You've got it. Done. No. Understand. I'll be there."

The buttery fragrance of chicken filled the kitchen. Warmth from the oven should've made the room cozy, but it felt claustrophobic. When Pierce hung up, he felt like a kid who'd just learned Santa's a fraud. Quinn stroked his cat but said nothing, letting him tell it his own way.

Or not, the voice of reason cautioned.

Her eyes were soft, the pupils huge in the dim light. No sharp angles or planes in the face he knew so well. Her body was curves and roundness. God, what he'd give to go to bed and just hold her. Feel her breath on his neck. Inhale her freshness. Her honesty. Her trust he didn't deserve. Being near her seemed to expand his lungs, help him breathe deeper, think more clearly. Air whooshed out of him. He forgot her loyalty to the weasel and to her brother and went with his gut.

"He's in trouble." Each word hurt his throat. He stumbled to the sink and ran a full glass of water. He chugged it down in one gulp, aware Quinn stood behind him. She was hugging Floyd, and he wished she'd grab him and hug him and make his day. "He wants to meet...tomorrow...see what we can do about this...fix he's in."

"Lord, Pierce."

A muscle ticked under his right eye. He rubbed the spot and stared into space. "He says Rex didn't steal the money. He says he made a big mistake."

She set Floyd on the floor. "He admitted that?"

Pierce nodded slowly. The movement hurt his spine. "Rex told the truth."

"He's innocent?" She didn't sound as if she meant the question.

"Maybe of embezzling the money." Pierce stared at a bubble in the sink.

"I am so sorry." She took a step, stopped, wrapped an arm around her waist. As an afterthought, she said, "Where is he now?"

"He wouldn't say." Impulsively, Pierce took her hand, curled her fingers into her palm and kissed her knuckles. "I need a minute...to think."

"Sounds like a plan." Meeting his gaze, she put her fingers against his cheek and held them there, infusing him with her compassion.

He accepted her offered arm and shuffled back to the adjoining family room. The room where yesterday Tony Franklin, apparently, drenched the white carpet with the blood of a chicken.

"Christ," he blurted, "do you think Tony's into something weird—like a satanic cult?"

"No."

The one word reassured Pierce, and he shouted, "Hell no!"

Not wanting to scare her, he collapsed into the recliner he'd designated as her seat to watch Bud, Lou and the mummy.

"You've had a shock." She fingered the remote. "Want the drapes open?"

What he wanted was to hold her but he said, "Thanks."

The drapes slid back and she gazed at the falling snow, giving him time to breathe. When she faced him again, she said, "What time are you two meeting?"

Don't tell her, Pierce thought. There was plenty she'd kept to herself. Such as the attempted mugging. The black Jeep. Whether she believed him about ratting to Edward.

"You don't have to tell me." A small smile lifted the corners of her mouth. She crossed her ankles and lowered her ass onto the floor, assuming the Lotus position as if it were natural and not torture. "I probably wouldn't in your shoes. I'd worry you'd call the police."

"Nine tomorrow night." He watched her drag an almost invisible piece of string under his feline's nose, jerking it away at the last minute. Hunched forward on his front paws, Floyd was in heaven. "At the office."

"Why not in the morning?" She dangled the thread over the cat's head. "He knows you're an early bird."

"He probably figures traffic will keep The Plaza cops busy in the afternoon. Or—" Pierce shrugged. "Frankly, I don't have a clue what he's thinking anymore."

She shivered. "How could you?"

The answer yawned at him from a pit of quicksand. Hating the sense of powerlessness, he said, "Unless you're really in the mood for Abbott and Costello, I suggest you go upstairs and try the soaking tub in the guest bathroom. I need to stop gazing at my navel and do something. Something physical. Release some testosterone."

"Such as?" She looked up at him and a piece of her hair came loose and framed her face like pictures he'd seen of a young Grace Kelly.

Mind-whacked, he looked away and mumbled, "Go for a jog. No problem with loose dogs or traffic..."

"And no problem with enough ice and snow on the streets to break every bone in your body?"

"Not every one, but point taken. I've got a great gym in the basement. I can lift weights. Tony and I..." He slammed the door on the images of their weight-lifting marathons and moved from the recliner to the leather and chrome chair molded into the shape of a vintage car's backseat.

Quinn rose and floated across the floor and climbed in next to him. "There's always loading the dishwasher. Or mopping the kitchen floor. Or..." She crawled onto his lap and flicked the tip of her tongue across his bottom lip. "Raw sex counts as exercise...doing something. Releasing testosterone."

"Jesus, Quinn!" Groaning, he sucked in oxygen like a gored ox. His dick hardened into a titanium pole, and his hands slid automatically under her sweater.

"Let's play doctor and nurse. See if we can lift your spirits." She rose on her knees and straddled him, laughing as he flailed to sit upright. Pressed against him, she teased his bottom lip, inviting him to explore her open mouth with his tongue.

He groaned louder. His depression appeared to be

lifting. She smiled. He said, "In your next life, you should go to med school, become a shrink."

"Can I use you as a reference?"

His fingers slipped inside her silky bra, caressing nerve endings until her nipples grew hot and hard.

She worked open the buttons on his shirt, then moved lower. "Hmmm. I do believe your erection is proof you'd benefit from further therapy."

His eyes flew open, and he pushed her away.

Astonishment took over her lovely face.

"Timeout." Trying to catch his breath, he put his palm above four raised fingers. "I promised...I swore...you spend the night and no-no sex."

She nipped his ear. "Promises are made to be broken."

He jerked away. "No foreplay, either."

"Fine. I'm ready. Let's do it right here."

"For God's sake, Quinn!" He yanked her up to standing, but held her at arm's length.

She stared at him. "What are you doing?"

"Keeping my word. I'm not ripping your clothes off. I'm not making love to you tonight." He took a step backwards. "I don't want your pity fuck."

"Fine." Quinn flashed a coy smile. "You promised me a back rub."

His hands shot out in front of him, and he took another step backwards. "Take a rain check."

"That's not right—going back on your promise."

"If I touch you—"

"C'mon. Take your medicine like a man," she whispered.

And he did.

****

The mattress moved so imperceptibly Pierce convinced himself that Quinn—not Floyd—was claiming more of the bed. When she snuggled into his backside, snaked her hands under the covers and cupped his balls, he stopped breathing.

"God, what a beautiful morning," she said her voice smiling.

Stunned by her nearness and the memory of making love, then going to sleep with her in his arms, he turned, slipped his arm under her neck and inched away from her glorious bod. "About last night..."

"Shhhh." Her smile dazzled him. "Today's Thanksgiving. Don't mention Rex or Michael or Tony. Let me wallow in denial a little longer."

"I still owe you an apol—"

"It's not as if we're engaged. Or going steady. Or even, God forbid, dating."

"We could be." He tilted her head so that she could see into his eyes. See his willingness to commit to her. Peer into his soul. "We'll have to work at the trust-thing."

"Let's go slow." She ran the tip of her little fingernail between his eyebrows. "Three crises may be all the tests we can handle for the next few days."

Knowing better than to pull her closer, he said, "And my crisis calls. I need to get to the office."

She stared. "Did you just say you're going to the office?"

Desire to repeat the magic of last night sucked him into a vortex, tempting him to forget Tony. He could stay with Quinn. Celebrate Thanksgiving. Close the wounds from Brittany.

"If I don't review Tony's records," he said quietly,

"I won't be ready when we meet tonight."

"Well, that sucks."

He laughed. "What a sweet talker."

"What about a quickie?" She propped herself up on one elbow and of course the sheet slipped off baring her rosy breasts. "I'm ready. Right now."

He placed the sheet over her shoulder and said words he'd never imagined speaking under torture. "My heart wouldn't be in it. There're hundreds of pages I have to digest..."

An emotion he couldn't read flickered on her face, then faded. She smiled and leaned in closer, their foreheads touching. "Could you use some help?"

"Thanks, but you've got forty people showing up—"

"Forty-two if you'll come." Her arms went around his neck, and she kissed him, eyes wide open and soft.

Since he wasn't a saint, he kissed her back, feeling closer to her than he'd ever felt to a woman. When he pulled back, she was smiling again.

"Seeing the lights. Eating great food. Doing something normal—putting Tony in the back of your mind for a couple of hours—might be a strategy that keeps you from going crazy."

"Waiting until nine o'clock for Tony to show up probably will have me gibbering," he said, still not sure if he could function at a party. "First, I'll need that brain transplant."

"Brain transplants are my specialty. Having you there might keep me from going crazier."

His eyes softened. "When you put it like that, how can I refuse?"

"In the spirit of full disclosure—"

A long, insistent peal from the doorbell interrupted.

"Probably a neighbor who doesn't know the password to my intercom." He scrambled off the bed, grabbed his jeans from the middle of the floor, hopped on one foot to pull them over his legs and hobbled into the hall.

"Maybe we can do that dance at The Bash."

"Count on it," he called, remembering Tony dancing at the last Christmas party.

****

The deep, smoky under notes in the woman's voice sounded vaguely familiar. Quinn froze on the bottom step but couldn't pick up the words from the family room. Was the woman crying?

Intent on eavesdropping, Quinn failed to pick up the silence of cat feet behind her. Floyd's tail brushed her bare leg on his charge to the kitchen. She yelped and grabbed the bannister.

Conversation in the family room stopped. Pierce appeared in the hall. His brows formed a V and his eyes narrowed.

Not happy to see me. Heart pounding, Quinn met his unblinking gaze.

"You'd better come in." He sounded as if the words burned his mouth.

Her heart stuttered. "What's wrong? Is there news about Tony?"

"Come in." His rigid, uncoordinated gait scared Quinn more than his stiff face and blank eyes.

"What's going on?" She became aware he kept both his hands at his sides as they retraced his steps to the family room.

"Hello, Quinn." The last woman Quinn ever

wanted to see sat in the middle of the sofa. Her dark eyes were huge, her milky skin translucent, her long black hair a controlled mass of gleaming waves.

Tears become her, Quinn realized, standing straighter, trying to control the slo-mo memories slicing and dicing her brain. She said, "It's been awhile."

Brittany nodded. "Four years. But you look good."

"Thanks." Hyper-aware of her bed-head, Quinn locked her jaw. Damn. Why couldn't she be standing there in her Thanksgiving dress—bronze velvet, low scooped back, full skirt—a dress fit for Cinderella?

Pierce broke the silence. "Brittany's here about Tony."

"I see." A lie, but Quinn wasn't about to ask for details.

"Since my divorce three years ago, we've gotten...close." Brittany touched a small, oval, diamond-encrusted sapphire pendant. "He's really been there for me."

"Your necklace is exquisite." Quinn thought she sounded reasonably polite for someone whose brain was as dull as an eggplant. "Did Tony give it to you?"

A tentative, shy little girl nod. "He knows how to pick up my spirits."

Worried she'd gag, Quinn shot Pierce a raised brow. Five million dollars should pick up anyone's spirits.

"I can't believe he's missing." Brittany focused on Pierce, her big eyes brimming with tears. "We talked yesterday morning after my plane was delayed out of O'Hare. We talked again at noon."

"By phone?" Quinn asked, wanting to get the facts.

"He texted me twice after that. At one and two-thirty."

"Where was he?" Quinn glanced at Pierce. They knew where he wasn't at two-thirty. At home.

Brittany shook her head. "I assumed he was at work. He talked about tying up loose ends so we could enjoy the long weekend."

"Did he meet you at the airport?" Pierce asked.

"He'd ordered a limo. I expected him to meet me at The Plaza Marriott. I got there at six." Tears deepened her voice. "Champagne and roses and chocolates, a spectacular view...but no Tony. No messages. No reply to my texts or calls."

"He called me at 7:18." Pierce spoke as if his lungs were collapsing. "He didn't say anything about meeting you."

Brittany shrugged—like a woman exhausted by her troubles—except every hair lay in place and every lash was mascaraed perfectly despite tears gliding down her cheeks. "No surprise, right? How'd he sound?"

"Like he was stressed."

"No surprise, right? He's wanted to tell you about us for a long time."

"He had other things on his mind."

Quinn felt the pull of Pierce's pain, took a step—a second behind Brittany. Quinn withdrew, assaulted by old memories of Brittany and Pierce glued to each other.

"C'mon. Sit." Brittany took his hand, led him to the sofa, sat down, then pulled him down next to her, holding his hand, squeezing it, patting it.

Dizzy, Quinn felt invisible. Pain squeezed her heart.

Surprisingly, Pierce broke away from Brittany's

comfort before she appeared ready to retreat. He said, "Quinn and I have to leave, but we can drop you at the Marriott. Tony might show up there looking for you."

"What time will you come back?" Brittany spoke in the hesitant, scared voice of a five-year-old being left alone in a spooky house.

None of your business.

Heat seared Quinn's scalp. She said, "You may remember I throw a Thanksgiving party at the office every year. We may still be going strong past nine or ten."

"Tony made dinner reservations for us at seven. If he doesn't show up, I'll probably order room service."

Damn.

Quinn saw Brittany's wistful tone push several of Pierce's guilt buttons and wanted to shake him.

Instead she said, "If he doesn't call you or show up by five, you can always come to my party. Cab over whenever you want. I'll ask a guest to take you back to the hotel."

"Oh, that sounds wonderful." Brittany spoke to Pierce. She reiterated a variation of her gratitude at least six times between his house and the Marriott.

Quinn was in favor of dropping their passenger in the circle drive, but no one asked her opinion. Ever the gentleman, Pierce left the engine running with the heat on high while he escorted the distraught Brittany to the elevator.

The snow had stopped overnight. A golden sun hung in a cloudless, acrylic blue sky. Short rays bounced off the ice-encrusted landscape, but at the edge of Quinn's mind, blackness hovered.

Ten minutes crawled by, giving her ample time to

rewrite several versions of her mental movie.

No matter the beginning and the middle, each rewrite ended with her finding Pierce and Brittany in her hotel bed.

Chapter 16

As soon as Quinn saw Pierce emerging from the hotel, she started singing, "Over the river and through the snow."

He climbed behind the wheel. She continued singing. She would not give him the satisfaction of asking why he needed fifteen minutes to walk a hundred feet to the elevators. Or ask how much he'd told Brittany.

"You want my balls in a vise or my head on a platter?" He pulled away from the curb without glancing behind him.

Despite his king-of-the-road driving 'tude, the white Mercedes SUV gave her a sense of safety she missed in the Corvette. So if he was trying to rattle her, he was about to meet with miserable failure. She ignored his stupid question and his reckless disregard.

"Brittany looks great, doesn't she?" He sped down the salted streets, clean and dry for the thousands of revelers arriving later for The Plaza Lighting Ceremony. "She's really worried about Tony."

"Uh-huh." *Brittany's worried about Brittany.*

"Any guesses why Tony didn't tell me about their relationship?" Foot on the accelerator, Pierce sailed through a yellow light. "You think he felt I'd disapprove—since she and I have a history?"

"Duuh." Face burning, Quinn whipped around to

face him. "Why would your history with Brittany bother Tony? Maybe he doesn't mind going to bed with your former lover. You are his mentor...someone to look up to. Someone to admire. Someone..."

Her breathing sounded as if a Sumo wrestler sat on her chest.

"She's nothing to me." Pierce kept his eyes on the road but took his hand off the wheel and reached for her. "I can't explain why I was an idiot."

"I can. You're terrified by the big C. You—" She shook her head angrily, but managed not to jerk away from him like a melodrama diva. "Let's stick with the plan. We'll pick up my party clothes, go back to the office and check Tony's records under a magnifying glass. Feel free to skip The Bash."

"I'm not your father, Quinn. I'm not going anywhere without you." The sympathy in the glance he shot her almost undid her.

Almost. She looked out the window and pressed her back against the seat. Mentioning Daddy was unfair. Below the belt. Cruel. She retreated to the place she'd gone after finding Pierce and Brittany half-dressed in her office and found the cool, distant voice she'd perfected.

"You can wait in the driveway. I have all my stuff ready. "

"Take your time."

"Like you took with Brittany?" Before he came to a full stop, she opened her door, jumped out of the car and punched the remote.

She jogged inside, closing the garage door behind her without checking if he'd followed. Okay, call her childish. Petty. Bitchy. Sue her. He was arrogant.

Baiting her with Brittany. But worse, far worse—he opened wounds she'd exposed to only one other person. Her lungs released a quavery sigh. She fumbled at the kitchen door's lock. Dropped the key. Picked it up. Rammed it home. The ache Pierce's tactlessness had brought to the surface hammered her heart.

Sunshine spilled through the window over the sink. Her pink and lavender African violets, rows of oversized cookbooks, antique wall plates from mother—all looked normal and inviting. A white envelope propped in the middle of the green pine table sent her hammering heart through the top of her head. Her full name, Sarah Quinn Alexander was typed in caps on the expensive, white linen envelope.

Her scalp tingled with sweat. In her peripheral vision, the walls shrank, bringing the basement door closer. It's locked, she thought. It's always locked.

Like the door into the garage? Her throat closed. Was someone else in the house? Her skin tried to crawl off her arms. She strained to pick up a smell or an awareness of menace in the morning quiet.

She forced her trembling legs to carry her to the family room. No place to hide in there. In her mind's eye she saw the foyer. Coats and umbrellas and boots and fuzzy slippers filled the closet she kept meaning to clean. Upstairs...

Dry-mouthed, she imagined climbing the stairs to her bedroom. Scenes from *Psycho*—a movie she'd never been able to watch from beginning to end— flashed in quick, subliminal bursts. Her breath caught. She backtracked to the kitchen. Picking up a snake held more appeal than picking up the envelope, but she grabbed it and stepped into the garage.

No way she was going up those stairs. Not alone. Not until she'd read the contents of the envelope. Alone. Without Pierce offering his opinions.

The dank odor of clay failed to mask the cold sweat oozing from pores she never knew she had. She flipped on the two-hundred-watt bulb over her potter's wheel, exploding bright memories of nights spent working her pots. Calmed, she slid a knife under the envelope's flap.

Four typed lines seemed to leap off the single half sheet of white, watermarked paper. Nausea coated her throat. She swallowed, but couldn't breathe. Couldn't understand. The message made no sense. She read the lines again, out loud, word by word:

Carter Quinn Alexander is alive and well.
He has a new family he loves dearly.
He never loved you, Sarah Quinn.
Ever.

The letters swam together, blurred, cleared and cha-chaaed in a meaningless rhythm of gibberish. She blinked, shook her head, looked in the distance. The shovel she'd used two nights ago stood in the corner. No ghost of her father hovered there. No voice groaned her name. No slasher charged out of the shadows, yelling at her in a crazy woman's voice. The silence was broken only by the rattle in her chest.

Several quick inhales evened the cadence of her breathing. Oxygen fed her overheated brain. She stared at the envelope and loosed the fury coiled in her belly.

Dammit, no one had to jump out and scare her. She was doing a damned good job of teetering on the cusp of melodrama all by herself. What a wuss. The wonder was she hadn't peed her pants. Or tripped over her paralyzed feet, hit her head and—

Her cell phone rang. Her lungs seized again. All at once adrenaline jolted through her, making her ready for flight or fight. *It's only the phone.*

Her fingers closed around the phone in her pocket. She'd check the LED. If she recognized the caller, she'd answer. If not, she wouldn't. And if she didn't answer, the phone wouldn't detonate a bomb planted inside the house.

Only in the movies. The second ring chimed. She removed the phone, read the LED and retraced her steps toward the kitchen door.

"There a problem?" Pierce asked in a composed tone laced with sarcasm.

"Nothing I can't handle." She passed through the kitchen and family room and foyer with the phone to her ear. She stuffed the note in her pocket and climbed the stairs, looking up—in case a wannabe Mrs. Bates came flying at her intent on mayhem. She reached the top step without an appearance by Mrs. Bates or anyone.

"Pop the trunk for me, okay?"

Five minutes later, Quinn insisted on loading her clothes bags and makeup case into the trunk. Pierce sputtered a few curses, shook his head, slid under the wheel and barely waited till she closed her door to back out of the driveway. They drove past the golf course. An elderly man, dressed in bright yellow pants with a green-plaid jacket, stood on the snow-covered fifteenth green. He took aim, raised his club and sent an orange ball arcing toward the sun. The golfer trudged across the course, and his single-mindedness focused Quinn.

Daddy might be alive. He might even have a new

family. But she absolutely refused to accept he'd never loved her.

Sitting on his lap. Listening to him read her favorite bedtime story for the fifth time. Playing catch with him in the park. Kissing his smooth, citrus-scented cheek after he'd shaved. A storehouse of memories—vivid, real and verified by her mother over the years—made the last statement in the note a monstrous lie.

"The elephant riding between us could blow up any minute," Pierce said, slowing. "Talking will make you feel better."

"Men and their fix-it mentality."

"Okay, talking will make me feel better." He tapped the brakes and made a right turn onto Country Club Lane, populated with sprawling Tudors set in spacious front yards as pristine as a Hallmark card. He drove to the dead end, stopped, killed the engine. "You have to know I don't have feelings for Brittany. I sure didn't tell her about meeting Tony tonight. Or his confession."

"Brittany's a topic for another time. Right now, I want to know if you ever told Tony about my father."

To his credit, Pierce didn't miss a beat. He met and held her gaze. "Nope."

No undertones of anger or defensiveness or curiosity. Typical Pierce.

"Want to offer any ideas into how he might know more than the bare facts—since I never told him?" Her full name was a matter of public record.

"Who besides you and your family knows more than the bare facts?"

"No one." Her jaw ached from the death clench on her molars.

"Any chance Michael confided in his best bud?"

"None." Anticipating the question failed to stop a rush of hot anger from discharging. "And if he had, how could Rex get in my house?"

"Someone broke in your house?"

"No. The inside door to the kitchen was locked. No signs of forced entry. But someone left me a note...and my vote is Tony."

Pierce stared at her as if she'd dropped out of the sky. "When'd you give Tony a key?"

"Maybe he copied yours. The one I gave you..."

He let a few charged seconds pass. When she didn't finish her thought, he said drily, "The one that fit the locks you changed four years ago?"

She punched his arm. "Do you always have to be so damned logical?"

He grinned, pulling her to his chest, stroking her hair. "I figure you're not yelling at me because you've already reached the same conclusion."

She took a deep breath, sat back in her seat, and stared at nothing. "I think I've had a small mental breakdown. My life feels like a soap opera."

"Hell, Quinn your life's been a soap opera since that nut in the garage. My money's on him for your dead battery...and the attack on the golf course."

"No, no, no." She shook her head. "No, no. Huh-uh. You were that target. Your house was vandalized. The Jeep belongs to Tony. Whether or not he mowed me down on The Plaza, we know he played chicken with us yesterday afternoon."

Spasms under Pierce's bleak eyes stopped her. She laid her hand on his morning stubble, careful not to press the sharp whiskers into his cheek. She didn't have the heart to remind him about Tony's confession. About his missed date with Brittany. About a mind so brilliant he could outwit dull imaginations, outsmart security systems, and outmaneuver a trusting mentor.

Air whooshed out of Pierce's lungs, and she imagined the dread crawling into his gut. "Okay. His confession...the attempted head-on with us...They make the circumstantial evidence more damning. But I still don't see a motive or means for him to leave you that note."

"Only one of the mysteries we have to solve."

He nodded, took her hand and kissed her palm, shooting electricity into her veins. "One mystery we don't have to solve...Brittany's place in my life. She's in my past, you're in my future."

His pause invited Quinn to jump in, but she called on years of practicing tai'chi and slowed her heart rate. She'd always thought her father was in her future. Turned out he was in her past. Not an irony she wanted to discuss with Pierce.

He tipped her head back, balancing her chin on his thumb and index finger. "I hope you believe me, but if you don't, I intend to walk the walk. Understand?"

Because she longed to believe him, she said the words he wanted to hear. "I understand."

He apparently missed her ambivalence and started the engine without pushing her. The steady whap of their tires on the salted asphalt let her mind twist back to thinking about the note. Michael, not Pierce, was the logical person to talk to about the secret they'd kept buried as kids.

Pierce squeezed her hand. "Don't let my past hard-ass reputation fool you. I'm not going to ask to read the note, okay?"

Her stomach and heart and lungs expanded. His reassurance soothed the dryness in her throat with honeyed surprise. They weren't going to argue. Capitulation without an argument was a first with Pierce. He loved to argue.

Loved more to win.

Suspicion wiggled into her, infecting the tendril of hope she'd started nursing. Had he laid a trap for her? Was he waiting for her to toss out a smart-ass comeback he'd have to return? Then she'd go on the offensive, and their cycle of verbal lobs and volleys would intensify. Dammit, could he resist ragging her to read the note? Could she trust him?

Her throat closed. His jaw remained relaxed, his hands easy on the steering wheel, his gaze focused on the street. No signs of deceit.

"Okay." She nodded. He either understood or he didn't. She wasn't elaborating. Not when she still had to tell him she'd invited Rex.

An honest oversight, Dr. Freud.

****

Two clothes bags weighing at least a ton tested Pierce's arm muscles, but he stood like a patient bellboy at the lobby desk and listened as Quinn chatted with Joe about The Bash that night. Pierce managed to bite back a snort as she added two new names to the list of attendees.

They entered the elevators with his heart rate stampeding. He said zip, giving her a chance at explaining. She punched her floor, then set her shoe case and makeup bag at her feet.

"I'll state the obvious." Lips pursed, she imet his

gaze head-on. "I should've told you earlier about inviting Rex. I started to—last night. But we got distracted."

Her tone softened on distracted, and he assumed she meant making love was the diversion. In spite of being pissed, he grinned.

"I should've told you after I found the note." The elevator stopped, and she mashed the OPEN button. A good sign she didn't want to maim him? "Or maybe after I invited Brittany."

The small jab nicked his thin skin, but did no real damage. He held onto their clothes as Quinn unlocked the door to her office and turned on the lights.

"I meant to thank you for asking her," he said. "Under the circumstances, you went above and beyond. I guess, under the circumstances, I can give you a break on inviting Rex."

"Generous of you." She took her bag from him and hung it in the coat closet.

"Mr. Generosity. That's me." He put his hanging bag next to hers, told himself she didn't need more grief, and faced her. He wanted to grab her. Kiss her. Hold her. Reassure her they'd find whoever left the note. Lying felt wrong, so he went with hooking a stray chunk of hair behind her ear. "Tony's confession doesn't change how I feel about the weas—Rex. But I'll steer clear of him tonight. It's one way I can thank you for helping with this fiasco."

Tears brimmed in her eyes. For a second, he thought she'd come into his arms. Instead, she threw him a shaky smile, stood straighter and gave him a high five.

Not a gesture he'd ever expected from the woman

who drilled clients in delivering firm, no-nonsense handshakes before sending them out on interviews.

Pierce figured work offered the best way to push the damned note out of her mind. Work offered him the best way to act like an intelligent adult instead of like a horny teenager. In his office, he asked Quinn to search Tony's desk. He'd go over the books one more damned time.

But he couldn't forget she was nearby. He got up after the first hour, unsure he wasn't dreaming. She threw him a keep-your-distance look and kept digging in a bottom drawer. Reassured she wasn't brooding over the note, he reset his brain and returned to his office.

There had to be a clue. Anything. Something he'd overlooked the first dozen times.

Two hours later, dry-eyed, brain buzzing, the only clue Pierce had was he didn't have a clue what he was looking for. The proverbial needle was moving in the proverbial haystack. Reams of paper—mostly computer printouts—covered the long conference table, credenza, chairs, sofa, floor. And more where that came from.

A yawn propelled him to his feet. He kneaded the cramped muscles in his low back, ready to take a break. Enjoy—

"Pierce." Quinn appeared in his door, her face rosy, her hands behind her back like a kid hiding a treasure. "Look what I found."

Excitement vibrated off her. Pierce came around his desk. "Does it clear Tony?"

A nearly imperceptible slump of her shoulders gave him the first warning. Her hesitation confirmed his question was all wrong. His hope misplaced.

"I'm sorry." She held out a small silver jeweler's box.

"Open it, will you?" He didn't trust his shaky fingers.

Her jaw closed, but she opened the hinged box.

"Jesus!" Disbelief ricocheted around in his head like a racquet ball. "Diamonds big enough for Elizabeth Taylor."

"Think Oprah. She's the diamond earring fashionista. Elizabeth Taylor's dead."

"Any idea what earrings like these cost?"

"Sixty-seven thousand eight hundred and ninety dollars." She dug a sheet of folded paper from her pocket, smoothed it flat and gave it to him. "I found the receipt and the earrings buried in his top drawer. Along with a card addressed to Brittany."

"Holy shiiit." Pierce read the amount on the receipt—paid for in cash—shook his head, felt his guts twist. "What the hell was he thinking?"

"That he loved her?" Quinn showed him the signed card. *With all my love forever, Tony.* "He wanted to show her he'd spend the big bucks on her. Wanted to show you..."

Pierce ran his fingers through his hair and tugged. "Makes no sense."

"Not to you, not to me maybe, but..." Quinn took pity on him and stopped.

"He didn't have to embezzle five million bucks to afford those earrings. I pay—paid—him enough he could afford double the price. He drives a Jeep for God's sake."

Quinn looked away, but not before Pierce read more pity in her eyes. He could hear her thinking,

Pathetic.

*He drives a Jeep...*God, what a stupid, illogical and pathetic comment.

"Call Brittany. Tell her to take a cab here," Quinn said in that sweet, gentle voice mothers used with their bullied five-year-old sons. "Get nosy. Find out what else he's given her. Ask the price of that pendant. I'll see if I can hack into his computer files."

His lizard brain grabbed onto the ideas as if they might save Tony. He gave Quinn the go-ahead and went back into his office to call the Marriott. It took him a minute or two before he could see to Google the number.

Jesus, Tony. Jesus, Jesus, Jesus. Means and motive to steal guaranteed receiving a long prison sentence and breaking the hearts of two of the finest parents Pierce had ever met. For what? For Brittany?

Whatever Brittany said, would he understand how Tony had derailed? Asking personal questions could lead to asking intimate questions he didn't want to ask. Pierce rubbed the back of his neck, exhaled, and reached for the phone.

"Oh, hello." Brittany made no attempt to hide her disappointment.

Pierce sidestepped asking the obvious and said, "Grab a taxi. Come to the office. Look at something we've found."

"What?" Her tone flat, without interest.

"I'd like you to see it." A metallic edge of impatience sharpened his tone.

"Can't you bring it to the hotel? What if Tony calls?"

Pierce tipped the silver box sideways. The earrings

dangled in an anemic ray of sunshine slanting across his desk. The light splintered into red and green and gold shards. "Won't he call your cell?"

"I...I don't want to risk missing a call." Tears muffled her voice.

And I don't want to risk hurting Quinn. He shook his head as if Brittany could see the gesture. "Ask the hotel to forward your calls to your cell phone."

Her sigh was long, dramatic—a reminder of a trait he remembered too well. When he said nothing—as he'd generally done when she'd pouted during their short-lived affair—she sighed again.

He waited a beat before saying, "See you in fifteen minutes."

"Wait!" Her voice rose to a wail. "Could you at least come get me? I'd like to talk to you...alone. Without Quinn around."

"Why?"

"Quinn hates me. Not that I blame her...I know she asked me to her party, but I don't feel comfortable...I'll wait in the lobby. You don't have to come inside."

"Fifteen minutes." He hung up, stood and straightened his shoulders. What the hell? He liked walking through fire.

****

"Just a sec."

Pierce was glad just to watch Quinn as her fingers flew across the keyboard at Tony's desk. Her bottom lip was caught between her teeth, her eyes bright.

Her strangled cry scared hell out of him. He jumped over a couple of paper mounds like a startled goat, nearly breaking his damned neck to get to her.

"I've got it. I've got it. I've got it." She pumped

her fist in the air.

"Better be damned good," he groused. "I came close to having a coronary."

"Ooohhh, poor baby." She shuffled through a thick file and removed a single sheet of paper she studied as if he'd disappeared. "Ever heard of BOT Nets?"

"Short for remotely controlled software. RoBOTS, right?" Talking blurred fantasies of her dragging him to the floor and tearing off his clothes. Since he should be thinking of Tony, he shrugged, reined in his libido and recited, "BOTs can spam a couple of million users at once and bring sophisticated computer systems to their knees."

"Bingo." Quinn's eyes widened, and she smiled at Pierce as if he'd invented computing. "Hackers and spammers and geeks. They use the technology so creatively—stealing passwords, bank account data, credit card info..."

At the end of his technology savvy, Pierce rocked back on his heels. "Cyber-baddies make dummies robbing banks in masks, waving guns and toting a paper bag sooo ho-hum."

Despite his lame attempt at a joke, Quinn threw him a mind-stunning smile. She pressed her thumb against her bottom lip, waited until he raised his brows, then asked, "Want my definition of BOT?"

Pierce shrugged, kept a straight face, drawled, "I'd rather hear you say you're dying for me to rip off your clothes. That you want to rip off my clothes. That—"

"Band of Thieves," she said. "Thieves because we're talking about a world-wide network of cyber-criminals. They sell their specialties for cash or trade illegal services for the latest virus or access to a compromised system. Nobody's exempt."

Pierce stared at her as if she'd dropped through the roof. "Thank you for speaking slowly and simply. But Steve Cutter and Tony spend a fortune on every new anti-virus software and network firewall that hits the market."

She highlighted a line on the paper she held, then met and held his gaze. "You know BOTs are designed to hide from virus scanners."

"Tony makes damned sure we install system updates as soon as they're available. An independent security audit every week gives us five stars." Dumping on Quinn required breathing, so Pierce inhaled, but his brain kept churning. Where were they going? Was Quinn deliberately trying to make him look stupid?

"Has Steve Cutter figured out what happened on Monday to the security camera? User error makes sense." Her tone, sympathetic and warm, melted Pierce's defensiveness.

"Steve let George off the hook. Says the old guy knows what he's doing. Tony sent me an email that he was checking a camera malfunction, but...I don't know...it's pretty cryptic."

"Unlike my very specific love-note." Pain and confusion overrode her forced brightness.

"Christ, Quinn!" He jumped over the pile of papers, missing the last mountain, stumbled, slipped. His legs did the splits. Time stood still. She fought back a laugh. Time sped up. He crashed sideways, slamming his knee on the side of his desk. "Yowwww!"

"Yowwwwie." Smiling like an angel, she eased down next to him.

Certain he'd messed up his chance at fathering

children, he swallowed his pride and managed a feeble smile. "And for my next amazing act of agility and coordination—"

"Gotta dash into the nearest phone booth and emerge in the cape and tights before leaping tall buildings, Dude."

When he opened his mouth to laugh, her tongue slipped inside, a feather of flame scorching every place it touched. The kiss released a reaching-out in her Pierce had never known before. He didn't give a damn that he looked like a complete idiot.

Her body pressed against his, curling into him with the familiarity of a long-time lover. Her heart banging his rib cage confirmed he was actually awake. Electricity jolted through him, exploding in his groin. The need to show off or crack wise or make silly promises evaporated. He held Quinn and let the tenderness radiating from her soak into his starved system.

Now I get how women bring men to our knees.

As much as Pierce wanted to stay there holding her, his knees finally mutinied. He had to move or never walk again. He shifted his weight and groaned. "That's a romantic overture."

She laughed, pushed to standing and offered her hand. "So taken."

Pride dictated he leap to his feet, but his aching knees won the debate. He let her haul his ass off the floor, then pulled her into him. "Sorry I reminded you about that damn note."

She tapped her index finger against his bottom lip. "Searching those records created a retreat. For a while. But I never forgot the note. Right now, I'm pretty sure

I'll never forget it. Not even if I find out who sent it."

He kissed the top of her head, then tucked it under his chin. "Okay, but forget about me doing more slapstick."

"Deal." She sniffled and kept her nose pressed into his chest.

"Do you think Tony's part of a band of thieves?"

She pushed herself to arm's length and stared up at him, her eyes and mouth soft. "He's smart enough. He's had opportunities. And—"

"And he's already admitted he embezzled the money."

"Someone helped him." She picked up the papers that had spilled into the outer office. "I'm sure he didn't act alone."

Pierce said nothing.

Had Tony written Leonard and Yeager because he wanted some kind of legal immunity? Did he want to shift the blame on someone else? Did he trust lawyers more than he trusted Pierce?

"My timing's lousy here." He pinched the bridge of his nose. Too many questions, too few answers. "But Brittany wants me to pick her up."

Quinn touched the tip of his nose. "Surprise, surprise."

His mouth twisted, and he swallowed, the tendons in his neck hard as rocks.

But he locked eyes with her. "No surprise I was the world's biggest idiot either. I hope—with time—I can prove I've changed."

She stood still, tilted his head forward, cradled his stubbled cheeks in her hands and kissed him, her eyes open, her fingers pulling him forward. The kiss deepened and she folded her body against his, moving her arms around his neck.

Leaving him dazed, she broke the kiss and whispered. "Go, Kemosabe."

Chapter 17

Focus, focus. Stop thinking about that damn note. Quinn gnawed her bottom lip and entered a new search argument. Stop thinking about Pierce declaring he's changed. Stop thinking about him walking into Brittany's hotel room. He's an adult. A male adult. Not even Brittany can force him to have sex.

Any more than you can force Tony's computer to reveal his secrets.

"Unauthorized User" appeared on the monitor yet again, and Quinn gave up. She pushed away from the desk. Break time. Think about something else for a few minutes. Strange she couldn't find a web site for the jeweler. Granted there wasn't a web address on the receipt, but there wasn't a street address either. Ritzy or shady?

A tap on the outer door sent her heart pounding. Then George called her name. Lord, would she ever stop being on edge? Exhaling, she got up and opened the door.

The older man's smile was so normal she smiled back—like a normal person with nothing more pressing than a party for forty-two—make that forty-three—guests for the moment.

"The caterers are unloading in the garage," George said, his smile deepening. "They're early. Worried about the weather, I guess. Mr. Jordan cleared them on his way out."

She thanked George, adding, "I'll come down in half an hour or so."

Pierce should be back by then, and she wanted to see Brittany's reaction to the earrings.

"What time are you coming to the party?" she asked George.

"My turn this year to come at seven. See the lights go on." He talked on for a few more minutes, reiterating as he did every year, how much he looked forward to The Bash since his wife's death. "Makes me forget for a while I don't have family."

Melancholy overrode Quinn's embarrassment at the old man's situation. Afraid the tears choking her would spill out, she let him talk. When he finally left, she reached for the phone. She'd waited long enough to hear from her baby brother. In years past, they'd have chatted at least three times before The Bash started. This year she'd talk one minute. She'd express her good wishes fast and forget the induced-labor conference with Rex. Rex wasn't Michael's family.

"Gobble, gobble, Quinn." Traffic muffled Michael's greeting.

She blurted, "Don't tell me you're in the car?"

"Okay, I won't."

Silence. Pointed. Hostile. Quinn felt as if he'd called her names.

"How else do you think I bring home the turkey? Luce sure didn't feel like cooking. So, it's off to Kroger's I go. Tra la la la, tra la la la, tra la la LAAAAAH."

Quinn flinched. "I'm sorry. I assumed you'd spend the day with Luce's parents."

"The doctor ordered a very, very, very quiet day for the parents-to-be."

"How is Luce?"

"Exhausted. Scared. Miserable."

"How about you?" Static crackled on the line.

"Exhausted. Scared. Miserable. Not the PC-admission of a first-time daddy, right?"

"I know it's been tough." Careful with the brilliant insights, Quinn.

"You don't know the half of it, Big Sis. But let's change the subject."

Against her better judgment, she followed his lead. She couldn't ruin the day by mentioning the note. She wouldn't let it ruin her day—or his.

"Thanks, by the way, for asking Rex. I know what it means to him."

"Things may...be looking up for him."

"My big sister, miracle worker."

She flinched at the ugly little slur of sarcasm edging the words. She touched her stinging cheek, saying hurriedly, "I can't give you details yet."

"No problemo. I understand ethics, Big Sis."

"I'm worried about you," she said, cutting him a break because he didn't push her on the details of Rex's job and because he'd gloat over Tony's fall from grace and because he must be whacked.

"Should I come to St. Louis tomorrow?" Let Pierce deal with Tony's ruin?

"In this weather? It's snowing here again. Another reason I'm headed to the supermarket. They're predicting three to four feet tonight."

"What if Luce goes into labor?"

"Russians drive Mercedes. We'll make it. Gotta go.

Don't call me, I'll call you later, okay? For some reason, Luce gets upset every time the phone rings. Say hi to Rex."

Quinn listened to the dial tone for two inhales and exhales, then hung up, telling herself the hollow feeling in her stomach was hunger.

****

Roses bloomed in Brittany's milky cheeks, but the line between her perfectly plucked brows was almost as deep as the parallel tracks between Pierce's eyes. Quinn scanned his stone face for a clue, came up with nothing.

Brittany glanced around the office. "Nothing's changed, I see."

"Everything's changed." Pierce glanced at Quinn as if she'd confirm the complete redecoration he made a day after Brittany disappeared from his life.

Brittany's tiny shoulders moved. "What about your office, Quinn?"

None of your business, beeeyach. Quinn's smile flickered, disappeared. "My office manager's a natural at interior design."

"Nothing from Tony." Pierce moved to Quinn's side and bussed her behind the ear, muttering, "Something's up."

"I'm sure he'll show up at the hotel, surprise me," Brittany said in a tinny, upbeat voice that jarred Quinn.

"Did he hint at a surprise?" Quinn pitched her voice low, fake friendly.

Brittany supported her chin on her right thumb and middle finger. Her index finger tapped below her cheek and she pursed her lips. *A woman thinking before speaking.* Her index finger traveled to her bottom lip, tapped twice.

She said, "Well, he did say he had something for me. Said he'd give it to me at dinner."

Pierce glared. "Any idea what that something is?"

Brittany took a step backwards. "You ask more questions than a lawyer."

"This is important, Brittany." Quinn filled the void of Pierce's speechlessness. "No more questions if you'll tell us everything you think might help find Tony."

"I've already told you." Tears threatened, but she recapped Tony's sudden invitation a week ago to visit Kansas City for Thanksgiving, all arrangements made, all expenses paid. They'd talked every day since— three, four, five times a day. "Tony's such a sweetie. He knows how hard Thanksgiving is for me. Being alone, no family."

"Did you think he was going to ask you to marry him?" Quinn spoke as gently as she could, avoiding eye contact with Pierce.

The tip of Brittany's tongue flicked her top lip, disappeared. She swallowed, nodding once, hard, fast, and whispered, "He said he loved me."

A sound escaped from Pierce—disbelief, sorrow, maybe.

Quinn slipped between him and Brittany, patted the other woman's shoulder, put a hand in the middle of her back. "Let's go into Pierce's office. You can sit down. Take off your coat."

"What about what you found? It's something of Tony's, isn't it? Is it for me?"

A little pressure by Quinn between Brittany's shoulder blades guided the other woman into the office. Feet shuffling, Pierce followed like an old man. He let Quinn open his top drawer, remove the exquisite box, hand it to Brittany, sitting on the edge of the wing chair, her coat unbuttoned, her oversized purse on her knees.

"Oh, my—" Brittany sat back in the chair and splayed her fingers over her heart. After a deep breath, she turned the box to the right, the left, back to center before lifting the top.

She slipped one pendant earring off its velvet bed, held it between thumb and index finger and raised it to the light. Removing the back of the earring, she cocked her head. Her dark hair fell to one side in a cascade of waves. Eyes closed, she slid the post into her earlobe and slipped the back into place.

As if alone, she repeated the steps with the second earring, puffing her hair up away from her ears, turning her head from side to side so Pierce and Quinn could see.

"This was with them." Quinn presented the small, unsealed envelope. Brittany opened it, glanced at the card, then stuffed it back in the envelope.

"Have you ever...seen such dazzling...earrings? I'm never taking them off."

"Diamond and jeans?" Pierce muttered, his face grim.

"Tony obviously knows your taste." Quinn silenced Pierce with a frown.

"Diamonds and jeans are all the rage." Brittany tossed her head at Pierce, but spoke to Quinn. "I saw a pair on the Internet I loved. They don't compare to these—don't come close. These surpass those!"

Several turns of her head gave Quinn her cue. She bit back saying, *They're decadent* and said, "They're exquisite."

"Not long ago I was having a bad day...I never got

squat in the divorce. I sent the earring link to Tony. He called me. Pumped me up. Said when he made his first million . . ."

Standing, she let the sentence trail off and crossed the room, purse over her shoulder. "I need a mirror. Your executive bathroom still here?"

Without waiting for a reply, she pranced to the washroom, entered and closed the door.

"Vanity, vanity," Pierce whispered too loudly.

"Shhhh." Quinn motioned him to stay put and tiptoed across the thick Aubusson rug.

Heart thudding, she pressed an ear against the door and held her breath. Pierce was so quiet she heard atoms bumping into each other. Deeper silence. Silence that muffled the thud of her heart. Silence that lasted a lifetime.

So quiet, but...she'd swear she detected the faint snap of a cell cover closing.

Pierce touched her shoulder. Adrenaline pumped into Quinn. She jumped away from the door and stared at him. He held his wrist up, tapping his watch.

When Brittany emerged a second later, smiling like an alligator spying two sitting ducks, Quinn was bending over his shoulder studying the receipt.

"I should go back," Brittany announced. "I'm certain I'll hear from Tony soon."

"Have you checked your cell phone?" Quinn asked. How the hell could she get her hands on that phone?

A headshake put Quinn in imminent danger of going blind.

"It hasn't rung since I left the hotel." She glanced at Pierce. "I'm ready to go back. I want to take a long bubble bath. Do my nails. Put my hair up. I want Tony to see these earrings the minute I open the door."

"That shouldn't be hard." Pierce moved away from the desk with all the enthusiasm of a condemned man walking to the electric chair. "You coming, Quinn?"

"I should check with the caterers. Do a few other things." Like wonder why Brittany showed zero curiosity about where they'd found the earrings. Strange she'd forgotten Brittany had the brain power of a twenty-watt bulb.

Ten minutes after they left, Quinn called Pierce. "Your mission, should you accept it...get a look at her cell phone."

****

Pierce tooled into his office at 2:03 grinning with such self-confidence and power Quinn's skin crackled with excitement.

"Not only did I accept your mission," he announced, pulling her from behind the desk and waltzing her around chairs and a coffee table, "I left no trace of my mind-boggling deviousness."

"Help me, Fairy Godmother." Quinn bit her bottom lip. She and Pierce did not have a good dance history. They both wanted to lead.

Without warning, he tilted her backwards until her head nearly touched the floor. Gravity pulled blood into her brain. She exhaled. "Don't drop me."

"Drop you? A master sleuth who ran into a snowbank, tended his passenger, knocked her purse on the floor, swiped her cell—"

"Whaaaat?" Quinn's neck whiplashed as he swung her upright.

Pierce laughed, made an exaggerated, theatrical

bow, and planted a loud kiss on her gaping mouth. "And yes, I checked her Messages Sent."

A cocked eyebrow accompanied his drawn-out pause.

"Don't think I won't hurt you." She punched his arm. "Who'd she text?"

"Not Tony. At least it's not a number I've used with him."

"Let me see."

He took the phone from his pocket and held it by one corner over their heads. "About that undeserved and inappropriate physical retaliation—"

The phone on his desk rang and Pierce's laugh was positively evil. "Want to guess who that is?"

He handed the cell phone to Quinn, took his time walking to his desk, checked the LED and flashed another snarky grin before picking up. "How're you feeling, Britt—"

Anyone who didn't know him might think his soothing, composed tone reflected concern, Quinn realized.

"No, I don't have your cell phone," he said, telling the truth since Quinn had it and was puzzling over Brittany's last text.

Perfect plan. Love the gift. Can't wait to show you. Yours, B.

"Sure, I can go check the SUV. I'm sure it's not there...Yes, I understand how important...Yes, I'll go down right now. In the meantime, go through your— Okay, okay. I understand you dumped everything on the bed...Give me ten minutes. I'll call you back." He disconnected, laid the receiver in the cradle and patted his left shoulder. "Should I take up a career as an actor?"

"I think you should. After you look at these other texts."

They spent ten minutes reviewing a dozen texts to the same phone number. They agreed the messages didn't help them a damned bit. Most were as cryptic as the one she'd made from Pierce's bathroom. Attempts at accessing voice mail without a password failed. They tried the phone number she'd called ten times in the last two days and groaned when it was out of service.

Pierce's cell phone interrupted their groanfest. He motioned Quinn to stand next to him before speaking.

"Bad news. Your phone's not in the SUV. I guarantee it."

"You're right," Brittany said, her voice breathy. "I feel so dumb. I found it. When I dumped everything on the bed, the phone must've fallen underneath. I got on my hands and knees..."

Quinn rolled her eyes at the same time Pierce rolled his. Like most liars Brittany peppered her story with too many details.

After she finally ran down, he asked, "No word from Tony?"

"Not yet. But it's still early." She let that comment hang, then said, "Is the invitation to Quinn's party still open?"

"It is."

"Okay. I may or may not see you later."

"Let me know if you hear from Tony."

"You, too," she said and hung up without agreeing to call Pierce.

"Pinch me," Quinn said. "I don't know if I'm asleep or awake."

His dark eyes flashed, then he grabbed her, crushing her to him, taking her mouth, anchoring her head in his strong, magical hands. Desire swelled and she pressed against his crotch, taking delight in his erection, repressing worries about commitment and love.

He slid his mouth off hers, feathered kisses in the hollow of her throat, placed and held her hand on his zipper. "Are you dreaming?"

"I'd say no—off the top of my head." Legs shaky, she held onto his elbows, inhaled and took a step backwards. "Romantic that I am, I suggest you sit behind your desk. I'll go back to checking Tony's computer."

He stood still, letting her hands slip off his arms. "With my mission accomplished, I do expect a reward."

"Which will be that much sweeter—later." Quinn danced away from him, stopping in the door to the outer office. "Asleep or awake, I can't figure out why Brittany lied to us. It's so damned blatant."

Pierce shrugged. "Makes me wonder what else she's lying about."

"Despite Tony's confession, I can't wrap my head around them as a couple."

Pierce snorted. "Not even if they were the lone survivors of Armageddon."

"Will you ask him about her tonight?" Quinn hugged her waist.

"Hell, I don't know what I'm going to ask him. Why for starters. And if he tells me he stole the money to give Brittany baubles..." Pierce shook his head. "If he tells me that, I'll probably need that brain transplant before I can call the cops."

Her heart felt suddenly electrified. "You'll call the police?"

"Unless he convinces me he stole money to save someone's life."

"His mother sounded fine. In good physical health. I thought the Franklins were bummed Tony was missing Thanksgiving with them. But I'd bet they aren't taking anti-depressants. Pioneer blood runs in their veins." Quinn rubbed the sudden rash of goose bumps on her arms. "There's always his cousin. What if she's ill? Or was hurt in an accident? Or needs experimental medical treatment."

"Whoa." Pierce held up both hands. "If any of those scenarios are true, no cops. You and I paid to keep this quiet, so I vote for keeping it quiet. But I still want to know why. And I want to know how Brittany figures into this clusterfuck."

Love's as strong as blood, Quinn realized. At least Pierce's feelings for Tony were as strong as if they shared a blood tie.

Wanting to avoid thoughts about Pierce's betrayal with Brittany, she said, "I got nowhere with his computer, but I could hack Molly MacIntyre's medical records pretty fast. If they're negative, I'll check the Endicott newspaper for accidents."

Pierce gaped at her. "You're wading into deep legal water."

"No. Not wading." She shook her head and wallowed for a minute in the gentle rebuke in his voice. "I'm swimming in deep legal water. With luck, no one will ever know."

Pierce grimaced. "Think that's what Tony said?"

The question, purely rhetorical, hovered between

them. Quietly, she asked, "Does he know you footed the bill for Rex?"

"Yes. It was his suggestion, believe it or not."

****

Working alone in his office did zip for Pierce's concentration. Quinn was a narcotic, and he needed his fix. Maybe Tony felt the same way about Brittany. Acid spewed into Pierce's gut. And maybe cows and pigs and horses flew. Brittany knew how to stoke a guy's libido, but loving him, giving of herself, helping him become a better person? Elephants would fly first.

The truth about his own shallowness slapped Pierce between the eyes. Brittany never set a trap for him. She'd seen him for what he was—unlike Quinn who'd seen him for what he could be.

He cringed, remembering commitment becoming a dirty word—despite his parents' forty-five years of marriage. They'd made life together look too easy. They'd loved him, let him skate too often, bailed him out more than once. Cute and charming and selfish, he'd developed the maturity of a spoiled brat. He'd betrayed Quinn because he never grew up.

Pierce pushed away from his desk like a drunk waking up from the mother of all hangovers. Christ, no wonder Quinn couldn't trust him. Calling her name, he jogged into the hall.

Wide-eyed and pale, she met him halfway. "What's wrong? Did you find proof?"

"No." He cushioned her face between his hands, kissed her on the tip of the nose and hoped she read in his eyes the admiration and respect and desire and love filling him with the hope she could see he'd changed. "I found proof I was a bastard for letting you down.

Betraying you. I know I said I'd give you time, but if you'll have me, I want to spend the next fifty years of my life with you."

"Fifty? You'll be ninety and I'll be—"

"The woman I love. Have always loved—even though I never deserved you."

Tears shimmered in her eyes, spilled over, pooled on the tip of her chin. "Damn, why can't I cry like they do in the movies? I'll have to see a plastic surgeon if I don't want to terrify forty guests tonight."

"Now you're fishing." He dabbed at her chin with his handkerchief. "Resorting to your feminine wiles."

She laughed. "Dream on."

"More sexual banter," he growled.

"How well you know me." She snuggled into his chest, resting her head over his heart, wrapping her arms around his middle, making him feel ten feet tall—even though he was hyper-aware she'd sidestepped his second proposal.

Chapter 18

In her bathroom, Quinn leaned against the lavatory and massaged the caravan of goose bumps marching up her bare arms. Crazy reaction since the memory of Pierce's hands on her twenty minutes earlier still burned her nerve-endings. Thank God she'd insisted they dress in their separate offices. She removed the last hot curler with fingers shaking like those of a ninety-year-old woman.

Ninety? Dear Lord. The thought of living with Pierce into old age intensified the ache to belong to a man who loved her. Only her. Who would stick with her. Only her. Had Pierce really changed? What if Dim Bulb hadn't jumped out at her? Would Pierce have ever made the first move toward reconciliation? Would he wait four more years for her answer? Arms trembling, she ran her fingers through a mass of waves. If she thought he had changed, why didn't she let him read the note from her kitchen?

She'd let him take her to bed, but she'd refused to let him into her soul. Her stomach growled. Stress always made her ravenous. Time later for armchair psychoanalyzing. She dusted a sprinkling of gold and silver glitter on her cheekbones and went into her outer office for a final inspection.

"Looking good." Titan-haired, sporting at least thirty earrings in her right ear to balance out her triple nose rings, Nancee, of Nancee's Catering, gave Quinn two thumbs up.

"You've outdone yourself, Queen of Catering."

Masses of potted bronze, purple, and white mums sat on the floor, on the desks, and at each end of the buffet. Everywhere Quinn looked, she saw bronze, silver, or gold candles. Nancee would light them around 4:30, turning the room into a fairytale. At seven, when nearly a third of a million lights set The Plaza ablaze, she'd extinguish the candles until everyone tired of oohing and ahing.

A low wolf-whistle interrupted the chat with Nancee. Pierce walked around Quinn in a wide circle. "May I see your license, Ma'am?"

"License for what?" Blushing, she pirouetted.

"To drive men mad." He touched her bare skin, exposed by the dress's daringly low, scooped back.

"In this ole rag?" She laughed. Her repayment of the embezzlement money meant she'd wear the five-hundred-dollar rag for the next twenty Thanksgivings.

"Men could drop dead from heart failure before they go mad." Pierce growled, his eyes all pupil, his nostrils flaring.

"So you like ze dress?" Quinn danced away, feeling frivolous and shallow and edgy. She'd found nothing online indicating Molly MacIntyre was ill or recovering from an accident. Pierce had found zip pinpointing Tony's guilt.

"I like ze dress." Pierce grabbed her wrist and kissed a spot at the nape of her neck. "I like even more what's een ze dress."

Flirting lost the mental battle between teasing and behaving. She needed a break from being so damned serious and weighed down. She batted her mascaraed lashes. "I can see your thong underwear."

"I don't wear—" The pulse in his temple went crazy. "Who are you?"

She brought his face to the hollow of her throat. "How do I smell?"

"God." His groan raised goose bumps on her arms. "You smell unlawful."

"That good, huh?" She sniffed his cheek, then dragged her tongue down to the tip of his ear.

They held their breath as if suspended in a bubble and gazed into each other's eyes. He asked, "You gonna kiss me, or am I gonna kiss you?"

"I can never figure out where my nose goes." Lips parted, heart fluttering, Quinn moved to meet him.

"You need practice. Practice makes perfect." Laughter jitterbugged in his dark eyes. He lowered his lips closer and closer and closer...

WHACK! The front door crashed open. They jumped. She clipped him under the chin, and his molars clacked.

"Sonuva—"

"Looks like my timing's perfect," Rex yelled in a hearty voice that sounded like John Stewart.

"Perfect," Pierce's curtness telegraphed danger.

Secretly grateful for the interruption, Quinn resisted the impulse to pat her hair. Instead, she tweaked Pierce's cheek.

"I'll check with the caterers," he said.

Quinn gave him an eye roll Rex couldn't see. "Thank you."

He sauntered away whistling *Over the River*.

"Now I see why you've been so busy." Rex came

closer on a cloud of musk, his mouth twisted into a bared-teeth smile. "When Michael said you aren't a woman who takes no for an answer, I thought he was just sounding like a brother."

"What the heck are you babbling about?" Quinn exploded. "Do you know what time it is? What are you even doing here before five o'clock?"

His eyes widened in mock surprise. "I'm here at your invitation. And I'm babbling, as you call it, about Pierce giving a reference to my prospective employer."

"You think—" Quinn stared at him. Not eyeball to eyeball, because he gave her the "good" side of his face, with its even colored-skin tone and good bones.

Air hissed through her lips. She paused, said, "Here's a newsflash. I don't use sex to achieve business goals."

In the past four years since she'd left Pierce, she could've taken vows as a contemplative nun.

"You don't think my chances of getting that letter are better now than they were yesterday?" Rex grinned at her as if they shared a delicious secret.

Quinn grabbed his elbow, guiding him toward one of the undecorated back offices. "Whatever your chances are, they have nothing to do with my relationship with Pierce."

Crimson suffused Rex's ears, his entire face and the roots of his brassy yellow hair. His birthmark turned the color of a raw steak. The vein pulsating in his left temple reflected a purplish shine.

Tough. Quinn fixed him with a glare. "My relationship with Pierce is none of your damned business."

His eyes narrowed to tiger-slits, and his lips

disappeared into a thin, hard line. "So the bastard's turned you against me too."

His whine grated her nerves like a buzz saw.

"Wrong again." Quinn rushed on. "You turned me against you."

"Michael swore you'd fight for me."

"I don't think Michael will be disappointed." Her cutting tone masked her doubt.

"No, I'm sure he'll see your attitude as supportive."

"I think I know my brother pretty well."

Quinn felt Rex watching her watch him as she tried to resist the impulse to slug him. Ridiculously, his fingernails, bitten to the quick, made her feel like crying.

Sucker. Can't disappoint baby brother.

Slouched against the doorjamb, Rex stuffed his hands in his pockets, crossed one foot over the other and pointed his toe into the floor

"This is me," he said, "being multi-talented. I can talk and piss you off at the same time."

There was too much truth in the statement for Quinn to laugh. She wanted to say, Yeah, and I'm out of estrogen, but lucky for you I don't have a gun.

"If Pierce had cracked wise like that," Rex continued, "you'd fall down laughing."

The truth in that hit too close to home and Quinn's stomach cramped. She said in what she hoped was a neutral tone, "Do I have to point out you're not Pierce?"

"Would you kick me instead?" Naked contempt blazed in his eyes.

Quinn didn't allow herself to flinch. "I'm sorry,"

she said. "That was vicious."

And she'd had enough vicious for one day. The note in her kitchen conveyed enough viciousness for at least a decade. A sharp, bitter taste flooded the back of her throat. She pushed the note onto the back burner of her memory.

"I owe you an apology." She pressed her tongue against the roof of her scalding mouth.

The beat of silence stretched into discomfort. Did he want her to grovel?

More silence before Rex stood straighter. He didn't quite shrug as he drawled, "Sorry if I'm a little slow on the uptake. I don't get many apologies."

"Maybe I'll start a trend." She couldn't bring herself to touch him, but she moved closer.

"Be still my beating heart."

His lame attempt at humor rang more of sarcasm than wit, but Nancee had just set fire to the first candle. A light in the darkness, Quinn thought.

A wiggle of her fingers brought the bartender to her side. "Two glasses of champagne, please." She met and held Rex's stare.

As she'd dressed, she imagined her first toast with Pierce. After which, ever the romantic, she'd planned on asking him to make Rex's Thanksgiving by rehiring him on the spot.

The best laid plans... Quinn raised her glass. "Happy Thanksgiving, Rex. I'm glad you're here."

"Glad to be here, Quinn." He clinked his glass against hers—a little harder than necessary.

****

Smiling, Quinn greeted the first guests and ushered them into the transformed office. A live string trio played Vivaldi. The multitudes of candles threw off pools of soft light and illuminated the deepest corners. Three buffet tables groaned under the weight of a feast. Nancee and her servers in their formal black pants and spotless white shirts stood at the ready with trays of champagne and canapés.

"Check out the dessert table first," Quinn teased a friend from college.

Rex appeared at her side. "What tempts you? Missouri Mud Torte, I bet."

"Cranberry-pear crisp." She hoped he'd take the hint and move along.

"I'm a pumpkin-bundt-cake guy, myself. I'll have to pump iron for three months to take off half that cream cheese frosting."

A new wave of arrivals squelched their scintillating conversation. Next to her, Rex extended his hand, smiled, and gave every indication he was her date—the official host for the evening. Where was Pierce?

"Head straight for the dessert table," Rex advised the guests and threw Quinn a sly look.

"Go mingle." Her smile felt tight enough to pop off her eyebrows. "I certainly don't expect you to stand here all night."

She didn't add that she wanted Pierce acting as host.

Rex gave her a one-shouldered shrug. "Tough job, but someone has to do it."

Yes, and she wanted Pierce doing it—even if she wasn't willing to say she'd marry him. Her heart missed a beat. Would he wait four more years for her answer?

Another throng of people stepped off the elevator. Rex whistled and said under his breath, "How many people did you invite? Must cost a bundle to wine and dine a horde like this."

Her stomach fluttered and Quinn snapped, "Why does everything always come back to money for you?"

His mouth twisted. "I'm a computer analyst. Or, I used to be. Can you deduct your expenses as a total tax write-off?"

Quinn stared. Money didn't consume Pierce, who was born a banker.

"I'm not being nosy," Rex said. "I'm interested. Someday, I want to throw a bash like this."

Longing or hope or some emotion Quinn didn't recognize sucked her in. "I invited forty friends."

Plus Brittany and you. She bit her tongue and swallowed the remark.

More guests came through the door, hugged Quinn, and entered Nancee's fairyland. Waiting for more arrivals, she said, "For your information, I don't deduct this on my taxes."

"Why not?" His yellow eyes narrowed—as if she were pulling a joke on him.

"Because I have no intention of discussing business tonight. This is a Thanksgiving celebration."

"Why here? Why not in your home? You have a great house."

A little shiver tiptoed down her back.

"I've only seen it from the outside, of course. Three years ago, remember?"

His eagerness made it impossible to say no. She nodded. "You took me to dinner at Plaza Three the night Pierce hired you."

"That was about the best night of my life."

Afraid he expected the same admission from her,

Quinn said, "To answer your question. I hold the bash here so we can see the lighting ceremony without getting trampled."

"Makes sense, but it's gotta be expensive."

Quinn sighed. God, how had she stepped in this snake's nest? Where was Pierce? She slid her eyes away from Rex. "I paid Nancee four thousand dollars—about what I'd pay in a good restaurant. Would you like to see the itemized bill?"

A sheepish look passed over his marred face, surprising her.

He turned both palms up. "Like I said, I've always wanted to go all out like this."

Less subtle than Quinn, he looked around, his yellow eyes taking in all the details.

Itemizing the cost of the flowers, the food, the wine, and the service? She pressed a knuckle against her bottom lip.

He finished his inspection and looked her straight in the eyes. "You know when you're supporting a sick mother, you don't have an extra four-K lying around for blowouts like this."

Quinn felt as if she'd just kicked a puppy. Before she could backtrack, three more guests arrived. Her Self-anointed Host with the Mostest greeted them as if they were his best friends. No one even glanced at his birthmark. By the time Quinn finished chatting with the arrivals, he'd disappeared.

Thank God, she no longer had to explain who he was and why he stood at her side. Pierce caught her eye and waved from across the room. Their ESP was tuned into the same channel. They zigzagged through the packed bodies. Quinn's heart missed several beats then settled into a soft flutter.

The slow, sexy smile Pierce threw her melted the bones in her toes.

People closed in on all sides of them, but she felt as if everyone except them vanished. Michael's face flashed, but she stopped and cocked a hip toward Pierce, enjoying the quiver behind her knees.

He closed the distance. His hand rested in the small of her back, sending several megawatts of electricity tingling up her elbow. He whispered, "You and Rex joined at the hip?"

She turned in a small circle. "Where is he, do you know?"

Pierce snorted, and his nostrils flared. "Vampires don't eat regular food, do they? He probably flew down to The Plaza to see if he can find some fresh blood."

"Yuk." She stepped back, recoiling from Pierce's sarcasm.

"Sorry. Guess I resent his acting like your lover more than I realize."

"Are you insane?"

"Yes. I had a small mental breakdown while he played Squire of the Manor." Pierce laughed, but there was no humor in the sound. "Was the weasel hitting on you—or does he have indigestion?"

"Will you shut up? He's less than ten feet behind you."

"And your point is?" Pierce turned slowly.

"Stop flaring your nostrils," Quinn hissed.

"Habit. It's a guy thing."

Rex stood alone in a darkened corner—away from food and drink. The intensity of his stare raised the little hairs on the back of Quinn's neck. She fingered her earring. From this distance, she might have described his birthmark as a heavy five o'clock shadow.

"What if he heard us?"

"Think he read your lips? Believe me, he wants to do more than read them."

"That was a mega-breakdown, by the way."

"Okay, I lied."

"Let's mingle." She squeezed his warm hand. "We can talk later."

Wherever she went around the room, she sensed Rex's eyes boring into her skull. He wasn't eating, but she caught him chugging champagne as she flitted from one group to another.

When Pierce brought her a plate piled with food, he asked, "Is Count Dracula's Cousin Rex from New Orleans by any chance?"

"Stop calling him that." Instead of shame, she felt an almost hysterical urge to giggle.

"Okay," Pierce capitulated. "But is he from New Orleans?"

Trying to keep her eyes away from Rex's corner, she shook her head. "You know he's from St. Louis."

"Well, he must have Louisiana ancestors then 'cause he's either trying to hex us or spook us with that steely look of his. Don't let him get any of your hair or fingernail clippings. That way he can't make a voodoo doll—"

"Pierce. Please. I'm getting uncomfortable. We're acting like adolescents."

He shot her an unreadable look. "Okay, I'll back off. And to show you my heart's in the right place, I'll even go over and talk to him. Will that count as sufficient penance?"

Her ears rang. "Not a good idea—"

He'd already turned away, headed toward Rex like a man with a mission.

"Ohhh, damn." Cold sweat slid down her sides.

When in a state of high anxiety...it was either eat or wade in and separate the two men. Stomach fluttering, she picked up the plate Pierce had brought her. She'd better fuel up in case she had to kick their butts out.

The fragrance from the miniature beef Wellingtons distracted her long enough to take a first bite. Out of the corner of her eye, she saw Pierce's head snap back. Her whole body flinched. Crisp phyllo dough stuck in her throat. Her heart did a double somersault, and her chest refused to expand.

God, had Rex slugged his former boss?

A roar of laughter drowned out music, conversation and the clink of silverware. Quinn's accountant and his fiancée ambled over to Rex and Pierce. In thirty seconds, everyone in the corner was howling—including Pierce. Another twosome joined the first group, chuckling almost the instant they stood still. Four more guests pushed into the widening circle around Rex. They guffawed immediately.

Quinn overheard one of the servers say to Nancee, "That guy does great impersonations. He looks and sounds more like Woody Allen than Woody Allen."

Nancee whispered, "My God, look at those earrings."

Brittany stood in the doorway like the queen waiting for homage. Quinn made her way through the crowd, her face frozen in a rictus smile. *Chill. Or people will think La Brittany still makes you nervous.*

"It's so late," Quinn said, "I'd hoped your other

plans came together."

"Not even a phone call." Brittany's voice was high, brittle, but she managed to move her head to show off the earrings. Their glow put the candles to shame. "Is there anyone here I know besides you and Pierce?"

Before Quinn could respond, Brittany pointed at the circle of laughing guests. "What's going on over there? I could use a good laugh almost as much as a glass of champagne."

A discreet signal from Quinn brought the champagne. The server left and Quinn said, "That's Rex Walker. He worked with—"

"With Tony! I remember!" Brittany held up her empty glass. "Tony couldn't stand him. Sometimes I thought he was almost jealous."

"I doubt that." Quinn took a second glass of bubbly.

Brittany tossed her head, putting Quinn in danger of diamond blindness. "For the past six, nine months, Tony's ranted—absolutely ranted—about Rex. How he was going to make sure he didn't get the promotion Tony wanted. I'd call that jealousy."

Several heads turned their way. Quinn smiled and spoke to the nearest guests. Brittany glided toward Rex's circle.

Quinn's heart sank. Damn, one more motive for Tony framing Rex.

Chapter 19

The headache banging in Pierce's skull deserved its own TV commercial. How Brittany got off suggesting Tony was jealous of Rex...

Hold on. Pierce pinched between his eyebrows. He just had to hold on. Quinn was trying her damnedest to herd the last guests into the hallway. The dozen diehards—with Rex still the center of attention— ignored the open elevator and stood chatting.

God, they were going to spend the night. Pierce wanted to shove them down an open shaft. Instead, he stood next to Quinn as they praised the food, marveled at the lights, yakked and yakked and yakked until he thought their tongues would fall out.

The hangers-on crowded into the elevator on a wave of hilarity. Brittany wiggled up next to Rex. Someone begged him for "one more" impersonation.

"Jay Leno again."

"No, Seinfeld."

"No, George on Seinfeld."

Quinn waved, right up until the elevator doors snicked shut. "Brittany and Rex. Who'da thunk he'd be the life of the party?"

"Yeah, who'da thunk Tony would embezzle five million dollars?" Pierce pinched his nose. "Recess time is over, boys and girls. Time to get to work."

Quinn held her tongue and headed toward her

301

office to change clothes.

Any excuse to escape his radioactivity. And avoid giving him a straight answer to his proposal. Determined to regain control, he sat on the edge of a stuffed chair and swallowed several wise-ass comebacks about undressing her. Sexual banter and foreplay held zero appeal when his heart wasn't in it.

At that moment his heart lay like a boulder in the pit of his stomach.

True to her word, Quinn returned in five minutes. Dressed in dark slacks and matching sweater, her hair a mass of flyaway curls, she gave him a tentative smile.

His heart didn't lift, but at least it beat faster.

"Let's go," she said. "The caterers will handle this."

"You're sure?" Quinn, The Perfectionist, letting go, letting someone else take charge? Had to be a sign she was worried. About Tony? About him?

Bastard that he was, he grabbed her hand and dragged her into the elevator.

"My brain's been whirling like a damn blender ever since you told me Brittany's screwy theory. No one will ever believe that crap about Tony being jealous." Pierce tapped his foot double time, trying to speed them to the Penthouse.

A tiny line appeared between her brows, automatically setting off his internal alarm system. "Whatever it is, tell me."

She squeezed her waist. "I agree about Brittany's theory, and I understand about brain meltdown. I've felt off balance ever since Michael called about Rex."

"No comparison. Impersonations or not, you don't even like the guy. Tony's like my brother,

Goddammit." Heart pounding, Pierce got right in her face.

The blood drained out of her cheeks. She withdrew, but there was no place to escape.

"Suppose we were talking about Michael." He spit out Michael like it was poison. A memory flashed of her opening up to him in his office, but he couldn't stop his attack—maybe because he wanted—needed—her permanently in his life. "It'd be like finding out the Pope kicks puppies when nobody's watching."

Tears glittered in her eyes. "I-I can't imagine."

"Then spare me the empathy." Disgust stung his heart for wanting her to understand. If she understood, she'd give him a straight answer to his proposal.

"How about Rex? You think he'd understand feeling betrayed? Let down? Hung out to dry? Or do you think he's too repulsive to have feelings?"

"Frankly, m'dear, I don't give a shit about his feelings. I told you I should've fired him months ago."

"Does that mean you won't rehire him? Not even after Tony's confession? "

"What do you think?"

The elevator doors opened, but neither of them moved. Quinn looked over his shoulder at an invisible buddy. Adrenaline hummed in Pierce's ears. He felt like kicking something. His own ass, for starters?

The elevator door whapped against the foot Quinn held in front of the sensor.

"Move," Pierce said, "and I'll put my head down there. Then, I'll apologize."

"Sounds messy." Ice crackled on each word.

"About what you'd expect from a jerk."

"You're stressed." No signs of thawing evident to

him.

"Uh-huh. All stressed out and no one to kill, so I go for you. Nice guy, huh?"

"Not at the moment."

Whap, whap. Would he ever learn that Michael was the only man who could run the pity play on her?

"Give me a second. My meltdown was temporary. Sorry I went off on you."

"Sooner or later, we have to reach closure on Rex."

"Closure. I hate that word." He snorted. "But no problem. I've reached closure on Rex Walker."

"A closed mind isn't closure. Firing him wasn't right, Pierce."

"It felt good, though."

"That's probably the best sign it wasn't right."

"Oh, hell. You just won't give up, will you?" He hated seeing that disappointed shadow in her eyes.

"I know meeting Tony comes first, so I'll back off. But I'm not giving up on you rehiring Rex."

"Got it." Would she agree to marry him if he rehired the weasel?

"Maybe if you got out of the elevator, you'd feel a little less...trapped." She stepped into the hallway and lifted his spirits by holding the door open.

"Good idea." He didn't consciously feel trapped, but being hemmed in probably didn't help him think straight. He blinked. Why was his reception room black as a cave?

"The damn lamp must've burned out." Backlit by the light in the elevator, Quinn kept her hand in front of the sensor. Pierce fumbled along the wall for the switch, flipped it and cursed.

Had Tony arrived early and turned off the

304

electricity?

Pierce rubbed the chilled skin on the back of his neck. How could Tony do that? Software controlled all the lights in the building. Because of the party, the ops gurus had programmed the lights on Quinn's floor to burn full blast until midnight.

He snapped his fingers. "The overheads cycle off because it's a holiday."

He breathed easier, sure he was right about this detail.

"If Tony comes by and the whole place is dark, won't he leave?"

"I swore I wouldn't call the police."

"That probably reassured him."

Nursing his stung pride, Pierce said, "I see your point."

She ignored his pathetic barb. "Think about it."

"I don't have to," he growled. "I know you're right."

"On the other hand, maybe he's using a flashlight."

"Make up your mind. We're looking for simple answers here."

"Do you know how to override the software?"

"I can spell C-O-M-P-U-T-E-R. You already know I'm limited to spreadsheets, yada, yada, yada."

"I assume George knows how? Maybe Tony assumed it would be dark?"

"Lots of assumptions." Pierce pulled out his cell, dialed, waited, slammed down the cover. "Honest to God, that old man has a bladder the size of a peanut."

"He had a prostate operation six months ago. He told me you visited him in the hospital."

Feeling as mean-spirited as Scrooge, Pierce didn't

try to defend his faulty memory. "I forgot I visited him six months ago. Even if it was six years, ago, he's entitled to go to the john. No way being in the dark's his fault."

"Do you have a flashlight?"

"In the emergency kit." Pierce exhaled. "Which since it's dark, I can't find."

"I have an emergency kit. If we hustle, we can get down and back before Tony gets here."

When he didn't move, she said, "Unless you've got a better idea?"

A longer exhale. "This is your way of making me pay for being a jerk about Rex, isn't it?"

"I'll take that as a no." Her tone sounded warm and kind, the way most people spoke to the mentally challenged—or to the true morons of the world.

****

Nancee was one hundred percent sure she had a flash in the van and handed over her keys to Quinn, who opted to check her emergency kit first. She couldn't hold back a subdued whoop of triumph. She waved an industrial-sized red flashlight and a pocket-sized blue one under Pierce's nose.

"Cover your eyes." Quinn pointed both flashlights at Pierce.

He placed the heels of his hands over his eyes. The bigger flashlight blinked, went out.

"No spares?" He nodded at the dead batteries Quinn had dumped on the desk.

"Not in the emergency kit." Grabbing Nancee's key, Quinn didn't give him time to rub it in. She led the race to the elevator.

In the garage, the smell of burned gas hit her

between the eyes. She blinked and stopped dead in her tracks.

Pierce, cussing as if he'd invented a new language, rammed into her.

"He's already here." She stated the obvious...in a quavery whisper. She stared at the black Jeep. "How'd he miss hearing us clatter around like clowns?"

Why didn't he look their way? Or, move?

Maybe he's resting. Her mind scrabbled for an explanation of Tony's hunched position over the steering wheel.

May he rest in peace.

The idea slithered out of her subconscious like a snake. Her heart dropped. Of course he wasn't dead. Dread settled in her full stomach. The bitter taste of gasoline fumes stung her throat. Her fingers found Pierce's hand.

"Stay here." He squeezed her fingers. "You may need to...get help."

"No." She clung to his hand. No matter how hard he squeezed her fingers, she wasn't listening to reason or letting go.

Oh, God, don't let her pee her pants.

Hand-in-hand, they tiptoed across the cold pavement. A foot or so from the car, Pierce called Tony's name.

"Where's George?" she said more to herself than to Pierce.

The old man had come up to the bash about seven and stayed no more than half an hour. Quinn remembered hustling him out as soon as he started quizzing her about the incident in the garage.

"Tony?" Pierce repeated softly, glancing at the

security monitors.

"Let's go inside."

"Not until I'm sure." Pierce pried her vise-fingers off his arm.

He reached for the handle, and the garage exploded in light.

****

The chairs in the ICU waiting room were waaay too comfy for Quinn.

Every five or ten seconds, the need to sleep overpowered her. Her chin then fell forward, her whole body relaxed, and she teetered on the edge of consciousness. Sleep beckoned. She could feel herself drifting away from the waiting room.

At the last second, her head snapped back. She jerked awake. Her tongue felt as big as a beached whale in her dry mouth.

No sleeping. Not while sixty-three-year-old George Johnson's condition remained critical. Not if she didn't want nightmares about Tony.

A curtain crashed down in her mind. Don't go there. Not without Pierce. He'd promised to come by the hospital once the police finished questioning him. He'd solemnly promised he wouldn't call the Franklins unless she was with him.

What in the world would they say to Tony's parents after they said hello? The KCPD had offered to call the sheriff in Junction City. If he knew the Franklins, he'd probably go to their home. If he didn't, he'd notify a friend or a relative or a neighbor. Someone who knew them well would have to be there for their shock of a lifetime.

Tony Franklin was dead—apparently by his own

hand. Quinn groaned. Disgust at her weakness spiraled through her and her legs quivered. She planted her feet on the floor and lurched out of her chair. She scrubbed her eyes and kneaded her lower back, walked the hundred miles across the waiting room and tapped on the window to the ICU-nurse. The secured door swung open. Alcohol, antiseptic and other hospital smells assaulted Quinn's nose. Her heart pounded high in her chest with each step toward George's bed.

The petite nurse at his bedside shook her dark head. "No change."

Doubt and hope grappled in Quinn's shattered brain. The clack and whir of machines punctured the eerie silence and grated on her nerves. She fought the ridiculous urge to check under the bed. Lord, deliver her from a stint in ICU.

A vision of Luce exploded, vaporized by the constant read-outs of George's vital signs. Tubes in his arms and chest, plus a huge bandage around his head reminded Quinn of Frankenstein's monster. She bit her bottom lip, patted George's icy hand, shivered. Most meat lockers were warmer than his curtained cubicle.

The minutes she stood next to him crawled. Her mind went numb and her feet felt like slabs of ice. Why, why would Tony hurt this old man?

Wake up, George. Give us a clue.

The monitor beeped. George moaned. Muscles in his face twisted. The nurse appeared out of nowhere, checked his pulse, said, "Let's give him a break. He's a little agitated right now."

****

Relieved four-minutes were knocked off her fifteen minute visit, Quinn turned tail and ran for the waiting room. A thin, middle-aged man sat in a chair, chin forward on his chest, eyes closed. She knew from an earlier conversation his ninety-year-old mother had gone into cardiac arrest ten minutes before he arrived to take her out to Thanksgiving Dinner.

An unforgettable Thanksgiving. Quinn poured another cup of the coffee. The stuff was thick as mud and bitter as dandelions. It could substitute in a pinch as a pacemaker. She swallowed and her body jolted awake, followed by her brain. Her legs no longer trembled as she carried her styrofoam cup into the hall.

Discovering patterns in people's work histories was a daily task for her. Ditto for figuring out exactly what an employer wanted in an employee. Both processes began with questions. Lots of them. Lord knew there were more than enough questions about Tony as an embezzler. Maybe, before Pierce arrived, she'd discover a pattern in the unanswered questions.

"Why would Tony hurt George, then kill himself— only minutes before meeting Pierce?" She skirted a bank of chairs between her and the door to the hall. Talking to herself helped her think.

"Not a good first question." The overhead fluorescents buzzed. "Why did Tony embezzle the money?"

She drained her coffee cup. "Follow the money."

A secret account in the Caymans or Switzerland?

As a banker, Tony must know the ins and outs of off-shore accounts. But his house and Jeep and outward lifestyle gave no sign of extravagance. Those diamond earrings...

Her heart beat a little faster. The erratic rhythm wasn't because of the coffee. Off-shore deposits made more sense for Rex. A tidy sum for cosmetic surgery and a new life with a new face.

"Problem is, Rex is innocent." She retraced her steps into the ICU.

"Follow the money," she repeated.

She crushed her cup, and a trickle of coffee seeped onto her hand. The world's most preferred drug.

Drugs!

"Oh, my God." Quinn stopped breathing.

Her Inner Puritan was convinced she and her mother were the only people in the Western world who hadn't used drugs. A week ago, she'd have scoffed at the idea of Tony Franklin into drugs. Tonight...the idea glittered with perfect logic. Drugs meant blackmail. But who would blackmail Tony? Surely not George.

Then why try to kill him? Why did Tony kill himself?

"Back to square one." Quinn sighed.

"Don't you know what they say about people who talk to themselves?"

"Pierce!" Quinn whirled around, her heart heavy as lead.

His moaning repetition of her name drove her crazy. She imagined forgetting her doubts and fears. She'd tell him she'd marry him. Whenever he wanted— as long as he held her. Her whole body shook. Unable to get enough of him, she unbuttoned his shirt, dragged her tongue into the hollow of his throat, felt his back stiffen.

Her mind protested, but, she drew back a little. "What else happened?"

Pierce flinched. "How's George?"

"Critical. Potentially permanent brain damage."

Pierce groaned and Quinn couldn't seem to shut up. "Did the police find a hammer?"

"I don't think so." His voice strangled with pain.

"The doctor thinks George was hit with a hammer." Thank you, O' Blabber Mouth.

Pierce's shoulders slumped like someone fending off an attack. "Can we sit down?"

"Here." She eased him back against the wall, pushed him down to the floor and sank down next to him. "What's wrong?"

His tired, drawn face hurt her. Needing to touch him, she patted his cheek.

A beat, then he said hoarsely, "The police need to talk to you before we call the Franklins."

Her heart rate spiked, then plummeted into the black hole in the pit of her stomach. She swallowed once, twice, finally whispering, "No problem. When?"

Pierce squeezed her fingers until she worried he'd break them all. "Now."

The vibration behind her eyes intensified, but she nodded. "Okay. It's not as if I haven't had lots of practice talking to the police recently."

"You're sure?" The tic under his left eye unnerved her.

"Absolutely." If she didn't faint or throw up first.

"Why don't you stay here? I'll tell them you're ready."

"Great idea." Especially since her legs had forgotten their purpose in life.

Pierce leaned into her, chucked her under the chin and planted a kiss on the tip of her nose. On impulse, she grabbed his head and gave herself mouth-to-mouth resuscitation. Heat stirred in her stomach. For the first time since they'd found Tony, she felt safe. Melded with Pierce, she knew the world hadn't toppled off its axis.

Smoking-hot tension arced between them, but he pushed her away, flashing his famous lopsided smile. "There are two cops. One's a character."

"Okay." Once more, Quinn's fingers had lost all feeling.

Pierce walked backwards, calling, "I can stay with you during their questions."

Whatever sense of relief had started to lull her fears vaporized when the door to the ICU waiting room opened. A short, overweight man with a patch of skinny dark hair lumbered through the door first. He registered in Quinn's mind the way wallpaper registered. She knew it was there, but unless the pattern or color was outrageous, it faded into the background.

It was the second cop who didn't fade but grabbed her attention like scarlet roses on purple-striped paper. Tall, with an athlete's lean build, he strutted through the door, a green-eyed stud dressed in black. His long, reddish-gold pigtail swung behind him like a snake.

"Yo, mama." A blast of cinnamon hit Quinn's nose.

****

Homicide Detective Ken Smith made the intros. Like him, they were short. "Detective J.R. Ryder, Narcotics."

Mercifully, neither policeman offered his hand.

Quinn spoke to Ryder. "Where's your mask?"

"In the car," he drawled. "Damned thing gives me a migraine after the first twelve hours."

Out of the corner of her eye, Quinn saw Pierce's

mouth drop. The cop was obviously way too cool to lose his laid-back 'tude.

"Mind if we take first things first?" Detective Smith pushed his bifocals up on his button nose. The gesture softened the edge in his raspy voice.

"Please." His partner rolled his hand in front of him, bent at the waist, and nearly touched his thin nose to his knees.

Detective Smith flipped through a pocket-sized black notebook. Pierce moved in next to Quinn. His arm slid around her waist. She was surprised no one mentioned how loud her heart was pounding.

"I understand you knew the deceased," Detective Smith began.

He means Tony. Quinn nodded. Pierce pulled her closer, but she thought he'd stopped breathing.

"From the conversation with Mr. Jordan," Detective Smith continued, "I know you think the deceased's wounds were self-inflicted."

The floor under Quinn tilted. Her stomach pitched and bucked, dragging her mind along for the roller-coaster ride. She turned to Pierce. "Someone-someone killed him?"

A muscle ticked furiously under his left eye. "The police found a knife...in the Jeep."

"We have to do lab tests," Detective Smith interrupted. "Unlike TV-cops, we're pretty sure the knife we found is the weapon."

Detective Ryder, lounging against the wall, snorted.

Tears jammed Quinn's throat, strangling speech. An unreadable emotion flickered across Pierce's face, and Quinn pressed closer to him, hating the dread she'd seen on his now granite face. He massaged tiny circles in the small of her back.

"Is the knife Tony's?" Pierce's tone could've sliced steel.

Detective Smith locked eyes with Pierce and refused to drop his gaze. "Rex Walker personally reported it stolen on Monday. The duty sergeant remembers the report. Says Mr. Walker was pretty strung out—"

"Getting fired leaves a lot of people strung out." Quinn glanced at Pierce, regretted her outburst, and dug her nails into his wrist. Did he think Rex killed Tony?

His hold on her waist stayed firm and steady. "I told them the firing was ugly."

"So noted." Detective Smith made a check mark in his little black book. "The fact is, Sarge says Mr. Walker was upset for another reason."

The phone conversation with Michael flashed in Quinn's mind. Should she drag him into this? Why? Whatever had upset Rex, it couldn't be Michael.

The detective apparently assumed she was listening to him and continued talking. "He claimed the knife was the only memento he has of his father."

The words detonated in bright bursts inside Quinn's aching head. She said, "I don't know anything about a knife, but I do know Rex left my party at eight-thirty."

Detective Smith ran his index finger down a page in his notebook and frowned. "The security guard, Mr. George Johnson, called Dispatch at 8:46. Can you give us the names of the guests who left with Mr. Walker?"

"Then," the other cop drawled, "I have a few questions."

Chapter 20

Why didn't Quinn simply forget Brittany's claims? Confirm Rex hated Tony? Not the other way round. Then, they could phone the Franklins. Mystified, Pierce fumed and tried to make sense of Detective Ryder's questions.

The guy must watch too many cop shows. His questions jumped around like water dropped on a hot skillet. Pierce growled under his breath.

Quinn glanced his way but threw a question at Ryder. "You're not going to tell us why Tony was a suspect, are you?"

Ryder stopped fingering his pigtail and sat up a little straighter. "What makes you think he was a suspect?"

The knots Pierce's neck spread to the base of his neck. The cop's earlier innuendo that Tony was involved in drugs washed everything in a red haze. How could Quinn stay so damned calm?

"Why waste your time coming to the garage if Tony wasn't a suspect?" she asked.

"Who said I wasted my time?"

"So who's your sus—wait a minute." Quinn's look of outrage gave Pierce no clue why her jaw cracked, but the hairs on his neck prickled anyway.

"Am I a suspect?" she demanded, her voice dropping.

"Should you be a suspect?"

"When eating too many Lamar's becomes illegal."

Ryder covered his mouth—but not before Pierce caught his chuckle. Quinn let the cop's stupidity pass—maybe because he kept tossing out questions that made no sense. A look passed between the two cops. Within seconds, they'd folded their tents and faded away. A faint whiff of cinnamon hung in the hall—the only reminder they'd ever been there. Pierce and Quinn stared at each other.

"This must be what it's like when aliens kidnap you." He pulled Quinn into an embrace.

"Surreal." She pressed her ear against his heart, and he wished they could stay there forever. She'd say she'd marry him, and they'd find a desert island...

Before he caved to that fantasy, he said, "How do I break this to the Franklins? Make sense of this nightmare?"

The damp spot on his shirt prepared Pierce for the tears in Quinn's eyes when she lifted her head and met his gaze.

"You won't make sense," she whispered, "but they know you loved him too."

****

The sheriff in Junction City picked up at 2:17 and informed Pierce in a tired voice that Mrs. Franklin's sister was waiting for him ten minutes away. "Give us half an hour to get out to their place."

The intervening thirty minutes gave Pierce time to visit George Johnson. The nurse stated the older man was resting much better. Pierce took this statement on faith because frankly, George looked the way Pierce felt. Like hell.

On the other hand, a little piece of Pierce's mind envied George. ICU-patients didn't have to make phone calls that would destroy the world of unsuspecting, loving parents.

Thank God, Quinn would be there when he talked to the Franklins. What the hell could he say to them? Could he even talk?

The crystal ball in his brain fogged over. He stopped trying to imagine who would say what when and concentrated on George's steady breathing. His own pulse slowed. There was good news in this nightmare. At least he wouldn't have to tear the Franklin's heart out by raising the suspicion their son had killed a sixty-three-year-old man.

Pierce stumbled through the ICU doors into Quinn's waiting arms. Holding her, inhaling her scent of roses grounded him. He knew, somewhere deep in his brain, he held her too tightly for comfort, but letting go of her felt like letting go of a trapeze bar. His heart would drop, and he'd plummet down, down, down. Her hand in his prevented his free-fall.

Blind with fatigue, he opened his mouth to swear he'd learn to like Michael, that he'd rehire Rex, that he'd tell his mother in no uncertain terms Quinn deserved her respect. A thought he couldn't grasp slipped away, and he stumbled over his feet. Quinn piloted them around sofas and tables in the waiting room without speaking, opened the door into a private waiting nook, and pushed him into a chair.

His mind went as blank as a disconnected TV. Quinn massaged his shoulders. He unclenched his hands, reached for the phone, recoiled.

"Want me to dial?" Her hand was a butterfly on his

shoulder, but the lightness stiffened his backbone.

"Maggie, it's Pierce." He heard bones crack in Quinn's hand but found loosening his hold on her fingers impossible.

Miles away, Maggie Franklin said in a low, urgent plea, "What's happened to Tony, Pierce?"

Her anguish turned a switch on in his head, and he found the balance between too much detail and not enough. A gun to his head couldn't have dragged from him a syllable of Tony's confession.

Frame after frame of images fast forwarded in a blur. Then they sharpened as Pierce saw the Jeep and Tony hunched over the wheel. His grip crunched more small bones in Quinn's hands.

No details on why he and she were in the garage around nine o'clock on Thanksgiving night, but how they saw the Jeep...and Tony. Next to Pierce in real time, tears clouding her gray eyes, Quinn managed a wistful smile.

No mention of who called the police. Or that George lay in ICU. Time for those details later. After the police cut through the chaos.

Pierce choked the phone, but spoke clearly. "The police don't know much yet...except how he died."

The pause at the other end sped up his pulse. Disbelief and denial rushed into his head. He blurted, "He...he was— God, Maggie! I... He was stabbed."

Silence screamed. Pierce heard a sharp intake of air. Panic kicked him in the stomach. Quinn laid their interlaced hands over her heart. The panic receded. There were no hysterics and only one question—for which he had no answer.

"When can we bring him home?"

319

****

"You're insane."

"I don't need your permission." Quinn jutted her chin, but her heart wasn't in it. Not after Pierce's phone call to the Franklins.

Her chin came down, and she softened her tone. "Until George regains consciousness, why not use the time productively?"

"Because going to your house—alone—at three in the AM—to pick up a damn laptop isn't productive in my opinion. It's a good way to get yourself killed."

"Who'd want to kill me?" She wasn't into drugs.

"Duuuh. Whoever killed Tony."

Rex's name hung between them like a gong waiting to be rung.

"I understand what you're saying."

"Good." *End of subject* hummed between them, unsaid, but understood.

So far she hadn't confided her hunch that clean-cut, boy-next-door Tony's embezzlement had supported his secret life of drugs and blackmail. Ryder's presence on the case supported her theory. Not so for Pierce. She knew him too well. Without hard proof of Tony's guilt, Pierce would think she'd lost her mind for sure.

Because he was right on one point. Someone had killed Tony.

He was wrong that anyone had reason to kill her.

"Don't forget that note in your kitchen. And we know Tony's not a suspect." Worry—not triumph— vibrated in his reminder.

Goose bumps shrank the skin on Quinn's arms and raised images of the snowball-attack. Which had occurred in another lifetime. She said, "I'll call Hector.

He can go inside with me—"

"When they sell timeshares in Hell." Pierce sighed. "Let's sit down. We're asleep on our feet. We'll know more about George in a couple of hours. Then, we can go to your place. You can do your computer searches until you pass out at the keyboard."

Quinn put her arm around his waist. If she said she'd marry him—even if she still wasn't sure—maybe he'd capitulate. Her insides clenched. Tony's murder—and her note—overshadowed talk about lifetime commitments.

They staggered like drunks past the tables and chairs and collapsed on the sofa. Pierce pulled her closer, shifted his shoulder for her cheek and dropped a kiss on the top of her head. His thick shoulder provided the sense of being safe.

Quinn luxuriated in the break for a moment before saying, "If I can find the password for BOTN, we'll have all the answers we need. I'm sure of it."

He groaned, but didn't open his eyes. "Sleep."

His order to sleep, together with his closeness, had the double whammy of strong black coffee. Quinn closed her eyes, but her mind sped up. Random thoughts spun like planets breaking free from gravity. Yet she whirled back to the same conviction.

BOTN held the answers, dammit. Pierce didn't understand cyberspace or he'd agree.

"What if you took a taxi to my house?"

He sat up and scrubbed his ashen face. "How many hoops would you like me to jump through along the way?"

Heat scalded the back of her neck. The intensity in his eyes pulled her into his soul. "Sorry." She interlaced her fingers with his. "I'm not used to people worrying about me."

"How about protecting you? Want me to throw you over my shoulder and haul your cute little butt into the nearest cave?"

"That's a little neanderthalish."

"Uh-huh. Observe my knuckles dragging the ground." He threw her a look of pure disgust. "I already see I've lost this round, but I make the rules for the next round."

Her heart dropped. Banker Pierce Jordan and his rules.

"I'm sure you want to hear the rules?" The brittle edge to his tone flashed a warning. There was a time to do battle and a time to rest.

Quinn rested, softened her shoulders and nodded.

Stating the rules took ten seconds flat. Pierce flicked them off on two fingers. "Stay with George. Or, stay near the ICU door until I get back."

"Got it, chief." Quinn saluted.

A vein in his temple bulged, and his eyes narrowed. Regretting her mistake, she grabbed his hand. "I'm sorry. Thank you. No more playing stand-up comedienne."

He traced the line of her jaw from ear to chin. "Not to be melodramatic, but I will never forgive myself if you get hurt."

Quinn swallowed, but her throat swelled, cutting off speech. She patted his cheek, then hooked her arm through his and walked him to the elevator, hoping he didn't refuse at the last second to retrieve her computer. The selfish part of her wanted him to stay. The logical part of her wanted him gone. She simply couldn't think with him around. And she needed to think if they wanted to find Tony's killer.

The elevator doors snicked shut, and she bit the inside of her mouth. *Do not call him back. He has enough on his plate.*

In the claustrophobic waiting room, she turned her back to the wall clock, kicked off her shoes, and rummaged in her purse. When she finished digging, she aligned a clean pad of paper, three pens and a highlighter on the clean desk. Now all that was missing was her real brain—her internal computer.

Pierce returned at four o'clock to wads of paper overflowing the trash can. The deep lines around his mouth and eyes made her forget the hundreds of attempts at guessing Tony's password. His color was a paler shade of white than the snow.

"The Baby Ruth's brain food." He laid the candy bar on top of her laptop, his smile lopsided, his eyes glassy, his shoulders so rigid she winced. Tony's murder had gouged soul-deep cracks in Pierce's cockiness.

"Here's a small down payment on my IOU." Quinn rose and dragged her tongue along his bottom lip. His desire spiraled into the pit of her stomach.

Arms wrapped around his neck, she teased the corners of his mouth, received a quick but intense shock from the stubble on his chin, then slipped inside his welcoming mouth. The anxiety that had crushed her heart and lungs during his brief absence receded, allowing her to breathe. Her nerves quivered as he repressed a groan. The head of his cock pressed hard against her. Lord, she wanted him inside her, reaffirming they were alive. Offering hope they might grow old together.

Without warning, he stepped back and exhaled like a man jumping in a mountain stream. "We either stop right now or..."

"We don't," she finished, amazed by the reasonableness of her tone.

"The electric chair holds more appeal than stopping, but I will...You think you can find something—anything...?"

The hope in his voice beat back the disappointment zinging through her. She nodded. "Why don't you find a couch and take a nap?"

"Why don't I sit here?" He pulled an imaginary zipper across his mouth.

The smart response dictated shaking her head, but he'd already moved to the other side of the desk and sat down, stretching his legs in front of him, owning the space. He watched her every keystroke in silence. Heart pounding, she entered a mental cave and concentrated on a strategy to hack into the site she suspected held the key to the embezzlement.

Nobody had to tell her BOTN probably allowed one sign-on attempt. If she mis-guessed the user-id on her first try—a near certainty since she assumed Tony never used his mother's maiden name or his astrological sign or anything mundane—BOTN access would be blocked.

Sweat slicked her palms. The scenario she'd dreamed up earlier—Tony signing onto BOTN with a fake ID that pointed to Rex—lost some of its plausibility. If Tony wanted to frame Rex for the embezzlement, he'd choose an obvious user-id. If his obvious became obvious to her, several traps still loomed.

She exhaled. First things first.

Words and icons melted into one illegible stew. She groaned, snapped her mouth shut and glanced at Pierce. His head lay twisted at an odd angle, and he breathed softly through his mouth. The facial stubble and tics in his jaw twisted her heart. Whatever level of sleep he'd entered, she doubted it was restful. If she ever figured out a damn user-id, maybe they could go back to his place and sleep for a week. What better sleeping pill than making love?

Quinn pinched the inside of her elbow, turned over a clean sheet of paper and drew several cat caricatures. This damn search was all cat and mouse. Her hand trembled with exhaustion, but she drew another cat. Instead of adding ears and whiskers, she drew a heart. Inside the heart, she mindlessly traced their initials— SQA + PHJ.

For God's sake. Face burning, she glanced at Pierce. His eyelashes curled like miniature brushes against his cheeks. Her heart stampeded. God, she had let him back in her life so easily.

She stood and scrubbed her burning eyes. No wonder she couldn't think like Tony thinking like Rex. Looking for patterns in Tony's mind was an exercise in chasing—

"Ghosts. Phantoms," she said out loud, nerve endings tingling.

Pierce made a noise but his eyes remained closed.

"Phantom—no *s*," she whispered, wishing Pierce would wake up and congratulate her.

Phantom fit.

If Tony had, in fact, tried to frame Rex.

What if she'd subconsciously bought into Tony leaving obvious pointers to frame Rex?

The irony stuck in her head like a nail. Ironic twists worked on TV shows, but in real life...Was she making this too easy? How did Tony know about BOTN? How did he embezzle a small fortune to support a drug habit no one suspected? Why had Rex suspected?

A memory of Detective Ryder flashed. Why had he suddenly shown up in the parking garage? What did she know about Tony that would help an undercover narcotics cop?

Logic said, wake Pierce, get his input. She hesitated. Tension knotted the muscles in her neck and shoulders. She imagined Pierce's strong fingers melting her bones while she checked out—what, exactly? His touch would drive her nuts—overriding the search for clues implicating Tony in BOTN.

Because...the last thing Pierce wanted was proof that Tony had masterminded the embezzlement.

****

Pierce's mouth tasted like a small, furry animal had crawled down his throat and died. He jerked awake, needing a heartbeat to figure out where he was and saw Quinn bent over a pad of paper.

"Mornin'," he mumbled.

Her head came up. "So soon?"

The purple smudges under her eyes sliced into his heart. When was the last time she'd slept all night? "Why'd you let me sleep so long?"

Standing, he realized he sounded belligerent and mentally kicked his ass for taking out his frustration on her. "Sorry. That's my male ego showing."

She stood and leaned toward him, risking death by

his dragon breath. "You're not used to sleeping on the job. Too bad I don't have more to show."

"Nothing pointing to the weasel?" He took a step backwards, hoping she wouldn't notice how bad he looked and how worse he smelled.

A quick headshake. "But I'm not giving up."

"I should check on George."

"The nurse thought he was resting more comfortably at ten past five."

"If there's no change, let's go to my house. Grab a shower. Eat something. Maybe even nap for ten, fifteen minutes. We can be back here in less than ninety minutes." When she didn't interrupt or shake her head, Pierce thought he'd convinced her, but the spooky glitter in her eyes caused his gut to spasm. .

She shifted her gaze to her pad of paper, staring at it like some kind of crystal ball. "You go. I'm close...to a breakthrough."

"Close to falling on that damn keyboard and breaking your nose." Pierce snapped his mouth shut before he made it worse by telling her he wanted her with him.

"Phantom thief," she mumbled as if he'd evaporated into the ether.

"Whatever." Jaw muscles tensed. He swallowed a dose of bad breath. Question after question popped in his cotton-filled head.

Secretly, didn't he want Quinn to drop her search? Forget finding evidence proving Tony was the embezzler? Prove, instead, that Rex was guilty.

Blood scalded Pierce's face. A jolt of adrenaline brought back Quinn's accusations he'd sabotaged their relationship by shutting her out. Keeping his deepest thoughts to himself. Hiding his darkest secrets from her.

He exhaled and almost gagged. Did she consider his contempt for Michael sabotage? Were dinosaurs extinct?

"Indecision," he announced, aware her mind swam in cyberspace, his dog-paddled in the shallow end of the pool. "Indecision is the key to flexibility."

The stupidity plummeted like an anchor dropped in a lake. He shuffled his feet. God, he was pathetic. Expecting a response was...stupid. Childish.

As if reading his thoughts, she raised her head. The corners of her mouth curved, and the tenderness in her smile soothed his ego. Even before she floated toward him, he felt his hard edges soften.

They stood for a few minutes without talking. His legs were beginning to protest when she looked at him with eyes that broke his heart. Oh-oh.

"On the last day I ever saw my father, I put a note in his lunch..."

"I see," he said as gently as if speaking to an injured child.

"You know, when you're a little kid, you think everything bad that happens is your fault."

He nodded, though she hadn't asked a question.

"From the beginning, that very first night he didn't come home, Mom told us he didn't leave because of anything we kids did." She nailed Pierce with an unwavering gaze, but he suspected she was seeing her mother.

"Your mom's one smart lady."

"That's why I wanted to believe her. After a while, I did."

"But?" The *but* churned his stomach.

"But I never told her...never owned up to writing the note to anyone—except Michael."

That explains a lot. Not who left the note in her kitchen, but a lot.

"I'm honored." Pierce hoped that didn't sound too hokey.

"Better hear the whole story." Her eyes looked hot with unshed tears.

Her hand went limp in his, but he squeezed her fingertips and held her gaze. "I'm listening, but you had nothing to do with your father's disappearance."

The deep breath she sucked in hurt his lungs, but she spoke in a clear, strong voice. "I wanted a puppy. A neighbor's black cocker had seven of the cutest wigglers..."

A faraway look clouded her eyes. "I wanted the runt. The black and white one. I had a name picked out. I went over every day and came home begging for Spot. Original, huh?"

Pierce stopped breathing. Quinn went on. "Daddy said no. Every time. No. He almost never said no to anything I really wanted."

How could he, unless he had a block of ice for a heart? Pierce stroked her hand.

"He said I was too young. I remember feeling insulted. Hurt and misunderstood, but mostly insulted. So, I wrote him a note."

She stopped, looked off into memory again. "I told him I hated him, thought he was a bad daddy and wished he'd go away because then I could have a puppy."

"Your mother didn't notice?" Sarah Alexander had always struck him as the kind of mother who never let her kids get by with anything.

"I don't know where she was. She usually knew everything Michael and I even thought of doing."

"If she was like mine, she had eyes in the back of her head," Pierce offered.

Quinn nodded. "I remember, I wrote the note right before I went to bed. Slept with it under my pillow. The next morning, while everyone else ate breakfast, I stuffed the note in his coat pocket."

Tears leaked out of her eyes. "He didn't come home that night and I knew why."

She clutched Pierce's handkerchief—a soggy, useless mess.

"I know." She sniffed. "I know he didn't leave us because of my note."

"Good." Pierce figured she meant she knew this in her head.

"I'm not so neurotic I spend every day feeling guilty or pining after him."

"You're a low-maintenance babe, sweetheart." Hard-headed, feet on the ground, he almost added.

Her lips twitched, and she sighed. The sound raised a bruise on his heart.

"That note in my kitchen—that note really—" The Quinn he knew, the one who said sighing was a character flaw, sighed again.

Pierce jumped in. "That note was cruel and spiteful and untrue."

"Not a coincidence, though. Can't be. With a little more time, I'm certain I can find the connection between my note and Tony's confession." She didn't give him big eyes or kiss him or make a move on him to elicit the response she wanted.

The temptation to remind her of the trust she'd just given him scalded the tip of his tongue. He clenched his hands at his sides so he wouldn't betray that trust. He said, "Okay. I'll wait for you at home. Call me when you're ready for me to come get you."

"Thank you." The intensity in her voice spilled down his spine.

"Two hours max," he muttered. Then, by hook or by crook, he'd get her in his bed—where he'd make sure she got some sleep—after which he'd get her yes no matter what.

****

Minutes later, in a mild state of disbelief at Pierce's departure, Quinn tapped her pencil against her upper lip. She'd have plenty of time to tell him she'd marry him. After she proved Rex had thumbed his nose at all of them, embezzled the money and killed Tony. Proof would make her *yes* that much sweeter.

Frowning, she entered PHANTOM. To hell with worries about getting sucked into quicksand. If she was wrong, about case sensitivity or passwords or keystrokes, she was wrong. She didn't have to do the police's work for them. And she didn't have to cogitate and ruminate until hell was serving iced cold beer, either.

"Everything should be made as simple as possible, but no simpler," she said to the computer screen.

Opera went with phantom the way birds went with bees and milk went with honey. Her pulse revved up. She pounded the keys on her keyboard. O-p-e-r-a.

For a fraction of a fraction of a second, her computer screen hung. She held her breath. Please, please, don't let the password be case sensitive.

A flash...the main BOTN menu came up. Quinn whooped. Fingers tingling, she studied the menu with its eight categories. Nothing fancy. But why would elegant screen design appeal to a band of thieves?

The casual user might see nothing unusual. With minor variations, the categories appeared on the main menus of all kinds of Internet portals. The listing of BANKS leaped out. Quinn ignored the prickle on the back of her neck, clicked on TRAVEL as a test and received the message to enter her password.

A second click on TOOLS confirmed her suspicions. Each category required a password. She gnawed her bottom lip. BANKS might even require additional verification of her identity.

Damn, leave it to a bunch of sociopaths to set up more safeguards than honest people ever considered. BOTNers could have a BOT installed tracking her every keystroke, recording every hesitation, analyzing every mistake she made. She probably had less than ten seconds before her operating system crashed. She exhaled and stared at the screen. Her eyes were grittier than sandpaper, and logic neurons refused to fire. Pierce was right—she needed sleep.

Shiiiit. She'd washed out as cybercop. She squeezed her mouse. The jig was up. The masks were off.

Masks. "No *s*." She fought the impulse to yell.

Her fingers flew across the keyboard. The drums in her aching head faded as a new group of sites appeared.

Laundering Institutions/ Unnumbered Accounts: Swiss, Caribbean, Latin American

Robberies, Greatest 20th Century

Federal Reserve Updates

Embezzlement/Scams/Etc.

"Yessss." Her hand shook on the mouse. She waited, then double clicked on the only subcategory that held any interest.

Chapter 21

"Nooooo." Quinn turned her back on the Embezzlement menu and glared at her cell phone. She grabbed it, inhaled twice and punched TALK.

"There's a taxi waiting for you at the main entrance," Pierce announced.

"I'm in the middle—"

"Of a pointless computer game. Come home, Quinn." His impatience gave his words a melodramatic edge that sounded so unlike him, she blinked.

"I need half an hour to finish my pointless computer game." She made no effort to soften her own impatience. Too many adrenaline highs. Too little time since Pierce had left.

"This can't wait. Get over here. Right now. You won't believe your eyes."

She held the phone away from her ear and stared at it. Pierce had hung up on her. Incredibly, she'd swear he'd spoken in exclamations.

Tough. Exclamations didn't make his big kahuna one bit more important than her miracle of breaking into BOTN. Irritation at him jumped a notch or two. She didn't have much to show for her mental gymnastics except brain paralysis. Her break-in of BOTN proved slightly more enlightening than breaking into a pet store. And Michael had disappeared off her radar.

Her eyes burned and her back ached and her jaw felt ready to crack. Maybe Pierce had a point about sleep. Maybe. She logged off before she changed her mind, but anxiety hammered the top of her skull.

What if she forgot the passwords? Pierce was distracting...and she was tired enough to forget her own name. She scribbled phantom, opera, mask on a scrap of paper and stuck it in her coat pocket. Her fingers grazed the envelope she'd forgotten—thanks to spilling her insides to Pierce. More muscles bunched in her chest. She stuffed the cell phone in her pocket, grabbed the laptop and tore out of her cocoon.

Whatever Pierce had discovered, it had better be good or she'd fall asleep in his face.

****

"Want help up them steps?"

A gust of wind swept across Quinn, dry-mouthed, disoriented, and slumped in the backseat of a taxi. She rubbed her gritty eyes, shook her head and thanked the driver. Where the heck was Pierce? After his phone call, shouldn't he throw open the taxi door, pull her into his arms and sweep her up the stairs like Rhett with Scarlett?

The driver let her feet touch the ground, then slammed the door and raced around the front of the cab. Sleet danced like thousands of miniature bees in his headlights. Shivering, she tottered up the marble stairs. The laptop's weight stirred a snapshot of the parking garage. Like in all the horror movies she'd ever seen, the front door was cracked a fraction of an inch. When she knocked, the door swung open. No squeaks though. Not in Pierce's house.

"Pierce?" Quinn scurried inside, disappointed the

scent of coffee didn't tickle her nose.

Silence magnified her footsteps. She frowned, set the laptop near the closet and walked to the kitchen. Where was Floyd? Her heart lurched. If either feline or human jumped out and surprised her...Pierce knew she hated surprises.

The note sat propped against a bottle of olive oil on the island. A snapshot of the note in her kitchen flashed. Sweat trickled down her back. She clenched and unclenched her trembling fingers, then picked up the note in front of her. She read the scrawled line in a single glance.

Come upstairs as soon as you get here. P

Relief poured over her in a wave of heat. She smiled. Impatience to see him overrode her lingering irritation at his bossiness. Interesting what he took for granted.

Or not. She reached the top of the stairs and stopped to catch her breath. His bedroom was the only room she'd visited on the second floor. Anticipation didn't vaporize exhaustion, but she felt more alive than dead on her feet. What better time to accept his proposal?

Her heart drummed in her ears, her head spun. Was she nuts?

Calling his name, she turned the door handle to the master bedroom.

The stench of musk punched her stomach.

****

"Close your mouth, Quinn," Rex drawled. "You'll catch flies."

"Oh, my—Michael!" The room swayed. She grabbed the brass handle.

Tied to a straight-backed chair, her brother strained against the rope and made frantic, unintelligible noises through his gag. A crimson welt stood out on one cheekbone.

"Isn't this nice? A family reunion." Rex sat at the foot of the king-sized bed. He kept his birthmark turned away from Quinn.

"Wh-what's he doing here?" she croaked.

Blood rushed to Michael's face, and the vein in his left temple throbbed as he tried to speak. He rocked his chair back and forth on the thick carpet in a frenzy.

"F*amily reunion?*" Rex's visible eye glittered. "You can see how excited ole Mike is."

The chair tilted on two legs and Quinn's throat jammed shut.

"Mike simply couldn't stay away." Rex crossed one leg casually over the other, keeping his birthmark turned to the wall. He could pass for a model in a men's glossy magazine.

The gun he pointed at Quinn looked shiny and lethal.

"What's going on?" she whispered. "Where's Pierce?"

Rex leveled the gun at Michael. Her heart flip-flopped. "Hear that Baby Bro? She's more worried about His Pierceness than she is about you."

Michael's blue eyes danced with fury. His response was garbled. A purple bruise intersected with the wound on his cheek.

"Is Pierce hurt?"

"What if I told you he was dead?" Rex arched a brow.

Because her trembling legs were about to collapse

anyway, Quinn slid down the wall. Her ears rang. Little black dots danced like gnats in front of her eyes. "You're-you're lying."

"Aren't you gonna say you'd know—if His Pierceness was dead?" Rex taunted. "You hear that line all the time on soap operas."

"I don't watch soap operas."

"Go ahead, Quinn. Rub it in. You have a life." Rex sniffed and raised his chest. His voice came out in falsetto. "Oh, no, Pericival, you're lying. Reginald couldn't possibly be dead. I'd know, you see, if...he was dead."

"Wh-where is he?" Quinn felt about as tough as a squashed bug.

"Where you always wanted him," Rex drawled. "At your feet."

Her back against the wall limited her view, but she could see Pierce wasn't lying between Rex and the bathroom. Standing meant she'd fall down, her brain warned. Her legs paid no attention to the old cliché, where there's a will, there's a way. There was no way willpower could heave her to her feet.

Michael kicked the floor and grunted like a four-year-old having a major tantrum. A vein jumped in his temple, and his eyes pled with her. Through her lashes, Quinn watched Rex watch her. Dammit. He knew she couldn't resist the bait he'd thrown her. The only way she'd know if Pierce was hurt—or dead—was to see for herself. Michael had to wait.

Head down, staying wide of Michael's flailing feet, Quinn crawled toward the far wall. A sweet, metallic smell hung in the air. Her heart jammed in her throat. She rounded the corner of the bed and tasted salt. She put her hands over her mouth. Her stomach bucked.

"Alas," Rex sighed. "Beauty is only skin deep, right, Mike?"

Pierce lay on his back, his arms wide. Purple and red bruises tattooed both eyes—which were swelled shut. A flap of skin dangled from his right cheek. His bottom lip looked like a wet, black caterpillar.

"Mike swears you don't faint at the sight of blood," Rex said.

Her stomach rolled. The skin on her arms and neck was clammy, and her fingers felt as useable as fresh sausages. "I don't faint. Period."

"Blood gives a nice sheen to black hair, don't you think?" Rex ran his stubby fingers through his yellow crewcut.

Quinn swallowed her nausea. "His nose looks broken,"

"You should see the other guy."

Warm air chilled her neck. Heart lurching, she whipped around.

Rex leaned over her shoulder. "Our Pierce looks like he didn't survive the train wreck."

"What's wrong with him?" The question clanged in her ears, too loud, too tinny.

"I'd say a concussion."

"Why'd you hurt him?" Pierce's harsh breathing constricted the air in Quinn's lungs.

Rex clicked his tongue. "Something bad happens and the ugly guy's always it. Is that your logic, Quinn?"

"You hate him," she flared, terrified to touch Pierce.

"Right." Rex moved the little silver handgun up and down. "I forgot."

"He needs a doctor."

"You think?" Rex pursed his lips.

"If he dies—"

"Boo hoo, boo hoo." Rex wiped away an invisible tear and threw Quinn a ghoulish grin. "Not to worry. Pretty faces are a dime a dozen. In some cases, several dimes."

"You signed on to BOTN and got a shock, right?"

"Not a shock. A surprise." He parroted Pierce's speech pattern with near perfection.

"Once you killed Tony—"

"Hard to do when I was *amusing* your hoity-toity friends into the wee hours. Brittany alibied me to the cops."

Michael made choking noises.

"Goddammit." Rex spun around and held his arms straight in front of him—probably the way he'd seen on TV—both hands wrapped around the gun's butt.

Quinn squeaked once—a tiny, pitiful sound.

Waving the gun, Rex looked over his shoulder.

Sweat dripped off her eyebrows, but she widened her eyes. Wide eyes failed to divert him, and despair dropped like a boulder in her stomach. What now?

She crabbed a couple of feet after him. "Who besides Brittany gave you an alibi?"

"Wanna bet, Michael, the next question is *where* did you entertain the friends?" Rex leaned over Michael's shoulder. "Could be a toss-up. Maybe it's how long did you entertain them?"

Suddenly, from under the cream-colored bedspread, a tiny razor whipped out, slicing Quinn's thigh. She gasped, but a soft groan from Pierce sent her scrabbling backwards, dismissing ridiculous concerns about rabies.

"What's wrong, Michael? Are you pouty 'cuz Big Sis has forgotten ya?"

"Stop saying that." Quinn found Pierce's thready pulse. "I thought you were his friend."

Rex cackled. "Who says we're not best buds? Who says I wouldn't do anything for my ole bud Mike?"

In the middle of his bluster, Rex laid the gun on Michael's jaw, stared at Quinn, taunted, "Didn't I trek into the mother of all storms to save my ole bud's ass?"

"They could make a TV movie based on your odyssey." Quinn held his gaze and oozed sincerity. Had she imagined Pierce's groan?

"Damn right." Rex nodded. "Hear that, Mike, ole bud, ole bud?"

Silently, Quinn begged Michael to nod. He squeezed his eyes shut and bobbed his head. Pierce lay absolutely still. Floyd peeped from under the bedspread.

"How's that for an endorsement?" Rex crowed and pranced toward Quinn.

The big orange and white head disappeared.

"A ringing endorsement." Her obvious phoniness terrified her he'd become suspicious.

"Careful now," Rex towered over her. "That comment teeters on sarcasm."

Quinn swallowed, speaking slowly. "I'm tired. But I meant what I said."

"Well, Missy, being nosy does take a lot of energy." Mimicking John Wayne in speech and action, Rex twirled the gun on the end of his finger.

Her heart slammed into her rib cage. "Stop that!"

"Not to worry. I've got a license. Plus, I'm a damn

good marksman. One of my many unappreciated talents."

A whisper of sound raised her scalp and froze her vocal cords. The flattery she'd intended to lay on him clogged her throat. God, she should've told Pierce how much she loved him. Wanted to marry him... Grow old with him.

Rex cocked a hand behind his ear. "Hark, methinks Sleeping Handsome wakens."

Quinn whipped around to check. "He needs a doctor."

She caught the tiniest ripple of the bedspread out of the corner of her eye a breath before Rex sauntered closer.

"Poke him." Rex stood on tiptoe, looking over Quinn's head. "He's playing possum."

Floyd, hissing, claws curled, scraped Rex's exposed ankle.

"Jesus!" Rex kicked sideways.

The next flash of claw was accompanied by a hair-raising yowl.

Rex backtracked, hopping from one foot to the other.

Floyd stuck his head from under the spread, bared his incisors and streaked between Rex's legs.

Stars gyrated behind Quinn's eyelids.

Maybe her rep as a hard head was overrated. She'd never had a gun bounce off the top of her skull. Unlike feisty female cops on TV, she didn't leap instantly to her feet.

On the other hand, neither did Rex.

Writhing and punching and screaming failed to dislodge twenty pounds of feline fur and fang. Floyd clung to Rex's neck with the ferocity of a mountain lion crossed with a Rottweiler.

Dazed, Quinn squinted. Nothing came into focus. Panic snaked down her spine. Where the hell was the gun?

Across the room, Michael went nuts. Neck muscles bulged as he screamed into his gag. He kicked his feet, bucked his body, jerked his head up and down.

The gun's barrel protruded from under the bedspread.

Quinn telegraphed Michael she understood. She saw the gun—and almost wished she didn't. She'd never seen a real gun until half an hour ago. Dummy that she was, she'd expected to live her whole life without seeing or touching one.

Michael stamped his feet—a non-verbal command. *Pick up the gun.*

Easy for him to say...tied up like a Thanksgiving turkey. She wobbled up on all fours. The room whirled. Her stomach dropped. She swallowed, glanced over her shoulder, froze.

Rex's screams had died to whimpers. His fetal position brought little relief from Floyd's full-fanged assault. Strangled screams from Michael demanded her attention. She crawled toward the bed.

If she watched more TV, she'd know how to pick up the damned gun. How to handle it.

Muscles and nerves trembled. Fear spread through her like a mutant virus. A little stretch—two, three inches at most—and her fingertips could graze the gun's barrel. Her heart stopped. She'd rather kiss a snake than touch that cold metal.

What about Pierce?

Would she rather let him die than pick up the damn gun? He'd never know she loved him and wanted to marry him.

Shaking all over, she formed pinchers with her thumb and forefinger and dragged the gun by its barrel from under the bed. Michael bucked his chair across the thick carpet. She picked up the gun by the butt and faced Rex.

Before she got the feel of the handle, he rolled onto his back. Floyd clung to his arm. Rex screeched and hammered a fist down on the old cat's head.

Quinn screamed. Floyd dropped to the floor. He lay unmoving. Eyes closed. Chest still.

"Bastard." Tears stung Quinn's eyelids. She gripped the gun, felt for the trigger and let her gaze stray for half a nanosecond to the motionless cat.

In that fraction of a moment, Rex's foot shot into the air. The toe of his shoe connected with her wrist, then smashed into her calf. The gun flew out of her hand. Her knees crumpled. She collapsed on top of the weapon. The barrel stabbed her ribs like a stake.

Rex piled on her back—bleeding and sobbing and swearing—a parasite determined to survive. He pummeled her spine and ribs with wild, frenzied blows.

She chewed her bottom lip. Tried to breathe. Couldn't. Her ears felt ready to explode. Rex pounded her. "Don't you know...a *gentleman* never...hits a lady?"

"Bitch." His voice thickened with tears. "You're like all the rest, bitch."

The ultra-thick carpet was smothering her. She risked a concussion and turned her face sideways, whispering, "Bitch is politically incorrect, you know."

Then, she tried to buck him off her back.

Her attempt earned her a harder rib-jab and a smack to the back of her head. She sucked in air, but tears rolled down her cheeks. The carpet swam in and out of focus.

Unconsciousness...one more head blow away. She bucked again.

"Give it up." Rex cuffed her on the temple for a little variety.

"...can't breathe." She huffed, her ears roaring.

"Poor baby." He wiggled a hand under her chest in search of the gun.

"Shiiit." She bit back a shriek.

His fingers were like having a snake crawl down her blouse. Years of yoga came back. She stopped fighting, balanced on her left wrist and raised her neck and shoulders in a modified salute to the sun.

The movements distracted him enough he pulled his hand out from under her. She whipped her head out of range of his open palm. Somehow, she grabbed his little finger between her teeth. He screamed. She bit down. Bones crunched.

He rolled off her back, moaning, "Oh my God. OmyGod. Oh. My. God."

He rocked back and forth, his finger in his mouth. Michael made noises and kicked his heels. Warning her, she supposed. A broken finger wouldn't stop Rex now. He had to have the gun. To get it, he'd kill her and Pierce and his best friend.

Sweat spurted off her. She groaned and made another tripod. Her ribs felt like burning fuses. Michael banged his chair like a wild man against the side of the bed.

"Give...a...minute," she gasped.

A minute wasn't nearly enough time to refine the plan. The basics emerged clear and rational. Retrieve the gun. Untie Michael.

The details didn't quite come together in Quinn's aching head. A mental movie unwound. She saw Michael call the police while he kept Rex in line with the gun. She took care of Pierce. The most important part of the movie was more nebulous.

How could she untie Michael and hold the gun and guard Rex?

Sucking his mangled finger didn't fool her any more than his hair-raising howls. Instinct warned her he'd spring on the gun the instant she lifted her body off it. If she moved her limbs and upper body any slower, they'd all die from old age. Her mind sorted and prioritized.

Call an ambulance and the police. Take care of Pierce and Floyd. Don't take her eyes off Michael and Rex.

The cat's lifeless body brought a sting of tears. Michael yelled incoherently into his gag, his face an unhealthy purple. Quinn inhaled and pushed upward. Rex halted his hysterics and watched. Watched her weak wrist collapse. Watched her slump back to the floor.

Then Pierce moaned.

Her heart yo-yoed. *God, what if he's choking?*

Muscle-memory from yoga ignited. Slowly, slowly, slowly, she lifted her hips. Her fingers closed around the gun butt, then around the trigger. Rex slithered sideways like a snake. Sweat soaked her clothes, threatened to blind her, slicked her fingers, but she pulled the gun from under her trembling body and pointed it at Rex's heart.

Her wrist shook, terrifying her she'd drop the gun. She whispered, "Don't. Move."

Rex cringed. "You're making a big mistake."

"A line from the soaps?" In her mind, she measured the distance to Michael's chair.

Understanding flashed in her brother's penetrating gaze. He frowned, dug his heels into the carpet and pulled his chair toward her like a mutant snail.

"You don't understand." Rex sounded like a small, scolded boy trying to make his mother feel guilty for his punishment.

"On your stomach." Quinn tracked Michael's progress out of the corner of her eye.

"You should listen—"

"On. Your. Stomach." She pointed the gun barrel at a spot on the floor. "Slide under the bed."

"Are you nuts?" He eased down on one elbow.

"Bingo. Slide under all the way."

Propped on his elbow, he said, "Your hand's too weak to pull the trigger."

"Maybe." A million hot needles stung her wrist. He kicked harder than a kangaroo. "But I'm pretty sure Michael's feet aren't too weak to stomp the shit out of you."

Grunts and muffled roars reinforced her assertion. Rex's mouth twisted. He must've realized she'd shoot him. He wedged an arm and leg under the bed.

"I can't go all the way." His voice rose in a poor-me whine.

"Of course not. Not a hulk like you." Quinn motioned Michael to turn his chair so she could reach him easier.

"Get your head under there, and turn your face the other way. It makes me sick." Fool that she was, she felt a jab of guilt speaking this truth.

Another groan from Pierce.

Her heart lurched. "Hurry."

Fire burned under her ribs. She bit down on her bottom lip and curled her fingers around the back of Michael's chair. Her calves and thighs shuddered, but she rose to her knees. The effort froze the air in her lungs. She swayed like a drunk. Behind her, Rex giggled. The sound snapped in her brain like an over-stressed rubber-band. Rage steadied her. She yanked the gag off Michael's mouth, nearly decapitating him. His ragged gulps echoed her own labored breathing.

"Don't talk, okay?"

Eyes glittery, he nodded, then croaked, "You're toast, Rex."

His wrists were a violent red, the skin raw and bloody from rope burn. Every time Quinn touched the knots, he flinched. Even supported by the chair, her whole body shook from staying on her knees. Her fingers fumbled at the Gordian knots Rex had woven.

"Pull the rope over one thumb," Michael ordered.

"Who knows what evil lurks in the hearts of men?" With the right side of his body under the bed, Rex slapped his left hand on the carpet, then imitated the spine-tingling laugh of The Shadow. She and Michael had listened to tapes of the old radio program for hours.

"Shut up," Michael said, his voice low, disquieting.

"Maybe I will, maybe I won't." Rex threw Michael's own voice back at him.

She tugged at the ropes and shivered. Rex's voice

switches came one after the other, sounding eerily natural. Attempts to keep up with each of his personality changes frayed Quinn's nerve-endings.

"Sit still," she hissed at Michael. "This is hard enough."

"Quinn..."

Her stomach flip-flopped. Her fingers shook so hard she stopped pulling at the ropes. "That's Pierce. I need—"

"You need to get me untied." Michael jerked his head around. His face was stone. His eyes looked right through Quinn.

"Need me to help the poor baby?" Rex asked.

The skin at the back of Quinn's neck crawled. The image of Rex touching Pierce revolted her. She said, "You need to stay exactly where you are."

"Quin-n-n-n?"

Her heart fired too fast, making her lightheaded. "I'm coming, Pierce."

"Sounds like a dying man if I ever heard one," Rex said.

She whipped around and nearly lost her balance. The gun banged against the back of Michael's chair. "Shut up."

"Don't drop the damn gun." The sharp menace in Michael's command dropped like a rock in her belly.

"Oh, no. Don't drop the damn gun." Rex sounded so much like Michael that another shiver shook Quinn.

"You can't take care of Pierce and police Rex." The easy rhythm of Michael's voice modulated his tone, capturing the essence of his old self. Confident. Logical. Familiar.

"Oh, Mike, you sly, sly, sly dog."

"Go to hell, Rex."

"Been there, Mikey, done that."

The last knot refused to give under Quinn's stiff fingers. Something in Rex's taunting Michael triggered a barrage of questions in her brain. What if Pierce hadn't called her name when she arrived because he'd been unconscious? What if she had her priorities all wrong? What if untying Michael put Pierce's life in jeopardy?

The acrid smell of her own fear engulfed her, numbing her fingers, her muscles, her brain. Panic clawed at her stomach. Pierce. He needed her. Now. She couldn't rescue him and Michael at the same time. For a moment, Quinn felt as if she'd stepped off the roof of a twenty-story building.

Michael said, "You're doing great, Quinn."

Uh-huh. She twisted the ropes. Monkeys used their opposable thumbs more efficiently than she ever would. Despite the faux encouragement in Michael's voice— intended to dupe Rex into thinking she was adept at untying knots?—she was too clumsy. Too worried about Pierce.

Let Michael get free on his own. She tapped his shoulder, ignored his scowl and mimed the rope sliding over his right hand.

Lying through her teeth, she announced heartily, "There! You're free."

Her kid brother knew her well enough to follow her lead. "Check on Pierce. Give me the gun."

"Might wanna rethink who holds the gun." Rex inched further under the bed.

At a loss where to put the thing, Quinn laid it in Michael's lap. "Better flex your fingers a couple of times first. We don't want any accidents."

Under the circumstances, she was surprised she could utter words.

She mouthed, "Be careful," and crabbed away from Michael's chair.

Tears blinded her as she passed by Floyd. Focus on Pierce. Nothing else. Just Pierce. *Hold on. I love you. I love you. Please let me tell you.*

Terrified, she rounded the corner of the bed and checked over her shoulder.

Michael flexed his fingers and shot his free hand in the air.

"Yessss!" For a heartbeat, Quinn sagged with relief.

Chapter 22

"Pierce? Pierce, I love you." Quinn's voice sounded so much like an angel, Pierce thought he'd died and gone to heaven.

The drum corps in his head stopped practicing. He drifted into blessed silence on a cloud of Quinn's rose scent. He held out his hand, but could raise only one finger. One eye was completely swelled shut. The other let him see shadows and movement, but not her face. He wanted to tell her he was okay, but his throat hurt too much. Something haywire between his brain and fingertips. He couldn't even squeeze her fingers to signal...

"You need a doctor." Her tears slithered down his cheek, pooled in his right ear and gave him hope. He was conscious.

"Don't even think about moving, Rex."

Michael's terse command came from another planet, but Pierce groaned.

"Shhhh." Quinn touched the side of his head that didn't feel like raw meat. "Michael has a gun."

Rex whimpered. "I need a doctor too."

"Go to the back of the line," Michael said.

Pierce clenched his jaw and thought an invisible floor sander had scraped the back of his throat. The need to tell Quinn something kept him from passing out.

"Don't move," she ordered in a breathy rush. "You may have a concussion."

The drum corps started practice again, and Pierce felt his head separate from his body. God, tell her...something...important. A small dot of white light slammed into his head.

Pierce heard the sharp intake of Quinn's breath as she examined the marks on his throat. "Everything under control, Michael?"

"Nothing to control," Rex said. "I'm hardly breathing."

"What do you need, Sis?"

"Call 9-1-1."

Pierce still couldn't squeeze her little finger.

"Got it. You stay with Pierce."

"You're sure you can manage?" Pierce heard her reluctance to leave him.

"He can manage the whole damn world with the gun," Rex hollered.

Air in Pierce's lungs ran out. Quinn faded in and out of his line of vision. The pinpoint of light flashed again. *Careful, careful*, he gurgled.

****

The explosion boomed like a freight train derailing.

Stunned, Quinn fell across Pierce. The mewing sound he made terrified her, but there wasn't time to examine him for additional injuries. She remained with her arms and legs splayed in four directions, shielding most of his vital body parts. Her heart drummed high in her chest. Any second, she expected a chunk of ceiling to brain her.

"Don't move," she whispered to Pierce.

"Quinn?" Michael's wail turned her stomach

upside down.

Pierce emitted low, guttural noises. She scrambled off him, but realized she couldn't stand. Salt flooded the back of her throat. A hot, metallic stench suffocated her. Slowly, she raised her head up over the edge of the king-sized bed.

Opposite her, Michael turned the gun over and over. He spoke to it instead of to Quinn. "He grabbed my ankle. When I started for the phone..."

"Is he..." Quinn's throat jammed.

"Why'd he grab my ankle? I told him we'd work everything out..."

"Call 9-1-1." Quinn thought she'd never sounded so calm.

She didn't trust Michael.

She didn't trust herself either.

One or both of them was going to throw up if they had to wade through the sea of Rex's blood to reach the phone. Or, if they didn't stop staring at the gaping hole in his chest.

Sweat beaded her brother's forehead. A green cast tinged his five o'clock shadow and made him paler than Pierce. She swiped at the droplets rolling off her own eyebrows. Michael's blue eyes glittered feverishly. She blinked rapidly.

The body at their feet didn't disappear.

"Lay the gun down, Michael." She gave the order a sing-song tenderness.

His gaze swiveled to hers, then back to his hand movements. Her tongue felt gargantuan in her hot, dry mouth. If he kept turning the gun over and over, he might shoot himself in the foot. Or accidentally shoot her.

She took a baby step. "I have to call an ambulance."

He flinched. The tempo of the gun-twirling sped up.

Heart drumming, mind racing, Quinn froze. "Pierce needs a doctor."

No mention of Rex. They'd played the let's-pretend game for years. Pretend Daddy hadn't left them. Pretend he'd taken a trip. Pretend he'd come home someday. Pretend everything would be the way it was before he left.

Cloud Nine dipped, and Quinn gave herself a hard mental shake. She held out her hand, pitching her voice to the big-sister tone she'd used with him forever. "I'll take care of everything, Michael."

The old magic worked, but it took a little longer. After what felt like a century, Michael handed her the gun and said, "Luce..."

"After I call 9-1-1, okay?"

****

"Your brother needs a lawyer." Detective Ryder touched Quinn's shoulder, drawing her away from the paramedics loading Pierce onto a gurney.

Her brain buzzed. "For self-defense?"

"Without a lawyer, it could come down to voluntary manslaughter."

"But-but..." Quinn sputtered, her stomach on fire. She was going with Pierce.

Pierce's critical condition justified forgetting about Michael. The paramedics suspected a deep contusion to Pierce's brain and laceration of his jugular vein. The chaos of dozens of police and crime-scene worker bees drowned out every thought except one. So far, she was doing a crappy job of taking care of Pierce and a lousy job looking after Michael.

"Hey," someone yelled, "this cat's breathing."

"We're outta here," the tallest paramedic yelled.

"I'll take care of the cat." Ryder pressed a cell phone at Quinn. "Call a lawyer from the ambulance."

****

"To pace or not to pace, that is the question." As the only occupant in St. Luke's surgical waiting room at 11:40 A.M., Quinn hugged her ribs and tried to take a breath deep enough to blast her brain with oxygen.

The shallowest intake made her rethink that strategy. Fire spurted into her ribs hurt. Especially when she sat. Or stood. Or moved. Or thought about moving.

Sympathy pains for Pierce. Had he heard her repeatedly declare her love?

A glance at the clock told her he'd been in surgery less than twenty minutes.

"Ten hours minimum," the neurosurgeon had told her. "Probably twelve."

He'd also suggested she call someone to keep her company. "About three, three-thirty, you'll be climbing the walls," Dr. Delgado said over his shoulder.

Michael was the logical person to hold her hand. But her brother had his own troubles. Images of him stamping out license plates looped in slow motion through her mind. A deep breath zapped the reruns. Despite the searing pain, she felt calmer. During the eleven-minute ambulance ride, she'd called Nikki Dawson, legal counsel for Alexander and Associates.

Nikki, like hordes of other shopaholics, was Christmas shopping on The Plaza. But she answered her cell and became all business once Quinn stated why she needed a criminal attorney. She immediately recommended her husband—at home with the kids.

Hope had fluttered in Quinn's chest. "They took Michael to the Brookside station."

****

Detective Ryder danced into the waiting room with canary feathers dropping from his mouth. He brought with him the scent of cinnamon, triggering for Quinn memories of Thanksgivings past—apple crisp, pumpkin pie and mulled cider—superimposed by flashes of their oh-so-recent-garage-encounter.

"Good news. Your old cat's gonna live. I'd say he's a whole lot better 'n you."

"I'm fine." Her knees shook, and her pulse wobbled. Remembering her ribs, she hugged her waist. *Pierce will be fine too. He has to be fine. He's as tough as Floyd.* "That's not good news," she shouted. "It's wonderful news."

Ryder jumped back, clapping his hands over his ears. The feather flurries slowed to a dribble.

Quinn's heart thumped. Cold all over, she eyed him. "Is this a good-news, bad-news scenario? Is there a problem about Michael?"

God, she'd forgotten him. "Did his lawyer show up? Where is he?"

Ryder held his hands up like a traffic cop, performed one of his dry-land double-axles, and moved closer. "Slow down. I know it's been a tough day. That's why I thought you could use the news about the cat."

The hollow in her chest contracted, painfully squeezing her heart and lungs. But the tiny invisible antennae behind her ears shot up like periscopes. They caught his real message before her mind nailed what he was doing.

Her breath hitched and certainty built. He was playing cat and mouse. Exactly the way he'd dropped hints in the garage. Teasing. Taunting. Daring her to take his bait.

Except she didn't know what he was dangling in front of her.

"You haven't answered me." Terse, low and pissy.

"Because you won't like what I have to tell you."

****

Dr. Roberto Delgado slipped into the waiting room at 3:28. His mask swung like a little green basket around his neck. Quinn still felt overwhelmed by Ryder's pessimism about the possible charges against Michael. She stood numb and mindless, trying to get the surgeon to come into sharper focus. He flexed thin, square fingers. Dread crawled along her arms.

"Pierce?" Images exploded of him in the ambulance—too white, barely breathing, but probably able to hear her descriptions of their wedding according to the EMT.

"Eight, maybe ten more hours." Dr. Delgado tilted his head to one side and massaged his neck. "His condition's more critical than we thought."

"Will I be able to see him tonight?" The cold, antiseptic smell of alcohol, kindled a spark of hope. "Just for a minute. I need to tell him something. Something important."

"We'll chat after surgery." The doctor straightened, sidled past Quinn, then sprinted through the door without looking back.

"Ask me if he excelled in Bedside Manners 101."

She turned to Ryder for confirmation.

The scent of cinnamon hung heavy as incense, but her angel of mixed tidings had left without a good-bye. Surprisingly, he'd left her laptop on an easy chair. She stared at the chair as if it held a bomb. In the chaos of rushing Pierce to the hospital, she'd forgotten leaving the computer in his kitchen. How had Ryder noticed?

Undercover narcotic cops probably notice everything,. She frowned and tapped the cover on the laptop a couple of times. Why had an undercover narcotics cop shown up at a murder investigation anyway? Narcotics cops played no part in the choreography of protecting the crime scene. Homicide interviewed Michael. She'd climbed into the ambulance without mentioning her cybersleuthing.

So, why had Ryder responded to the 9-1-1 call? She dug her cell phone out of her coat pocket. Cop or not, she didn't trust him. Not after his stunt in the parking garage. As the BOTN main screen came up, she balanced the phone between her ear and shoulder and dialed Michael. She keyed in *Phantom* and *opera* with the concentration of a bomb-maker.

"You've reached voice mail..."

"Damn." What if Luce went into labor before the police finished their questions?

Thoughts of Luce re-fired a question that had nagged Quinn the moment she'd entered Pierce's bedroom. What was Michael doing in Kansas City?

Something to do with Rex no doubt, but what?

If Michael hadn't pulled that trigger—

Without warning, a slow-motion video of the dead man unwound. Quinn blinked, but a close-up frame filled with blood, drew her again and again to the crimson pool like a shark. She shook away the memory, dialed Pierce's house, keyed in *m-a-s-k*, the password for "Unnumbered Accounts in Latin America."

The screen flashed. She leaned closer, and an invisible knife slipped between her ribs. She didn't recognize the clipped voice on the phone. She identified herself, asked for Detective Smith and bit back a childish scream when she was put on hold.

Calm down. Use the time...She scanned the computer screen. Whatever happened to user-friendly interfaces? Were all the BOTN users geeks? The design of BOTN flaunted accepted programming conventions and ignored common user practices. Her first search sent her down a cyberhole. A second attempt wound through so many levels she lost track of her location. She finally ended up back at the main menu rehearsing her first words to Pierce.

"Give it up, Sherlock." Pain from her ribs radiated up her back, into her skull.

Whatever Tony had found that allowed him to frame Rex eluded her. So did hard facts proving Tony had embezzled the money. Both men were dead. Pierce faced months of recovery—maybe even memory loss. What if the truth never came out?

Her heart hammered. Michael would have a new baby and a new job. He wouldn't have a free minute—certainly no time to clear Rex's name, though she felt sure he'd try.

Pain ratcheted up behind Quinn's eyes. She blinked and stared at the ceiling. She'd talk to Michael. Make sure he didn't go into a funk. Damn, what a mess.

Worse than a mess for Pierce—hurt so bad he might not know she loved him.

Detective Smith came on the phone. "Your brother left about two minutes ago."

Quinn closed her eyes and covered her mouth. Her heart yo-yoed, but caution uncoiled in her queasy stomach. "Does that mean—is he a free man?"

"We don't usually send guilty men home."

"Of course not." Tears thickened her voice.

Of course not, because the police should give Michael a medal. Two medals, she amended. One for her life, one for Pierce's. An adrenaline jolt brought the tears. Tears of joy and hope and pride. Her brother, the hero.

She repeated the phrase in her head once more, but couldn't drown out two louder questions. Why had Ryder been so negative? What did he know?

Enough to warn her Michael needed a lawyer.

Quinn tasted copper. Laughing and crying at the same time, she swiped at her eyes and dialed. When Michael didn't pick up, her heart dropped. She said, "Call me, Baby Bro. I'm at St. Luke's. Pierce is in surgery." Her voice cracked. She recovered, adding, "Love to Luce. I hope this time tomorrow you and she are holding the newest Alexander."

Unstoppable tears streaked down her cheeks. She bit down hard on her bottom lip. She clicked the phone's OFF button. She would not ruin her brother's happiness by spilling her worst fears. Pierce might never recover his full memory. She squeezed her eyes shut, reveling in scenes of Michael and Luce—first with a pink bundle, then a blue one. The ache in her ribs blurred more details.

Determined to hold onto the fantasy, she set the laptop aside and lurched toward the hall. Two steps and she became seven years old pushing an imaginary baby carriage. How many times had she and Michael pushed her favorite doll around their cul-de-sac? Mommy, Daddy and Baby. Her stomach plummeted and she stumbled. Daddy. How many times had she dreamed of putting her very own wiggly, black Cocker Spaniel puppy in the same carriage?

The imaginary baby carriage disappeared. Quinn hugged her waist and hobbled back to her coat. A part of her knew she teetered on the cusp of hysteria. The trembling in her arms worsened as she tore the envelope out of her coat pocket. Her brain gyrated like clothes in a dryer. Her throat muscles refused to swallow. She collapsed into a nearby chair and focused on the block printing. Her lungs pumped oxygen into her brain. She sniffed the expensive paper.

Only one way to know for sure. Her hands barely shook as she ripped the single, folded sheet out of the envelope.

Seeing was believing. The next to the last line jumped off the page.

He never loved you, Sarah Quinn.

"Sarah Quinn." Her ears rang.

In her mind, she saw a row of dominoes toppling.

****

Quinn shuffled to the restroom like a long-dead corpse. She splashed cold water on her face. When she lost feeling in her fingers, she stood and dried her face with a paper towel. She avoided her reflection. The skin on her whole body felt as if it had shrunk on her bones. She swished her mouth out twice, but couldn't wash away the metallic taste of fear.

The fear expanded and contracted in shorter and

shorter cycles. Her pulse hammered as she picked up one foot, then the other, lurching toward the ICU waiting room. The hall was deserted. The nurses remained behind closed doors. No one could see her from inside the unit. The perfect setting...

Her legs quaked. The truth about who wrote the note convulsed in her stomach as if she'd taken a vicious punch. She laid her clammy hands against the cold metal bar on the waiting room door.

Now or never. She pushed the bar, charged inside and faced the nightmare she'd denied for too long.

Sitting on top of her coat, Michael held her laptop on his knees. The corner of a white envelope was visible in his shirt pocket.

Chapter 23

Hope ruptured inside Quinn like a toxic balloon. She licked her lips. "Why didn't you return my calls?"

Michael's head snapped up from the computer screen, and he scrubbed his red-rimmed eyes. "I don't call you every time I get a hangnail, Sarah Quinn."

"Murder's not a hangnail."

"I should never have called you on Monday."

"You should've called me eight months ago."

His laugh raised several generations of goose bumps on her arms. "So you figured out the bank gave me the axe."

Disbelief choked Quinn. "I swallowed your Federal Reserve story like a fish swallows bait." Her heart felt as if she'd swallowed a rusty hook. "I can't believe you haven't had a job for almost a year."

"I've had a job." His gunmetal eyes flashed contempt. "Leaving all those cyber-clues pointing to Rex was hard work."

She winced and stared, clenching her jaw. Did he want applause? "Why didn't you get a real job?"

"Try being married to Luce and see what kind of real job you need. Take my word. The woman spends money like the golden goose lives with us." He swiped a hand under his crimson nose.

Quinn made an umpire's time-out sign. "I'd have helped—"

"Newsflash, Sarah Quinn. I am your baby bro, but you can't always help me." He scrolled down a page, glanced at her, clicked the mouse with lightning speed. "Besides, crime pays. Selling coke, you don't have to worry about stock options that aren't worth the paper they're printed on."

Her vocal cords tightened, but she whispered, "What about going to prison?"

"I'm not going to prison." He slammed the laptop shut.

Her shoulders snapped back. "Won't Patagonia feel like prison without friends or family?"

"Ta-daaah!" He pounded imaginary piano keys on top of the closed laptop and flashed a ghastly grin. "Cybersleuth Quinn Alexander found the bank account in Argentina."

"It wasn't so hard once I figured out—"

"Bet you didn't know Bariloche's called the Switzerland of South America."

"I know you used Daddy's name on your unnumbered account."

"Another bingo for my favorite cybersleuth."

She felt like shaking him—except she doubted she could shake him long enough to get his attention. She wasn't sure she could even touch him. "Daddy's name with your social security number makes me wonder if you want to be caught."

His bark of laughter gave her the willies. "Wonder no more. I see skiing every day in my future."

"How about throwing snowballs?" She didn't wait for an answer as the night on the golf course unwound in her head. "You could've killed Pierce."

"Boo hoo. I should've cut him off at the knees

before you got in his car. Right up until you and the bastard sucked face, I thought you might help me."

"Where was Tony while you were zooming around in his Jeep?" Quinn took a long shot—one that felt like shooting at the moon with a dart.

"Tied up in the back of the Jeep. Right behind me." Michael set the laptop on the floor. "I never planned on killing him."

Her heart stopped.

"I had to kill him," Michael said, his voice reasonable, untinged by remorse.

"Sounds like the only rational solution." She dabbed her eyes.

"Tony was like you—a Goddamned bloodhound. He saw right through the system clues and cookies I left in BOTN. Took him awhile, but he figured out I'd made Rex the scapegoat."

"How?"

"Like you did. Dumb luck, mostly. He sniffed and searched and poked around until he found a trap door I forgot. By Monday morning, he was breathing down my back—ready to tell Pierce he'd made a mistake about Rex."

"What makes you think so?"

"A letter. I routinely hacked into Tony's files. Which he did not suspect."

His bragging tone taunted Quinn, but she let it go for the moment. She had to understand. "A letter to—?"

"To a big KC law firm. Tony was so worried about His Pierceness. Afraid Rex might sue once the truth came out that yours truly had been having a little fun."

"Rex wasn't in on the scam?" Quinn massaged a spot under her left breast.

"Not until he got pierced. Then, he started poking around. Found enough interesting stuff he demanded a meeting. Didn't give a damn about snowstorms or that Luce was losing it."

Dozens of questions danced in Quinn's head, but she only wanted to know about Tony. "Why—"

Talking more to himself than to her, Michael continued. "Rex had his uses. Like imitating Tony in that call to His Pierceness." In a dreamy voice she recognized from their childhood, Michael said, "Of all people, my ole bud should've known better than to threaten me."

Her scalp prickled. Message received, but she didn't understand. She said, "What time did you leave St. Louis the day you kidnaped Tony?"

"Three A.M. One of the many blessings of coke— you don't need sleep."

"Coke?" Quinn repeated the word like a moron.

He laughed. "Now I've shocked you, huh?"

Another piece of the puzzle dropped on her like a lead pipe. Ryder hadn't waited in the garage for Tony. He'd waited for Quinn—figuring the love of coke ran in the family?

"Don't look so cow-eyed stupid, Big Sis. Everybody uses."

"I don't. Mom doesn't." She jutted her chin at him.

"No, you and Mom are too cool for school."

"Cool enough to know you're crazy to use that stuff."

"I use that stuff so I won't lose my mind. It's not like I'm an addict."

"Of course not. How many people would you've killed if you were too cool for school?"

He wagged a finger. "Watch the sarcasm. For the record, I saved Pierce's neck. Rex had every intention of killing him."

Whether it was the casual tone or her wobbly knees or something she couldn't fathom, Quinn couldn't move. Her brain simply couldn't wrap around the disconnect between the man she'd known as her brother and the murderer sneering at her denseness.

"Did you come here to kill me?" Time slowed. He avoided her gaze, and she took hope when he didn't answer right away. She loved him. He loved her. They'd sworn an oath...

His mouth curled. "I don't know."

Shaken by memories of them gazing at the stars, giving voice to their childish hopes that Daddy would return, swearing eternal loyalty to each other, Quinn said, "Why don't you know?"

As if taking pity on her, he shrugged. "You thought I'd say no, didn't you?"

Unshed tears choked her. "Silly me."

"What about me? You gonna turn me in?"

"What other choice do I have?" Every breath she took hurt her ribs. Dammit, she should've taken the Vicodin they'd offered her in ER.

"Let me leave. You know I've already bought my one-way ticket to Buenos Aires. You and Pierce paid off the bank. I'm off the hook for Rex. The cops won't figure out for a while who killed Tony." He turned his palms up. "Looks like a happy ending to me."

Each sentence hit Quinn between the eyes like a jackhammer. "What about—what about Baby Quinn?" *What about Pierce? What if he doesn't know I love him?*

Michael shook his head, then focused on the ceiling. "Honest to Christ."

"You wouldn't abandon your unborn baby?"

"Duh." He ground his forefinger against his temple. "Leave the country, go to prison. Either way, my kid never knows me."

"Luce could bring the baby—"

"Hold it." Michael formed a camera with his fingers. "Let me get a clearer shot of this—Luce coming for conjugal visits with the wee bonnie babe."

Heat stung Quinn's cheeks, and she wished she'd kept her mouth shut. He didn't seem to notice. Or care.

He said, "Luce's already figured out that, thanks to our old man, I'm genetically unfit for raising kids." The stranger set the imaginary camera aside. "Too bad she didn't figure it out nine months ago. She got damned huffy when I suggested an abortion."

"Imagine that." Quinn's stomach rolled. "I don't buy your bad-gene theory. Daddy wasn't a bad man, and you weren't always like this."

Grinning like a caricature of the brother she'd known, he winked. "You mean I didn't tear wings off flies or torture animals or build bombs in the basement—so I must've been normal?"

"That about covers it."

His gaze—flat and cold—locked with hers. "Believe it or not, I've always been a little bent. Two guesses why I hung with Rex—and compassion isn't one."

When Quinn just stared at him, Michael sighed a my-stupid-sister sigh. "Scapegoats serve useful functions, you know."

"That's sick."

"Huh-uh. Honest. It was a game Rex and I played all the time. Getting any attention beats getting no attention. He loved it—right up to the end."

"Right up until you shot him?"

"He didn't like leaving any witnesses." Michael stuck his right hand deep in his coat pocket. "It was Rex or you..."

****

Two giant orange eyes glared at Quinn.

"Don't even think about it." Michael yanked on her arm and pulled her out of the snowplow's path.

She bit down on her lip. Any movement—especially quick, jerky ones—hammered her ribs, and the icy wind swirling in the parking lot knocked the breath out of her.

Michael took no notice she walked hunched over. He said, "We're not in the movies. You can't jump up on the plow and escape."

Jump up on the plow? Her ribs felt like sticks of dynamite as the hot pain swelled around them. Did he think she'd lost her mind?

A shovelful of snow topped off a nearby mound. Huge fluorescent lights turned the piles an ugly blue. Gears grinding, engine roaring, the gas-propelled dinosaur lumbered away. Quinn shielded her eyes from the stinging sleet.

"In the movies, you could push me under the blade," Michael said. "I'd end up an ice sculpture, and you'd end up a heroine."

Conserving her breath, Quinn kept her head down as he dragged her forward. Could she kill him in such a gruesome way?

Was there any way to stop him without killing

him?

Think about how he hurt Pierce.

Wind slammed them in a frontal assault. She stumbled, he jerked her upright. She cried out, but he didn't slow down. Her feet were useless.

"Why didn't you park in the garage?"

"A parking garage is like dropping a rat in a maze," he said. "Out in the open, with a hostage, I'm in the catbird seat."

Intuition found no fault in his logic, but her brain had long ago turned to ice. Michael could say he didn't intend to kill her, but if she tripped over her frozen feet, fell down, drove a rib through her lungs and died instantly, would his intentions comfort her? Would her death cause him a moment of grief?

"Dead ahead." His laugh rose to a chilling cackle. "No pun intended."

A thin blanket of snow covered the car she recognized immediately recognized. Surprise exploded under her ribcage. "Pierce's Corvette?"

"Rex coveted it." Michael held her elbow, popped the trunk, but stopped the opening with her laptop. "Get ready for a shocker."

He removed the computer. The trunk snapped up. The sparkle of earrings flashed before her mind registered Brittany's neck at an odd angle, her eyes open, a bloody slash across her forehead.

"Oh, my—"

"The earrings are fake. So was the affair with Tony—as I'm sure you've figured out." Michael tossed the laptop on the curled body. "Brittany made Rex's mistake. She thought she was more important to me than I did. In my book, sex fails to trump survival."

Salt burned Quinn's throat and her head filled with white noise distorting Michael's calm, factual report of his year-long affair with Brittany, her part in the scheme to discredit Pierce, her misguided attempt at blackmailing Michael...

The slam of the trunk lid cracked like the gunshot in Pierce's bedroom. Heart leaping, Quinn felt her legs wobble. Her body began a slow descent.

Michael yanked her upright and hauled her around to the driver's door. "Get in, slide over."

His confession of a third murder had stripped his normal bass of all traces of familiarity. Her apathy earned her a vicious shove that sent a hot knife slicing down her spine. She bit back a cry and called him sadist—half expecting a blow to the back of her head.

Instead he laughed. Terrified, she supported her ribs with both hands and scrabbled across the bucket seat, then the gear box. Something hard in her coat pocket cut through fabric and flesh and bit into bone. Between jabs and curses from Michael, she ignored her cell phone. *Conscious, stay conscious.*

He climbed behind the wheel and started the engine. "Rex wanted the 'Vette as a getaway car."

"That Rex. Always thinking ahead." Quinn rubbed her numb hands together.

"His idea of total, absolute bliss was taking you with us to South America."

"Taking me—?" Quinn squeaked like Minnie Mouse.

"C'mon." Michael grinned. "You women always know when a guy's ga-ga over you."

"Are you craz—" The nasty taste in her throat swelled. She clamped her mouth shut. If she threw up, would he shove her out of the car?

"Excuse the cliché, but I'm crazy as a fox. Rex had wet dreams about you."

The skin on her arms crawled like a snake crossing a dry rock. She dug fingernails into the top of one hand.

"Buckle up." He clicked the locks in place. "And forget those movies where the heroine jumps out of the car."

"I'm not an idiot." She snapped her seatbelt.

"Does that mean you won't grab the wheel and steer us into a tree or a snow truck?"

"Now there's an idea." She laid on the sarcasm, wanting to throw up on him until he came to his senses.

"Think Brittany. Her smart mouth put her in that trunk."

What'd she say? Quinn closed her eyes. Forget Brittany. Where were they going? Mother Nature's little tantrum must've socked in KCI—maybe airports as far east as O'Hare and as far west as Denver International.

Could coke keep Michael awake five hundred miles to Dallas?

The clack of the wipers ratcheted up the dull ache in her side to a searing, unrelenting pain. Could she take advantage of his fatigue—somehow turn the tables on him? Could she send him to prison?

God, why hadn't she told Pierce sooner she loved him?

"Hellooo." Michael spoke from a distant planet. "I hear those cerebral cogs turning, turning, turning."

Her brother the stranger. She opened her eyes. As kids they'd read each other's minds so frequently they'd amazed themselves.

"I was thinking about what happened at Pierce's."

"Nosy, nosy, nosy."

"You and Rex screwed up the plan." At this moment, she doubted she'd ever had a clue how her brother's mind worked.

"Quite a deduction, Sherlock." Michael shifted into neutral and glided to a stop. A city street department truck spewing salt lumbered into the intersection at Westport Road and Southwest Trafficway, blocking all four directions.

Slamming his fist on the steering wheel, Michael swore, then tapped her temple. "Those guys can't help you—so don't do anything stupid, because I don't have a damn thing to lose."

His accuracy about her intentions took her breath away, but she said evenly, "Mom raised us to use our heads. Which I usually do except when it comes to you."

"Can I help it if I filled that tender spot in your heart?"

"I loved you." *Please, hang on, Pierce.*

"Trusted me, too, right?"

His sarcasm twisted her insides, turned them to liquid. She switched her gaze out the misty window. Another car had drawn up next to them.

Her pulse sped up too fast, then plummeted. Deductions about the driver's gender and age amounted to pure conjecture.

"Couldn't resist my charisma, could you?" Michael's sing-song cadence mocked her.

"You know me too well." She willed the driver to look at her.

"Oh-oh. Those itsy-bitsy mental cogs are spinning

at the speed of light." Michael stopped drumming his fingers on the gearshift and turned her face toward him. "Forget sucking in that guy."

"FYI, I was curious who'd drive in this weather." Her attempt at sounding indignant came off pathetic.

He patted her shoulder. "Uuuh-huh."

His long, melodramatic sigh nagged her. Told her reading her mind required zero effort. Reminded her he knew her like a book—a short, simple primer with wide margins.

"Give it up, Quinn. Five minutes max, the road crew's finished, the light changes, the guy next to us goes about his business."

"And then what?" Time was running out. She shifted toward Michael. "Where are we going? What about Pierce? What—"

"Calm down." He tapped his index finger against her bottom lip. "Just be glad I saved you from a life with Rex in South America."

The cell phone bit into her hip bone. Her mouth went dry. Michael gazed at the traffic light and kept talking—in love with his own voice. "Some people consider Buenos Aires quite charming."

Make him think you're listening. She deliberately turned her shoulder away from the other car. "How's your Spanish?"

He grinned. "Money speaks every language."

"Silly me." She slipped the phone from her left pocket into the folds of her coat. Careful, careful. Trying to bash his brains out with the phone in her left hand would be like trying to fly by flapping her arms. "I forgot the money."

"It'd be a fortune if Pierce hadn't fucked us up."

"How'd you fool Pierce so long?" Carefully, slowly, she shifted the phone to her right hand. Images of Pierce helped repress memories of kissing Michael's boo-boos.

"Newsflash! Pierce is a legend only in his own mind."

"He does have a strong ego." No stronger than this embezzling murderer next to her. "And a good heart."

"Mr. GoodHeart sucked your brain out the first time you met him."

He didn't hear her intake of breath as she raised her hand. Didn't read her mind. Didn't turn until she slammed the phone into his right temple.

"Jesus!" Unlike a TV character, he didn't flick the pain away like a gnat. He clasped his head with both hands.

She forgot he was her brother and hit him again. This time the phone connected with his nose. Blood spurted like a small fountain.

"Unlock the door." Tasting the coppery dregs of horror, she smacked the horn.

"Stop that!" He swatted blindly at her with one hand.

"Unlock the door." She cracked his wrist.

His screech sounded sweeter than the Mormon Tabernacle Choir. Sweeter still was his need to suck at his wrist and nurse his head and nose at the same time. Quinn seized another horn-smacking opp. This time the horn blasted. A hand waved from the de-icing truck as it passed through the intersection.

"For godsake! Stop, Quinn." Michael threw himself face down across the steering wheel but not before she saw blood trickle down his chin.

His moans sounded pitiful, but she didn't trust him. He wasn't out yet.

Damned inconsiderate of him since her ribs burned like Roman candles. Slivers of green flashed through the misted windshield. The left-hand turn arrow.

On a roll now, she smacked the phone between his shoulders. He howled like a wounded ape and jerked upright. She whacked the horn again.

Soft, nearly inaudible knuckles rapped Quinn's window. "What's wrong?"

Hope flared, but she didn't turn. Michael somehow managed to protect his face with one hand and punch the window down with the other.

"No problem," he called in a jaunty tone.

A cold breeze shocked the skin on Quinn's neck.

"Call the police," she yelled, pressing her cell phone into her thigh.

"No problem." Michael repeated and threw a bloody salute.

In the corner of her peripheral vision, she caught a snapshot of a muffled-up man with steamed-over glasses peering into the Corvette. "Call the police!"

The man took a step backwards. "The police?"

"Now!"

The left-turn signal flashed yellow.

"No!" Michael grabbed the gearshift.

"Call them!" Quinn slammed the cell phone down on her brother's knuckles.

His howl raised the hairs on her nape. The other driver rattled her door handle, demanding they open up, warning, "I'll call the cops."

"Do it, dammit."

"Wait."

The click of the locks was softer than Quinn expected. The other driver jerked open her door. Icy air swooshed inside.

"My wife's strung out," Michael said with incredible lucidity. "Got some bad coke. I'm taking her to St. Luke's."

"Help me." Tears spurted out of her eyes. She reached for the driver, who wisely didn't stick his head inside the car. "I'm hurt."

"She's strung out," Michael insisted. "Can you believe it? She attacked me with a cell phone."

"He's kidnapping me." The car's dash blurred.

"Broke my damn nose."

The driver whistled. "Looks bad, man. You need a doctor."

Quinn shoved her phone at the other driver. "He's insane. Call the police."

The Good Samaritan ignored the phone, and Quinn's ribs refused to support extending it toward him any longer.

He said, "You know St. Luke's is behind you."

"No shit?" Michael said. "I guess I'm disoriented. I probably have a concussion."

Mr. Innocence. Praying Mr. Samaritan would wake up and take the damn phone, Quinn blurted, "He's killed two men. There's a dead woman in the trunk."

"Jesus!" The driver lurched backwards but grabbed the door jamb.

"She's hallucinating. I need to get her to ER."

"Maybe I should follow you," the stranger said without conviction.

"No. Please." Next to Quinn, Michael growled. She tensed, waiting for him to peel through the red light, plowing into the salt truck.

"Take me with you." A current of electricity passed between Quinn and the stranger. She edged her hips toward the open door.

Michael said, "You should go with me."

"No. I'm hurt."

Against all logic, after she'd beaten him to a pulp, she expected him to remember all the times she kissed his hurts, read him bedtime stories and promised she'd always be there for him. She'd failed him miserably, but surely he knew she'd never meant to abandon him.

"That okay with you?" the stranger stayed behind the open door.

Quinn's ribs screamed. She put one foot on the frozen ground. Please don't let her fall. Let the Samaritan offer his hand. Let Michael let her go.

Finally, he said, "Sure. Meet you in ER."

Chapter 24

8:50 A.M.—December 22

"Why don't you sneak over to your house and catch a nap before work?"

Quinn's hand jerked and slipped off the doorknob in Pierce's bedroom. Heart racing, she shot a glance at the bassinette next to his side of the bed, then whispered, "God, I'm sorry I woke you."

"You didn't." Pierce sat up in bed, dark hair tousled, eyes deep bruises against the yards of white gauze and tape bandaging his right arm and shoulder. "You're quiet as a shadow."

"Ryder's waiting. Can you go back to sleep?" She tiptoed to the bed and spoke in the whisper that had become second nature with Baby Quinn snoozing. "Fifteen straight nights of our girl screaming..."

Pierce shook his head and replied in a conversational pitch. "When she's an international opera star, we'll remember she started practicing in the crib." He paused, then added, "Well, maybe I won't remember."

Quinn's heart jammed her throat, but she crawled onto the bed, taking that fraction of a second to find words she hoped would comfort him. She pressed her lips against his ear. "You'll remember. You remember more every day."

His mouth twisted. "Business details. Nothing about what put me in the hospital. Or why you look so sad every time I mention adoption."

"Not sad. I look like The Bride of Dracula."

He tilted her head backwards and gazed into her eyes. "You need a new mirror, m'dear."

A lie, but she managed not to cry. "Thank you. But we both know I've just insulted the count's bride."

"Shhhh. You look like the woman I want to marry. And I do want to marry you, Quinn. Once I'm fairly sure I won't become a vegetable or an invalid." He kissed away her protests, held the kiss, then murmured, "Whether married or not, I intend to make sure I provide for our future opera star."

"Our star has you bewitched." Quinn laid her cheek against his stubble, imagining the screams of his parents if he pursued adopting the baby of the man who nearly killed him.

He stroked Quinn's hair, and her raw nerves stopped jangling. "Admittedly, I am bewitched. But I owe that tiny creature, you know. Carrying her in my good arm gets me ready for P. T. next month."

"Riiight." Tears stung the corners of Quinn's eyes, but she laughed—because of Pierce's obvious attempt at cheering her up. God, how could he be so gentle with Michael's child?

****

Forty-five minutes later, Quinn placed her hand on the doorknob at Alexander and Associates. The stink of grease and sugar hit her in the stomach. Dèjá vu. The parking garage and the image of a black-caped Ryder flashed. She closed her eyes. The queasiness and memory passed.

God, what she'd give to be at home with Pierce, snuggled next to him under the down comforter, the house quiet...She indulged in five seconds of fantasy before she straightened her shoulders, opened her eyes, turned the doorknob and stepped into the reception area.

Ryder had Leah, Janelle and Sami eating out of his hand.

"Make mine chocolate." Quinn forced a cheery tone. Lamar's had become a habit with the red-haired detective.

"Yo, Mama Quinn." Powdered sugar stuck to the corners of his mouth. He shifted the box past Janelle to Quinn. "Looks like you could use at least two."

"Baby Quinn didn't sleep last night?" Sami delicately licked the tips of her fingers.

"Baby Quinn did not sleep last night." Quinn hung up her coat, fussing with it in the closet. "My baby niece went AWOL the day they passed out the sleeping-at-night gene."

She bit her tongue, afraid she'd add what her mother had told her. From birth, Michael had been an owl, rarely sleeping more than an hour at a time.

Do. Not. Go. There. She realized Ryder had fixated on her fists. She forced her fingers to relax. Her heart drummed in her ears. Baby Quinn would be okay. Perfect. Nothing like Michael.

"My mom says I didn't start napping before I was two," Janelle offered.

"Thank you for that ray of hope." Quinn tried to imagine twenty-three more months of sleepless nights. Had lack of sleep turned Michael into a monster?

Get a grip.

"On a different note," Ryder offered—noticing her shiver?—"my mother says my three sisters slept like babies from Night One."

Quinn bit off a chocolate sprinkle. "Consider me encouraged."

Sami opened her mouth, shut it, shot Leah and Janelle a get-to-work glare.

"Sorry." Quinn shook her head. "Hormone overload."

After a beat of awkward silence, Sami hustled to her desk. Fun time was over. Quinn tried to usher Ryder into her office. He stayed put. Maybe he didn't want to be alone with her any more than she wanted to be alone with him. Or, maybe he was trying to lighten the mood which had gone South as soon as she opened the door. For whatever reason, he made a production of passing the pastry box off to Leah. Everyone but Quinn cracked a couple of jokes. Her chocolate confection tasted like cardboard. She slipped into her office and spit the greasy ball into her napkin, wincing at a twinge in her ribs.

Ryder closed the door, flopped into the wing chair and adjusted his orange pig-tail, letting it lie on his chest. "Tough week?"

"No worse than last week." Or the week before. Nothing like the first week. Pierce in ICU. Baby Quinn's birth. Luce falling apart. Michael vanishing.

"Sounds like progress."

"Absolutely." Quinn closed the collar on her jacket—just in case he could see her carotid pulse hip-hopping.

"How's Pierce?"

His nosiness irritated her, but she said evenly,

"Better, now that he's out of the hospital."

What did Ryder want?

"How's his memory?"

"The doctors are hopeful." Quinn heard the edge. As a gesture of goodwill, she added, "They don't think he'll ever remember what happened in his bedroom, but every day, he recalls more and more business details."

He didn't remember—or was it that he didn't accept?—Tony's murder.

Watching Ryder study her, she picked up the top message on her desk. Despite Pierce's denials, she knew his headaches mimicked migraines. "Right now, he loves having Baby Quinn with him. He says he might work at home, stay with her until she's thirty, maybe forty."

Ryder chuckled. "Sounds like a man in love."

"A man besotted." Quinn's heart slowed. "He's the one person who can soothe her at night. Or whenever she goes nuclear."

Ryder leaned forward. "Has your sister-in-law signed over her parental rights?"

"Twenty-four hours after she gave birth. Her parents didn't want their grandchild, either." Quinn pinched the bridge of her nose, trying to block out the memory of the grandparents' venom. She sighed. "They hate Michael. Never want to hear his name or see his child or do anything but spit on him in hell. If spitting gives him any relief, they'll shovel on more coal."

A long whistle. "They blame him for their daughter's breakdown."

A statement, not a question. Quinn exhaled and nodded. "Absolutely. If Luce had never married Michael—" Before she realized it, her bitterness erupted. "They'll have the marriage annulled as soon as she recovers."

"Blood's always thicker than water. They could change their minds—if Luce never picks up all her marbles."

Quinn felt her mouth twist. Ryder. What a silver-tongued devil. "Not quite the term the lawyers use, but that's their concern...that she won't ever pick up all her marbles. We assume her parents will never reclaim their granddaughter because Luce suffered such great emotional distress."

Shut up, Quinn. As if dismissing the whole mess—which she rarely mentioned to either her mother or Pierce anymore—Quinn waved. "I definitely have to cut back on sugar."

Ryder laughed. "Cut back on sugar. Your advice to me in the garage, remember?"

"Vaguely. That scene feels like a movie I saw years ago."

"Think this would've played out differently if I'd told you up front I was a cop?"

A slow headshake. "I'm pretty sure a happy ending wasn't in the cards."

"You're a realist, Quinn."

Face warm, heart thumping, she said, "Is Michael dead?"

"Officially, no."

To her surprise, he hesitated, avoiding her gaze, steepling his fingers. He might think she was a realist, but he must also think she'd crash and burn if he got too graphic.

"Officially because you haven't found a body?"

An image of Pierce, unconscious in ICU, steadied

her when she said body.

"That's right. I check with my informants every day. Nada, zip, not a peep. Which is very strange."

"Why?" The single word caught in the back of her throat.

"There should be some kind of buzz over a guy who stole fifteen million dollars of coke from the Hoàngs." Ryder turned his palms up. "But if the Hoàngs don't want us to find his body, we won't find his body."

As if in agreement, Quinn nodded. Poor Baby—

Stop. She pinched the back of her hand. Right this minute, Baby Quinn was fine, safe at home with Pierce. Safe. That was all that mattered right this minute.

"With any luck," Ryder said, "Your niece won't start asking questions about bio daddy for a few years. Time enough for you to figure out what to say."

"Uh-huh." Thinking she sounded ungracious, Quinn added, "Thanks for the vote of confidence."

He stood. "Ain't no roadmaps for where you're going, Quinn."

"That's a comfort." She smiled. "I'm roadmap-challenged. I prefer landmarks."

A light danced in his moss-colored eyes. He extended his hand. "You've got my number. Call if I can ever help."

A little shock hummed through Quinn. "Does this mean you won't be stopping by every week?"

"Only if I'm in the neighborhood. Which isn't likely." He jammed his hands in his pockets. "I'm working with the Feds on a couple of cases that cross state lines."

This added layer of transparency raised the hairs on

Quinn's arms. "And to think I'm one of those people who believed drug dealing happens in another galaxy."

"A common misconception." Ryder made no move toward the door, and Quinn's antennae snapped up. What was going on? He stroked his moustache, fueling her unease. "Why do I get the feeling I'm missing something?"

"Busted," he said, face and voice serious, scaring Quinn silly.

"Tell me," she said, her tone harsh and cold. She'd figured out a long time ago his clown facade worked to his advantage.

"Okay. I have a question. A personal question."

How personal? She didn't have a second to squawk like an airhead because he rushed on. "You'd tell me, wouldn't you, if your brother contacted you?"

Her jaw dropped, and the gerbil in her brain jumped on the treadmill. "I broke his nose for cryin' out loud."

"And cooperated fully with the police—after you regained consciousness. I'm not blaming you for his getaway."

"Gee, how big of you,." She moved toward the door and hoped her legs didn't collapse.

"I had to ask." He rose and readjusted his pigtail.

"No, you didn't."

"Okay. Just remember I brought Lamar's every week, so I can't be a total jerk, right?"

"You think you're pretty sure of what I'll say, aren't you?" She turned the knob.

"Yep. I've been around. I'm a damned good judge of character."

She opened the door. "Merry Christmas, Ryder."

****

Fresh from her bath, smelling of violets, Baby Quinn lay in the middle of the bed, kicking and cooing, the poster-child for contentment. For the moment, at least.

And it might be only a moment.

"Want to talk to your mama, Sweetheart?" To hell with waiting for Quinn to call at 10:30. If Ryder was still in her office, he'd overstayed his welcome. Pierce punched AUTODIAL, dangled his clean handkerchief in front of the baby, laughed when she squealed loudly. "That's a yes."

"Ryder just left." Quinn's voice sounded thin.

Pierce traced the tip of the handkerchief across the tiny nose he loved.

A loud meeooow interrupted a gurgle.

"Ole Jealous Eyes wants in the bedroom."

Quinn laughed and he wished he could make her laugh again. She rarely laughed these days. Hardly even smiled. She never talked about marriage. He didn't either. No freakin' way he'd sign on as an invalid-husband. But Quinn worried about saddling him with a baby who cried more than she slept.

"Our gal's on the bed, and Mrs. Taylor informs me Floyd has threatened to call the Humane Society."

Quinn giggled. "You are insane."

"Mrs. Taylor figures Floyd, as a hero and all, thinks he should get first dibs on the bed."

Idiot. Pierce mentally kicked his ass for the oblique reference to the day he hated but couldn't recall. Then Quinn snickered, and he shut that window into his soul. He knew about Floyd's heroism from her. The rest he'd blocked out. He prodded her once more about the meeting with Ryder, but didn't push when she changed the subject. She'd tell him when she was ready. Too bad he wasn't ready to bring up marriage.

"Any chance you can come home early? Mrs. Taylor's begging for quality baby-time."

"The doctor says—"

"I'm not fantasizing sex, Quinn. Holding you's probably the best therapy for my head right now." Bastard that he was, he didn't hesitate to punch her guilt buttons.

"I'll probably fall asleep."

"Good. That's probably the best therapy for you right now." Especially if her dreams didn't haunt her. "Let Floyd stay on the bed, and I bet we can dissuade him from calling the Humane Society."

An anemic chuckle, then she said, "It's worth a try."

****

Sun streamed in the window behind Quinn's desk. Too tired to get up and close the blinds, she let the heat lull her. God, her eyelids weighed a ton. Surrendering to temptation, she laid her head on the desk and faced the warm, golden rays. *Just for a few minutes.*

Or long enough to review the upcoming holidays. The goal was to keep the festivities simple, so why did she feel so out-of-control? Weepy? Overwhelmed? Her mother arrived tomorrow afternoon. Pierce's parents would show up Christmas morning. Yet she'd shopped for no gifts. Had no gift ideas for anyone—not even Pierce. Her mind raced and her stomach churned.

Eyes watering from the glare, she lifted her head and stood. Thank God, she'd written bonus checks—fat checks—for Sami, Leah and Janelle. They deserved the checks. They'd seen her wig out over Michael. They'd heard most of the gory details about the scene in Pierce's bedroom. They'd held the fort while she went to St. Louis to bring Baby Quinn home, then managed the end-of-year business demands while she spent day after day after day in the hospital with Pierce. Her three right-hands deserved gold and silver and diamonds, but maybe, just maybe, they'd appreciate their bonuses more if she threw in an unexpected vacation...

When she yanked open the door between her office and the reception area, their chatter and soft laughter stopped. Pressing her back against the door jamb, she wiggled her fingers.

"Santa's been keeping a list. He's impressed, I'm grateful. So go home and don't come back till next year."

They whooped and hugged her and ad libbed a chorus of *Santa Claus Is Coming to Town.*

She walked them to the elevator and teared up only once when Leah declared, "I bet the worst is over, Quinn."

"I can live with that." She gave high fives all around and retreated to her office on a cloud of youthful optimism.

By the time she reached Pierce's house twenty minutes later, she'd made two phone calls—one she considered the most important call of her life. The first went exactly as she wanted. Mrs. Taylor jumped at the chance to spend the night with Baby Quinn. Giggling like a teenager, the housekeeper promised to trick Floyd into forfeiting his cushy spot on Pierce's bed. And of course she swore not to warn Pierce of Quinn's early arrival. With any luck, he wouldn't hear the garage door over Baby Quinn's screams.

Shivers of excitement carried Quinn from the garage into the kitchen. A bottle of champagne on ice, two glasses, a platter of finger food and three fat candles sat on the nearest counter. Quinn laughed, danced a little jig and whispered, "Santa has come to town."

Lord, she'd forgotten the fun side of surprises. If Pierce wasn't surprised by what she had in store...she stopped and cocked her head.

Silence. Deep. Quiet. Natural.

I remember silence. She threw a triumphant fist in the air. No operatic cries or screams or shrieks. What better sign from the universe than Baby Quinn sleeping that her plan was destined to come off without a hitch?

She ran up the stairs, opening the top three buttons on her blouse, and called in a low, sexy cadence, "Honey, I'm home."

"Honey, I'm speech...less..." Pierce's slow easy grin widened as Quinn stopped in the doorway, hiked one corner of her skirt above her thigh and did a little bump and grind.

"My, what big teeth you have." She leaned forward, giving him an eyeful of cleavage.

"C'mere." He threw back the comforter, but Quinn continued her slow bump and grind toward the bed, where she pushed him back into the pillows.

"Who are you?" he asked, his voice hoarse, his eyes all pupil, his hands hot and demanding on her breasts.

"The woman holding you to your proposal—your *two* proposals. The woman who felt pushy marrying you while you were in a coma for two weeks. The woman who loves you. Has always loved you. Will always love you."

"I don't have a ring—"

She laughed. "Doesn't matter. I'll wear the pull-tab from a beer can—till we go shopping for a pear-cut diamond."

"Pear-cut, huh? Sounds like you know what you want." He nuzzled a spot behind her ear and she moaned shamelessly.

"Definitely. A family ceremony—your parents, my mother, Baby Quinn, Mrs. Taylor, and Floyd. In the living room. On Christmas Day. At dusk. Lights from The Plaza in the background—"

The buzzer on the front gate interrupted her fire-hose declaration. Chucking Pierce under the chin, Quinn punched the intercom, nodding as an unseen deliveryman from Monique's, her favorite boutique on The Plaza, said, "Package for Pierce Jordan."

She nipped Pierce's lower lip, then said, "I'll be right there."

Pierce shook his head, but kept his hand on her nipple. "Must be a mistake. I haven't ordered anything."

"I've already picked out my dress. Actually, I asked Monique to send three. We'll decide together." She kissed him, inserting her tongue into his mouth, keeping her eyes wide open, willing him to understand how safe she felt.

How many single mothers found a father for another man's child? She didn't know, she just knew Pierce had wanted the adoption at the lowest point in her life. He wasn't a quitter, she thought, suddenly wanting to tell him again she'd always loved him.

Some men stuck through thick and thin.

Daddy and Michael did not.

Pierce did.

A sensation of floating carried her downstairs. She flung open the door, and the deliveryman took one look at her grinning at him like a sex doll and jumped backwards. He thrust an iPad at her for her signature, exchanged his electronic toy for a dress box, and jogged down the front stairs without looking back.

As she bumped the door shut, a three-by-five white envelope slipped off the box and fell face-down on the tiles.

Her heart missed a beat and the memory of the envelope in her kitchen surfaced. Knees weak, she stared at the envelope at her feet. Logic said it contained a congratulatory note from Monique.

"Helloooo?" Pierce's voice broke through Quinn's numbness.

She set the box on the floor and turned over the envelope. Her stomach lurched. She whispered, "Dèjá vu."

Her breath came in ragged puffs. The envelope faded in and out of focus. She bent over it like a puppet on a broken string. Blood drained from her head, but she read the ornate computer script at a glance.

Sarah Quinn Alexander.

Her hand shook as if she was picking up a bomb. It took three tries before she slid a nail under the flap. The letters danced, but she managed to read the single sentence.

Tell Baby Quinn someday her daddy loved her and won't forget her.

A word about the author...

Allie Hawkins lives just off the fast lane in Silicon Valley. She walks every day, writes every day, and dances Zumba every chance she gets.

Thank you for purchasing
this publication of The Wild Rose Press, Inc.
For other wonderful stories of romance,
please visit our on-line bookstore at
www.thewildrosepress.com.

For questions or more information
contact us at
info@thewildrosepress.com.

The Wild Rose Press, Inc.
www.thewildrosepress.com

To visit with authors of
The Wild Rose Press, Inc.
join our yahoo loop at
http://groups.yahoo.com/group/thewildrosepress/

C0-A00 763

Books edited by Robert Wechsler and available from Catbird Press

COLUMBUS
À LA MODE

Parodies of Contemporary
American Writers

by Robert Wechsler

CATBIRD PRESS

© 1992 Robert Wechsler
All rights reserved

No part of this book may be used or reproduced
in any manner without written permission,
except in the context of reviews.

CATBIRD PRESS
44 North Sixth Avenue
Highland Park, NJ 08904
908-572-0816.

Our books are distributed to the trade by
Independent Publishers Group.

To learn about Catbird's other humor books,
see the back of this book or write us for a catalog.

The author would like to acknowledge the extraordinary,
unparalleled, downright ineffable editorial help of
Arthur Goldwag. I would also like to acknowledge
the authors of two recent books about Columbus which,
more than any of the others, stripped Columbus of his myths
and, thereby, made his clothing that much easier for me
to try on: John Noble Wilford, author of *The Mysterious
History of Columbus,* and Kirkpatrick Sale, author of
The Conquest of Paradise, whom I rewarded with a parody.

Library of Congress Cataloging-in-Publication Data

Wechsler, Robert, 1954-
Columbus à la Mode: Parodies of
Contemporary American Writers
/ Robert Wechsler
p.   cm.
ISBN 0-945774-16-8 (alk. paper) : $12.95
1. Columbus, Christopher—Humor.
2. Parodies. I. Title.
PN6231.C6114W4 1992
818'.5407—dc 20   91-38929

To Jill, without whom . . .

CONTENTS

INTRODUCTION
à la Robert Wechsler

What you are about to read (I hope) is a hybrid, something like those wondrous mythical creatures such as the centaur (horse and man), the sphinx (woman and lion), the griffin (lion and eagle), and the catbird (bird and parodist). This book is an ulnography (parody and biography), named in honor of the ulnar nerve, which is set off when you hit your funny bone.

A lot of the excitement in writing as well as in reading comes from the bringing together of unlike things. This is as true of humor as it is of poetry. When they are forced to spend a little time together, two ordinary things can rise to the level of the extraordinary. They can also squabble.

Biography is something very ordinary. It seems that biographers will go to almost any extent to make their books ordinary. It's become mandatory to have at least one sexual revelation about the subject (preferably illicit), and almost mandatory to have one political revelation as well (preferably fascist or communist). And at least one of the subject's bubbles has to be burst, if not the subject himself.

Literary parody, on the other hand, is hardly ordinary. In fact, it's an endangered species. Literary parody has a long history but a short present, and its present is getting shorter all the time. The ancient art of parody survives today primarily in parodies of magazines, movies, and television shows. There is also the occasional parody of a long-dead author, which was never quite the point. It is much more pleasing for the parodist to know that the author might actually read his parody and take his criticism as well as his enjoyment to heart. When the author is among us, it also makes the parodist feel that his work is itself alive and not simply the echo of laughter in a museum.

So, biography is too ordinary and parody too strange. Perhaps, I thought, bringing them together would make biography extraordinary and parody a bit less strange, while making both of them more enjoyable. The idea is something like this: since any reader is only going to be familiar with some of the authors I choose to parody— even if they're all famous contemporary Americans—a familiar hero and story might make each parody fun even to people who have never heard of the particular author. Just as the story of Columbus can be made more palatable with a scoop or two of comedy, literary parodies can be made more palatable with a scoop or two of a character who has everything it takes to be the hero or subject of a contemporary novel, biography, book of journalism, newspaper column, or whatever.

And Columbus has it all. He was lustful and lustworthy, violent yet sensitive, adventurous and obsessed, spiritual yet down-to-earth, or -sea. He was a businessman, a professional, a politician, and a religious zealot, and he hobnobbed with everyone from ship's boys to the Queen. In short, he was protean enough to step into the shoes of such contemporary characters, real and fictional, as our recent presidents, Nathan Zuckerman, Lee Iacocca, Rabbit Angstrom, and Gary Gilmore. His family, too, has the ability to roleplay. His mother can play Frank Sinatra's mother, his wife can play a character out of Joyce Carol Oates or Anne Tyler, and his mistress can be a lone heroine right out of Toni Morrison.

In *Columbus à la Mode,* I have created an ulnography that brings together a fifteenth-century Italo-Iberian explorer with contemporary American writers, in parody form. As with a genetic experiment, the result might be a higher being or it might be a monster. It might even turn out to be both. The result might infect our literature by reproducing rapidly, or it might be just another mule. The only thing I can guarantee is that *Columbus à la Mode* will not read like anything else.

The Columbus you will read about in this book is essentially a realistic portrait. He was a man divided against himself, and he was not easy to stand. Since he was one thing and the other, there's a lot from which to pick and choose. But there's also a lot we don't know about Columbus, and I have not been shy about filling some of the holes. For example, we don't know how his wife died or even whether he simply left her back in Lisbon. So I brought in Stephen King and let him kill her off in his royally gory fashion. We don't know what drove Columbus to so obsessively seek to cross the Ocean Sea, so I left it to modern psychology to give him a complex about his father and I left it to his wife to do the rest. One artistically licentious liberty I took was making Amerigo Vespucci Columbus's nemesis; in fact, the two explorers were friendly acquaintances, and the New World was named for Vespucci after both of them had died.

The parodies have a range similar to Columbus's. There is everything in this book from imitation to burlesque. Where the author has a distinctive style, that is parodied. But many of the writers, especially the nonfiction writers, have little style to speak of, so their attitude toward the world and toward their characters is parodied instead. Sometimes the parodies are tight and book-oriented; sometimes they're broad and author-oriented. Sometimes Columbus narrates; sometimes the story is told by a major player or a minor observer; sometimes the author is dropped into the fifteenth century and reports directly on what he sees. Columbus's mother, wife, and his only known mistress get their own parodies, and his brothers and sons also play a part (his brother Bartholomew even has the luck to play Alexander Haig).

There is also a wide range of writers parodied here. There are serious novelists, popular novelists, serious biographers, a popular biographer, and a few autobiographers, all of them presidents or would-have-runs. There are journalists, humorists, and inspirationalists, travel writers, children's writers, and a dog. Because so few poets are recognizable and poetry parody requires more recognition than prose, the only verse parodied here is that of Dr. Seuss, who died soon before this book went to press.

Enough introduction. On with the ulnography.

When Christopher Columbus was born, parents were the people chosen by God to provide you with the social status that would keep you in your place throughout your life. These days, parents are the people you choose to blame for all the neuroses and psychoses that keep you rushing to (and from) therapists throughout your life.

When it comes to showing what havoc parents can wreak on their children (not to mention uncovering illicit affairs), no American writer can compete with Kitty Kelley. Although she has become famous for her behind-the-smile portrait of Nancy Reagan, her octave-lower-than-gravel portrait of Frank Sinatra fits in better with the life of Columbus. In fact, Columbus and Sinatra share something in common: mothers from Genoa. However, as many people say of Kelley's books, the scandals here are manufactured. But possible.

VIA MIA

à la Kitty Kelley's *My Way: The Unauthorized Biography of Frank Sinatra*

His mother's name was Susanna Fontanarossa, but she was so haughty and overbearing they called her Regina. She came from a proud old Genoese family of weavers, merchants, and slave-traders. She could speak each of the city's dialects, but it is a wonder she ever learned, since she never let anyone get a word in edgewise. Regina was so imperious, she proclaimed that, over her dead body, no one would ever say a word about her to anyone. It is over her dead body that *Via Mia* was written.

It was a shock to the Fontanarossa family when, on New Year's Day 1451, Regina brought home a Sicilian boxer named Domenico Columbus. While Domenico seemed nice enough, it appears that he had taken a few too many punches. He came from a vague line of illegitimate Sicilian beggars, scoundrels, and numbers runners. The quiet, asthmatic boy wasn't anything special. He had never learned to read or write (although he was good with numbers, like his dad), and he had never held a job, even as a front. The one thing Domenico was good for was being sicked on anyone who bothered Regina. She chose him the way one chooses a watchdog or the way I choose to treat people in my books.

But her family could not understand this. Where was love, honor, family pride?

"Her mother said to her, 'Gina, I thought you had a good head on those man-like shoulders of yours,' " said Maria Passatempo, a plain-looking neighbor who was going steady with Domenico when Regina walked in and selected him as her pet. " 'What you want with a southern baboon like Filippo?'

" 'That's *Domenico*, you moronic bitch,' Regina said to her mother. 'And he's what I want. And whatever Regina wants, Regina gets.' "

The next thing Regina got was pregnant. Not from Domenico, but from Giuseppe Vespucci, best known as the father of that famous explorer Amerigo Vespucci, the great nemesis-to-be of Regina's first-born son. Giuseppe was ten years older than Regina. Cutting an aristocratic figure, he was tall and broad-shouldered, he had hair combed up into a pompadour, and he was the love of her life. Unquestionably, it did not hurt that his mother was a distant relation of the Medicis.

Since Regina had not wanted to get pregnant and never intended to marry the dashing, irresponsible gigolo, she figured pregnancy would not have the gall to happen to her. But it did. And the wedding was still two months off. So off she went to the local abortionist.

"It was a disgusting place," said Maria Impudico, a neighbor whom Domenico got pregnant a few weeks before he married Regina. "The old hag had twenty cats and never let them out. And she didn't have no kitty litter neither. I did everything I could—threatened to get Domenico arrested for seduction, tried to get taken into the local convent, even considered insisting it was a virgin conception—but finally I decided not to cut off my nose to spite my face, and had an abortion."

Regina did not. She took one look at the place and nearly had a miscarriage. You see, she was obsessed with cleanliness. Psychiatrists have interpreted this mania for cleanliness, especially constant hand washing, as a person's attempt to cleanse himself of real or imagined guilt. You know, like Lady Macbeth, the one from the Shakespeare play. And like Lady Macbeth, Regina's guilt was certainly real enough. I could write a whole book about the guilty things she did, if she were only famous in her own right. As it is, however, it would not make it into the chainstores, even with my name on it.

In the middle of the wedding reception, Regina disappeared.

"We all thought she'd gone to the ladies room," said Maria Pettegolo, one of Regina's bridesmaids. "But even Regina could only freshen up so long. One of the bridesmaids, Maria Spia, found her in a closet with Giuseppe Vespucci, whose mother had once been one of the lesser Medicis' mistresses. And they weren't even drunk!"

"Regina was a lively girl," said Maria Invidioso, the

older sister of one of the ushers. "She had a mouth that would make a gondolier blush and a way of dancing that would wear him totally out, even if he was only *watching* her!"

Soon after the wedding and just before she started to show, Regina went off on an extended visit to Florence ("to enrich myself," she told everyone). She stayed with the family of the best man, Giuseppe Vespucci, best known as the father of that scandalous model Simonetta Vespucci, who posed for Botticelli—in the nude—as Venus-on-the-Half-Shell. Botticelli's patron was a Medici.

One day, Domenico showed up in Florence. Striding into the Vespucci household in the crude Sicilian manner he had, Domenico shocked Regina so much that she began to give birth. Fortunately, the baby was late, and Domenico thought it was the fruit of their wedding night. Even if Regina had not let him near her all night long.

"The birthing room was like a boxing ring," said Maria Allevara, the midwife, who was an abortionist on the sly. "Two men—the father and the godfather—were battling to see who could do more and say more to make sure the kid turned out to be a boy. It would've been a draw had Domenico not knocked out Giuseppe —the son of an upstairs maid to one of the Medicis—a few minutes before I made the only botched delivery in my career."

Through his contacts with the powerful and glamorous Medici family, Giuseppe Vespucci had Domenico thrown in prison and the key tossed into the harbor. This was not the first time Domenico had been arrested. He had been charged with stealing an eggplant, arrested for being disorderly when he sang Christmas carols loud, off key, and on Easter Sunday, and he pled no way *(nolo contendre)* to a charge of seducing a nun. And it would not be his last arrest either.

After letting Domenico stew in his own juices for a week or two, Regina hired a sponge-diver to dive for the key and she had Domenico freed from the dungeon. "She and her Sicilian husband arrived at the Vespucci household drunk as skunks," said Maria Domestica, the Vespuccis' upstairs maid, "and the Mrs. proceeded to call my master a 'son of a Sicilian bastard.' Then she said, 'It's raining horse gnocchi and dog lemonade,' and she promptly undressed in the salon, before the servants. Mr. Columbus, who, they were saying in the kitchen, had never seen her naked, just smiled and stared."

Now, where was I? Oh, yes: When the baby finally came out of its mother's womb and Regina learned that it was, indeed, a boy, she cried out, "He will be just like his father!" Meaning Giuseppe Vespucci.

Domenico was shocked by his wife's words and said, "No, he will be nothing like me. Nothing!"

"The first words that came into my mind as I held Regina's baby and wiped him off," said Maria Allevara, the midwife/abortionist, "were, 'This little thing is so weak and scrawny, and I pulled him out like it was my maiden voyage; he'll never amount to a thing. Especially if he grows up under the thumb of that bossy broad.'"

No one knows what sort of child Columbus was. Was he that perfectly behaved sort of boy who grows up to be a mass murderer? Was he a bully who forced the kids in his neighborhood to give him a percentage of their earnings to finance his youthful adventures?

I don't know the answer, but I don't think you'd be risking the farm if you bet he was a dreamer. The sort of peculiar kid who never gives the expected answer or shows interest in ordinary things. The sort of kid who appears in every novel, because that peculiar sort grows up to be a writer who seeks revenge against all those run-of-the-mill bullies who made him feel like the peculiar kid he was.

Childhood is something Robert Fulghum, one of America's most popular inspirational writers, knows a great deal about. After all, he hasn't learned a thing since kindergarten, so there isn't a lot standing in the way of his childhood memories. Here is Columbus standing in for Fulghum.

ALL I REALLY NEED TO KNOW I LEARNED ON THE STREETS

à la Robert Fulghum's *All I Really Need to Know I Learned in Kindergarten*

Popes, Cardinals, and Borgias was the game to play on the streets where I lived as a child.

We would walk to a churchyard and, when the excitement of our gang had reached a critical mass, one of the bigger boys would yell out, "You have to decide which you are—a POPE, a CARDINAL, a BORGIA, or a COMMONER. If you don't decide right away what you are, *I'll* decide for you."

Each of the kids would call out not only *what* he wanted to be, but often *who*. Sometimes certain cardinals were popular, sometimes certain Borgias, especially the one who was Pope until I was seven. There was a tacit agreement that only the oldest, strongest boy could be the Pope. Me, I would say I wanted to be the captain of a pirate ship.

You see, I always wanted to play pirate and trading ship. I wanted to imagine myself on the rolling main, a wineskin in one hand and a freshly grilled fish in the other, lying back and watching the horizon just sit there beautifully, day after wonderful day. I only threw in the pirates for a touch of violence. But the older boys would always insist that piracy wasn't violent enough, certainly nowhere close to what was happening in Rome and Florence. And they were unable to imagine a churchyard as the deck of a ship, dipping and climbing through wave after endlessly bobbing wave.

I liked to take the churchyard's point of view. It was always a churchyard, day in and day out. Bishops and cardinals, even the occasional Pope or Borgia, walked through it all the time. It had seen burnings, stabbings, and beheadings galore. What it wanted was a change of scenery: whitecaps, sharks, sails flapping in the wind, the huskiness of ancient sea chanteys. And why shouldn't it be able to play like us children of the street?

But the older boys would just yell at me and tell me to be the landlubbing commoner I was. They would glare at me as if to say that their fathers were mates and captains of ships, and that they wanted to play something they wouldn't become. And then they'd kick me.

You can kick a churchyard and it will lie down and be nothing but a churchyard, abandoning its dreams of the sea. But the love I held for my dreams was stronger than the fear I had of being kicked to death. So I would never give in.

If I'd only been able to give each of them a box of Crayolas—the big box of 64 with the sharpener inside—things might have turned out fine. I knew they were better people than I thought they were. But I would never resign myself to being a churchyard who abandoned my dreams. So day after wonderful day, my pirate ship blew all those popes and cardinals and Borgias to smithereens. And only *I* got to enjoy the spectacle.

Dreams do exist. I know. I have held one's hand, and it squeezed mine back. But the only ship I've ever really sunk was my own.

Although as a child Columbus was in love with the sea, when he reached adolescence he wasn't quite so sure. In fact, he wasn't quite so sure about anything. In other words, he was your average, everyday, mixed-up adolescent. And he did—or so I'm assuming—what all mixed-up adolescents who can't simply go off to college do: he ran away from home and tried to find himself. Also like a typical adolescent, Columbus hoped that someone else would show him the path he should take. In his day, such decisions were handled by angels and other denizens of Heaven, sometimes—if you were one of the elect—by God Himself. So Columbus wandered and waited for celestial guidance.

Mark Helprin, best known as the author of *A Winter's Tale*, is one of America's best novelists of the fantastic coming down out of the sky and stirring up a poetic chaos in something like a real world, but not exactly. This parody of his most recent novel involves one of Helprin's typical epiphanies, a modicum of his superlative-laden language, and a bit of his mystical-seeming dialogue.

A Soldier of the Absolutely Greatest War Ever

à la Mark Helprin's
A Soldier of the Great War

Christopher stood by the side of the road, laughing. His smile was the perfect and uncontrived smile of a child, although he was rapidly approaching that state of man known as manhood. His laugh was the laughter of angels who have never before visited earth.

An old man with white hair, like a halo of the light reflected by snow after one of the most terrible storms of the century has buried a village under an avalanche, ambled toward him rapidly. The old man was going so fast, Christopher almost put out his thumb for a lift. But then, with the suddenness of the greatest passion of one's life, the old man came to a stop in front of Christopher.

"Where's the fire?" Christopher asked the old man.

"The fire's in my soul," the old man answered.

"And what do you stoke it with?"

"The fire or the soul?"

"How do you walk so quickly for one so old?"

"I welcome pain. It's an old friend of mine, the only one that's still alive from the absolutely greatest of wars against Naples. Come walk with me, if you dare."

Christopher was happy to have company. He was at that point each of us reaches at least once in our lives, the point where our fate is to be decided. Because he knew he wanted to do great things and that he did not have connections, he found the life of a warrior most appealing. The choice, then, was a relatively simple one: one if by land, two if by sea. First he would check out the land by wandering through Europe like a scholar-gypsy waiting for a spark from heaven, and then he'd go to sea, hoping not to be struck by another sort of spark from heaven. Perhaps the old man could teach him a thing or two, or even make his decision for him.

They walked together in a silence more silent than the silence that will follow the last judgment. Then what seemed to be more birds than had existed *in toto* from the moment of creation burst out in song, like a waterfall cascading onto the most beautiful of women and the most handsome of men bathing together below.

"Do you hear?" Christopher asked.

"Have I given you reason to suppose me deaf?" the old man answered.

"I mean," Christopher asked, abashed, "do you hear something more than birds singing in the trees?"

"Do you mean, do I hear angels or lost souls or that sort of claptrap? No, all I hear is birds. Zillions of them. This place must be infested with insects. But not for long."

Christopher tried again. "Have you ever heard anything more magnificently beautiful, more overflowing with great cadences and harmonies?"

"Yes, in fact I have. The sound of one woman moaning beneath me is more beautiful than the racket of all these birds. And the memory of her having dumped me for a man half my age is more deliciously painful."

A beam of light broke out through the clouds above and lit the way before them. Unbent beneath their lack of encumbrances, the young boy and the old man began to climb a mountain that rose majestically into the clouds.

"The mountain didn't look so steep or high to me from where I was standing when we met," Christopher said.

"Nor to me," the old man said.

"Why do you think that is?"

"I don't know what your problem is, but I happen to be blind."

"But I was given no reason to suppose you blind."

"I'm not into self-pity, my son. But didn't you wonder why I'm wearing sunglasses on a cloudy day?"

"I have a great deal to learn, sir."

"You certainly do. You are the apotheosis of ignorance. Boys aren't what they used to be, back when the ages were dark but the pupils shone with the light of good discipline. Back when men believed that anything could be accomplished. What you children need is delusions of grandeur. You've got to believe that beauty is truth, that might is right, and that pain is pleasure."

Christopher looked back down the road he had taken with the old man. In the distance, a mountain range undulated, more like the sea than the sea itself. Suddenly Christopher realized what the old man was getting at: land or sea, it didn't really matter. All you have to do is believe that you will be greater than any man has ever been, that your achievements will be more important than any man's before you, and that nothing can stop you now.

Although blind, the old man was teaching him how to see. If only the old man were deaf, perhaps Christopher could learn how to appreciate the sound of a woman moaning beneath him. But what did it matter. Now Christopher knew he'd meet an old deaf man who would teach him to hear, and that he'd meet a paralyzed man who would teach him to feel, and that he'd meet a wine connoisseur who would teach him to taste. Smells were far too abundant to require any sort of education at all.

Christopher stood lost in thought. Then, suddenly, the beam of light that had lit their way shone right into the boy's robin's-egg blue eyes. The beam grew brighter and brighter until Christopher cried "Uncle!" and promised he would fight his battles at sea and never bother with the land again.

The beam retreated back into the clouds, and Christopher stood frozen, afraid to open his eyes and discover that he, too, was blind. After leading him a mile or so up the mountainside, the old man finally resorted to one of the most ancient ruses in any book: "Get a load of that milkmaid!" he cried out, and Christopher looked all around him. Alas, he did not see a milkmaid, but he did *see*. And from then on, he felt that the pure, virginal act of simply seeing was a thing of magic, the greatest gift ever given to mankind.

Columbus went to sea, but he was thinking more about trade and warfare than exploration. To get where he was fated to go, he was in dire need of another revelation. Since he was, after all, a young man, his next revelation would most likely come in the form of a love interest. There is nothing like the comforting, confidence-building attention of a loved one to put you on the road to adulthood. That is, nothing except the nasty, confidence-destroying putdown of an unrequiting loved one, which can burst the loveliest fantasy faster than you can say, "No!"

One of the most clever American novels of the last ten years is Philip Roth's *The Ghost Writer*, in which Nathan Zuckerman discovers that Anne Frank is alive and well and living in Massachusetts. Marriage to her would be the answer to everyone's doubts about Zuckerman's Jewishness.

Doubts about Columbus's Catholicism also have been hypothesized, one of the principal pieces of evidence being how amazingly devout he always appeared. In fifteenth-century Europe there happens to have been a young woman who could wield a mean candle to Anne Frank, at least in the public's heart. But she, too, was dead and had left behind nothing but her story. Or so everyone assumed.

THE GHOST WARRIOR

à la Philip Roth's *The Ghost Writer*

It was the last daylight hour of an August evening in 1476, more than twenty years ago—I was twenty-four, had just fought my first naval battle and, like many a *Seeschlacht* hero before me, was already contemplating my own massive *Seeschlacht*—when I woke exhausted after a six-mile swim from my sunken ship. I lay at the base of a steep crag, on which sat a late-model fortress. I climbed the crag with great difficulty, and was greeted at the top by a man who wore the full uniform of an admiral in the Portuguese Navy.

I told him that I was the sole survivor of an armed commercial squadron, flying the Genoese flag, which had been attacked by Portuguese and Burgundian ships. He was effusive in his apologies for the piracy of what had once, he said with sorrow so immense it seem feigned, been the great Portuguese Navy.

As the great admiral was telling me how he missed the heat of battle and boudoir, and how hawkish, even Jewish, my nose was (I insisted it was aquiline), a door was opened by a woman who might have been his wife or a servant, it didn't much matter. Through the door I could see what appeared to be a young woman (because her hair was very short, it was hard to be sure of the gender) sitting on the floor, swathed in a French tapestry—by now a very old, outmoded look in Genoa. Her legs were drawn demurely up beneath the expanse of tapestry, but I could see her ankles, and they seemed to me the ankles of a woman. And I am an ankle man.

Where had I seen that severe, masculine, heroic beauty before? Was it the tomboy who used to highdive into the bay with me, or was it my Uncle Abe, who cured salami (all-beef)? Although she looked nothing like the admiral, I assumed that he had kidnapped an attractive nun and that this was their daughter. I assumed that she dressed and wore her hair like a man because it could be dangerous to keep so beautiful a woman alone in a fortress protected by so many un-provisioned troops. Immediately I assumed more than that. The wife-servant had not even set the tray down on the chest beside me before I saw myself married to

27

the *infanta* and living in a small fortress of our own not so far away.

The great admiral noticed me staring through the door and looked at me with the sternness of a father who doesn't like to watch his daughter be undressed by the eyes of a stranger. "Your daughter?" I asked.

"She's no daughter of mine," he answered with a laugh. "My daughters have all been married off to princes and dukes, except for the lucky one who eloped with a common sailor. This one's not even a woman, in fact; she's—*he*'s the best damn student of warcraft I've ever had. Why, he could strike the medals off most of the lieutenants who served under me, back when."

Without, apparently, knowing I was there, the student entered the room, patted its belly, and said, "How much longer did you say it would be?"

"Giovanni, meet Christopher Columbus. He just survived the naval battle we watched for today's lesson. Christopher, meet Giovanni, my dearest student."

The student sat on a bench by the doorway. "They ought to construct a monument to your patience," the Admiral said to his student.

The student gestured vaguely toward its stomach and said in a rather forced bass, typical of teenage boys, "You can't eat monuments." And then the student said to me, "The Admiral always says, 'When you're lost at sea and out of provisions, you can eat rats, you can eat masts and sails and rope, you can even eat other sailors, but you can't eat monuments.' "

"Nor," the teacher added, "can they eat you."

* * *

That night, while I was lying in bed, I heard some muffled voices on the turret above my window. Figuring it was a couple of guards about to go on a binge, I rolled over and began to prepare straw to stick in my ears. But before I had rolled the straw into a couple of perfect little balls, I recognized one of the voices as Giovanni's—or Giovanna's. I hopped out of bed, went to the window, and tried to make out what was being said.

A light thud directly overhead. What was Giovanni/a wearing at this hour? "I can't live here, I can't live there. I can't *live*."

"Go to sleep," came an older voice, which I assumed was the Admiral's.

"Let's talk."

"We've talked."

"I love you. I even respect you. The others are all dopes. Let me sit on your lap."

"You're nearing port. Be patient."

"Tell me a story about one of your battles. Sing me a sea chantey. Place your hand between my legs."

The Admiral chose *b*, although I felt his voice was more appropriate to *a*. When the chantey was over, I could hear Giovanni/a crying, but I wasn't sure if it was the quality of the singing or the student's secret tragedy that had stirred this response.

"Don't wallow," said the Admiral. "Hold the course and it will hold you back."

"But I'm going off the plank."

"You know what you have to do."

"Yes, tell. Tell!"

"No!" And there was the sound of a smack. I don't know who smacked whom, but I could guess. There was no more weeping and no more talking and, thank God, no more singing either. If only I could learn to handle a woman—or even a man—so well.

It was only a year earlier that Giovanna had told the Admiral her story. She had just come from Orleans, where they had been reenacting the battle Joan of Arc fought against the troops of Henry VI of England.

"It wasn't the pageant; it was the people watching with me, especially the women, who thought how wonderful it would be to be a virgin again: pure, chaste, and childless. The women cried throughout the epilogue, when Joan of Arc was tried for sorcery, wantonness (dressing and wearing her hair like a soldier), and blasphemous pride (answering directly to Her Commander instead of to the Church). The part of Joan's recantation that made the women bawl the loudest was where she swore she was not a virgin, and the part of her repudiation of her recantation that made them whoop with the greatest joy was where she swore she *was* a virgin and would go to the stake pure and chaste as the flame itself. From the moment the fire began to lick the toes of the dummy on the stake till the glorious pageant came to an end, all the women were bursting with joy and beatitude.

"I wanted to tell them that I, and only I, knew that Joan was not only not a virgin, but that she was a mother as well. You must keep my secret: I am Joan of Arc's great-granddaughter, the daughter of the daughter of her daughter, all children born during their mother's sixteenth year, just like Joan of Arc's. No one but the four of us has ever known who we really are. In fact, no one else has known that we were women, except the men who fathered our daughters (and my mothers carefully disposed of *them*). It seems that each generation is weaker than the last, and that mine is the weakest and, perhaps, the last, because I have now told the man who will father my daughter, and I could never bring myself to take your life. But this debilitation was not what my great-grandmother had intended. She believed that one day one of her descendants would win the ultimate victory, that she would be the Second Coming of Jesus Christ Our Lord."

Clearly, God had destroyed my ship at the Battle of Toro and forced me to swim six miles to shore solely in order that I would meet the direct descendant of the heroine who lit up my life: Joan of Arc, the only human, the only saint-to-be who had all the qualities I respected: a penchant for visions and cross-dressing; a direct line to God, whose orders were the only ones she would follow; the need to fight with everyone against her, always against her; and a talent for creating the myth of her life and keeping the myth alive generation after generation by means of a brilliant idea.

And her great-granddaughter was in the room above me, pregnant with the Admiral's daughter, training to be as great a general—or at least an admiral—as her great-grandmother. Perhaps she would bear a boy and would have to try again. Perhaps she would turn to someone younger and taller and virile in the true, Italian way. Perhaps she would prefer a man who did not know who she was or who his child would be—or so she would think. Perhaps my blood and Joan of Arc's would mix together for generations to come, and result in God's return to earth and the salvation of mankind.

Then I had a better idea: we would marry. I had often been accused by my family—especially my mother—of having forsaken the Church (even of being Jewish), of traveling to lands and having relations with women who have never heard the name of Jesus, of the Holy Ghost, even of Mary.

Who could question the faith of the husband of the only true, *living* remnant of Joan of Arc?!

The next morning I had all my plans set for impressing Giovanna. But she had other plans. The first words she spoke to me as we passed in the hall were, "Goodbye. I'm sorry we were never able to talk. I would have liked to hear about your battle. I love battles." She was dressed now in the uniform of a soldier. Her face even seemed to be covered with the peachfuzz that precedes a beard. Not a bulge, not a woman, not a descendant of Joan of Arc. No, the only one of us whose lineage would end with the Second Coming was mine.

"How old are you?"

"Sixteen," she said.

Making her just the right age to add another branch to the willowy family tree of Joan of Arc.

"Where do you come from?"

"Venice."

"Do you know your parents?"

"Unfortunately. And yours?"

"You wouldn't know them. They're nobody."

"The Admiral's been awfully generous to me."

"He's a generous man."

"And he's been an awfully good teacher."

"He's a good teacher."

"But he thinks you'll come to nothing. That you don't

have an ounce of warrior in you. And I agree. He told me not to tell you, but there it is."

Then and there, I decided to change careers. I didn't really enjoy the battle I had just fought—especially since we were blasted out of the water and I had nearly drowned—but I still loved the sea. From then on, I would give up war and take up exploration. God had chosen this moment to show me my true calling, and I have been a true believer (and explorer) happily (and not so happily) ever after.

Columbus set out to sail the two seas of his day, visiting ports of call all around the Mediterranean and up and down the Atlantic coast, from Iceland to the Gold Coast of Africa. But eventually, he grew bored with the life of a common sailor. He was in a hurry to get somewhere fast. So he stopped off in Lisbon after a trip to Madeira, he asked around the convent schools and, after appearing suitably uninterested, he got himself introduced to a young convent girl named Felipa Perestrello e Moniz. Felipa just happened to be the sister of the governor of Madeira, a beautiful Portuguese island off the coast of what is now Morocco, and a popular base for the gold-and-slave trade in Western Africa.

Joyce Carol Oates is a writer who knows how to get into the heart and soul of adolescent women (among many sorts of people who people her novels and her stories). For those who wonder what sort of woman married Columbus, here's a literate guess.

FELIPA: A WIFE?

à la Joyce Carol Oates's *Marya: A Life*

It was a night like any other night in my novels: patchy dreams, strange voices, trembling trees, and Felipa, too, was trembling. Strangely. Patchily.

Felipa had fallen in love. (Her mother would put up her straggly hair, light a cigarette, and say, "Felipa? Who would want a smart-aleck like her? And so ugly!")

Felipa comes out of her room at last. Her mother stands in the doorway to the kitchen, flicks ashes over her shoulder, and says, "So you think you can fall in love like any girl?" Felipa smiles. Her mother's hair has come undone and is smoldering softly on her shoulders. "Don't you get smart with me, you," her mother says.

"I'm not *getting* smart. I've *been* smart all along."

"You little savage, you," Felipa seems to hear, but she wakes to find herself still in her room at the convent. Still in bed. Just a dream. Is Christopher just a dream as well?

Felipa listened and heard strange voices. Patchy voices. She smelled breakfast and nearly gagged. She imagined looking at herself in a mirror: she was just as ugly as everyone was afraid to tell her she was. And her breath was just as bad. She was afraid to look too closely at herself for fear of seeing something forbidden: her father's glassy stare and saliva dripping from the corners of his pale, thin-lipped mouth. Was her father really dead? (Are we all really dead? It made her smile to think that her cousin Antonio might be dead.) Well, if nothing else, Felipa had beautiful hair, long, gorgeous, mesmerizingly luscious hair. But the way life went, someone would be sure to destroy even this tiny inkling of pride by shearing it off. (As sure as, in a mystery, someone will use a loaded gun.)

Christopher almost seemed to like the fact that she was different, although he wished she would let him have her like he had the other girls in the convent school, the other girls, who giggled and billed and cooed and talked about how nasty and conceited Felipa was, just because her brother was the hotshot governor of a measly island like Madeira. Christopher was tall, broad-shouldered, muscular, several years older, and bound to be rich and famous (at least with her brother's help). She could take his long, semi-reproachful silences. She could listen as he made his repetitious arguments with others—his father, his captains, God—by way of her. She could bear the way he kissed too rough and grabbed her with greedily clutching hands, drowsily fidgeting under her clothes as long and far as she let him. With her cousin Antonio, in an abandoned dinghy, she had learned how to get into stone, to close herself like the fossil of an oyster, not to give in, not to seem like all the other, fun-loving girls. What she had never learned is why that sort of response turns so many guys on.

When she was thirteen, Felipa began to write. She wrote about three novels a year, as well as two short-story collections, two essay collections, one book of poetry, the occasional play, and dozens of reviews, articles, and school papers on everything from household poisons to household gods. The nun who taught her wrote at the end of each of her papers, "You have a most *feverish* imagination." Felipa loved her imagination almost as much as her hair. But just as her hair became tangled and ornery, her imagination scared her out of her wits.

When she was fourteen, Felipa began to study philosophy and the classics. And when she was fifteen, Felipa began to study the sciences. By the time she was sixteen, she had read everything in the convent library, and what she hadn't read, she'd written. It was then that she concluded that the earth was round. It was this certainty (contrary to all that the others around her, *beneath* her, believed) that made everyone think she was a smart-aleck. Superior. Flirtatious. Provocative.

Felipa never told a soul about her discovery. Not even her cousin Antonio, who would grab her by the throat and wring her neck like a chicken. Not even her mother, the only person who didn't seem to notice that she'd changed. Not even Father Paulo, the only man she'd ever wanted (before she met Christopher, of course), the man who, when he placed a wafer on her tongue, gave her a thrill of ecstatic certitude.

"Ain't-I-hot-shit Felipa," was what they called her. They waited behind trees to jump her. They invited her to parties that had never been planned. They told everyone she'd done it with Father Paulo. But Felipa never cried. She told herself again and again that she must never seem weak or they would go for her like wild animals. The words of Father Paulo echoed in her mind: "All experience is terrifying." And he had proved it by grabbing her hand and saying to her, "Don't be afraid, I can show you *the way.*"

Then she met Christopher. An expert at being *not-there,* suddenly she wanted to be *there.* Where he was. But he seemed to think she was *nowhere.* His silences reproached the other girls, the ones who giggled and billed and cooed. So she pursued him. She plotted to get him with an anguished stubbornness that was new to her. Not that she wasn't already stubborn and anguished, but this time it was different: the stubbornness wasn't contrary, and the anguish felt better than ever.

She had gotten up the nerve to talk with him only because the puddle she looked into that night was muddy: she looked pretty swell to herself. And she'd had a few too many glasses of communion wine. Those eyes; that mouth! She wasn't sullen, she wasn't obnoxious, her eyes didn't bore holes in anyone and her mouth wasn't narrow and foul. She was suddenly suffused and infused with power, ecstasy, glory. Yes. Today. Here. Now. Christopher. Columbus.

She took Christopher to the abandoned dinghy she

used to frequent with Antonio, and she told him she had a secret she'd kept for one whole year. And she hadn't told a soul. It was a virgin secret, she assured him, and she was prepared to give it to him, him alone. He said he was interested in her gift of another sort of virginity, but she attacked him for not being cool: How could anyone want a virgin any*more*?! This secret was really something special. Something only she knew and something she would only tell to the man she would marry.

After she had stopped his grabby groping for the fifteenth time, he relented and said, "Okay. Tell me already."

And Felipa did. As if it were her first orgasm, the secret suffused her body and poured out of her in a cry of wonderful agony: "The earth is round! The earth is round!"

Christopher looked at her as if to say, 'Everyone knows that, Felipa.' But all he said was, "Will you marry me?" And even though her eyes said, 'Yes,' her bitter, ironic, sarcastic, foul, smart-alecky mouth said, "No."

As in all screwball comedies, Felipa Perestrello e Moniz eventually came around, married Christopher Columbus, and moved with him and her mother to the island of Porto Santo, a few miles from Madeira and not far from the coast of Africa. There, Columbus could enjoy her brother's patronage and could grow into the explorer her father had been.

There was one more step left in Columbus's maturation from dreaming child to courageous explorer of new worlds: he had to decide to risk his life and go looking for those new worlds. But he was married now, and he had a baby son and a good job on a good, gentrified island. So where was the incentive? Why should Columbus be hungry for anything more than what he had?

He clearly was in need of another good epiphany, but he had pretty much had his share of them by now. So it was Felipa's turn. Fortunately, America has a novelist who can turn an epiphany with even more élan than James Joyce: Anne Tyler. All she needs is a few eccentric characters, some family tensions, and Wham! someone walks smack into an epiphany and her life takes a whole new tack.

NAVIGATION LESSONS AT AN ACCIDENTAL RESTAURANT

à la Anne Tyler

She didn't know why Chris had picked this restaurant of all the restaurants near the harbor. It didn't have a view of the ships coming in; it didn't have the freshest fish or the spiciest pepper. It wasn't even one of the many restaurants her brother had a strong opinion about one way or the other.

What did it matter what her brother thought? Well, it mattered to Chris. Chris was obsessed with her brother's every like and dislike, like a lapdog with rabies. He seemed to be the source of each of Chris's decisions. But not this one. This one had no explanation. It appeared to be an accidental choice.

She found herself remembering their first meal together. Chris was everything her brother had been at that age: tall, handsome in that special, early Renaissance way, arrogantly taking life by its throat, as if life were a sinner before the Inquisition.

The way he had ordered dinner for her that night, smoothly, easily, without a sign of effort. Nothing was hard for him then, and everything was hard for her. She had reached the end of the stories she had to tell, and he was full of sea tales from all over the world, and dreams of living in Paradise, or Iceland perhaps.

Chris looked across the table at Lipa. Dreaming, as always. All she ever did was dream. She dreamed of her literary life in the convent. She dreamed of having a man she could push around. She dreamed of squid and all the different ways to cook it. He was more realistic. Her brother had given him a good position: good pay, good status, and little work. He was a patronizing nincompoop of an in-law, but he paid the bills. And her mother had recently given Chris all her husband's sea charts. Chris had never had so much fun poring over anything, even a woman's body. What more could he want?

His own mother had never given him anything but grief, and his own father had been unable to hold a job. His father wove wool and tended gates or sheep or whatever he could find. Since the day he and his brother-in-law Abe had invented Genoa salami and lost the patent to the father of that Florentine horsetrader

Amerigo Vespucci, his father had turned his back on life. And on his wife as well. Chris and his brothers had left home almost as soon as they could; there was no future in Genoa for them.

One scene from his youth stuck in Chris's mind. Father was tending the Olivella Gate that year. Like Chris, he tended to be clumsy and had never perfected a graceful pulling-to of the gate accompanied by the appropriate bow. And he could never remember to bring the olive oil, so that the gate cried out to each passer-through, like a child whose doll has just fallen into a sewer.

One day the Pope was in town—Chris forgot now which—and was said to be heading toward the Olivella Gate. When a crowd gathered around his father, he refused to let the crowd see how nervous he was. He tried his best to pull himself together by drawing his sword and swiping at a few of the people standing in the gateway. When he successfully nicked a boy about Chris's age, he suddenly smiled. It is the only smile Chris could remember his father smiling. Chris, too, smiled, because the boy had been one of several bullies who persecuted him for his father's clumsiness. He smiled at his father and his father looked across the crowd and smiled back. His father took another swipe with his sword, but then realized the moment was over and let the habitual frown of failure return.

Lipa looked across the table at Chris. He was angry, even though she hadn't said a word. He was always angry. His pride had slowly descended to anger, and it looked as if his anger might quickly descend to the bottom of a bottle of madeira. The waiter came and she ordered squid and she flirted with him a bit. Chris didn't seem even to notice.

"I'm not hungry," he said. And he began tinkering with a knot. He never seemed to eat. Her brother seemed to do little else. If only she could bring them together, like two ships seeking out favorable winds and finding that all they have to do is go in the same direction. But Chris couldn't bear the sight of him; all he would do was cash his paycheck. It wasn't enough.

Suddenly, as if it were the most natural thing in the world, Lipa rose and walked out the door. Not a word to Chris or even to the waiter. The squid would be cold, but she liked them that way, too. She walked to the edge of the harbor. The sun was going down, the sky was nearly dark. Two ships were moving in the harbor; one was going out and the other was coming in. A sailor stopped next to her and watched the ships, coming in and going out.

"Think there'll be a war?" he asked her.

She wanted to say, "I hope so," because she wanted so much for something to happen. But she was afraid of the consequences, as she was afraid of all consequences, and so she said, simply, "I don't know." And then she told him how it was between her and Chris, how he was a man who had come to the edge of the world and stood there as if the earth were flat and if he took another step he'd fall right off into eternal damnation. She told him about her brother and his father and her mother and his mother and their little baby, Diego, as well. And he listened the way a sailor will, especially when the speaker's brother is his boss.

Finally, Lipa thanked the sailor for listening to her so patiently and went back to the accidental restaurant.

Chris was still there, and the bottle of madeira in front of him was empty.

"We are looking the wrong way," she said to him. "We are looking at the ships going to Portugal and coming back from there. We should go to the uninhabited western side of the island and watch the desolate Western Sea, where there is no one, where anything is possible, where there might be more treasure than in all of Africa and no one to fight for it. There all ships travel in the same direction, if they dare travel at all. There you will find the mythical isles of Brasil, Antilla, Cipangu, Ymana, St. Brendan's Isle, Ventura. There is your future, your immortality, your wealth."

Columbus nodded, and beckoned her to him, and said, "I will go. If someone will pay my way."

Once inspired, things began to go more than just peachy keen for Columbus. Before running off to discover a new world, some historians believe he became a rather wealthy man. Most of us like to separate the passion for wealth from the passion for power and immortality. But in his ongoing, multi-volume biography of President Lyndon B. Johnson, Robert A. Caro found a case in which the two passions coexist and feed on one another. If being filthy rich was good enough for LBJ (with help from his wife, Lady Bird), then it was certainly good enough for CC (with help from his wife, Felipa).

À la Caro, this chapter also includes a version of Columbus's military career that is very different from the one Columbus himself gives above in "The Ghost Warrior."

Myths of Ascension

à la Robert A. Caro's *Means of Ascent:*
The Years of Lyndon Johnson

There are two threads—dark and bright, thick and thin, soybean and mung—that run side by side through the life of Christopher Columbus, sometimes parallel, sometimes perpendicular, sometimes all knotted up. One is his seemingly bottomless capacity for deceit, deception, delusion, illusion, illicitness, and downright lying. The other is the fact that, occasionally, he could almost, for a few moments, be a semi-decent human being, with an ounce or two of concern for others.

He was a tall, gangling, awkward youth, humiliated, ridiculed, and kicked around throughout an impoverished boyhood in a city that he considered "the end of the earth." His family was the laughingstock of Genoa. "I saw how it made Chris feel," said Fernanda Genoese, a childhood neighbor. "And I cried for him. I had to cry for Chris a lot. He was the saddest, gawkiest creature I ever saw."

Once he left town, Columbus was suddenly the wonderkid of the sea, rising with spectacular speed and displaying a genius for discerning a path of ascension that consisted of utter ruthlessness, obsequiousness, manipulation, and domination. His goals were two. First, there was power for the sake of power, ascension for the sake of ascension. Then there was money.

His life was spent becoming the brightest star in a new galaxy rising over the maritime horizon. He would never be the shooting star his father had been, a meteorite plunging precipitously to earth and crashing into smithereens too late at night for anyone to see and too faint to seem romantic to the few young lovers, wherever they are, that may still have been awake. No, he would ascend into the sky, join an appropriate constellation, and stay put.

Columbus kept his life shrouded in secrecy and surrounded by carefully cultivated myths. For example, everyone believed he was a hero in war.

On August 13, 1476, the story goes, Christopher Columbus was wounded in a sea battle, his Genoese commercial squadron attacked by French and Portuguese ships. Everyone died but Columbus, who—with gangly body and awkward strokes—swam several miles to the Portuguese shore, surviving thousands of stings from the tentacles of a squadron of Portuguese men-of-war. A great storyteller, he had a great story to tell and he told it greatly.

In fact, Columbus was on a Burgundian ship and was

doing the attacking. And he didn't swim six miles, because he couldn't swim an inch. Yes, like most sailors, Christopher Columbus was unable to swim and, rather than learn, he spun the tale of his heroic swim to make it seem as if he not only could, but that he was a champion at it. The truth is that he landed on Portuguese soil with a pirate's intent to despoil a few villages and women. "He set fire to my hovel," said Maria, a short, obese woman with skin nearly as dark as her hair, which was a porcupine of split ends. "And when my sisters and I ran out, he grabbed us, ordered us to strip, and chose the one he liked the best. It was me, of course."

Another myth involved his business affairs. Columbus gave all the credit for his remarkable business success to his wife, who stayed behind in Porto Santo while he was off sailing. There was, he and all his associates, including his wife, insisted, no favoritism. The fact that her brother was governor of the Madeiras and that her father had drawn many of the maps she was selling had nothing to do with her business success. The fact that Columbus was a new supernova in the constellation of King João II of Portugal, for whom Columbus raised funds and made maps, also played no part. "It was all his wife's doing, and don't let anyone tell you different," said his attorney in Lisbon. And Felipa did do a great deal. But without Columbus's contacts with besotted captains and the king, her small beginnings would never in a million years have turned into an empire.

In few businesses is the role of royalty as crucial as in being a commercial agent and chartmaker. Since all international commerce, with the exception of smuggling, is regulated by state apparatuses, since no one buys a map that has not been approved by the king, since every ship requires the king's protection, and since Portugal's king told everyone that he had been anointed by God, it is extremely difficult to believe that Columbus's meek, hard-working wife—as bright and competent as she may have been had Columbus not dominated her so ruthlessly and mercilessly—could have made a king's ransom out of her office in an overturned dinghy in the harbor of Porto Santo. (Columbus liked nothing more than keeping the overhead down, as long as he didn't have a dinghy overhead).

What was Columbus's secret? What was his path to commercial ascension? What drove him to pursue wealth as vigorously and with as full and imaginative a stable of myths as he pursued power for the sake of power?

One question at a time, starting with the last, since it's the most fun to talk about. Columbus came up with a series of mythical voyages that led to mythical maps, further mythical voyages, and an increasing number of monopolies. First, he said he went down the coast of Africa, further south than anyone and further west as well, finding—or imagining—new islands for his maps and new tribes with new types of precious stones and foodstuffs to trade. To get to these new tribes and to find these new islands, you had to go through Columbus. Then he went to Iceland—or so he insisted, calling it Thule—and he returned with a map of the undiscovered North. His name became synonymous with the North, and anyone who wanted to trade with the Vikings had to go through him to get to King João. Of course, the Vikings had excellent maps of their own, but since Columbus controlled trade with them, he made sure they were unavailable. And who smuggles maps when six-foot blondes of both genders are selling like hotcakes?

Columbus's path of commercial ascension was not all a matter of monopolies based on myths. Before he came up with his bestselling myths, he had to beg and threaten for money—"finder's fees" he called them—until mariners coughed up what he demanded. At one point he was offered a lucrative priesthood by an immensely wealthy shipowner who had come under Columbus's domination, but Columbus insisted that he'd never be a great mariner if he accepted it. It became clear that money was only his secondary passion—after all, there were lots of absentee priests—and that what he wanted was not to be just a successful businessman, not just a great mariner, but something even greater, a Discoverer, an admiral ruling over all other admirals. But since Columbus was an extremely passionate man, his passion for money was extremely strong itself, strong enough, in fact, to lift a crate of sugar with one hand tied behind its back.

And Columbus's secret? Why, fear, of course. He was terrorized by the thought of being poor, humiliated, the laughingstock of any place on earth. One of his favorite stories was of being carried on a sedan chair to his ship in a distant African port. Noticing that the porter was white, he struck up a conversation. It turned out that the porter had once been a ship's captain. Columbus never felt secure. It could all come down around his oversized ears; his star could plunge to earth; the king or his brother-in-law could die and he would have to start all over again. No incentive is more powerful, more overweening than fear, not fear of failure or fear of spiders, but fear of becoming your father.

If Felipa had had daily nightmares that she had become her mother, who knows how much more successful her business might have been or what lands *she* may have discovered herself.

The story goes that on Porto Santo, Christopher Columbus met an old sailor who had actually sailed across the Ocean Sea and, by accident, had discovered an Other World. This old sailor is said to have given Columbus directions. The story goes on to say that before he could tell anyone else, the old sailor died; some assume that Columbus resorted to mayhem to protect his secret.

Of course, the myth was designed to make Columbus look both lucky and cruel. Although this might very well have been the case, I thought it might be nice to come up with an alternative myth. No American novelist is more adept in myth-making, and writing about myth-making, than John Barth. Here's the version he might have written, in the style of his latest novel, coincidentally about stories told to and by another famous sailor, Sindbad.

THE FIRST VOYAGE OF
CHRIS FROM COLUMBUS

à la John Barth's *The Last
Voyage of Somebody the Sailor*

The table was full and the wine barrels were being emptied with the speed and spew of a whale clearing out this cavity or that. At one end of the table besat Christopher Columbus, in the seat of the brother of his wife, which brother was governor and toastmaster general of the island. Columbus toasted King João and his queen, Lisbon and Oporto, white grapes and red. He toasted the Father, the Son, and the Holy Ghost, and Matthew, Mark, Luke, and John. Then, as his mind floated further into the heavens, his toasts fell down to earth: he toasted all the whores on Porto Santo (each by name) and the ones on Madeira as well. At last, he toasted his wife and her brother.

Looking up without a clue as to where his next toast was coming from (although he knew very well which side it was buttered on), he espied a stranger in strange garb standing in the doorway, faint with hunger and exhaustion. He ordered three of the finest rabbits the chef's assistant could catch and sat the stranger down beside him.

"And what might your name happen to be?" Columbus asked. "And what might be your game?"

"My name," the stranger said, "is Chris, and I'm from Columbus. Ohio. Of the Columbus Columbuses. I'm a journalist, a graduate of the Columbia University School of Journalism. After graduation, I was based in Colombia and then I went freelance and did research for a book in a small Brazilian town called Colombia as well. From there I was hired by a congressional committee and moved to the District (of Columbia). The last thing I remember, I was vacationing on San Salvador, one of the lesser known and, therefore, quieter Caribbean islands, where I went for a well-needed rest after my boss was indicted on eight counts of insider information and child molestation. That's the story of my life."

Throughout this highly repetitive speech, given in rudimentary Portuguese with a very strange accent and style, the throng around the table sobered and stared at Columbus. Columbus, Columbia, Colombia, Colombia, Columbia. Was this stranger some sort of cheerleader? A wandering advertisement in story-telling form?

The interloper ignored the murmurs and continued his story. "I had rented a deep-sea fishing boat for a week, just me and my girlfriend and a captain who knew when we wanted him to disappear and when we wanted him to watch or participate. A week out, smack dab in the middle of the glorious, fish-filled gulfstream, a storm came out of nowhere (my girlfriend insisted she couldn't relax, or even sleep, without playing her cherished CD collection of new-age hogwash, so we never heard a single weather report) and we capsized. I came to in a Portuguese fishing boat that had been blown hundreds of miles off course, and here I am."

"Here you are," Columbus echoed. "And you seem to like my name."

"*Your* name?" the stranger queried.

"*My* name," Columbus echoed.

"Which might happen to be?" the stranger queried further.

"Christopher Columbus."

Chris from Columbus, Chris the Castaway and Cast-about, cast now as an intruder in an intrusive land, knew well with whom he was talking. He had not arrived at this tavern by pure serendipity. He was here to find his way back, back to the District. "And what, if I might ask Your Honor, is *your* game?"

"Brasil." To which the company laughed, for *they* knew Brasil was imaginary and that Columbus took the imaginary for the real. "But I am reconsidering. Perhaps it should be this District of yours, or that San Salvador from which you voyaged to Porto Santo."

"And to which I would give anything to return, if I ever returned anything (never lend me a book). Perhaps if we told each other the story of our voyages, they might intersect and let me go back where I came from (please lend me an ear)."

"But I don't have any voyages," Columbus of Porto Santo insisted. "At least none of my own, not yet."

"Okay then," said Chris from Columbus, "I'll tell mine and perhaps your listening will let me return. I'm game for anything, as long as I'm fed and clothed and given a warm bed with an even warmer woman."

"That's a deal," said Columbus the sailor. "And the better the story, the better the woman."

And so began

The First Voyage of Chris from Columbus

I grew up in Columbus, Ohio, on the same street James Thurber, the famous humorist, had grown up on. It was a nice neighborhood of people who told stories about beds falling down and dams breaking through and ghosts getting in. But the only prepositions I really cared about, at least after I passed into double digits, were "in" and "out."

There was a pond deep in the woods not far from my house that only I knew existed. Every time a good-looking chick would smile at me, I would ask her to come swimming with me in my pond. But she didn't believe that such a pond could exist (just as your friends here doubt the existence of Brazil). If there were such a pond, everyone would know about it, naturally. My story, each chick insisted, was just a way of getting her alone in the woods and doing to her what boys do to girls. I would tell her, no, it was what girls do to boys that I was interested in, but that there really was a pond.

At last I propositioned a girl who wasn't the least bit afraid of me or what I might have in mind. The fact that she was two years older, ten inches taller, and captain of the girls' basketball team might have had something to do with this. But I was innocent and didn't realize she couldn't wait until I made a move, so she could try out some of the martial acts she'd been learning in her martial arts class.

When we reached the pond, I kicked off my shoes, pulled my shirt over my head, shimmied out of my pants, and then dove into the cold, clear water. She (her name was Dizzy, 'cause she was so tall) stripped to her panties as naturally as if we'd been married for twenty years and then—I was electrified almost to the point of ejaculation—she slipped *them* off, too, and slowly walked toward me, took my erection in her hand, and promptly added its liquid to the liquid she hadn't believed for a second would be where I said it was. And then she let me do it to her.

Two weeks later she came to the pond on her own and we had a space-and-time-transcending fuck like the one I hope to have with the woman you award me with tonight. Dizzy wasn't a virgin, she told me, but no one had ever made her feel so tall.

This story, on the other hand, *is* a virgin. I wouldn't tell this to a soul, except to secure my return to the District, via San Salvador. I hate our government, I hate the District, my apartment is tiny and noisy and I'm afraid to walk around the neighborhood at night, and it's exciting to be back in the Renaissance (which I haven't studied since high school), but I want to go home. I want to transcend space-time once more.

The Genoa Columbus looked at the Columbus Columbus and thought about the tale he'd told. There was a body of water and the body of a woman and

54

there was a land that was reached (the land of experience). But it wasn't much of voyage, not a thing compared to sailing down the shore of Africa or up to Iceland and beyond. And he told the stranger so.

"But," added *the* Columbus, "even though your story merits nothing more than a toothless old witch, I would give you my wife if you would tell me everything you know about Brasil."

"In Brazil," Chris the Castaway began, "the women are incredible. Their skin is dark and luscious, and they display it in great profusions on the beaches and during the season of Carnival. And they've got the dampest crotches in the world."

"No," Columbus the Discoverer of New Worlds corrected him (he was getting tired of his namesake's obsession with sex). "I was thinking more in terms of where this island is located."

"But it's not an island," our very own Chris from Columbus reported. "It's one of the largest nations in the world. Or at least it will be, once it's discovered by Amerigo Vespucci."

Vespucci! That cannot be. That *will* not be, Columbus the Avenging Mariner resolved. But what he said was, "And is there a lot of gold there?"

"On the women there is. And on a lot of the men as well."

"And this San Salvador? Is there gold there as well?"

"It's a small island. But there's gold everywhere tourists go."

Columbus of Porto Santo, sailor and brother-in-law of the honorable governor and toastmaster, looked around at the throngs of his brother-in-law's drinking buddies. Some were asleep and the others were laughing amongst themselves, saying that Columbus had truly cracked at last, that he had paid an equally crazy friend of his to play word-games with him about mythical lands and a future that would never come to pass. So Columbus, who looked West and desired to sail to Brave Brasil, decided not even to take the Stranger with His Name aside, but asked him right in front of the besotted masses what were Brasil's coordinates.

Chris from Columbus simply shrugged, much as Atlas would have in the same situation. But he didn't want to leave his host in the lurch, so he took a damp map out of his pocket and handed it to the man who would supply the woman who would get him back to the nightlife of Georgetown and the girls and guys who were waiting to fulfill his every fantasy. It was a map of San Salvador and it showed its coordinates clearly: $24.35°$ N, $75.58°$ W.

Columbus the sailor, Columbus the Discoverer-to-Be of Brasil (damn that horsetrader Vespucci, who would never discover his own navel now), Columbus the man cities and nations would be named after excused himself and, before our New World Chris could get through more than a single fantasy of the woman he would have that night, his namesake had returned with Felipa, his very own wife. And happily ever after, she fucked our Chris, from Columbus, Ohio, and the District of Columbia, via Colombia and Brazil, until he fell asleep into space-time and woke in the arms of a Felipa look-alike at the base of the Columbus Monument on the island of San Salvador, Bahamas.

Eventually, business was so good, Chris and Felipa moved back to Lisbon to be closer to the king and to all the money he was handing out for exploration. Columbus still went on voyages here and there. While he was off cavorting, Felipa was stuck at home alone.

In those days, a woman seeking private advice would go to her mother or her priest. But let's imagine what Felipa would have done if Ann Landers were there to ask about what was eating her.

Devoted Wife or Liberated Woman?

à la Ann Landers

Dear Ann Landers:

Please tell me if I am the greatest fool who ever lived or just another, run-of-the-mill flibbertigibbet.

My husband is a sailor. He brings in a decent income (from working for my brother), and I get royalties from the treasure maps he has drawn of the African and Scandinavian coasts and from his charts of islands in the Ocean Sea. He has given me a son I can be proud of, even if the boy is more insolent than his father and insists on treating me like the help. I know my husband fools around, but what can you expect when everyone else he knows has a girl in every port.

I have an adequate apartment in Lisbon, my son is off at a monastery school, my husband is off at sea, and I am surrounded by a number of admirers, whom I keep at arm's length with strategies even Odysseus's Penelope could never have thought up. It is my increasing skill in inventing strategies to keep the suitors coming—but not too fast or furious—which has led me to reconsider my position. In other words, I think I've got something. A special talent. And I want to market it.

Just imagine! *20 Ways to Keep Them Guessing*. Followed by *20 More Ways to Keep Them Guessing* and *Keep Them Guessing Some More*. As a bonus, patterns for weaving your husband's shroud. Think how they'd sell in a country where shipboard jobs are increasing at the rate of 35% a year! Talk show appearances, signings, a newspaper column like yours, foreign rights sales, *Keep Them Guessing* widows' walks and telescopes. Who knows how far it might go!

But, of course, there's a catch. If I go public with my schemes, my husband will find out that I've been encouraging the attention of other men. And he'll have my hide (he's not slavishly loving, like Odysseus).

So here's my dilemma: do I remain the devoted wife of a philandering man, employing my strategic skills solely for my own benefit, or do I become a liberated woman and share my skills with the world, become rich and famous, and risk a violent death at the hands of my husband or my son? Please advise me. I don't know what to do.

—Between the Devil and the Deep Blue Sea

Dear Devil:

You have an opportunity to make it on your own and a husband and son who couldn't care less if the Inquisition were to drag you away in the middle of the night. I've heard your story zillions of times, but I still feel the pain again each time I hear it. Fortunately, there are experts and organizations that have helped others in your predicament. Write to: Get Lost, a Sicily-based group (P.O. Box 666, Palermo Station) that makes sure sailors get lost at sea and children get lost on their way home from school. Or find a nice villa in the Algarve, take a pen name, and don't let anyone know where you are except your agent. By the time one of your devils gets back from the deep blue sea and the other one gets back from school, you'll be long gone, incognito, and raking it in.

Remember: neither sex has a monopoly on abandoning a spouse and child.

Well, there was no Ann Landers in the fifteenth century and Felipa wasn't about to ask a priest about making money by encouraging adultery. She was most likely working on the first draft of her first book when she heard that her husband's ship would arrive in Lisbon that night.

Where there's Stephen King, there's fire. And blood and mysterious happenings. And death. What this all has to do with Columbus's return to Lisbon, you'll learn by reading the big type below.

SPIDERKEEPER

à la Stephen King's *Firestarter*

It wasn't until he'd reached the sanctuary of a Spanish monastery that Christopher Columbus could look back on the horrors of the last week. It was all his fault, not his sweet, young, innocent son's. The boy couldn't help it. A great mariner like himself should have foreseen it all and formed a strategy guaranteed to nip the horrors in the bud.

Diego wore a bright red dress with blue epaulets and green tights. His mother's dress was black and fell to the floor. Her sleeves were long and her face was long, too.

Diego was busy in his room. He was playing with his spider collection. The spiders were alive. They were crawling everywhere.

His mother was busy in the kitchen. She was making dinner. Her husband, Chris, was coming home from sea.

Diego was excited to show his father his spider collection. It had been very small

(as had Diego)

when they were back in Porto Santo. But here in Lisbon, Diego had found many new species, most of them imported. And they all had names. Latin ones. But the pride of his collection had come from Porto Santo: *Geolycosa ingens*, the wolf spider.

Although Lisbon was crawling with spiders, none of them could hold a poison sac to *Geolycosa ingens*. The mascot of Porto Santo, it was the only creature native to an island whose plantlife was rapidly being decimated by imported rabbits. It was also the rabbit's only predator. Diego'd been so happy in Porto Santo.

(crawling with wolf spiders, wolf spiders, wolf spiders)

When his parents came to take him to the boat, to take him to Lisbon, to take him away from Porto Santo, his eyes ripped holes in their flesh. He vowed right then and there that they would pay. And the earth trembled with spiders thumping their endorsement (or was that just the rabbits?).

Christopher Columbus was pulling into Lisbon harbor after a long trip to the top of the earth. Word had just reached him that his wife was seeing other men. By San Fernando, it had only been a year since he'd seen her! Goddamit, didn't she have the slightest bit of patience? They were all alike.

Ah, but Diego would be a big boy now. Almost ready for the Ocean Sea. He would be strong and hardy, just the way he himself had been at five, and he would have interests to share and wisdom to gain. If only he has forgotten the Big Bad Thing or remembered how big and bad it is and told it where to go. Either would be just fine.

The first thing he'd do when he arrived at his home

would be to get on the boy's good side (if he still had one) and see whether the Big Bad Thing was active. And if it was, he would do everything short of destroying the boy in order to stop it. For good! And if that was not enough . . . he dared not think.

Chris's welcome-home dinner was burned. Felipa was so afraid that her husband had heard the false gossip (or even the true gossip) that was going around the Alfama, she had lost her sense of time. Only the utmost fear, driven by vibrations in the ground beneath her feet, could make her lose this, her deepest, most powerful sense.

She was afraid how Diego would greet his father. What would he remember? How would he feel about this big, burly hunk of a man who would stride into the room like a ram into a pen full of waiting ewes? No, that was *her* feelings. What would this sudden return, after a long, long year, do to the Big Bad Thing if it were laying dormant within Diego?

Felipa had protected Diego from the encroaching outside world and she had shielded him from all emotions as well. All he felt was love for his spiders and disdain for her, as if she were nothing but a servant seeing to his needs. That was good. Hard, but good. However, Chris would not let anyone treat him like a servant. Especially his son. And he wasn't wild about spiders either. And maybe the Big Bad Thing had been developing in Chris as well! She was terrified. So terrified, she'd burned the welcome-home dinner.

Christopher Columbus strode into Felipa's house like a ram into a pen that contains his only lamb. Passing

Felipa as if she were a servant (that is, with a good smack on her ample behind), Chris strode on into Diego's room and took him up in his arms.

The spider Diego'd been playing with fell onto Chris's leg and gave him a good, swift bite. "Shit!" Chris cried out. "Shit! What is *that*?"

Diego said, proudly, "An African red, fresh off da Gama's ship. I went down to the docks myself to get it."

(at least I wasn't playing with my wolf, my wolf, my wolf)

Chris managed a puzzled smile and brushed the spider onto the floor, crushing it under his great boots carefully so that Diego didn't see. "You should've seen the whales around Thule! They could pack a mighty big bite themselves!"

Chris laughed the first laugh in a long, long year at sea. Felipa heard it in the next room

(can't believe I'm listening at the door)

and could not decide whether to laugh or cry, whether it was the diabolical laugh of the Big Bad Thing or Chris was so deathly afraid he'd lost his sense of dignity.

"I've got dozens of 'em," Diego cried out to his father. "Put me down and I'll show you."

But Chris didn't want to put his beautiful son down and he didn't want to look at another goddamn spider.

"Put me down, I say." And Chris hugged the boy tighter for his manly authority.

"Put me down *or else!*" And Chris felt his son vibrate mysteriously, and the ground beneath him vibrated as well. And the spider cages, too, seemed to shake, as if the spiders would all escape at once.

Chris put his son down and the floor stopped shaking.

* * *

At that moment, Felipa entered the room. "Dinner ready?" asked Diego. "I'm starved, and so are my friends. And this here's Daddy. Daddy, meet Mommy."

(mommy's a lousy cook)

They exchanged a bow and curtsy. Then Mommy told her men that she'd burned dinner and they'd have to go out to eat.

"Out on my first night home!" Chris declared. "Out when I've just come in!"

"Don't want go out," announced Diego. "Don't want. And *they* don't either."

"But there's *no* more food in the house, Diego," Felipa pleaded. She was breathing hard. "I'm sorry. I'm *sorry.*"

"You'll be sorry, for sure," Diego swore, and he looked up at his Daddy with a Big Bad smile.

Suddenly there was quiet, as if they were no longer in the middle of the greatest, busiest port in the world, as if they were in the eye of a hurricane that was destroying everything in sight but them. Then everything began to shake: the china (blue china from Southern China), the Swiss-made, walnut grandfather clock, the crucifixes (some with drops of real blood dabbed on), and the spider cages, made from a special African teak. There was a strange, subdued light in the room.

Chris wanted to grab Diego and challenge the Big Bad Thing man-to-whatever, but he was suddenly so tired he couldn't move. He looked down and saw two teams of little white spiders crawling up his legs. He couldn't budge. He couldn't remember the Lord's Prayer. He couldn't even swear an oath to San Fernando.

Felipa wasn't frozen. She was ripping at her dress and screaming to highest heaven. She ripped layer after layer, but Chris still couldn't see what was wrong. She seemed insane, more insane than ever before.

And Diego. Diego was laughing at Felipa and giving Chris a smile of pride.

(this is your gift, Daddy, the gift you really wanted deep in your heart)

Felipa flailed and Chris froze and Diego laughed.

I should have foreseen this. I should have known that the Big Bad Thing would not go away simply with age. I should have known it would sense how angry I am with Felipa.

Finally, all the layers of Felipa's skirts had been ripped away and Chris could see a spider bigger than any he'd ever stepped on, even in Porto Santo. A wolf spider! That island was cursed, and rightly so, considering that Felipa's brother was its governor. That horse-trader! Felipa was wrong to let Diego keep his collection and wrong to let it become an obsession. How could she not have realized that the Big Bad Thing feeds on obsessions? Now she was paying for her poor judgment.

Felipa let out yelp after yelp until, finally, she crumpled onto the floor. Dead. It was over.

The sounds of Lisbon returned, as did all the spiders to their cages. Diego hugged his father and looked up at him with beaming expectation. Chris was able now to raise his hand and slap the boy, but he realized that could mean he'd join his wife on the floor. Dead. So instead, he patted the boy on the head and said, "I'll have to teach you how to use your spiders for greater ends.

For example, there's this Portuguese king who keeps turning me down for a loan. . ."

Okay, no one really knows how Felipa died. In fact, some historians have speculated that Columbus left her behind in Lisbon when he went to Spain to get money out of King Ferdinand and Queen Isabella. But he did take his son along, he did find a circle of supporters at the La Rábida Monastery near Palos, and he did hang out in Cordova, where he took up with a circle of intellectuals and financiers who met at an apothecary and tried to help realize Columbus's dreams. He also took up with Beatriz Enriquez de Harana, a cousin of one of his apothecary mates, who helped realize Columbus's fantasies.

The reason Columbus went to Spain is that he had struck out with King João II of Portugal. The Portuguese king had thrown all his support behind a route to the Indies via Africa's Cape of Good Hope, which Bartolomeu Dias would round in 1488. Columbus's next step was to get into the good graces of Queen Isabella, a most devoutly Christian woman, but a woman nevertheless.

One of the most important first meetings in recent history was that between Ronald Reagan and Mikhail Gorbachev, at least to Ronald Reagan. My parody closely follows the Reagan description of this first meeting, which is how he introduces the story of his life.

MEETING ISABELLA

à la Ronald Reagan's *An American Life*

Beatriz and I awoke early on the morning of May Day 1486, and at the first glimmer of daylight, we looked from our bedroom at the long gray expanse of the Guadalquivir River. In the distance we could see the majestic high minarets of the Alcazar.

Below, the river was shrouded in a dull mist. Above, the sky was a dull curtain of dark clouds. In between, there was nothing at all.

It was a dreary, miserable, foreboding, yet strikingly beautiful panorama.

I had looked forward to this day for more than a year. For weeks, I'd been given detailed information about political currents in the Spanish court and the complexities of the war against the Moors. In my diary the night before, I wrote: "Lord, I hope I'm ready. And if I'm not, You'll have a lot of explaining to do!"

Neither Beatriz nor I had slept very well that night. We had spent the evening at the drugstore, having malts with Diego de Harana, Antonio de Marchena, and some of my other aides and their mistresses. Doctors said the malts would help me build my body in five or six different ways. And they taste good, too.

Juan Pérez told me that if the only thing that came out of this first meeting with Queen Isabella was an agreement to hold another meeting, it would be a success. But I wanted to accomplish more than that. I dreamed an impossible dream.

I believed that if we were ever going to break down the barriers that prevented us from crossing the Ocean Sea, we had to begin by establishing a personal relationship between the greatest mariner and the greatest ruler on earth.

During the previous five years, I had come to realize there were people in the Spanish court who had a genuine fear of the Ocean Sea and what lay beyond, who actually believed that God didn't want us to go there. I wanted to convince Isabella that God wanted me to discover what was on the other side and that she had nothing to fear from it; I had His assurances. So I had gone to Cordova with a plan. I had even packed my cordovan loafers.

The Spanish court had its team of diplomats and maritime experts (and King Ferdinand as well) and I had mine (but no King Ferdinand). However, I wanted a chance to see the Queen alone.

Since I had come to Spain a year earlier, Isabella and I had quietly exchanged billets-doux that had suggested to me she might be a different sort of Queen than the queens I had known before.

That morning, as we bowed and curtsied and I looked into her smile, I sensed I had been right and felt a surge of optimism that my plan might work. I also asked an aide to remind me to recommend my dentist to her.

As we began our first meeting in the presence of our advisors, Isabella and I sat opposite one another. I had told my team what I was going to do.

As our technical experts began to speak, I said to her, "While our people here are discussing the pressing need to cross the Ocean Sea, why don't you and I step outside and get some fresh air?"

Isabella was out of her throne before I could finish the sentence. We walked together about one hundred feet down a hill to a boathouse along the river.

As we descended the hill, the air was crisp and very cold. It might even have been called "brisk." I'd asked members of the apothecary staff to light a fire in the boathouse before we got there, and they had: Only later did I discover they'd built such a rip-roaring fire that it melted a gold reliquary containing hairs from the beard and lion of St. Jerome. The fire had to be doused with pitchers of water and then relighted a couple of hours before we arrived.

We sat down beside the blazing hearth, just the two

of us, and I told the Queen that I thought she and I were in a unique situation at a unique time. "Here you and I are, a man and a woman in a room, probably the one man and woman in the world who could lessen the distance between Spain and whatever lands lie across the Ocean Sea, stock full of gold to mine and souls to save. But by the same token, we may be the only man and woman who could let all that gold and all those souls lie useless and sinful."

Borrowing a quotation from an old friend of mine, I continued: "Isabella, You can't cheat an honest queen. And never give a sucker an even break. It's fine that the two of us and our people are talking about reducing the distance between Spain and the Indies, but isn't it also important that you and I should be talking about how we could reduce the distance between the two of *us*?" And we did.

In the preceding months I'd fantasized many times about this first meeting with Isabella. Nothing was more important to mankind than assuring its continuing expansion. Yet for all of eternity our fear of the unknown had kept the world under a shadow of ignorance. Our thoughts about the Ocean Sea had been based on a policy known as "Flat Earth and Eternal Damnation"— the "FEED" policy, but feed us it didn't. It was the craziest thing I ever heard of: Simply put, it called for us to look out to sea and not want to take a boat out there. We were just a few thousand doubloons from discovery.

I wanted to go to the negotiating table and stop feeding the FEED policy, but to do that, I knew I first had to upgrade my religious concepts so that I would be able to negotiate from a position of *strength*, not weakness.

That is why I had returned to the Monastery of La Rábida.

"We have a choice," I told the Queen. "We can agree to discover what lies across the Ocean Sea—or we can continue to ignore it, *which I think you know you can't do forever* (because France, Portugal, and England certainly won't). I will not stand by and let you maintain your superstitious ignorance. Together we can try to do something about ending the ignorance."

Our meeting beside the glowing hearth went on for an hour and a half, and when it was over, I couldn't help but think something fundamental had changed in the relationship between us. Now I knew we had to keep it going. To paraphrase Robert Frost and Sigmund Freud, there would be many mountains to climb before we slept.

As we walked up the hill toward the house where our advisors were still meeting, I told Isabella: "You know, you've never seen my cell, never been there. I think you'd enjoy a visit there. Why don't we agree we'll have a second rendezvous next week and hold it in my cell at the monastery? I hereby invite you."

"I accept," Isabella replied, then, with hardly a pause, she said: "But you've never seen the court in Seville." I said, "No," and she said, "Well, then let's hold a third rendezvous in Seville."

"I accept," I said.

My people couldn't believe it when I told them what had happened. They all laughed at Christopher Columbus. But who's got the last laugh now!

Part of the fun of a biography are those interludes that tell you what it was like to live in a particular place and a particular time, especially when the particular people are royalty, with lots of palaces, castles, and fortresses.

America doesn't have monarchs or even palaces, but it does have a president and a White House. George Bush hasn't had the occasion yet to write his full-length autobiography, so we'll have to settle for his dog, Millie, who seems to have had more than enough time, despite the occasional litter of puppies. It's nice to have servants, isn't it. And even nicer to have a master who decides to further the cause of literacy by showing that even a dog can write a book (submissions of manuscripts to book publishers have tripled since the book came out).

In the following parody, I begin to use Columbus's Spanish name, Cristóbal Colón. He had an Italian name, a Portuguese name, and assorted others, but I decided to stick with two. Believe it or not, there is a bit of method to this madness.

KATY'S BOOK
AS DICTATED TO ISABELLA OF CASTILE

à la Mildred Kerr Bush's
Millie's Book: As Dictated to Barbara Bush

The Alcazar in Seville is my favorite palace. It seems that we take over a new Alcazar just about every year, but none of them is as homey as this one.

Just walk in through the main gate and you will quickly see why. You walk right into the Court de la Monteria, which leads to a long gallery. That is where Kingsy sends me to walk myself when he is "busy." Iz insists that dogs must do what they do in the garden, but Kingsy is so "busy" he can't be bothered, and I dislike nothing more than digging. It's so . . . well, dirty.

The gallery takes you to the Court of Honor and its grand Mudejar façade. It's so graceful and intricate! Although I have sat in on my little masters' geometry lessons, I still cannot understand all those shapes. Iz told me that they are known as "arabesques," because they are the work of Arabs. That makes sense, even if the designs do not.

What I like most about the Alcazar is all the colonnades. There's nothing like a few hundred columns to get a dog excited. Who needs trees outside when there are the next best thing right in your own house. Talk about fantasies! Kingsy never had one as good as my reality.

But even Paradise isn't perfect. The Alcazar is also full of chests. I don't know what they keep in them, and I don't care. But they're everywhere, and they're such obstacles! Every time I get running real good, I slam right into one. I think they move a bit when they know I'm coming.

My favorite room is the Salon de los Embajadores. It is splendid! Magnificent! Too too! All those wild designs, all in and out and around and through. I have heard soldiers say that the reason they were able to take Seville from the Moors is that the Moors would smoke hashish, walk into this room, and freak out. For days, they were unable to fight; some never returned to normal. Sort of like lead and the Romans, the soldiers say, and add, "We won't make the same mistake with the New World and gold." And I believe them.

My favorite aroma comes from the Inquisition's barbecues. Nothing in the world smells so sweet. They have their barbecues right outside the walls, and when the wind is right I get to spend hours devouring the fumes. Once Torquemada became Iz's confessor and convinced her to make him Chief Inquisitor back in 1483, he collected together what must have been and still are the best chefs in Spain, or anywhere for that matter, at least judging by the pungent bouquet of their roasts. And you know it must taste good as well, because they never serve me a bite, not even a left-over bone.

But Iz became less interested in Torquemada and the Inquisition when this fellow Cristóbal Colón started coming around. I never before saw Iz so lively and excited. She acted just like a princess! She could talk about nothing but Cris and his trade routes and gold and souls and how she was going to be the richest and most powerful ruler in Europe, and maybe then, at last, she would dump Kingsy and take Cristóbal of the Indies as her consort. I didn't like to see her whispering about such things, but I couldn't tell Kingsy; he doesn't understand Dog. I tried every combination of whimpers and paw tapping and head shaking, but all he could think was that I had that "heat thing." That man has a one-track mind.

The Queen's Chamber is where I sleep, on a miniature bed that looks just like Iz's, but is not so high off the ground. Let me tell you about an important moment in the Chamber's history: the first time Cristóbal Colón came into it. It was early in 1492 and after a big row between Iz and Kingsy, it looked like Cris was in the doghouse. But one day, there Cris was in the Court of Honor, alone. He had left his entourage back at the apothecary in Cordova. Kingsy was out of town, of course. Cris insisted that he had made an appointment, but then he pulled out his calendar and realized it was for next month at the same time. "But while I am here," he added, "we might as well talk." He made a very strange face and some not so strange gestures (I'd seen Kingsy make them to the maidservants many times). Iz asked him to follow her. I followed, too.

Iz asked Cris to go into the Chamber first, but he insisted *she* go first. While they were bickering just the way she and Kingsy do about paying the bill at a restaurant, I simply decided something had to be done and entered the room first myself. Well, Cris reached down and grabbed me by the scruff of my neck and punted me through the Patio of the Dolls right smack into a chest. Ouch! I have never felt anything like that kick (even puppybirth), and I hope I never do again.

For almost six years, Columbus followed the Spanish court around as the Spanish fought the Moors and took long siestas between battles. The more Isabella rejected his petitions, the more money and titles Columbus demanded. Royal commissions said he didn't know what he was talking about (and they were, for the most part, right). And all of Columbus's supporters in court and among intellectuals and financiers could not make Isabella budge. Her heart and soul were focused on driving the Moors out of Spain. And she might even have enjoyed the way Columbus doted on her.

Then one fine day in 1492, Granada fell, the Moors were defeated, and Columbus was called before Ferdinand and Isabella one last time. Hope sprung eternal. At least for a moment.

Of course, behind the throne there was a great deal of political posturing and intrigue. No contemporary American writer has mastered the personal side of politics like Gore Vidal. His novelized American history is brimming with all manner of mannerisms, prejudice posing as opinion, and weak chins exposed for what they are.

1492

à la Gore Vidal

Luis de Santangel, King Ferdinand's chief financial adviser, was waiting in his office for the Queen's decision on the financing of the Columbus expedition. Although—and very likely because—his wife was nagging him for money to buy more shoes and his children were playing a combination of Doctor-and-Nurse and Hide-and-Seek in-and-out of his desk, Santangel was recalling his first impressions of Columbus, who was known to him and his circle as the Argonaut. Before the Argonaut had even opened his self-righteous mouth, with its full, red lips and its peculiar tic when anything religious came out of it, which was often, he had made it apparent to the world that he was an opportunist of the most consummate variety. But his opportunism was of an attractive sort, not too different from Santangel's own youthful ambition to control the finances of Spain, if not in name, then in reality. An ambition he had, of course, fulfilled.

Now here the Argonaut was, thrice rejected and then, after Granada had been taken and the Moors defeated forever and a day, given one last audience with the Queen. When he left, the Queen declared that she would see no one else before she had made her final decision. As a matter of fact, she never did *see* anyone. Santangel laughed at how many men had told him—as melodramatically as if they were playing a minor saint in a miracle play—that she had looked right through them during their audience and seen all they were, all they had been, and all they would ever be or—if she felt so inclined—would never be; in fact, the Queen was terribly near-sighted and had developed a knowingly blank stare that brought her great amusement through the terror it brought to the victims' faces, as if they stood naked before her. It was Santangel's dabbling in the young science of optics that allowed him to comprehend—and withstand—the moral as well as political siege her vision placed on her visitors.

The Argonaut, too, had withstood the Queen's siege from the very first, Alonso de Quintanilla, the court treasurer, recalled. That is why, from the mariner's very first visit to court back in 1486, Quintanilla—known to his associates as Quintessence—had taken money from the court's coffers to keep the Argonaut and his mistress living comfortably during what he knew would be several years of wooing the Queen. And no one wooed like the Argonaut wooed. He could woo her with financial figures, with quotes from obscure apocryphal texts, with catty observations about her ladies-in-waiting, even with stories about the bungled exploits of her husband, which bored her coming from lesser jesters, including that conceited ass Santangel, whose monstrous ego never let him see who really held the royal pursestrings. The Argonaut got her laughing so hard about the pretentious gavel-swinging mannerisms of Hernando de Talavera—chairman of the royal commission that studied the Argonaut's proposal and found it impossible, unnecessary, ill-advised, and overpriced—that the Queen ignored the commission's conclusions and continued to give the Argonaut public—and private—audiences.

"The Marquise de Moya," a swarthy servant called out from Santangel's door.

"Show her," said Santangel coyly, "in." To his wife he added, "Goodbye, darling. And take the children with you. All of them."

"Don't lay one hand on that Marquise!" Doña Santangel muttered over her breath. She always addressed her husband in the imperative, and her husband always disregarded her edicts.

In fluttered one of the most magnificent creatures to have decorated the court of the Most Christian Monarchs. She was dressed in the latest craze—a gown sewn from the uniforms of Moors who had fallen at Granada. So that there would be no doubt about her rank, her gown was made only from generals' uniforms and from gowns ripped off the generals' wives.

But no one, Santangel mused, gave one damn about

the Marquise's rank. No one even seemed to care about her cratered face, which she covered with a simple black veil, in mourning for her father twenty years after his venereal death. What gave the Marquise her elevated situation in court was the way she could sum everyone up in a single adverb/adjective duo. The Queen was overweeningly understated and King Ferdinand was a highbrow lowbrow or lowbrow highbrow, as you chose; Torquemada was catastrophically catechistic; Quintessence was quintessentially quiescent; and the Argonaut was devoutly devoid. She called Santangel himself, he had heard from one of the ladies-in-waiting, insatiably omnivorous, and this lady-in-waiting, in turn, was deemed meretriciously unmerited. Thousands of epithets had been invented for the Marquise, but none of them was good enough to stick. If she had one for herself, she had skillfully kept it mum.

"Well—?" she asked breathily.

"Well what?" Santangel replied as he so often did, with a question.

"Thumb up or thumb down?"

"No thumb at all," he answered. "Not yet."

"She'll send him packing, I can feel it in the middle toe of my left foot."

"And France will have all the gold that lies across the Ocean Sea. And all the slaves as well. They'll bury us under a slimy mountain of frogs and snails."

He had touched the Marquise's weak spot—her stomach. She rushed from the room and left Santangel alone to contemplate the perfect description of her. Sketchily skewed? Verbally vernal? Characteristically uncharacterizable?

"Alonso de Quintanilla." Another interruption.

"Show him in."

"The verdict is," said Quintessence, "in."

"And— ?" Quintessence took forever to get to a point, Santangel noted with a patronizing smile. Often he never arrived there at all. Lacking in moral fiber, he would make a splendid lackey to a country marquis, and no more. That is why Santangel had asked for his appointment.

"Look out your window, Luis. He's already on the outskirts of town, and he's riding a mule!"

"For a guy who boasts about being the Second Coming of Jesus Christ, he seems to be doing things rather backwards riding a mule instead of a donkey and going *out* of town rather than *in*."

"It does seem a bit . . . shall we say. . ."

"That ass of a queen! I worked my oratory to the bone keeping the Argonaut from going off to France to join his brother. This time she's overdone her overweening."

"Shall we seek an audience with Her Most Goyal Highness?" Quintessence guffawed at his pet name for the Queen, and he wiped saliva from his lips with a beige-and-green Egyptian cotton handkerchief given him by the ugly but promiscuous daughter of a Provençal knight-errant who had passed through the court in his quest for a son-in-law.

"We shall *demand* an audience."

As they sauntered out of the room, holding their sheaths against their legs, Santangel's servant marveled at how excited a couple of grown men could get about an Italian's cockamamie scheme to sink the royal treasury as surely as he would sink the ships he wanted the Queen to give him. If it was such a splendid idea, why wasn't the Queen putting her money on a true, *Spanish* sailor? Everyone knew it wasn't the Italian's oratory that had won her heart, and it most likely was not his oratory that had disappointed her so much she'd given him the gate at last.

Queen Isabella heard her two financial wizards clomping down the hall long before they appeared—out-of-breath—before her. She loved to watch Quintessence bow and scrape. And she adored nothing more than the way Santangel looked through her with the princely confidence of a conman. She and Santangel were far better matched than she and that Genoese ship's boy.

The finance wizards entered and rushed through their courtly protocol. "Dearest Queen," Santangel began, while Quintessence blotted his forehead with a jade-green and ruby-red silken handkerchief carried overland from China by one of Marco Polo's mistresses, "you can't let him go to France. If you do, you will be remembered as the Queen who turned her back on the future of Spain."

"I simply turned my back on that boorish Italian sailor. I had my fun with him. What matter is it of yours?"

"He is the savior of Spain," Quintessence said sincerely.

"He told me," the Queen responded crossly, "that he is the savior of *mankind*."

"What's the difference?" the clever Santangel asked.

"Touché," the Queen cheered, but then she put her hand over her mouth; French was not the most appropriate language for her response. "Santangel, make your case, and make it snappy."

"First, Your Dearest Majesty, there is what is closest to *your* heart: the glory of Spain, the fact that Spain was chosen by God to lead mankind toward the End of All Times. Second, there is what is closest to *my* heart: all the gold that is purported to be waiting for someone to discover it across the Ocean Sea. And third, the first cannot be accomplished without the second. With the Ottomans in Constantinople and Jerusalem, now is the time to raise a crusade to take back the Holy Sepulcher. And once we discover a short sea route to all of the world, it will be time to send Spanish priests to convert all the heathen, teach them Spanish, and set the stage for a Spanish Second Coming. Do you want Charles of France to be known as the greatest monarch in the history of Christianity? Do you want *him* to stand at the right side of God for all eternity? And all due to boredom with a man who knows more about satisfying fish than women?"

Isabella positively jackknifed to her feet and approached Santangel so that, for the first time in their long acquaintance, she could look him in the eye. She realized now that he was not doing this simply for his own glory, but for hers as well. She could see now that he had a pair of the softest baby blues she'd ever seen on anyone over three, including Columbus. She could see now that she would have to ask him to a private meeting when this business was finally put to bed.

She called out imperiously in the general direction of Quintessence, "Have that Genoese jack-tar brought to the throne room. Immediately!"

Columbus's scheme now had the full support of the throne. He was on his way to riches, power, and immortality. If he survived the voyage.

But how did royal support for an Italian's crazy voyage appear to the Spaniard-on-the-street? No American columnist takes the pulse of the people better than Art Buchwald, and Buchwald does a mean blood pressure test as well. Because he's a humorist, Buchwald's not so easy to parody; therefore, this chapter in the life of Columbus is more an imitation than a parody.

GOODBYE, COLUMBUS
à la Art Buchwald

The question on everyone's lips since Ferdinand and Isabella drove all the Moors and Jews out of Spain has been: Who's next? Or, more appropriately, Who's left?

I thought this question would give me at least ten columns-worth of funny hypothetical answers, but old Izzy didn't miss a beat. The answer is Italians, or so my friend Angelo told me the other day.

"Arturo," he said, "is it our gesticulations?"

"Is what your gesticulations?"

"Is it our gesticulations that's making them drive us out of Spain?" He was gesticulating in high gear as he spoke.

I asked Angelo why he was suddenly getting so paranoid, and would he please put his hands in his pockets. He tried, but his hands wouldn't stay put, so I tied them behind his back. As if I'd nearly zippered his lips shut, he spoke in a half-whisper, half-mumble: "I was there, at court, when they told that Columbus character—you know, that assimilated Italian who calls himself Colón—to get the hell out of Spain. And they even offered him ships. That stingy Queen. Imagine!"

"What exactly did she say?"

"She said, 'Sail off the edge of the earth if that's what you want! Or discover a continent. I don't care!' "

"Such a pious woman. She doesn't even know how to curse."

"That's what I thought. But then Ferdy said something similar. And I know *he* can swear."

"Columbus . . . Colón . . . ," I said, trying to place the name. "Isn't he the nut who talks about golden islands across the Ocean Sea and a shortcut to the Indies? Who cares if he *does* fall off the earth?"

"But Art, Columbus could fall off the earth in a dinghy. Why would the Queen offer three ships to get rid of just one nut? I tell you, the Italians are next. Isabella simply can't bear our pasta or our bocce and especially Sophia Loren. But most of all, she can't stand people asking, Who's next? First they ask who's going to be next to go and, if there isn't an answer soon, then they'll start asking who's going to be next on the throne. Sure as my hometown tower leans. They've been doing it in Italy for years. And Isabella couldn't bear to part with her china or those handsome courtiers of hers."

We batted around the alternatives—Portuguese, French, Basques, Gypsies, homosexuals. We agreed that driving out any of them would satisfy Isabella's subjects twice as much as driving out the Italians.

But then suddenly Angelo broke free from the knot I'd never been able to get right, even as a boy scout. And mid-sentence, he began to gesticulate right where he'd left off. It was then that I realized what the Queen was up to. Even Basques don't gesticulate like that; they just plant bombs. And all Gypsies do is purloin an occasional purse. Pulling a flag out of a drawer and singing the national anthem, I pointed to the door and, patriotically, I bade Angelo farewell.

Columbus had fought a long, hard battle and had obtained everything he desired. All he needed to do now was realize his dream, and keep it from becoming a nightmare.

When a hero makes it big, the first thing he does is thank the little people who helped him get where he is. America has had no better hero in this sense than Jimmy Carter, and so it is to Uncle Jimmy's autobiography that I turn for a bit of thanksgiving.

Keeping Score

à la Jimmy Carter's *Keeping Faith*

People along the route to Court, when they saw that I had gotten down off my donkey and was jogging, began to cheer and to weep, and it was an emotional experience for me as well.

DIARY, APRIL 17, 1492

I was on my way to be inaugurated as *Admiral of the Ocean Sea, Viceroy and Governor of Lands To Be Discovered, and Captain General* by Queen Isabella and King Ferdinand. As I rolled slowly off my donkey, the people seemed anxious and concerned about me. Perhaps, I realized, they thought the donkey was ill.

But then a shock wave went through the crowd. There were gasps of astonishment and cries of "First a donkey and now he's jogging! Will he skip on water next?!" The excitement flooded over me. It was bitterly cold, but I felt warm inside. It was one of those few perfect moments in life when everything and everyone seems absolutely right, except the heckler who said I couldn't sail a dinghy in a bathtub.

I would like to delegate authority in my role as Admiral of the Ocean Sea, etc., but I am not certain that would be best for all involved. Therefore, as sure as the Indies are across the Ocean Sea, I will do all that is within the bounds of human capability to do everything myself (including menial labor, which Beatriz and I enjoy a great deal).

DIARY, APRIL 24, 1492

When I went to Seville for the inauguration, I brought with me not only my personal family, but also my Monastery, Apothecary, and Italian families, which I like to refer to as my "team." I had made a private promise to myself, complete with secret handshake, to tap some of the talented Franciscans, Italians, and scientists who had served me as a candidate for Admiral of the Ocean Sea, etc. My decisions about how to use them were not made casually, but somewhere between informally and black tie.

I knew that other Admirals had been criticized for installing their "cronies," but as the first Admiral of the Ocean Sea, I didn't give a hoot what anybody might say, until, of course, they said it. My team had been tested in the political crucible and had all gotten at least a C+ in experience (with one exception among the Franciscans) and no less than a B- in competence (with one exception among the Italians).

As Beatriz and I planned our new life, I recalled how much some of these men and women had shared with me over the years. Let's see: Fra Juan Pérez and Fra Antonio de la Marchena had shared their wisdom and piety; the Count of Medina Celi and the Duke of Medina Sidonia had shared their financial expertise and cash; and the Marquise de Moya had shared her excellent espionage skills, not to mention her quips. And no matter what they might say, I *do* have a sense of humor.

Fra Juan Pérez was more seriously misunderstood and underestimated than anyone else who worked for me (I know, because I kept score). I would like to tell you why, but I am not quite sure myself. Perhaps it was his abuse of his former confessor-confessee relationship with Queen Isabella. Perhaps it was the way he let his monastery become a hideout for pirates and Italian immigrants without papers. Perhaps it was the monastery's great success in laundering money as well as robes, hairshirts, and tapestries. I can't really say.

Even closer to me personally was the Marquise de Moya. As a lady-of-the-night in Genoa, she had welcomed me to her house on many occasions. She was younger than the others, yet seemed to know more about pleasing a man. I know this only from the stories she told me, because although I had lust for her in my heart, our friendship never passed beyond a wet kiss on the hand. When she hooked that ancient Marquis, I knew she was the one to get to the Queen if old Juan did not have it in him anymore.

Before I knew it, the Marquise was Isabella's best buddy. They were inseparable companions at cards, bullfights, and shopping sprees. Throughout my long campaign, the Marquise was almost always by my or Isabella's side. I often grew exasperated with her when she went to Court late, forgot to carry out my orders, or peddled her wares to the King, but many people—and I among them—think that she was one of the greatest undercover agents of all time, and she certainly talked the best game.

It is difficult for me to explain how close Don Luis de

la Cerda, Duke of Medina Celi, was to me or how much I depended on him. He was calm, mature, and boyish. Surprisingly clumsy for so tiny a man, he described himself as having "the shape of a dinghy and just as much grace." But this did not stop him from participating in sports, even fencing. His unheralded courage led him to sustain terrible wounds while jousting, which is why everyone calls him Luis the Lance.

Don Luis had to make a great financial sacrifice to help fund my voyages but, like several others I had the goods on, he was more than willing to do so. However, if he had only known what he would be put through in the years ahead, he might have gone to his priest and confessed every single one of his sins (if he were keeping score). He was a good businessman, a good friend, and a man of charity. He even sent Fra Juan Pérez a great deal of his friends' laundering business.

Of course, no one has meant more to me through these years of pain, sorrow, and victory than Beatriz. Although a sweet young thing of twenty when I met her, she has been an excellent mother, a loving companion, a faithful friend and, on occasion, a fierce combatant. Everyone likes to say that she is far brighter and clearsighted than I, but fortunately no one seems to state the corollary, which is that I am dull and foggyheaded. She blinds everyone to my limitations, and even I could never ask more of anyone.

Well, we're almost there: the launching of the *Niña*, the *Pinta*, and the *Santa María*, which, like Columbus himself, really had other names, at least until Columbus laid his paws on them. But first Columbus has to get those paws to work and put together one of the most famous voyages in the history of mankind.

To do that, Columbus had to have superior management skills. And he had to manage in an age when there were no business schools, no junk bonds, and no books on excellence, quality, or ethics in the workplace. Fortunately, America has a man who overcame the very same limitations to take one of America's largest corporations over the brink of catastrophe and, despite the help of the earth's two most powerful commercial nations, back to the brink again: Lee Iacocca.

COLUMBUS

à la Lee Iacocca's *Iacocca*

At the age of forty-one, I was Admiral of the most important marine expedition ever. At the same time, I was virtually unknown. Half the people in the royal court didn't know who I was. The other half knew me only as "the big wop."

I'm going to tell you what qualities allowed me to succeed in putting together this marine expedition. I'm not doing this for the money; I'm donating every penny I earn from this book to The Home for Retired Admirals. I'm not doing this to get back at certain kings and queens and nobles for not backing me all the way; I've already done that by showing them all. No, I'm doing this to set the record straight. My way.

* * *

When Queen Isabella called me over to her throne-room to tell me what I'd been begging her to tell me for years, I found myself in a delicate position. I had bypassed dozens of more prominent explorers on my way up the maritime mast. In addition, I still had no real credentials as a sea captain. At this point in my career there wasn't anything that people could point to and say, "Columbus did that." All they could do was point *at* me and laugh. Or even worse, they could not point at me at all.

I was left with one major job to accomplish: get together three ships and three crews. But that was nothing to me, for if I had to sum up in one word the qualities that make a good admiral, I'd say that it all comes down to decisiveness.

Decisiveness is a matter of acting. That's what life is all about, and death isn't. It would be nice to be absolutely certain that the Indies were only a hop-skip-and-jump across the Ocean Sea, but real exploration just doesn't work that way. All you have to work with are myths, tenth-hand reports, and daydreams. At some point you've got to take that leap of faith. And if you're a real admiral, you won't take that leap alone. No, you'll scrounge around for three ships and a hundred men or so (to be paid for by somebody else) and you'll let them take the leap with you. If the leap turns out to have been a little longer than you thought, at least the chronicles will bail you out.

People say I draw my sword before the count of three, that I'm a sail-by-prophecy operator, but I'm really an average sort of guy, just like you. The only difference is that I know how to act with authority, to take authority, and to demand more compensation each year than you'll ever see in a lifetime.

It only took me two months to put together my first voyage. This might sound like a lot of time, but when you consider that ninety percent of Spain's ships had been chartered by Jews to get the hell out of Spain before the deadline—literally—it's something you've got to admit only a guy with the brilliant management abilities of someone who has never set foot in Salamanca Business School could accomplish.

It all comes down to motivation. My more learned associates would call motivation a coda to my theory of decisiveness, since motivation is nothing more than getting others to act the way you want them to. But I prefer to call motivation the way to build a team, to inspire people, to make them achieve all they can achieve. As long as they achieve it all in my name.

The first rule for motivating underlings is to talk to them in their own language. That's why I learned Spanish. And you've got to put yourself in their position. This wasn't hard for me, because I, too, had been out of a job before (for six years, to be exact) and I, too, was deathly afraid that I'd fall off the edge of the earth or be eaten by ferocious monsters from Hell. But for me the risk was worth it. What I could never understand about the sailors was why they'd take the same risk for a few measly doubloons.

Second, you have to sell them on your vision. Selling inspiration is no different than selling women. To sell a woman, you have to convince the prospective purchaser that he will look good with her on his elbow and feel good with her in his bed. Inspiration provides the same sort of warm, cuddly feeling.

And not only do you have to sell, you also have to let them know the game plan and let them in on the game. And you have to make them respect you. That is the key to it all. Sell them by letting them in on the action and by gaining their respect. It's simple as any con game in town.

What I told prospective sailors was this: "I, too, was once afraid of crossing the Ocean Sea, but I know so much about the voyage now, it is no more fearful to me than crossing the Guadalquivir River, and certainly easier than saying it ten times in a row. When we return, all of us will be honored by all of Spain for opening up the wealth of the Indies to the Spanish alone. I guarantee you that you will all become millionaires and that none of you will ever have to swab a deck again."

I could see each of the men reaching deep into his heart and saying to himself, "That's exactly what I wanted to hear."

Third, you've got to put your foot where your mouth is. I know people smarter than I am, men with more experience, more understanding, more virtue, more stamina, and more sense. And yet I've left them behind in my wake. You don't succeed for long by thinking and talking. To get people to respect you, you've got to kick them around. Because when they begin to respect you, they'll follow you to the death. There's not much more you can ask of a man, or I'd try.

After my first speech to the men of Palos, they continued to mock me in the streets, throwing life-size effigies of me over the local lover's leap and calling out, "A leap of faith right off the edge of the earth!" and "The Indies are across the Ocean Sea just as much as I still love my wife!" Taking this as a sign of disrespect, I snuck up to the cliff and kicked a couple of the clowns so hard they joined their dummies on the rocks below. And I threatened to do the same to anyone who didn't sign up for my voyage.

Which brings me to my fourth point. To succeed, to gain respect, you have to have protection. This is something my more learned associates call "protectionism," but I prefer to call it the "birds-of-a-feather" principle. I might have been slaughtered right then and there had I not promised the two biggest honchos in town that, if they'd back me, I would give them a healthy cut, or "quota," of all the gold we found. And since no one in the area would ever work again if they got on the bad side of these two guys, I had a crew in no time at all. I certainly showed those peons good!

I succeeded in manning my first voyage by being decisive and by motivating the men of Palos. I motivated the sailors by talking to them in Spanish, by selling the voyage to them as if it were a whore, by lying to them through my teeth, by threatening them, by making good on my threats, and by obtaining protection. That is the art of putting together a team that will stick with you through thin, if not—I discovered—through thick.

At last, Columbus shoved off, set sail, and got going. For weeks he sailed through waters charted only in mapmakers' dreams.

The contemporary king of writing about forms of transportation rather than places of destination is Paul Theroux. Since Columbus had nothing but a name for his destination (and "the Indies" was nothing but a vague term for the vaguely known continent of Asia), a parody of no other writer will do for Columbus's view of the First Cruise across the Ocean Sea.

THE OLD PHOENICIAN EXPRESS

à la Paul Theroux's *The Old Patagonian Express*

I chose to get to the Indies via the Ocean Sea because everyone else had already chosen the land route or was trying to find a way around Africa. What really matters in travel is the journey, not the arrival, so even if I fell off the edge of the earth, as I was warned I would by a few of my more cozily hypocritical friends, the trip would have been worth the bother.

Yes, I had been sitting around far too long, so I opted for the journey and took a risk on what the arrival would be. And what a journey it was. Each day, the sunrises and sunsets took part in an Olympic competition, the flying fish flew on flights of fancy, and the storms took me dozens of miles off course and let me see vast empty expanses the average tourist never sees. But there was also the nauseating companionship of ordinary sailors, incurious, sullen, even surly. There was something Polish about the resigned way they went about their work each day. They bored me profoundly.

Ten days out, I realized how torrentially irrelevant

the ocean is. It forces its being on you so heavily and humidly that it becomes something unimaginably vile. Its roar is loathsomely emphatic, and its spray is a joke without a punchline. But how gloriously so! I don't believe there ever will be another ocean like the Ocean Sea. *Blam, blam, whoosh, whoosh,* it goes all day and night. It is smug in its unblushing repetition, and it is highly erotic in the way it spreads itself out and calls for you to dive right in. "By San Fernando!" I thought as I set sail on it. "Is *this* my transportation of choice? This farcically, profoundly loony body of salty liquid? It's a poor excuse for a sea." But it kept right on going. It was weird how far it actually went, and not an eyesore in sight.

The Ocean Sea is not only the cup out of which all fish drink (as all sailors drink from the very same cup on board) but, as if that's not horrific enough, it is also the toilet into which all of them vacate their fishy bowels (as all sailors vacate their own over the side). So clear, so cold, so sadomasochistic, yet the sea is nothing but an oversized cesspool. And not half big enough for *my* tastes.

And then there was the food. If I never saw another saharan biscuit or ate another gnarled slice of fatback, if I never again gagged on another garlic clove or drowned anything else in olive oil, I would be a very happy man. But the bread was the most nauseating sustenance of all. I wouldn't touch a crust of it before nightfall, that is, until after I couldn't see the maggots anymore.

There is truly nothing more remarkable than the Ocean Sea, which is why I intend to remark at great length about it. It has none of the quaint insignificance of a village, none of the extraordinary anticlimaxes of a pilgrimage on land. In fact, there isn't a thing about it that is measly, niggardly, or dry. Yet nothing is as dreary and bleak, as constantly itself, as absurdly absurd. It is like a field of poppies from the viewpoint of a worm, a fishing pond from the viewpoint of a tadpole, and a seraglio from the viewpoint of a castrato. One moment it is calm as a river, the next it shakes and rises like the quaking earth. Yet it is always wet and deep and cold and filthy.

Suddenly the Ocean Sea abandoned its canny monotony for increasingly extravagant masses of greenish weeds. The sea changed its sound from *Blam, blam, whoosh, whoosh* to *hush hush glorp glorp*. It changed its appearance from an endless receptacle for feces to an endless dumping ground for the garbage from all the gardens in the world. It changed its smell from the overwhelming stench of sodium chloride to the even more overwhelming fetidness of rotting vegetation.

"You are the first captain to see all this," one of my mates said to me that night. "And you might be the last."

I tossed a bottle of rum overboard and replied, "No, the Phoenicians were here before me, boy. They were great mariners, part of a culture that originated in what is now known as Genoa. They discovered the route to the Indies, but they did it for a lark. They were a good-time culture. And as far as the Phoenicians were concerned, the Indians didn't have anything to trade with them. All the Indians wanted to give them was a pile of yellow stones. And what, they asked themselves, could anyone do with that sort of junk? All I can say to that is, 'Thank the Holy Ghost for progress!'

A couple days later we reached the Indies. Of course, I was the first one to spot land, although one of the men had the nerve to take the credit. He ended up a few fathoms under, as the result of a tragic accident while getting into a dinghy to go ashore. But the journey is all, so I won't bother describing my arrival.

It's hardly enough to hear Columbus's version of his First Voyage. There are dozens of others. I could turn to one of the mates, or a common sailor, or even a ship's boy. But there'll be time for them later. A more surprising point of view can be had through the account of an African stowaway, whose story has never been told, most likely because he never existed.

But if Charles Johnson can place an African American stowaway on a slave ship and win a National Book Award with a bestselling sea story, then why can't I put an African stowaway on Columbus's ship? Especially when it provides an opportunity to parody Johnson's freewheeling combination of dialect and intellect, brutality and lyricality.

FIRST PASSAGE

à la Charles Johnson's *Middle Passage*

Of all the things that could drive men to cross the Ocean Sea, the best one, I've come to learn, is gold. But I'm not going to talk too much about gold here, because I didn't see too much of it. An earring here, a calf there, that's all.

No, I'm going to talk about the Admiral.

I had run away from my home in Africa—a village that was about to be destroyed and enslaved for the umpteenth time or so, as if we were nothing but a race of hermit crabs inhabiting inflammable shells—and I had stowed away on a ship to the Canary Islands, where after a few weeks of dockwork I found myself still desirous of more adventure, for no amount was enough once my consciousness was raised. When I heard the rumor that the three ships in the harbor were on their way across the Ocean Sea to legendary lands whose streets were said to be washed with golddust, where men were said to be kind and considerate and women to do all the fighting and dying, I ripped off the first dinghy I saw, paddled out to the ship, and snuck past the watch, stealing his watch as well, as I was wont.

While trying to find a good place to hide until we were well under way, I ran into the back of a giant, who turned so fast I expected to be swatted off the ship like a fly. But he simply stared at me with eyes like the sky over the Sahara Desert, eyes bluer than Paul Newman's, bluer than the Blues themselves and, puzzled, he touched his well-groomed beard, whiter than the skin of the slavetrader's daughter who let me place my forefinger inside her, and it seemed to become brighter as he touched it and as the sun came out from behind a cloud and tapped him with a ray, and his hair seemed to shine like a full moon and to encircle his head in a beatific halo, just like the one floating on top of that poor bastard in all their paintings who's got blood splurting out of this place and that. But then suddenly the sun went back behind another cloud and the halo vanished, leaving behind it the face of a madman, with eyes clenched, teeth bared, forehead traced with secret maps of the Ocean Sea, and I knelt before this god-devil and bowed my head to ask mercy upon my soul, upon the soul of my people, and upon the soul of my teddy bear, too.

When I looked up, the god-devil had gone from scratching his beard to scratching his crotch. "Can you use another hand?" I asked him. "You never know when a black man will come in handy with the natives across the Ocean Sea. You know, we's all buddies, boss."

He nodded and said, "You never know. And then again, sometimes you do."

"You might have some use for a bodyguard before this trip into the unknown is over. Guarding bodies is my specialty, sir."

He nodded and said, "I might have some use for that sort of service. And then again, perhaps I won't."

"And I give a damn good job, Joe," was my final attempt.

He didn't nod and he didn't speak. Instead he kicked me in the head (I was still kneeling) and then, on his way to wherever he was going, he told an officer to sign me up and confiscate my dinghy. It had worked again.

It was a week before anyone said anything to me other than an order or a curse. And another couple of days before I learned the name of the *Gott-Teufel*: Cristóbal Colón, whom everyone called the Admiral. That was the night a meteor crossed the sky, silent as a seagull, fiery as a torch wielded by a messenger running from a lion, yet it seemed to take its time crossing the sky, sending out a tail more spectacular than a peacock's, more radiant than a woman's, and more soothing than a handful of 18-karat gold. As if we knew it was going to happen, we were all on deck that evening, finishing up small jobs, starting new ones, as if we needed some excuse other than the fact that our quarters down below made a burning hut with slave-traders waiting outside seem preferable.

It was a full two weeks before I had occasion to run into the Admiral. We were floating slowly in the middle of a green and yellow carpet of slimy ooze that looked as if the *genii loci* had had too much to drink the eternity before. To look over the rail at the ocean's ceiling was to add to the gods' work with one's own. When the Admiral approached me, I was praying to the gods to clean it all up.

He politely let me finish my prayer and then asked me whom I was praying to. "To the *genii loci*," I said. He told me that gods aren't local. That there is only one and that He was with us, not physically, but looking down on us and watching over our First Passage, above all others. Because, he said, he and his voyage were chosen, the elect, the one the one God loved to love. That is why he was Admiral and I was a peon, he explained. If my gods were worth their weight in gold, I would be Admiral and he would be my servant.

I would have quoted Kant had he written yet, but instead I remained silent, in awe of the white giant loved and chosen by a god whom he had the terrible audacity to believe was the top god, when he didn't seem to be a god at all, by my reckoning.

"Have you *seen* this god of yours?" I asked.

"No, but we've jawed a few times."

"What has he said?"

"He has told me that it is my mission to find the lands across the sea, to rule them, and to take all their gold and kill all their natives. He's a jealous god, you know."

"A bit unmerciful, too, I would say."

"Mercy is as mercy does."

The Admiral was clearly insane. His principle was Never Give In and Never Forgive; Give Nothing But Orders. He had power, would soon have wealth and fame, doubtless had had his share of women and men, and yet I pitied him. He had made or would make his mark on all these men on the ship, on all the men on both sides of the Ocean Sea, and even on all the animals and plants and bacteria and viruses, but no one had made a mark on him, no one, I was soon to learn, excepting his father. For his other principle was Never Be a Bum Like Your Father. If he had never had a father, like me, he would have had to come up with another sort of principle, something like There's Worse Things Than Suffering, or Adventure for Adventure's Sake (and Maybe a Little Gold As Well).

A week later, after catching me reading his secret maps of the Ocean Sea and whipping me with his metal-tipped cat-o'-nine-tails, he said, "Since every lug on this voyage is out to get me, from Pinzón down to the lowliest ship's boy, I need someone to tell me what they're all thinkin'. A full report, in tripl'c'te. I need someone to tell me when trouble's a-brewin'. A friend. 'Course, if you don't want to play ball, there's always the ocean. You can float for days with all that gunk out there, prob'ly till you starve or feed the sharks. Takes your choice." And then he proceeded to betray every man on all three ships, chronicling their secrets in a voice so sweetly venomous and so frighteningly rational I wanted to tie myself to the mast, cover my ears, and remember how good I had it trying to escape from those overweight slavetraders. In other words, I wasn't quite comfortable with the Admiral and thought our relationship could only lead to my eventual demise, at one faction's hand or the other.

Since I'm telling you this story, however, it is axiomatic that I chose to be the Admiral's "secret agent," if you'll pardon the expression. Since I'm so eddicated it makes even *me* a bit nauseous, it is self-evident that I survived the First Passage and got myself a bloody good *education sentimentale* at the best European universities (paying for it with the gold I brought back in my breeches). And since you've heard of the Admiral, it is perspicuous that he didn't become a bum like his father, and that, perhaps, he actually *was* chosen by his god or his devil.

Which brings me to the moral of my story: one man's god is another man's devil. Unless, of course, it's gold.

Land ahoy! Yes, it's finally October 12, 1492. After weeks of sailing through the Great Unknown, Columbus and his men are finally there, at least if there turns out to be any there there.

What better way to reach the shores of what appeared to be a whole new, fantastic universe than to the beat and rhymes of our childhood favorite, Dr. Seuss, who passed away soon after this book was written. Unlike most of my parodies, this one parodies only the author's style, applying his optimistic vision to a another can of worms completely.

For those of you who have repressed your childhood and don't have children yourself, the refrain parodies Horton's insistence that "A person's a person. No matter how small."

One last note: Amerigo Vespucci, whose descriptions of his voyages were much spicier and, therefore, much more popular than Columbus's, reported that, among some of the New World natives, the women would insure more pleasure from sex by applying insect venom to their lovers' penises in order to make them swell. It doesn't sound swell to me, but there isn't much men won't suffer to please a woman (and vice versa).

COLUMBUS DINGS A DONG

à la Dr. Seuss's *Horton Hears a Who*

One night in the year of the Lord ninety-two
With Columbus the sole one awake of the crew,
He thought that he saw land at last up ahead
And went and got everyone up out of bed.

They laughed when they'd gotten the sleepers
    all out
And couldn't see anything, squid, swordfish, or trout,
But when they got up late and came onto deck
Columbus was calling them things worse than Heck.

The crew got the sails down in time for the reef,
But the captain kept pouring on buckets of grief:
"You moronic morons, you ignorant igs,
You wouldn't know diamonds or gold dust from figs,
You're clods, ignoramuses, imbeciles, fools,
Half-witted harebrains who grew up on gruels,
Blockheads and fatheads and muttonhead dunces,
Dingbats and mooncalves who talk only in gruntses."

Just when Columbus had finished his spiel
The crew saw a sight that was really unreal:
Apparently humans apparently naked
Whose skin was apparently very well baked,
Males with large pendants, females with nought
Covering everything covering ought,
Children were ditto no matter their sex
And the sailors were torn between lust and perplex.

"What are those creatures?" said Sailor Indeed.
"Whatever they are, they do certainly breed.
There's hundreds, there's thousands, all ages
          and heights,
But they can't be humans, they can't have no rights.
They'll do all our dirty work, darn all our socks,
Clean out our outhouses, have our hard knocks,
Mine mines and plant plants and trade us some trades
Or we'll show them our pistols and cannons and
          blades."

Columbus was shocked when he heard the men cheer,
The creatures' humanity seemed to him clear.
He looked at his sailors and said they were rude:
"A person's a person. No matter how nude."

"Griffins and chimeras and dodos are nude,
Unicorns, duocorns, that sort of food,
But," said Sailor Say, "*they*'re surely not human,

Note the size of their ding-dongs and their lack of
	groomin'."

Columbus admitted the males were colossal,
But he'd seen something similar on a Genoese fossil.
"Just look at those women, don't they give you a thrill?
And when you have had them, there won't be a bill.
But the real proof will come when they're 'not in
	the mood.'
A person's a person. No matter how nude."

They landed and greeted and shook hand to hand
And they named the new nation Ding-Dong-Dingy
	Land.
The natives, or Ding-Dongs, in too many words
Announced that Columbus was a son of the birds:
He talked like a parrot and ate like a hawk,
And the wings on his seaship were like the
	Great Grawk.

Columbus announced that to him they were people,
And he ordered a church with a good Christian
	steeple,
He baptized them all, only ten of them drowned,
And he took all their gold, paying ten beads a pound.

The sailors decided it weren't bestiality
If they accepted female hospitality.
But the natives were restless and the sailors were beat,
So they told Old Columbus, "These are females in heat.
No woman has ever demanded so much.
These have to be animals, you can tell by the touch."
Columbus decided he'd set an example
And entered a hut to have a quick sample.
Two hours later, he staggerwaggered out
And to all of his men he gave a great shout:
"They're humans, I'm certain, and I'm very shrewd:
A person's a person. No matter how nude."

Discoveries are things of myth. Remember the first time you discovered that someone else was especially attractive. Lust had been around as long as apples, but this was something new, wonderful, fantastic, deserving of Homeric myths. So was what Columbus stumbled on, even if the natives called it Home, Sweet Home.

For a tour of Columbus's myths, here is Columbus himself speaking in the manner of humorist Dave Barry.

CANS OF BULL

à la Dave Barry

This place isn't all it was cracked up to be. First, there aren't any cities of gold. I haven't found a single place fit to be called a city, and no more than a few gold earrings, which the native women stick in their nose. There's not even anyone here named Goldsmith.

One of my men had the bright idea that if we found a dentist, we'd find gold. Ten men searched for six months and when they finally returned to the *Santa María* to make their report, all they had to say for themselves is that although they don't brush, the natives don't have any cavities. Paradise for sure.

Second, there aren't any cannibals here. With all the men that die at sea, we thought a few good recipes would help us if we were thrown off course by a hurricane and stared starvation in the face. But it turns out the natives don't eat meat, primarily because they don't have any cows or sheep or pigs or even ducks. But they think it's because their gods don't want them eating meat, so they don't even eat each other. Another example of sour grapes.

Third, the people don't have anything much to trade. I promised King Ferdinand and Queen Isabella that I'd open up valuable trade routes to the Orient or to a world we know nothing about, but when I offer the natives beaded necklaces and the other crap the Africans have always accepted with open arms, all they do is offer us beaded necklaces back. No pepper, no gold, no peanuts, no nothing. Not even any women.

Fourth, there aren't any Orientals. These people don't have those little moustaches and they don't wear those funny broad-brimmed hats. And they never bow. Maybe this is an island, like Antilla, or all that's left of Atlantis.

So I've got to decide: do I lie and say I found the Orient and it's full of cannibals living in cities of gold, or do I come up with a new myth? Lies will out, but myths require creativity.

Let's take a quick look at the history of myth. The earliest myths were about creation, for a logical reason. Creation started either with an egg or via birth from the head or bowels of a god.

Once man was created, the whole thing had to happen all over again to create woman and make her feel inferior. So woman was created from man rather than from a god. A slick trick.

Once the creation myth was all settled, the next step was to make a myth about history. Something about destroying all the other tribes, being chosen by God or gods, paying penance for minor crimes like coveting your neighbor's wife and having castration fantasies, and then setting up laws that would keep the powerful in power by making them priests, doctors, and celebrities.

Once that's been accomplished, history begins and eventually people start questioning the myths and the people in power, and then they come up with their own myths and take power themselves, *ad nauseum.* But that takes thousands of years. By then I won't be around anymore. Unless, of course, someone makes me a god.

So, let's start with a creation myth. And make it poetic, like Homer. How about:

> *In fourteen-hundred and ninety-two*
> *Columbus sailed the ocean blue.*
> *And on the merry twelfth of October*
> *A whole New World did he discover.*

There aren't going to be any eggs or bowels in my creation myth. Let's start with the middle of a starless, moonless night. I'm pulling an all-nighter. None of the other guys can hold their rum, so they've passed out cold. And then, suddenly, there it is on the horizon, shining with the unique glow of a land about to be dis-covered. I shake the men awake and one by one they come on deck and say they can't see a thing and that I've got the DT's again. But actually, God has chosen me to be the only one to see the land I am about to discover. Next morning, just as my vision foretold, we pull into shore, that grand, merry morning of the twelfth of October.

What we find, instead of cities of gold, are Solomon's gold mines deep in the earth waiting to be dug. What we find, instead of cannibals, are manlike creatures waiting to be civilized and saved. And what we find, instead of something to trade, is a big land to colonize and lots of slaves to do our work for us. In other words, Paradise.

So what if it'll be hundreds of years before our technology allows us to dig gold mines that deep. So what if the diseases we bring with us kill off millions of the natives, so that we end up importing slaves, and the crops we know how to grow don't flourish in a tropical climate, so that we have to make do with inedible stuff like corn and tomatoes. These are details for politicians and historians to argue about, not the stuff that myths are made of.

The folks who were living here when Columbus arrived never got an opportunity to write down their side of the story. What did they think of all those pale people covering their paleness with equally drab clothing? What did they think about the Spaniards' bad manners and feeble offerings to their gods? And what did they think of Columbus himself? Was he seen as a brave chieftain or a ridiculous clown? We'll never know, but it's fun to imagine.

To give the Native American point of view I turned to America's leading Native American novelist, Louise Erdrich, and her richly quirky prose. It's not easy being funny about a holocaust, but who said humor has to be easy?

TRICKS
à la Louise Erdrich's *Tracks*

I was the last of the Tainos left on Guanahaní, and though I no longer have eyes to see or ears to hear, although it has been many, many years, I remember the first sight and the first sounds of the white man as clearly as I remember the last time I had sex.

It began as a disturbance of the wind, the wingbeat of a dragonfly, the sigh of a woman three huts away. The first sight we had was of their great *canoas*—three of them in a row—coming out of the horizon. The first sound was of men laughing harshly, and then the words, "By San Fernando, getta loada that one!" And the first act was that of the man they called Admiral, who grabbed the naked breasts of my sister's nameless daughter, repeating, as if in prayer, "By San Fernando! By San Fernando!" in a language we Tainos had never heard before.

But Admiral chose the wrong Taino. The first act of a Taino toward a white man was my sister's nameless daughter's. She bit the Admiral's arm with those sharp choppers of hers, so deeply that he bled. He bled like a waterfall whose spirit is filled with the happiness of thunder and lightning. And yet he did not cry out and he did not strike her. He smiled at my sister's nameless daughter, naming her then and there Ardita. She called herself Ardita until all the others had canoed to the horizon (at which time she reverted to namelessness). In Admiral she had found her equal at last, a man powerful enough to yoke her with a name.

Ardita's scandalous story was one of the most popular in our village. Even the *kaseke* liked to embellish it after one too many papaya liqueurs.

The Tainos were not a prudish people. In fact, in the days before the sickness picked us up by the scruff of our necks and dropped us off a cliff, we were known as a good-time clan. But we did what we had to do to preserve our *paraíso,* which is what the white man called our island. The white man also called it San Salvador, after someone apparently as unlike us as possible. Salvador came from a clan, known as the Saints, which actually *tried* to suffer, and they enjoyed their suffering and believed it would lead them to *paraíso*. There is an old Taino saying: "Each to his or her own."

To preserve our *paraíso,* we created an intricate system of rules governing relations between us, known as *tabu*. It had something to do with satisfying the demands of the spirit of the waterfall, who threatened to have his way with all our women and then drown them in his pool. It is said that we stole the idea from some people who came over the other horizon in much smaller *canoas* than the white man's.

Ardita was the first to ignore *tabu*. She did not, like some young parrots, squawk about rights and freedom and the like. No, she simply acted as if *tabu* had never been handed down through generation upon generation of Tainos.

She built a hut next to the pool of the spirit of the waterfall of the mountain and invited her lovers to join her in its cool, deep waters. It was said all over that she prayed with evil chipmunks, read palm trees' palms, and sneezed like a porpoise in its season. She was a scandal, the greatest scandal in our history. But she was my sister's nameless daughter, and I loved and defended her. I invited her to my house often, listened to her stories, and played out her fantasies.

Then the white man came, and Admiral chose Ardita out of all the young women in our village. Ardita took his hand and led him to the waterfall. He wanted to dive right in to the first fresh water he'd seen in ages, but she mumbled something about swimming only right after you eat and led him to her little circular hut of branches and vines. She fed the Admiral a mixture of *yuca*, *batata* skins, and herbs she grew under a crag that overlooked the ocean, miles away across the island.

It was rumored that Ardita mixed love potions in her hut, but that is an old wives' tale. For only an old married woman would think that a bird of *paraíso* like Ardita would need anything more than her smile. It was certainly enough for me.

The Admiral ate Ardita's cooking and Ardita traded Taino words for Spanish ones. She emerged from the jungle the next morning with her white man, who was smoking away on a *tabaco* she had taught him to enjoy. She told the sailors to keep their hands off the merchandise unless they were willing to pay the price. But Guanahaní had only a barter economy.

The next three days were like a New Year's festival. Every ounce of food in the village was eaten, every man and woman was satiated with the pleasures of the flesh, and every story was told again and again until they flowed together into one great epic of the Tainos (with cameo roles for the white man). We traded quips and provisions and looks and jewelry and diseases and souvenirs. And we all ignored *tabu*. The way a rainstorm begins with a drizzle and ends with a flood, the deaths began.

When the party was over, the white man left in his great *canoas* and was never seen again. The sky grew barren and the waterfall slowed to a trickle and then, for the first time in the history of the Tainos, despite all the concoctions Ardita could concoct, it stopped, and the pool began to shrink until the spirit was naked as we, and fighting mad. Ardita began to shrink, in spirit, because now everyone was breaking *tabu,* and she was nothing special. She, too, became fighting mad and took it out on her fellow Tainos. Together she and the spirit of the waterfall took us one by one, giving us all sorts of agonizing sicknesses, taking pleasure in our pain as they had been pained by our pleasures.

It was Ardita who chose the order of death. She began with the old women who gossiped about her and the men who weren't man enough to make her come. Then she chose the best-looking women, who lured men away from her pool. Then came the men who were men, but not her equal, which was all of the ones who remained. Except me. And finally there were the ugly and quiet women, and the children.

Until all that was left was Ardita and me and the spirit of the waterfall. We were swollen with all the names of the dead, of all the people we had loved and hated, of all the people we had ignored. Suddenly, we began to speak their names in unison, and they filled the air for days, like bees whose hive has been destroyed. And they stung us just as heartlessly and died in the act, eviscerated.

Finally, the swelling went down and Ardita brought out a deck of cards. I licked my lips and the spirit howled with delight. We began a game that was to last for years. We ate almost nothing, we hardly slept, we did not move from our seats. Ardita dealt, I dealt, the spirit dealt, and trick by trick, game by endless game, we became weaker and weaker until at last the spirit faded away and vanished. Ardita and I continued playing without sharing or even trading a word. Our lives and our *paraíso* were at stake; we would have to play till it rained again, even if it killed us. And it did. At least Ardita. Just as the first drops began to fall, she opened her parched mouth for the first time in months (what an incredible poker face that woman had!) and caught a raindrop on the tip of her tongue. And then her *canoa* put out toward the horizon.

Me, I was drenched.

Guanahaní was *paraíso*, and it will remain so till all our *canoas* come back from the horizon, or the white man returns, whichever comes first. The spirit of the waterfall said that, in the long run, more white men would die than Tainos, which wasn't much comfort for someone who lives only in the short run. The spirit of the waterfall said that Admiral went from island to island, causing the local spirits of the local waterfalls to kill off one tribe after another, which was even less comfort. The spirit of the waterfall said that Admiral is considered a great man throughout the seven seas. But I do not believe him. Everyone knows there are dozens of seas. And that the spirit cheated at cards. So I do not believe the spirit had anything to do with the sickness. He just hated to see anyone else get the credit. Especially the white man, who had dishonored his pool with their laundry.

I have survived, but I have suffered more than Salvador himself and enjoyed it less as well. I was the one who gave Guanahaní its last blessing. I was the one who spread the rumor that San Salvador was not only haunted by the Tainos' vengeful ghosts, but also that it was covered with hazardous waste. All I can do now is tell my stories, play a few hands, and have a few drinks. But there are no Tainos to listen, no Tainos to take tricks against, and no Tainos to pick up the tab. That is Admiral's curse.

Now go ahead and cut the deck before I start telling you the story of my first marriage.

On March 15, 1493, Columbus arrived back in Spain from his First Voyage. He had happened upon a few islands, a little gold, and a lot of people. He had brought with him several natives, some native crafts (especially ones in which gold was used), and a parrot or two. It wasn't a lot to show for himself, but he did have a lot of adventures and, therefore, a lot of stories to tell. And he didn't want to do too much more than whet the monarchs' appetites.

The myth Columbus is best remembered for is the egg trick he did to show up the Spanish nobility upon his return. Egg tricks are not the specialty of any contemporary American writer, but no one can spin a tall tale like E. L. Doctorow, especially when it has a moral to it. Here, in Doctorow's current run-on-and-on style, we see Columbus from the point of view of a boy who shares much in common with Doctorow's recent hero, Billy Bathgate.

EGGTIME

à la E. L. Doctorow's *Billy Bathgate*

He had to have planned it, because all the other eggs were either deviled or chopped, julienned or pickled, whipped or painted with likenesses of Queen Isabella, King Ferdinand, and their dog, Katy, only this one was left untouched. Only this one was to go down in the history of famous foods alongside Adam's apple, Persephone's pomegranate, and Prometheus' liver.

Cristóbal Colón was not the most handsome man, with white hair uncombed and a ruddy face whose cheekbones seemed lost in flesh, all set on shoulders that held no neck. Even in the fine clothes he had to wear for this festival in his honor, hosted by the second most powerful man in the kingdom—the Archbishop of Toledo and Grand Cardinal of Spain, Pedro Gonzales de

Mendoza—he suffered a sartorial inadequacy as some people have leprosy or the plague.

Yet he was the greatest man I have ever come near, greater than any pope, soldier, or even toreador. Not that I came very near the Admiral at the festival, I was only a freelance servant boy, but gifted with extraordinary peripheral vision as well as a sense of judgment keener than the judges of the Inquisition and almost superhuman speed for a boy of an undetermined age somewhere in his early teens, I saw what I saw and even in motion I saw it clearly.

I immediately granted Cristóbal Colón all the powers of his reputation because of the way he walked clear cross the room to discover the only caviar of the feast. Five *hidalgos*, three ladies, and one questionable individual had asked me where it might be, and I had been absolutely unable to earn a doubloon letting them in on the secret. The great Colón's discovery that the caviar was sitting in a tiny bowl behind the grand head of a Pyrenees boar enabled me to earn five pieces of eight before the Admiral's extraordinary appetite had cleaned out the bowl.

The magnificent Admiral had recently returned from discovering islands across the Ocean Sea and, because the King and Queen had been usurping all of his time and hogging all of his stories, this was the first chance the nobility had had to rub shoulders with the first Governor of the Indies. He had waltzed into the hall, tangoed through the crowds, and was now sitting this one out and telling some of the tallest tales I've ever heard, about ten-foot natives who grilled human flesh on kebabs; about a violent hurricane on the way home and the message he placed in a bottle, thinking he'd never see Spain again; about his unjust imprisonment in the Azores and another brush with death in Lisbon; about the way his mistress Beatriz and his queen Isabella greeted the homecoming king. The Archbishop sat right in among the nobles, who hung on every one of his marvelous words, who were completely enchanted by the honeyed voice of the Admiral who could spin a tale tighter than his father the weaver, more wild than his mentor Odysseus, and softer than his mistress Beatriz' inner thigh. He had the nobles believing that the meek would inherit the Other World (and that Colón himself was meek, despite all evidence to the contrary), that righteousness was righter than might, and that the Cubs would win the pennant. The Admiral's honeyed baritone seemed to become sweeter and stickier, and the nobles seemed to cling to it as if he were the Archbishop revealing that Christ was about to return to earth and bring salvation to them and only them, leaving the poor and righteous to fend for themselves, the scum, and not only that, the great hall hushed and even the silverware ceased to ring out, the women swallowed their giggles, the men held back their belches, and the children fell asleep. The Admiral had an incredible technique, his technique was to have technique alone.

Then suddenly one of the grandest of the grand nobles made a late great entrance, tossing his hat and cloak into my hands, and then he tripped down three stairs and slid fifty feet or more on the freshly waxed marble floor, and his slide ended at the feet of none other than Cristóbal Colón, who stopped his tale and helped the man to his feet with a single, stupendous tug. The noble made a show of brushing off his clothes, but he was clearly thinking of what to say to the discoverer of a whole new world across the sea, and he finally thought of something and he even said it.

"Are you Cristóbal Cohen?" he asked.

"I am Cristóbal *Colón*."

"Aren't you the kike who says he was the first to discover a western route to the Indies?"

"No, I'm the *wop* who *did* discover a western route to the Indies."

"Ya know, if you hadn't happened to have a lucky break or three and get better weather than has ever been recorded on the Ocean Sea and have inside information from a sailor who ya killed after he stepped off a ship at Porto Santo and told the first guy he saw, who happened to be you, all about what was over there across the Ocean Sea and how to get there and that he was the sole survivor of the only ship that ever came upon it (and he was Spanish and the youngest although illegitimate son of a nobleman to boot), then some man, some real man, some Spanish man of a good, old family who didn't make such a big deal about Providence and destiny and all that kind of New Age crap, one of our many, many great geniuses would have made an expedition there as soon as credit loosened up. In other words, big fucking deal!"

Admiral Colón didn't say a word to the drunken bum of a noble, he walked across the room and reached under the table near where the caviar bowl had stood and pulled out an egg, a regular old hard-boiled egg, pure and white and ovoid, and he walked over to where most of the nobility of Spain had congregated around their challenging peer.

"Big fucking deal?" the Admiral said. "Well, if being

from such good old Spanish families makes you such geniuses, then one of you can surely balance this here egg end up on that there table in about two seconds flat, give or take. But don't go cheating by using salt or crumbs or that sort of crutch. It's gotta stand on its own lack of feet." And he laughed a hearty laugh at his joke, which was not shared by any of the nobles who had been bewitched by him only moments before. For with the age of chivalry nearly over in Spain, there were few real challenges anymore, and this one was a doozie, more original than a dragon or a giant or a damsel in distress.

For a thin minute it seemed that Colón had them licked. But then one of them grabbed the egg and delicately placed it on the table, and he tried this and he tried that, he prayed and he cursed, he whispered and he roared, but everything he did was worthless, and everything the others tried was no less worthless, and everything their wives suggested was every bit as worthless, too, and the children were still asleep, and oh around three in the morning the challenger, now sober as a man on the stake, finally groaned out, Uncle! and the Admiral of the Ocean Sea and Governor of the Indies, calm and patient Cristóbal Colón, took the egg from him, walked to the table, and gave it a nice easy squash, so that one end went flat and the egg stood there bolt upright, as if in the embrace of an egg cup or chalice.

No one had to say what the moral was and no one did, not even the Admiral (but I will): once something is done, everyone knows it can be done and how to do it, so if there be any justice in the world all the credit ought to go to the one who does it first.

I walked out into the street, where beggars slept in miserable piles of rags and children snuck back into orphanages and peddlers came out of holes in the wall to walk cross town to where they picked up their over-ripe wormy fruit to sell to people no better situated than themselves. And I thought about what I'd heard of the Admiral's tales and what the noble had said to him and what a great con artist the Admiral was, and I decided that I would go on his second voyage and learn the tricks of several trades, even if I had to row the whole way across.

Success breeds success, and Columbus's success was working away like a rabbit. Besides success, success also engenders fresh, unhallowed traditions, known as fads. It wasn't as if people were sailing across the Ocean Sea every week, but it's not too presumptuous to suppose that a lot of fads had already been sired, including jargon, career paths, lifestyles, and games.

This sounds a lot like the big boom of 1980s America—Wall Street—where out of almost nowhere, whole industries reared some pretty ugly, although well-manicured heads. Since exploration was the boom industry of the 1490s, the best way to introduce the non-risk taker to this industry's denizens is via a parody of Michael Lewis's bestselling Wall Street anecdotes collection, *Liar's Poker*, in which Columbus plays the part of John Gutfreund, admiral of Salomon Brothers in the 1980s and a sliver of the 1990s as well.

PRIOR'S POKER

à la Michael Lewis's *Liar's Poker*

I was a sailor on the Ocean Sea, in fact, on the biggest voyage ever to cross it: the Second Voyage of Admiral Cristóbal Colón and his brother Bartolomé. Seventeen ships, 1,200 men, including support staff, with a capitalization of three billion doubloons. I was one of two hundred trainees, or ship's boys.

The Admiral, it was said, often left his office and walked the deck of the flagship. He would wander here and there, unpredictably, and he would sneak up behind you while you were busy swabbing or bailing. An eerie sixth sense guided him to wherever a spot was missed or gold was hidden. Some said that Colón had a nose for golddust; others said it was just an allergy.

If you suspected someone was peering over your shoulder, you couldn't look, because your orders were not to turn around, on penalty of swimming with the sharks. You felt a chill in your bones, like a small furry animal about to be devoured by a bigger furry animal. But this one had neither fur nor fangs, only a size-fourteen boot with a reinforced toe. Or so they said.

Often as not, Colón would be off haunting another sailor by the time you realized he'd been there. But he always left his mark: a sticky chaw of tobacco that it took an hour or more to wipe off to the mates' satisfaction. You felt skinned alive, fucked over, and sticky. That was the way the Admiral operated.

Prior's Poker is the most popular game aboard. The story goes that the Admiral learned the game from the prior of the monastery that sold the King and Queen on an incredibly risky product guaranteed to open up the markets of the Indies, if there wasn't a crash. The philosophy of Prior Juan Pérez was a simple one: "If you believe in it, go with it. However, if it doesn't work, you're fucked." The Prior believed he was lucky, and more often than not he was right. But, more important, he *knew* that he was a great bluffer. He hadn't kept his oath of silence all those years for nothing: no one could control his emotions as well as he. And with all the collateral he had—both land and souls—no one could better afford to take a risk.

Prior's Poker is a game of pure bluff. From two to twelve people stand in a circle and hold in their closed fists a coin from any one of a hundred-plus kingdoms, principalities, duchies, palatinates, city-states, tribes, and pirate ships. In turn, each of them asks if anyone has a coin from this or that part of the world, becoming more and more specific (as the bets spiral higher and higher), finally getting down to the denomination. The game might seem childish, but when thousands of kilos of gold are in the offing, it becomes downright mature.

Since the Prior did not go on any of the voyages, Colón had to find another playmate on board. Vicente Yañez Pinzón, shipowner and captain of his own caravel, fit the bill. He was the best and the toughest, a far superior bluffer than Colón could ever hope to be. And he never forgave Colón for stealing his brother's maps and hogging all the limelight, which made his brother so sick with anger (and syphilis) that he died right after returning from the First Voyage.

It has become a legend of Colón's voyages and of the game of Prior's Poker—a visceral part of their mythical identity—that one day Colón ordered Pinzón's ship to come alongside his and then called across to him, "One coin, one island, no tears."

Pinzón wasn't about to give up a whole island, and he knew he was a better bluffer than ten Colóns, so he responded, "No, Cris, if we're going to play for those stakes, let's make it a continent."

It would have been just like Colón to accept, but since he hadn't yet discovered a continent, it was unbearable to think that when he did it would belong to a thug like Pinzón. So Colón said, simply, "You're good."

No, thought Pinzón, only very, very crazy.

Things have changed in the exploration business. All you used to need was an able body and some old caravel would give you a shot. No one was doing much more than cautiously trawling down the coast of Africa, finding a little island off the coast of Morocco that had been discovered ten times before, raiding a village that had signs on its outskirts: "No Gems or Women Inside! Honest!" No one ventured a day's sail from shore; no one took a risk.

And then Colón set up shop, and the stakes changed. He was backed by the Spanish crown and half the bankers in and out of Italy. Suddenly, everyone wanted a piece of the action (known popularly as "a piece of eight" for the number of lives explorers were said to have), and Colón Brothers had the biggest voyages in town. It wasn't enough anymore to have an able body; you had to have been at least a pirate, and not any pirate ship would do. You had to have been on one of the ones that raided the big flotillas. Admissions to the bar sinister grew so quickly, the rats finally decided the pirate ships were about to sink and returned to some of their former careers, such as spreading the plague and accompanying pied pipers.

From giving undesirable jobs to men who hadn't the stomach, spleen, or dash for piracy, explorers found they could now have the pick of the litter. And the best voyages had the whitecaps of the waves.

The first thing I learned when the ship I was on set sail was that the deck of a Colón Brothers ship is more jungly than a Caribbean island. If a mate doesn't want you, you're sunk. And if a mate *does* want you, it isn't exactly full speed ahead. I was as helpless as the female victim of an arranged marriage when she first hears the hideous belch of the man with whom she has to spend the rest of her life.

But I learned. I learned that the way to get ahead is to swear as fucking much as you damn well can. I learned that you say it, "Ready, fire, aim," and that you can't be afraid to bet the ship, even if it isn't yours. I learned that if you pat yourself on the back, the next sensation is likely to be a sharp kick lower down. But all my learning did was make me such an arrogant sonuvabitch that I ended up in bonds, high up on the mainmast.

After two months on board, I finally met the Admiral. Occasionally, when the cook's back was turned, I would grab a bite to eat from the galley. If you didn't, you starved. The mate who had put me in bonds came up to me and told me to report to the Admiral. I hadn't ever seen Colón, but apparently he was visiting my ship.

I walked in, remembering the stories I'd heard about the guy, about all the things he'd said and done. He liked to say, you have to wake up every morning "ready to bite the ass off a Carib." He kicked butt so hard, a lot of men went overboard and never surfaced again. He could sell blubber to a whale, find gold in a cesspool, and woo a lioness away from her cubs.

But when I entered his room, he was calm and deliberate. He talked about sins and duties and heaven. He spoke with an aristocratic accent and royal pauses. I had never met anyone so frightening. Not even a mate wielding a cat-o'-twenty-tails made me nervous as Colón.

He told me I'd been caught stealing food from the galley, and he wanted me to put back what I'd taken. He wouldn't listen to any explanations; sins are sins are sins, he said, and expiation is expiation. He couldn't figure out what went on inside the pointy little heads of little bastards like me.

When I reached the galley, I saw more mates than I had ever seen together, except during a storm. When I began to return what I'd taken, they laughed. They laughed and laughed and laughed, until all of them were coughing nearly to death.

When I was done, I turned around. Standing in the doorway was none other than the Admiral. It was a goof, a practical joke so big the Admiral Himself had joined in the fun. I'd been snookered by the King of the Other World. I'd finally made it.

While Columbus was gallivanting on the sunny shores of the Caribbean, his mistress, Beatriz Enriquez de Harana, was sitting home alone in Cordova minding their son, Ferdinand. Columbus stopped by to see her between his first and second voyages, but when he returned from his second voyage, he started wearing a monk's habit and acting very pious. He continued to send Beatriz money, but it's likely that he very rarely, if ever, visited her.

A poor, jilted, exploited woman with an illegitimate child happens to be the protagonist of Toni Morrison's powerful novel *Beloved*. The best way to parodically approach a novel so tragic is to turn it topsy-turvy. Here's my attempt.

DESPISED

à la Toni Morrison's *Beloved*

103-17 1/2 Apt. 3C was joyful. Too joyful. Full of a baby's giggling. Giggling so happy it attracted people from miles around, hundreds of miles sometimes.

At first, things had been quiet around the apartment. There was just Beatriz and Chris. Chris was in and out of work, and they lived from hand to mouth. Then came a little mouth named Ferdinand, and it wasn't long before Chris found a good job at last. And left. And then came the baby. That is, the joyful babyghost. Hopping and cooing and drooling and thumping. All day long, and all night too. Like a child's favorite video.

The first visitor was Juan, who looked in a mirror the baby made a funhouse one, and Juan couldn't get enough of seeing himself short and fat or tall and gangly. Then Glimp came along, and the baby couldn't bake enough cakes for him. He was off and eating. Eating, eating, eating. Then all the neighbors started coming by, and then people from the next block, and then people from across town. And all because of that joyful babyghost, making a racket they could hear clear across the Ocean Sea. It was the daughter Beatriz never had, but it seemed she would now have forever. A baby that would never grow up.

And where was Chris? Her man. Her sailorman. He never even knew about the babyghost. He had already gone off on his Second Voyage, and then she'd heard no more, except for an occasional check. But she might be wrong. Maybe Chris *did* know about the babyghost and decided to keep an ocean between him and it.

To get away from it all, Beatriz spent hours every day in a special little clearing in the woods, remembering each and every promise Chris had made (and broken), each and every job he had taken (and lost), each and every woman he had picked up (and dropped). Occasionally, she'd remember a new one, but she'd forget them all as soon as she set foot in 103-17 1/2 Apt. 3C and lost herself in the fun. After a while, she couldn't bear forgetting what a louse he'd been, so off she'd go again to the clearing, to remember.

Now her son, Ferdinand, was gone as well. Gone whoknowswhere. It wasn't that he minded the babyghost; he enjoyed it as much as the next elder child who gets none of the attention (and can never expect to get any either). No, he left because he was contrary. Since everyone came, he left. If everyone were to leave, he'd come. If a few came and the others stayed away, he'd come and go.

Then one day Paolo Q. appeared at the door. He

looked like he'd walked a few continents to play with the babyghost. But when the babyghost came up to greet him with a giggle and a coo, Paolo Q. ignored him as if he wasn't there. As if he didn't believe in ghosts. As if he didn't think a cooing babyghost was the cutest thing he ever couldn't see.

Beatriz knew Paolo Q. He'd been one of Chris's friends back in Lisbon. Maybe he knew where Chris was, what he knew, who he was sleeping with. After a little small talk that seemed like big talk (or was it big talk masquerading as small?), she got to the point.

"Where is he?" she asked.

"Across the Ocean Sea," he answered.

"That alibi again!"

"I call 'em as I see 'em. And I saw him set sail not six months ago."

"And Ferdinand?"

"At odds, Chris said. Godknowswhere. And you?"

"I'm alone."

"What about the hundreds of people crowded into your studio apartment?"

"They're nobody. Just here for the babyghost."

"No man?"

"No man."

"That all right by you?"

"That's all right by me. I've got my memories, at least when I can remember them. And I've got my admission fees. And I sew a little on the sly."

Suddenly, Ferdinand happened by for his semi-annual visit, so he could assure himself that staying away was still the contrary thing to do. The crowds and the babyghost were still there. But something seemed different. Yes, Mamma was not lost in the crowd as usual.

She was sitting and talking in the hallway. To a man. Alone.

Beatriz called Ferdinand over and got the introductions out of the way.

"How's FatherAdmiralSir doing?" he asked the strange man who was openly pawing his Mamma.

"Probably his usual," Paolo Q. answered: "Discovering discoveries, enslaving slaves, womanizing women. Nothing out of the ordinary, I wouldn't expect. He's not a man for surprises."

"Amen," Beatriz said, taking Paolo Q.'s hand out of her blouse.

Paolo Q. continued: "However, I did hear a rumor that CC had donned a monk's robe and sworn off women for better or for worse, but he hadn't given up booze or slaves or gold."

And then Beatriz asked him, "Won't you stay around? Everyone else does. Why be different? That's Ferdinand's specialty, ain't it, Hon?"

"Sure, I'll stay a while," said Paolo Q. "I wasn't doing anything anyway. But what is it with this babyghost?"

"That ghost is so happy it makes me puke," Ferdinand butted in.

"No," Beatriz said. "She's thankful, maybe, but I don't see how anyone could be happy spending every minute as the center of attention. I can't remember the last time *I* was the center of attention—even in all the books about Columbus, I'm sure I'll be little more than a footnote, if I'm not censored out—but I'm happy as a lark without any menbirds pestering me."

Beatriz suddenly rose and went out to her clearing and remembered the year winter came in a hurry at breakfast and stayed for lunch and dinner and even the midnight snack. She remembered how the day she met Chris the sun stood still and shone on them like a spotlight, while the rest of the world froze nearly to death. She remembered how the day the babyghost was born the earth shook and rent a chasm through the middle of the house (which is why it was 103-17 **1/2**). Nearly swallowed the babyghost up. Only it wasn't a ghost. Yet. But would be. Soon.

When she returned, the apartment was deserted. It looked tiny, as any studio apartment does when you get rid of the furniture. Which was just people, because there hadn't been room for furniture for years.

The apartment was deserted except for Ferdinand (who was unpacking his bag) and Paolo Q., who was telling Ferdinand what he'd done to rid the apartment of the babyghost, so he could be alone with Beatriz.

And then in walked Despised. That was her name, but no one wore it out. Just the sight of her was unbearable. Ferdinand began to pack. Paolo Q. tried to figure out how to *bring back* the babyghost, so that Despised would at least be lost in a crowd.

Despised had eyes like wells. Full of water as if there'd soon be buckets of tears. Tears like Noah's flood. A flood like Job's tears. Tears like . . . well, like tears. Because everyone despised her, and she knew she deserved it. She knew it so well, she sought new people out so she could prove to herself every day that it wasn't them, but her.

There was something else, too: she loved to see people fight over her. Over how much they despised her. Over similes to express how much they detested her. How much she made them suffer. How much they wished the dam would break and the flood of tears would flow at long last and maybe she'd drown in it or at least be washed away to another part of town. She loved to watch their expressions and listen to what they said and what they didn't say as well.

And then she left. Her daily ration of hatred had been consumed. Beatriz despised her because she hadn't been able to hate anything in years and had just realized how much she missed it; Paolo Q. despised her because he'd just managed to bring back the babyghost and he knew he'd never turn that trick again; and Ferdinand despised her because he hadn't yet come up with a simile as despicable as Paolo Q.'s.

But more than Despised, they realized, deep in their hearts, that they despised Columbus. The man who'd left Beatriz alone with the crowds of babyghost admirers. The man who Paolo Q. could never quite replace. The man Ferdinand knew he'd end up slaving for and someday, it came to him suddenly, even writing a biography about. Without being able to write one honestly hateful word.

Columbus's second voyage was far larger than the first and was intended to set up a settlement somewhere across the Ocean Sea. It was the beginning of the long process of Europeans taking the New World from the Indians and making it Old.

The laughs to be had here are basically in the form of black humor. That's why I turned to the contemporary American master of black humor, Kurt Vonnegut. I found that Columbus's voyages to the New World fit very well into the vision of Vietnam Vonnegut presents in his recent novel *Hocus Pocus*.

Mumbo Jumbo

à la Kurt Vonnegut's *Hocus Pocus*

My name is Jan Hus Hernandez, and I was born in 1473. I was named at the behest of my maternal grandfather, who was nothing but a groundskeeper at one of the twenty royal palaces in Spain, in honor of Jan Hus of Prague, Bohemia. Hus protested against the corruption of the Catholic Church and was burned at the stake in 1415, when I was negative 58 years of age.

The year is 1538 now.

If all had gone the way a lot of people thought it would, Jesus Christ would have come among us again, and we would all be in Heaven together.

No such luck.

If my mother hadn't been the village idiot and my father hadn't been a wandering minstrel and my half-brother had been whole, I might never have met Cristóbal Colón. And if I hadn't been a commissioned sales rep and errand boy for the most exclusive whorehouse in Seville, I probably would never have seen him with his pants down. Figuratively speaking, that is.

I had propositioned many sailors before, but never a skipper. Cristóbal Colón was my first. And my last. I was actually on my way back to the house with an important message from a client's admirer when I was stopped by an enormous paw. "What's the hurry, son?" the paw's owner said. When I saw that he was wearing a captain's hat, I painted the most magnificent picture of one of my clients, from her slender toes up to the long, bulbous lobes on her ears. It wasn't actually *one* of my clients, it was a collection of the best features of them all. I had worked hard on this description, just in case, and was proud to have delivered it so skillfully.

Captain Colón waited patiently throughout my spiel. Then I asked him what he would think of a visit to our establishment. "I'd laugh like hell," he said. But he didn't.

I began the First Voyage across the Ocean Sea as a ship's boy. I was the one who had last dibs on the food and no dibs on the rum. I was the one everyone could kick if he himself was abused by the one above him in the Chain of Being that is a ship.

The first time I was kicked, I went to the Captain, now the Admiral. He said it was nothing. I asked him what he would do if he were kicked by a sailor. "I'd laugh like hell," he said.

But no one ever kicked him.

The first sailor who kicked me was the first white man to die on the other shore of the Ocean Sea. He stepped off the rowboat onto what seemed to be a beach. But the sand was quicker than he was. I laughed like hell.

The second sailor who kicked me was kicked so many times by the Admiral that as soon as he returned to Spain, he went to work for the Admiral's nemesis, Amerigo Vespucci. It was this second sailor who first called the mainland "America" (he had a speech impediment for which a cure was found only days after the sailor died of yellow fever—or, possibly, a poison dart— on a boat-trip up the Amazon River).

The third sailor who kicked me was the Admiral Himself. I was swabbing the deck when he lumbered into me, hot in pursuit of another ship's boy. I don't think he noticed, or he would have laughed like hell.

By the Second Voyage, I had become the Admiral's mouthpiece. The master of his self-serving fantasies. I learned a great deal from the Admiral. I learned so much, I could probably convince you that I myself was the Admiral and that Colón was nothing but a conman. As it was, only the second half of this statement is true. I think. To this day, I have come to no firm conclusion how smart or dumb the Admiral was.

The first thing every woman asks me when she learns that I was on each and every one of the voyages of

Cristóbal Colón is how many Indians I killed. The first thing every man asks me is how many Indians I slept with. As it turns out, the answer to both questions is exactly the same.

If Jan Hus had not been burned at the stake in 1415, nothing in Spain would likely have been different. No one there had ever heard of Hus, except for my maternal grandfather. He always liked trivia. My mother let her father name me in return for his promise to finish all her crossword puzzles. Only he died ten days after I was born.

Life is rotten. Hopeless. Futile. Getting up each morning is like taking coals to Newcastle: so many other people are getting up as well, brushing teeth, skipping breakfast.

I know this because I was there. The New World. It was one big hallucination, but I found that I could adjust to it. I just couldn't adjust back.

When tribes of Indians approached us carrying gifts, it was my job to tell the boys that the food was laced with poison, the women were diseased, and the gold was pyrite. That left more food and gold for the Admiral, and if he was going to be celibate, then everyone else would have to be, too. The Admiral convinced me that it was for the boys' good, that only He could handle so much temptation.

When we chased the Indians into the jungle, it was my job to tell the boys that we were playing Capture the Flag, with new rules. The rules were that the Spanish Flag could fly securely only after all natives had been neutralized. "Neutralize" is a word I invented (and

I received a promotion for it); anyone can kill, but only civilized men can neutralize. I also invented the word "Colonization," in honor of the Admiral Himself.

I was also the one who, on the Second Voyage, got every member of the enormous expedition to sign a declaration that he had set foot on the mainland of Cathay. Even though we didn't see a single chopstick, not to mention a mainland.

The boys believed more and more of what I said, and what I said grew wilder and wilder. Eventually, I Myself began to believe my words; I've never liked being different. Now I can't believe that I said what I said and believed what I believed. Lethal mumbo jumbo.

Life is nothing but failure, shame, man's inhumanity to man *(Bartlett's Familiar Quotations)*. Jan Hus on a spit, village idiots signifying nothing, laughs like hell, Colonization, neutralization, and violation, Inquisitions for non-inquiring minds, tiny chapters for tiny attention spans, ship's boys kicked while they're down, kicks getting harder and harder to find, paradises lost. The works.

And this ain't no mumbo jumbo.

Columbus's Third Voyage was a disaster. The settlement at Santo Domingo became a center for rebellion; bands of men fought over gold mines and massacred the natives; even chaos couldn't reign over these Spanish hooligans. As it was, Columbus had the landlubbing job of Governor, and the one thing all the fighting bands could agree on was that Columbus and his brothers, Diego and Bartolomé, were corrupt, incompetent, and on the violent side even for a representative of the hardly peaceloving King. So the rebel leaders started sending messages to the King, who caved in to popular demand and sent over a replacement.

The United States is fortunate enough to have had one of its leaders replaced for corruption: Richard Nixon. (Okay, okay, he quit. But in a monarchy, justice is swifter, if less just.) I felt the best way to tell the story was through the eyes of the replacement: Francisco de Bobadilla, in the case of Columbus; Gerald Ford, in the case of Nixon. Some other Nixonian characters who make cameo appearances are linguist Alexander Haig, as Columbus's brother Bartolomé, and golfer Tip O'Neill, as opposition leader Moxie de Moxica.

A Time To Kneel

à la Gerald R. Ford's *A Time to Heal*

When on August 23, 1500, I stepped foot on the island of Hispaniola, tripped and fell flat on my face, got up and knelt on the shore, and prayed to God and King, I knew I was prepared. People thought I was low-key, unemotional, lacking in passion, even dull, but I knew I was as hungry for power as the next dictator. And I was ready to take it.

For fifteen months, things had been going badly in the Other World. Under the governorship of Cristóbal Colón, wage and price controls had everyone up in arms—literally—other expeditions (led by officers from the First Voyage) had taken gold and pearls without sharing a doubloon with the Crown, and lies were being told. Throughout my life as a knight (Order of Calatrava), I always believed what I was told. I was truthful to others and so I expected them to be truthful to me. I mean, fair is fair or chivalry isn't chivalry.

Well, Colón had been sending messages back to court that everything was fine and dandy in the Other World. But once the messengers were turned over to the Inquisition, they changed their tune (as well as their octave). It was my long-held belief that messengers should not suffer for their messages, but they really ought to tell the truth.

The last message that had come from Colón was that Francisco Roldán had made peace with the Crown and that everything and everyone was nice and peachy. But when I stepped foot on the island of Hispaniola, at the settlement known as Santo Domingo, I, Francisco de Bobadilla, saw before me seven good Spanish men hanging from a gallows designed for four. And there watching them with a big smile on his sizeable face was the youngest of the Colón brothers, Diego. I introduced myself and Diego said to me, "I'm sorry to say that only five men are scheduled to be hanged tomorrow. But if you like, I can send some troops into the jungle to catch some more rebels and make the execution more robust."

I told Diego (who was acting governor in Cristóbal's absence) that it was not for me to tell him how to run the Other World, but I did hint that it might be best if he waited for the Governor to return before he hanged another man. "And where *is* your brother?" I asked.

Diego shrugged his shoulders and walked away. And he didn't even trip.

Three days later, the middle Colón brother, Bartolomé, returned from Xaragua and visited me immediately. "I am in control here," he told me. "I just arrivaled from Cristóbal's ship. I want to alert you that things are deteriorating. The whole tournament may be over. Cristóbal may have jousted his last joust, raced his last race, fenced his last fence. I can't tell you what's going to happen, because I exclusived two chroniclers who work for the Seville *Post,* but you'd better start thinking about a change in your life, . . . Mr. Governor."

I had been called a lot of things in my life, especially when I tried to bring justice to Jerusalem, but this was the first time anyone had called me "Mr. Governor." I liked the way it sounded. I couldn't wait to try it out on my wife, Maria.

"And where *is* Cristóbal?" I asked.

"In Las Vegas," he answered. "It was a gamble, but his big toe assured him he'd strike gold. And there was a local rebellion as well. But he should be back any day now."

Seven days later, Governor Cristóbal Colón arrived in Santo Domingo. Bartolomé came to bring me up to date. "I can't tell you what's going to happen in the next forty-eight hours," he said. "I just don't know what the Governor is going to do."

"But you know what he's done," I said. "And what he hasn't done."

"He hasn't done a lot. But remember the exclusive?"

The next day, the Colón Brothers and some of their

aides and officers met with me at the café on the town square. The Governor began the meeting. "I would like to discuss the most important issue confronting the Other World," he said. "Gold, gold, gold, and more gold."

My God! I had assumed that this was going to be a momentous occasion, that Colón was going to come to grips with the threat to his Governorship, that he was going to announce his retirement and the founding of a Gubernatorial Library on his favorite island, Jamaica. Now I was convinced he was totally out of touch with reality.

"Goddamn that Amerigo Vespucci! He got to Vegas before me, supposedly searching for pearls. That's an old one. He was looking for allies, and he found one in Roldán. He was looking for men, and so he stole our slaves in the Bahamas. And he made the biggest gold strike ever in Las Vegas, and then began an even bigger gold rush in Cordillera. That's *my* gold. Mine, mine, mine, all mine!"

When Colón ended his speech, the silence was deafening. And even worse was the stench from the bodies that were still hanging from the gallows in front of the café. I was thinking, deep in my heart, that the gold was not *his* anymore. I had orders from the King, but I couldn't tell anyone. I had to remain neutral. I had to give the Governor a chance to come around. After all, chivalry is chivalry . . .

Although Roldán had made peace with the Colóns, the big rebellion in town when I arrived consisted of Aragonians, led by Adrias "Moxie" de Moxica. Mox was a close personal friend of mine. His first words to me were, "Listen, Governor [that title again!], while I have great respect for your honesty and integrity, and a bit of respect for your ability as well, our philosophies, values, and taste in women are diametrically opposed. Not to mention the fact that you're a lousy Castillian. I wish you every success in bringing our politically and geographically torn islands together, but as soon as your honeymoon is over, I'll be going around the islands kicking your ass in."

What a way to talk to the future Governor of the Indies, but it was vintage Mox. And rebellion is, after all, the essence of monarchy.

Bartolomé was the next to enter my office. He told me, "I can't tell what's going to happen. One moment I think he'll cave in, the next moment I think he's going to earburn the whole town down around us. That's all I can tell you."

Well, to make a long story short, after ten days of Bartolomé's telling me he couldn't "informationalize" me, my chivalry was stretched to its breaking point. I took my men, entered the Colón Brothers' office, and arrested the bunch of them. Since all their soldiers were on siesta, they went peacefully, in chains. And not one of them tripped even once!

The next day, I took them to the caravel *La Gorda*, put them in the responsible hands of Alonso de Vallejo, and said, "Goodbye, Mr. Governor."

Colón parroted, "Goodbye, Mr. Governor," then grabbed my neck and held it for a split second longer than advised. One of my men yanked his chains and threw him bodily onto the ship. The sails went up in a grand display, the wind caught them nice and full, and

I gave a final wave. Then I grabbed Maria's hand and said, "I can do it. I'm ready." As we walked hand in hand back to the café, I felt my chivalry pouring back into my bloodstream as Maria suggested that I ask the King to pardon Colón. He was addicted to gold and immortality, and that shouldn't be held against him, she insisted. And as I tripped on the body of a Colón sympathizer and fell flat on my face, I agreed.

Columbus arrived in Seville in chains. He was greeted with the popular Spanish cheer, "The chains in Spain fall mainly on the swain!" He was humiliated, and then some. The future seemed dark, dreary, even apocalyptic.

While chained in a dungeon, Columbus wrote a long letter to the King and Queen, which has come to be known as the *Book of Prophecy*. It set forth Columbus's mystical visions and the religious motives behind his voyages.

When you spend months alone in a dungeon, you start talking to yourself. So I figured it was a good time for a second-person narrative, something perfected by Jay McInerny in his claustrophobic look at a young cocaine addict in New York City, *Bright Lights, Big City.*

MIGHTY SLIGHTS, TINY DUNGEON

à la Jay McInerny's *Bright Lights, Big City*

You are not the kind of guy who should be in chains like this at this point in your life. God has walked out on you. He called you after they put you in chains and said He was through with you. Well, you've heard that line before. He'll be begging you to come back before you know it.

What did you do to deserve this sort of rejection? You do the dishes and you say your daily offices. Could God be angry that you say them Eastern Standard Time?

Is it your pride? You remember the way you put on the uniform of an admiral, even though you were nothing but a common sailor and a not very experienced one at that. You remember all those wonderful feasts you ate at all those marvelous palaces. The rare vintages you indulged yourself with. The women, the song.

But you assumed the itchy Franciscan habit a whole voyage ago. You stay only at little cells in religious houses. And you sleep on the floor or on deck. Repentance and humility, eczema and arthritis. What more can the Lord ask of you? Didn't He get enough kicks out of Job?

Once upon a time your mission in life was to obtain wealth and glory for yourself. But things have changed. Now your mission is that of St. Augustine: to wipe out all the gods of the peoples of this earth for the glory of the One and Only. Your mission is that predicted by Joachim of Fiore: to finance the recovery of Mount Zion, to recapture the Holy Sepulcher from the infidels, to hold bullfights where the First Temple once stood. And your mission is that of Seneca, too: to find the key to open the chains of things and reveal a new heaven and a new earth. Of course, the first chains you'd open are the ones they have you in right now. By San Fernando, what you would do for a stroll!

You feel yourself falling asleep at last, but when you near the point of no return, you're suddenly wide awake. You are shaking with a feverish need to have another rush, to light the fire within you. You turn around suddenly when you feel a sense of mortality creeping up behind you. But it's only a rat. You open your Bible to do some lines, but it isn't enough to make mortality (or the rat) go back where it came from. You do more lines until you find yourself standing at the base of Mount Zion. Only it's in the Other World. All the prophets are lined up to welcome you to your interview. But you realize that your soul is as disheveled as your clothing, and it itches even more.

You have always wanted to be a prophet. You see

yourself as the kind of guy who'd make a great prophet. Why, you're even going blind. And your rants get raves. But you haven't prepared for your interview. What kind of impression are you going to make? You turn and start walking away. You don't even wave. You take a nice long stroll through Seville and then go back to your dungeon, where you wake up and you're just as sleepy as ever.

You are at an imperceptible pivot in your life, but you perceive it. You are crossing a line that is harder to see than the equator, but you have no problem finding it. Either you will die in chains, humiliated, forgotten, and poor, or you will rise like a phoenix and lead Christendom to its redemption. You will be a divine instrument once more and by divine right you will divine the way to make yourself divine in the eyes of all the heathens on earth. Otherwise, the Portuguese will take over the whole hemisphere and use it as little more than a string of ports from which to catch cod. And then they'll most likely salt away all the treasures they find and let Christendom go to the Moors.

You can handle death. You can handle failure. You can even deal with ridicule and insult and ingratitude, which is all you ever get for your troubles, for there is no justice in this world. But you cannot live without God, without that special relationship you have as the instrument of His redemption of Christendom before the Apocalypse comes in 1650, assuming you didn't make any mistakes in your long division.

Without God by your side, you are prey to mere human beings. You hear one of them outside, humming some minstrel song. A small voice inside you (is it your best self or your worst self?) says, *They're out to get you.*

Another small voice (is it your worst self or your best self?) answers, *Let 'em*. You throw up your hands; at least you would if they were free.

When the door to your cell opens, you don't bother to turn around. But out of habit, you say, "Who is it?"

"The Unholy Inquisition. We're soliciting donations to buy firewood to burn all the people in Spain who do not worship the Devil."

You're not sure how you feel about the Devil. While you would welcome anyone's company, the Devil might be too much of a bad thing. His brand of comfort is hardly southern. Nonetheless, since you haven't seen a soul in weeks, you're even happy to see someone without one.

The Devil offers a cloven hoof to you and you apologize for not being able to shake it.

"Let's party!" he says.

"I really can't now," you say, shaking your head.

"I can get you out of those chains in two shakes of my tail," he assures you. "All you have to do is give me your worthless soul. I mean, what good is it doing *here*?"

"Not much. But it's all I've got."

"Not a single year, a month, even a day for old Beelzebub?"

"Sorry, Bub."

"Not even a prophecy I can burst?"

"You seem to be doing a good job as it is."

"No, *this* is all God's work. His motto is, 'Anything you can do, I can do better.' And He's almost as good as His Word. But I can assure you things will go better if you put your faith in me. You'll get the sympathy vote for all the ingratitude and humiliation you've suffered. Every woman will take one look at you and comfort you in her bosom. And if she doesn't do it willingly, I'll make her. Not a bad deal, huh?"

"I've had better. Like getting a percentage of everything I found in the Other World, and getting to be governor of it as well."

"I'm disappointed in you. You've worked your ass off all your life, and what for? To be treated by your sovereigns as if you'd handed the Other World over to the Moors? To be the instrument of a Guy who can take you or leave you? Hell, you could be the instrument of a hundred women who would take you places you still haven't discovered."

"Have you ever experienced this nearly overwhelming urge for a quiet year chained in a dungeon?"

"No. Hell is payment enough for me, thank you." The Devil reflects for a moment. "Wouldn't you like to take a nice stroll, breathe some fresh air, eat a real meal? Just a day of your soul would do *my* soul good. And God wouldn't even notice."

You think about it. What you'd really like is to throw this whole mess in the face of your Sovereigns. You've written them a long letter telling them who you are and what sort of relationship you have with God. You want to see if they've read it, if they care any more about you than God does. 'Cause if they don't, if they've taken away everything you've earned, then the Devil's offer might not look quite so bad. You're not so old that you can't start a new life and have some fun for a change.

You stare at Beelzebub for a minute or two, watching the way he shifts from one hoof to the other, the way his shifty eyes never meet yours for more than an instant. What you want to say is: you'll accept his one-day-only special offer. As the Devil says, there are lots of discoveries to be made right here in Spain. But you'd have to learn everything all over again, and you know you can't teach an old seadog to turn new tricks. So you refuse his offer.

"May God take you," you find yourself saying to the Devil in farewell. But he doesn't take your words as they were intended. In fact, he kicks you when you're down. Join the club.

After several months, King Ferdinand and Queen Isabella finally granted Columbus a pardon and asked him to come see them in Granada as soon as he was released from his dungeon.

Getting out of prison is a hard thing for American writers to describe. Few of them have ever been to prison for anything more serious than aggravated pornography, and then they are beloved martyrs to their fans, so the experience pays off in royalties. No one has gotten into the head of a freed criminal as well as Norman Mailer did in *The Executioner's Song,* his story of Gary Gilmore. Mailer created an incredibly chilling novel by taking the minimalist sentence to its maximum extreme.

THE EXECUTIONER'S PROSE

à la Norman Mailer's *The Executioner's Song*

The dungeon was dark, dreary, full of rats. The chains were a drag, too. Or were they? He was thinking that they were sort of a wedding ring. And as a devout Catholic, that meant a life sentence.

The word came from Granada. He was free. But he had to go to Granada. To see the King and Queen and thank them for their mercy. Shit! It took them long enough.

He walked slowly away from the monastery. "I'm really out," he said.

Around the corner, he tried to pick up a girl. Just came right out and asked her for it. He said, "It's been a long time and I'd like some right now!" It didn't work.

Two blocks later, he met another one. Her name was

Isabella. Just like the Queen. A real princess. It worked on her.

Isabella's father was a drunk. And a cripple. And had punched out three wives till they couldn't take it anymore. Her mother was the second wife, the one who took it the longest. And gave it back pretty well, Isabella liked to remember. Isabella had two sisters, three half-sisters, and a smattering of brothers. Half the smattering had been shot and the other half had ended up in prison for shooting someone. Sometimes a brother. The sisters traded boyfriends and husbands like sugar. Eventually, each man sifted through their collective fingers and went down the drain.

What attracted Isabella to Chris was the white of his hair, the blue of his eyes, the gold of his jewelry, and the way he fucked. She'd never come that many times before. They must be spiritually tied. Like Mary Magdalene and Jesus.

Chris thought he was Jesus. And Isabella was Mary Magdalene. A tempting chick. He would spread his Gospel to the heathens of the Other World. Make way for the Apocalypse!

"Let's get the hell out of here," he would say after they had stopped for an hour on the road to Granada. He didn't have much patience once they were done fucking. It wasn't long before he was getting on Isabella's nerves. They all did after a while. Men's karma was bad news.

He walked slowly away from the rest stop. "I'm really out," he said.

Boy, did Chris dress badly. Like a monk. Hairshirts hadn't been in for centuries.

And he kept mumbling. Like Dad. How he'd get so-and-so good. How he needed gold. Gold, gold, and more gold.

"Why don't you spend your gold on me?" she asked.

"It's for a crusade," he answered.

"Couldn't *this* be a crusade?" she asked. "If I didn't flip out once or twice a week, I'd have wanted to be a crusader more'n anything."

"You don't understand," he said.

Man, was she pretty. Her skin was nearly as smooth as his chains. And warmer.

Chris carried his chains in a bag. He would never part from them. His will directed that they be buried with him.

"I don't like all that clanging, Chris," Isabella said. "Can't you dump the trash? Let go, Chris. You're out. Really."

"They're not trash and I'm not dumping them," Chris replied.

Chris frightened her sometimes. In fact, often. She didn't know what it was that frightened her so much. Perhaps it was the fact that he was the spitting image of her father. Or that since the day she saw her first leper, she had always associated lepers with mumbling. And chains.

Sometimes he was okay. But only sometimes. They were all okay sometimes. Especially at first. And then the times grew fewer and fewer until they were only okay after they beat you. Chris hadn't beaten her yet. She wished he'd start and get it over with quick.

The next time they argued, she said everything she could to set him off.

"What are those chains for, if not to beat my ass?" she finally said after everything else had failed. "I think you are the most insensitive human being I've ever known."

"I'm not insensitive," said Chris, "to being called insensitive."

Chris was so pissed with her, he wouldn't oblige. Anyway, the chains were special. They meant something. Her ass was only something warm to squeeze.

They were almost at Granada and they stopped at an inn for a drink. Chris put his chains down on a table and went to the bathroom. When he came out, a guy was playing with his chains, and another was playing with Isabella. Chris kicked the guy with the chains, and they were throwing fists before you could stop it.

Maybe Chris was too tired from walking and fucking, but the guy split his eye with the first punch. The guy split his lip with the second punch. And he would've split his hairs with the third if Isabella hadn't got between them in time.

She hated to see her man have his ass whipped, even if he had thrown a blind kick to start things off. He was a cheater and a bully and obsessed with his chains and he frightened her and sometimes he was impotent and he smelled and he mumbled and he farted and he thought he was the Father, the Son, and the Holy Ghost all rolled up in one. But she loved him just the same. She couldn't help herself.

"The son of a bitch," Chris said to Isabella outside. "I'm Cristóbal Colón, and they can't hurt me."

"*I* can hurt you, he-man," she answered.

"Try me."

She kicked him in the balls. Right on target, as always. When he was done hopping around the inn a few times, he stopped and said, "You fight as good as you fuck."

A voice in her head kept sounding like an echo in a tunnel. It said, "I love him. I love him." But he didn't hit her once.

When they reached the gate that led into the fortress of Granada, Chris said goodbye. Like they'd see each other tomorrow at school.

Isabella said, "I'm going with you, all the way."

"We've gone all the way enough. I've gotta get a job."

"Who's gonna take care of you and your house?"

"No one takes care of Cristóbal Colón. And I don't live in no house. Just a ship."

"You're a sailor then," she said, excited.

He walked slowly away from Isabella. "You don't understand," he said.

The gatekeeper was on break. He was probably off drinking, just like his father used to do back in Genoa when he kept the Olivella Gate. A crowd was forming.

Chris grabbed a couple of bars with his bare hands and bent them good. Everyone squeezed through the gate. Except Isabella. She was walking back toward Seville with another tall, good-looking sailor. Only this one's hair was brown. And so were his eyes.

Although no one had a whole lot of respect for Columbus anymore (just like now), he did have a royal contract and he still had a few friends in high places. So he was given one last chance, one last voyage, his Fourth. The one thing he was told to do was to steer clear of Santo Domingo, where Bobadilla was still governor and didn't like competition. Of course, Columbus headed straight for Santo Domingo.

There is little doubt that if John McPhee had been alive at the turn of the sixteenth century, he would have done a book on Christopher Columbus. Columbus was both sufficiently exciting and sufficiently obscure to merit Mr. *New Yorker*'s attention. Here is a capsule version based on McPhee's recent maritime book.

Looking at an Admiral

à la John McPhee's *Looking for a Ship*

The Admiral was concerned. The last time he had returned from the Other World he was in chains. Now, as he stood looking at the four caravels that would take him on his fourth voyage across the Ocean Sea—the *Capitana*, the *Gallega*, the *Bermuda*, and the *Vizcaina*—he wondered whether he would return at all.

"It's not an easy business," he told me the day we first met, when I was doing a book on blacksmiths and he was getting his chains refitted. "One day, the world is yours—literally—and the next, your family's nothing but a chain gang."

Being a ship's captain is a profession as old as the Flood and just as messy and dangerous. Noah had to clean out the animals' stalls, since his wife was too squeamish and insisted her children were above that sort of work. Jason may have captured the Golden

Fleece, but he ended his life, many years later, crushed by the prow of his ship. Ahab spent eternity trailing Moby Dick at the end of a harpoon. And Kennedy was shot.

It's hard enough to be a captain; it's all but impossible to become an admiral. You have to put in a lot of years, sail vast expanses of water, manage thousands of the toughest men ever born, and kiss a lot of fish. There are ninety-five captains vying for each position. And they say four hundred and seventy-nine captains and admirals—85% of the admirals employed by European ships—applied to be Admiral of the Ocean Sea. The requirements for the job included: 34,000 man-hours at sea, with at least 20,000 of them as captain or admiral and 5,000 of those lost, shipwrecked, or pirating; membership in the International Admirals Union and at least fifteen of its locals; or the overwhelming admiration of Queen Isabella.

What sort of a person was the man that got the position in the end? What were the forces that molded Christopher Columbus into a great mariner?

"He's a mariner's mariner," said Frank de Bobadilla, governor of Santo Domingo until he ignored Columbus's warning and died sailing straight into a hurricane. "But he wasn't much of a governor. That's why they won't let him on dry land anymore. He's strictly a man of the sea."

Christopher Columbus was born in the Olivella district of Genoa. His father, Domenico, wove wool and warded gates. In the Admiral's youth, Genoa was the leading sea power in the world. Then Venice moved ahead, and the Admiral moved out. He moved to Portugal and the Portuguese island of Porto Santo. His ships traveled south along the coast of Africa and north as far as Iceland. While the other men were drinking, the Admiral was studying maps and reading books by such writers as Aristotle, Ptolemy, and John of Hollywood. At every port he went out of his way to ask sailors, young and old, what lands their ships may have happened upon during storms, what stories they'd heard from others, and whether they had a spare cigar. He not only sailed, but drew maps and became involved in the financial aspects of the industry. Today, the capital city of the state of Ohio is named after him, and nearly one percent of the boys born there are given his Christian name.

The Admiral runs a happy ship. But he has not won his hands over with fraternization. Except, of course, his brothers. He knows what a magisterial distance is (although most of his sailors do not), and he knows how to keep it (and the sailors are happy to let him).

"He's wrung more seawater out of his boots than I'll ever sail across," his brother Diego says of the Admiral, awarding him the status of a marine cliché.

The Admiral's face—bearded and nearly lacking in features—appears to have been the site of an epic battle. It is the only one the Admiral ever lost. As he moves back and forth on the bridge, he takes in the heavens with the empty gaze of a dreamer. His mind is taut, like a slip-knot. His body is chunky, like a candy bar. His character is immaculate, like a pair of newly-bought jeans.

A young, future Admiral of the Ocean Sea watches his every move with wonder. "Da Gama is nothing compared with the Admiral, sir," he tells me over rum, a few too many perhaps. "And Vespucci is strictly bush league. This fellow's the real thing, sir."

I ask the boy, a young Englishman named Horatio Raleigh, what he thinks they will find on this voyage. He answers quickly, as if no one could be in doubt, "A great deal of gold, sir. And women better looking than the horses back home. If you'll excuse my implications, sir."

I ask him about the discovery of new lands, and he tells me they've all been discovered already, although he expects they'll fill in a few holes on the maps. But land is not "his thing."

"Booty is what all of us are looking for, sir," he says. "Pearls and gold are all that matter."

Gold was first discovered by Eve. The traditional myth is that Eve gave Adam a forbidden apple to eat, but a recent excavation (which I attended as research for my next book, on the daily life of Middle Eastern archaeologists) has unearthed evidence that it was actually a gold ring, which Eve had made with help from Hephaistos. When Adam put the ring on his finger, which he named "ring finger," he was suddenly married. Eve was soon dressed, Paradise lost, and gold forever dangerous. Almost as dangerous as captaining a ship.

Frank had told me that the Admiral was not a landworthy man, but I wanted to see for myself. So after we returned from the Admiral's fourth voyage, I visited the great mariner at the court in Segovia. The mourning period for Queen Isabella had just ended, and now the Admiral was able to bullfight again.

"I love nothing more than I hate bullfighting," he

tells me as he skips out of the way of a rather senile bull. "I just can't wait to get back across the Ocean Sea. It'll be my Fifth Voyage, you know."

Acting as his own picador, the Admiral makes his first lunge with his pic. He wears the bull down slowly, carefully. His movements are straight and pure and natural in line. Even the bull is impressed. But it is not enough to satisfy the Admiral.

"I hate it," he tells me across the *barrera*. "I hate it with a passion. I hate it in spades, and hearts and diamonds as well. I hate it because I can't do it better. It's worse than being in chains. It *is* being in chains. On land all I can do is fight bulls. And I'm not even Spanish."

He handles the next bull just as skillfully. And the next. It was sad to see a king over men at sea acting as nothing more than a king over cattle on land. But not nearly as sad as seeing him skewered by the bull's horns when he turned to speak with me. That was almost tragic.

There's more than one way to unlock the secrets of Columbus's craft. In the following parody of George F. Will's bestselling ideologico-statistical look at baseball, exploration is the lock, the no-longer-Protestant work-ethic is the key, and Columbus is the manager.

MAN AT WORK: THE CRAFT OF EXPLORATION

à la George F. Will's
Men at Work: The Craft of Baseball

There is a sign on his cabin door: "Man at Work." That says it all. Christopher Columbus epitomizes the work-ethic.

People like to say that great explorers are "naturals," that they have a "good sense of direction" or "sea legs." They especially like to say it about Italians, but that isn't the case. This myth is false and pernicious. Italians get lost as much as the next guy or gal.

Exploration has become a realm of upward mobility for Italians. It's hard to believe now, but they used to say the same things about Phoenicians, too, who back in the early days of exploration were considered "naturally swift." Homer certainly had some choice epithets for them!

The fundamental fact is this: For an explorer to fulfill his or her potential, a remarkable degree of mental and moral discipline is required. And Columbus has it all.

Columbus was just a boy when he first shipped out of Genoa. His penchant for power and mutiny occasioned frequent references to his "instinctive" mastery, his "natural inclination" toward taking charge. The truth is that Columbus was, from the first, a superb craftsman.

Vasco da Gama, the first explorer to find the real sea route to the Indies, which he did in what many consider the greatest month any explorer has ever had—May 1498—calls Columbus the "complete" explorer and illustrates his point with this detail. As a rookie explorer, whenever he came on virgin territory, Columbus would practice planting the flag of whatever country was picking up the tab. It was not enough for him to do it in Spain or Portugal or even Africa. If his ship came upon a little seagull island, Columbus would take his flag, hop into the dinghy, and row out to it. Once there, he would carve a hole in the rock, he would plant his flag, and then he would kill a few seagulls to show who was boss. He got into his famous, Odysseian shape by rowing back to his ship, which rarely waited.

That is how Columbus got his career statistics. The first few weeks, he had the worst slump of seasickness on record, but the royal family didn't send him down and Columbus came through for them. On his First Voyage alone, he broke hundreds of records, including most islands discovered in a single voyage, most localities named after members of the royal family, most natives massacred in a single day, and most serious disease brought back to Europe (syphilis).

Exploration is a game of failure. Even the best explorers fail about 65% of the time. It is a humbling experience.

Take Columbus for example. He never has discovered the Indies. In fact, he keeps missing the South American continent, one time riding right by it in a heavy fog.

And he has never got close to North America. Yet he is great.

He is great not only in what he does each voyage, but in the fact that he has kept doing it voyage after voyage. It hasn't been easy. Nothing has come easy to Columbus, just as nothing comes easy in life. I wasn't born with the vocabulary I use in my columns, you know. I had to read each and every one of those *Word Power* books several times over, again and again, *ad nauseum*, to be able to toot all the notes on my horn. And I had to learn to tie a bow-tie, too.

Exploration ought to be fun. "After all," Columbus likes to say, "when you plant a flag, you say, 'I hereby declare this land to be *mine*,' not *yours*." (Actually, the rulebook says an explorer is only required to say the word *Mine!*)

Columbus certainly knows how to have fun. Nothing makes him happier than a long discussion with his mates about the fundamental details of exploration. His first mate said it best: "In exploration, you take nothing for granted. You look after all the little details or suddenly the whole thing will kick you right in the butt. If the skipper doesn't do it first, that is."

BARTHOLOMEW: "What do you think of the Caribs this voyage, Chris? Think they have a chance?"

COLUMBUS: "Never count anyone out, Bart. Remember: we're still an expansion club. We may be on top of the New World today, but we could find ourselves in the cellar if we don't work our rear ends off."

DE LA COSA: "I've been looking my charts over, Chris, and I think that if we go after them high and tight, they'll get so angry they'll make a mistake. Their tendency is high spirits, those Caribs. Wired tight. All we have to do is pounce on their first mistake."

COLUMBUS: "What about the Tainos? They're more powerful than they look."

DE LA COSA: "They have gap power, Chris. Their tendency is to go for the other club's weaknesses. My charts say that their chief tends to be streaky. Unfortunately, we tend to get him when he's hot."

DE HARANA: "I think we know most of their weaknesses, Chris. We just have to concentrate and work on fundamentals like threading the needle through a coral reef in the dark of night. But what do we do about that new tribe from Cuba? We don't even know if they *have* tendencies, not to mention what they might be. We don't even know if they play by the rules!"

COLUMBUS: "We'll shove the rules down their throat, Diego. And don't worry your little head off; they'll have tendencies alright. We all do, even me."

Exploration is a special sort of organization, not a democracy, autocracy, plutocracy, or mickyocracy, but a "palocracy," or government by old pals. Not like work or politics or families or anything. No, it consists of people who have, for decades, from the rocky days of piracy and the spartan ships of war, intersected, entwined, and occasionally exchanged wives. If you're not one of them, they say you're not an "exploratory person." If you're one of them, there's nothing left to say. That's why so many are strong and silent types.

What makes exploration great is the connection between character and achievement. Columbus is a saint of a man. He never swears, he never drinks, he honors his father and his mother, and he covets nothing but other explorers' discoveries. That is why his club has led the league each voyage. He is to exploration what Chaucer is to literature, what da Vinci is to the arts and sciences, what van Keilerjagen is to hunting boars. And his tendency is to have fun. Like the proverbial good girl, Columbus has truly shown us how far we can go and still have a good time.

Before you think there's no more story left, let us follow Columbus into his tottering days with parodies of two of our greatest novelists, Saul Bellow and John Updike.

The fourth voyage has just ended and Columbus is dining with his nephew. God knows whether Columbus had a nephew or not, but for the sake of fitting into Saul Bellow's *More Die of Heartbreak*, I decided to create one. Like Bellow's, this nephew is torn between admiring love and a need to quibble and deflate. As a parodist of this Nobel Prize-winning author, I feel much the same way as the nephew.

FEW DIE OF HEARTBURN

à la Saul Bellow's *More Die of Heartbreak*

Last year while I was out to dinner with my Uncle Cris (C. Colón, the well-known explorer) he passed through a crisis in his life. Ours was a relationship consisting of heavyweight conversations, in which with confused speculations we touched upon the complexities of existence in a tone of high-level seriousness punctuated by passages of poetry and methane. Cris had recently been commandeered by a new woman only weeks after returning from his fourth voyage to the Other World. He was always traveling, rushing across the ocean as if a husband were pursuing him for his crimes. Yet there were no crimes, at least not against husbands, at least not in Spain.

I have to tell you up front that Cris is built like a Gothic cathedral, complete with gargoyles. Like his soul, his body reaches for the heavens, but like both feet when he visits nuns in their rooms, it still must touch the ground. Although taken for nothing but another *meshugah* explorer, he is a person of magics who has left humdrum humanity behind. While our species continues to fall deeper into its fallen state, Cris keeps discovering fresh modes of experience, new kicks. Dante wrote that without hope we live in desire, and Uncle, who has the highest hopes of any washed-up man I know, proves the converse: that those who do not live in desire have hope. Although he has appealed greatly to women of all classes, ages, and races, he has never known what to do when their interest takes a literal, physical form. However, he simply cannot bear to let a woman down. Whenever our talk maneuvers its way from exploration to sex, and I have finished with my clever similes of the two, he quotes to me the words of Thomas Aquinas: "Three things are necessary for the salvation of man: to know what he ought to believe; to know what he ought to desire; and to know what he ought to do."

Of all the Italian greenhorns in Spain, only Uncle Cris discovered the Other World. He is a man like no other since the Heroic Age, yet he is far from satisfied with his victories or himself. With François Villon, he likes to complain, "Had I but studied in the days of my foolish youth!" But then he would have been a monk or a priest, and he would never have gone anywhere or done anything, to speak of, with anyone.

He is also unhappy with how the world has proceeded. "That is where I was born," he said to me, pointing out the window at the streets of Cordova. "On the wrong side of the river. And now look at it. It's another goddamn palace."

"But you were born in Genoa, where a palace hasn't gone up in fifty years."

"Fifty years ago I was a baby. Had I but studied in the days of my foolish youth!"

"But they didn't have the right maps to study. They didn't have the slightest idea what was across the Ocean Sea, or whether you'd fall off the earth for that matter."

"That's what was so exciting. I remember the day during my First Voyage when my boys couldn't take the suspense anymore. We'd been blown off course a bit and things were taking longer than I had calculated. Calculations weren't easy in those days; it was enough to have some idea where you were headed."

"Have you ever really known where you were headed?" I asked, carefully examining the lines on his forehead as if they were the entrails of an eagle. He was a child of a singular bent, a prodigy who required special care. He had a singular ability to wield power, to raise funds, to take take take. However, he understood nothing outside his field, especially himself.

"I have been a tool of Providence, just as Spain has been. Spain was ready, I was ready, and off we went."

"Spain was ready? At first, most of your capital came from Italians, all your education came from the Portuguese, and you were just about to sell out to the French when Isabella's fickle interest in you suddenly metamorphosed into support."

"Yes, Isabella played me a fool. If I had read Chaucer more closely, I would have known her for what she was and I would have known exactly what she wanted. It wasn't gold, it wasn't Glory, it wasn't even the fireside. Unfortunately, I still haven't read Chaucer closely, so I don't know what it was."

On balance, reviewing all the facts, Uncle is a sex-abused man. He is strong, but hardly silent, and women have always taken advantage of his babbling. It is Samson's hair, Quixote's books, the thirst of anyone who dined with the Borgias. To a woman, his largeness of appetite for food, power, wealth, and luck seems to include an unslakeable appetite for physical intimacy. His ability to take the initiative and have everything he wants makes women think he has foreordained and guided their advances. But he hasn't. Amid talk of the ways to discipline sailors, the ways to sift gold and determine its quality, the ways to get to heaven and yet be immortal on earth as well, what women from the Queen down to the daughter of a slave are slaking is not Uncle's appetite. It is something higher, something greater, something post-physical. It could even be said that it is the black hole of Uncle's death drawing them into the mythology of the life it soon will end.

"Chaucer would have been of no value to you," I insisted, "although he did say, 'Love is blynd.' To be loved by you is a privilege, and it's a weak queen who accepts a privilege from anyone but her king. You had to get her beyond that point."

It never dawned on Cris that Queen Isabella even had a point. To him she was just soft curves with a shrill voice that cursed servants and barbarians alike. That is why Uncle needs me to protect him. To him the world is just soft curves that require him to smooth them out. What he doesn't realize is that the world likes its softness and its curves. Fortunately, the world doesn't realize this either and, therefore, praises those who flatten it. Ironic for the man who proved it round.

"The point is that I am bunking down with a new woman. She may not be everything, but I've had that before. This one recalls the words of that wonderfully blasphemous John Wycliffe: 'by hook or by crook.' None of her words are capitalized, none of her statements have been deliberated, and all of her hypotheses are fresh."

I can't bear to have this kind of stuff laid on me. I wanted to force the truth down his throat, to push his head against a mirror so he would see himself for what he is: an aged explorer built like a Gothic cathedral who has been everywhere and done everything with everyone and is abused and manipulated by women who are fascinated by this explorer's age, build, and history. How can I protect a man who is open season, who cannot keep his mouth shut even while he eats or, presumably, during sex as well? What can I give him? What can he give me? Something's got to give.

I looked down from my thoughts and realized what it was: Uncle Cris had eaten so much and talked so much between bites that his nether parts looked like a great goat skin overflowing with wine. He started to belch at an awful volume and frequency (which is what made me look down from my thoughts). As his self-appointed protector, it was my duty to relieve him of his pain as well as to end the embarrassment he must have felt. So I asked the waiter for a skewer, and I let more hot air out of the old explorer's tummy than the King's bellows could ever vent.

The crisis was past. We could now go home to a troubled sleep.

In his last months, Columbus showed the same sort of perseverance he had shown in his years in Portugal and Spain, before his wild scheme became a venture worthy of others' capital. His principal interest was his suit to ensure his sons' inheritance both of his royal titles and of his title to royalties.

John Updike recently took Rabbit Angstrom into his waning years in *Rabbit at Rest*. Fortunately, Updike's skills are not waning, so his prose is as parody-worthy as ever. However, Updike happens to be an accomplished parodist himself, so I have taken special care in mocking this mockingbird.

SEADOG AT REST

à la John Updike's *Rabbit at Rest*

Standing amid the resplendent courtiers at the palace, Seadog Colón has a funny sudden feeling that what he has come to meet, what's floating in unseen about to dock, is not his son Ferdinand and daughter-in-law Maria but something more ominous and intimately his: his own death, shaped vaguely like a ship or, more precisely, like a dinghy.

It has been a year already that Seadog's been on dry land. Creaking louder than the boards of a ship caught on a reef, his bones groan out more regularly than the chimes of a grandfather clock. When his bones keep interrupting King Ferdinand holding court—poor old Ferd, alone without his Isabella—Seadog steps outside into the square.

Isabella is the same age as Seadog. Or was. Recalling to mind that night in the boathouse by the river, the fire roaring, the aides keeping Old King Ferd occupied with tales of golden palaces on the islands across the Ocean

Sea, Ferd not knowing what the hell was coming off, Chris—his outer name; only *he* still called himself Seadog, his inner name—watches a young mother spanking her daughter, probably for doing something she old-fashionedly thinks is naughty but which now, in this age of exploration, raises no more than one eyebrow in three. Isabella is dead now. Although she was on her deathbed when Seadog arrived home from his Fourth Voyage, Old King Ferd would not let her give him an audience. God knows what old Ferd told her about the latest voyage. Probably painted him as a pirate robbing priests, raping nuns, and letting others' slaves go free. This same man who stood, sat, lay, and even fucked in pain. The pain of nearing death, coming in like the ship carrying one's own illegitimate son and his luscious young wife, whom Seadog can recall undressing for her bath one evening: layer after layer, her skin like milk poured slowly over ivory, until suddenly, with her last layer falling to the floor like a feather worn in the hair of one of the Caribs at court falling off along with his head when he failed to pray to Our Savior, she revealed the only blemish on her form, a strawberry of a blemish just to the left of that soft, mysterious cleft hidden in the midst of a New World forest of down.

A flourish of trumpets. The ship is in the harbor now. Taking into account the slow pace his blindness and arthritis have forced him to take and his lifetime inability to walk across anything that isn't rocking to and fro, Chris decides to get an early start toward the dock. As he walks away from the palace, he turns and looks back at it, thinking that perhaps he'd change to salt and not be forced to play host to his boring prig of a son. It isn't that he dislikes his son Ferdinand; he doesn't think enough of him to harbor so strong an emotion. It's just that seeing his son means tension, tension makes his arthritis act up, and his arthritis makes him impotent. And most of all, he dreads to see the addition of hundreds of grey hairs on his son's head, each of them a testament to his own age and the nearness of death, slowly coming into shore, not rushing, not throwing out lines, in fact trading with the rowboats full of vendors of Santo Domingan sugar, Juanan cinnamon, and Isabelan children, but clear as the fact that the world itself is coming to an end, that the Second Coming will come like the ship slowly coming into shore, but with Seadog seated at the helm, and all the women on shore naked as the Tainos and even more interested in sex.

Where is he? Without the slightest knowledge of what he is doing, Chris has walked down an alley and into the middle of a flock of sheep. The bleating reminds him of Beatriz, Ferdinand's mother, when she tried to get him to make her an honest woman. "You seem honest now," he would tell her. "I would buy figs from you, even dates, and never check your weights." What more did the woman want? She had a handsome son, and she had a lover known worldwide in a world he himself had enlarged, and she had a few properties he had given her: a whorehouse, an experimental farm near Barcelona which grew Belgian endives, and a few shops taken from the Jews. Was it his fault the whores had aged, the endives got too little rain, and there was no one left to run the shops? He recalls the way her nipples reached into the sky like little minarets. Who wants an honest woman anyway? And who wants to be in the middle of a flock of bleating sheep? He forces his way out and continues shuffling on toward the dock.

Two hours later, the ship docks just as Seadog completes the last leg of his quarter-mile trek. It doesn't help that he is nearly blind and has trouble breathing. Wheezing, groaning, tapping every building with his walking stick and every woman's breasts with his hands, he arrives safely, soundly, and with a smile on his face.

"I welcome you," he says to a man he thinks is his son, but when he kisses and pinches the woman at the young man's side, the young man draws his sword. "Don't be angry with me," Chris pleads, taking the opportunity to fall to his knees, not to beg, but to rest. "I am just a blind old Admiral of the Ocean Sea, Viceroy and Governor of the Indies, etc., and I know not what I do."

"Well," says the young man, thinking for the first time that here was an old man he would like to grow up to resemble, "you have excellent aim, style, and selection for a man who knows not what he does." And after putting the sword back into its gilded sheath, the young man gives Seadog a hearty smack on his arthritic back and takes him to greet his son.

Maria gives Chris a big hug and kiss, but Ferdinand stands his ground and remembers how, all the way back across the Ocean Sea on the Fourth Voyage, his father swore he couldn't live a month on dry land, but all that litigation has kept him going, all those suits to get everything he could for Diego, the natural son. Not that Ferdinand is envious; no, Ferdinand would take his talents and independence over Diego's fawning ignorance any day. And then there's Maria, the greatest temptation any man could ever hope to resist; only Ferdinand is stalwart enough to resist her. But he can't wait to complete his masterpiece of a biography and make his father into the greatest mythical figure since Iago.

Seadog looks his son over. Nearly six-feet tall, long greying auburn hair, a noble nose, a mischievous mouth, a sizeable bulge under his tights—just like he was at that age. But his son is useless. He has no colonies, plantations, or ships to rule, and he doesn't even enjoy ruling it over his delightful Maria. He is satisfied with himself alone. Shaking back his hair, looking down his nose, giving his bulge a tug, Ferdinand seems more sanctimonious than ever, and he looks at his father with eyes that seem blanker than the pale blue sky this gorgeous summer Mediterranean day. How does his son see his father? As a great success that, no matter how heroically he strived, he himself could never bring off? Or as a tired, crippled, blind, dirty old fart of a man who would be better off under a monument in a cathedral somewhere?

Does Maria see the young ram in Seadog, who was everything her husband only seemed to be? Does she long to see if the old dog still has it in him? He acts as though he has forgotten her greeting, takes her up in his arms again and kisses her with the apparently befuddled passion of an old ram long gone to pasture. Is her response a matter of sympathy, or lust? Whatever it is, it isn't bad, but it sets his arthritis to work compensating for any pleasure he dares feel, and the arthritis sets his mind to work recalling that it was not his son and his daughter-in-law he actually lumbered all the way down to the dock to meet, but rather his death, shaped vaguely like a ship, like the caravels he led across the Ocean Sea and back, even like the canoe to which the

Taino girl Maria's kiss reminds him of took him that first night on San Salvador. And without the slightest hint of sympathy at all.

How-to books have existed for a long time. Soon after Columbus died, Niccolò Machiavelli wrote a how-to book for despots, so you can imagine how much was being written for larger audiences.

The most popular how-to book the last few years has been Charles J. Givens' *Wealth Without Risk*, a title akin to *Victory Without War* or *Birth Without Sex*. Of course, there *is* wealth without risk—via inheritance and, to a lesser extent, marriage—but that isn't what Givens is talking about. Actually, his book is pretty dry, full of things like esoteric tax loopholes, but his introduction is representative of the new econo-inspirational literature that has taken the U.S. by storm. I just couldn't help parodying it by applying its style and vision to Columbus's greatest skill: discovery.

Discovery Without Risk

à la Charles J. Givens'
Wealth Without Risk

Although my father worked as hard as he was able all his life, he died without a discovery to his name. And his name is my name, too. So I didn't start out with a single discovery to build on, or much of a name either. In a great, expanding, monarchical country like Spain, I thought at the funeral, this is unpardonable and I hoped he would burn in hell for thousands of millenia. I swore an oath to myself, and to God as well, that this would never ever happen to *my* son. I would discover something really really big, so my sons' only problem would be living *up* to their name.

After all, my friend, there's no downside to discovering, say, an entire hemisphere. There are winners and there are winners. Only elsewhere are there losers, those people who complained that the lands were already inhabited and that discovery would spread diseases and destroy the ecosystem. Loser is such an ugly word. It is not what you want to be, my friend, no sir.

To be a winner all you have to do is follow my simple strategies. There are a lot of routes to a lot of places, but I can provide you with the x-ray vision necessary to show you where they go and which are best to follow. Discoveries do not behave according to the rules of common sense; you need uncommon sense for that, and my sense is the most uncommon in Christendom.

My strategies are safe, practical, and immaculately conceived, and you don't have to be a nautical wizard to put them to work for you. The sea is not complicated. It's just a body of water, hydrogen and oxygen fused together by a process you don't have to worry your little head about. It has waves, and things float in it, especially ships, unless they run into a coral reef. Do what I say and frustrations and failures will become a thing of the past, at least of *your* past. Just don't worry about your friends' frustration and failure. If they're too cheap to buy my book and follow my strategies, that's their problem.

The first thing to remember is that where you are is where you are. You've got to start somewhere, so don't make any excuses about how far you live from a body of water bigger than a creek. Get off your ass and get ready to go.

The second thing to remember is that there is nothing more important than direction. You can't just go around in circles, my friend. If you have direction, if you have the slightest idea where you want to end up once you get going, then you can turn the power of a paddle into that of a gigantic gust of wind. Start out with ten units of effort for every unit of result and, by means of a eucharistic sort of hocus-pocus I will call "momentum," one unit of effort will give you ten units of result. All you need is my strategies and your dream.

For starters, try an unlimited dream. For example, a forty-year-old woman raced me over on my Third Voyage, and although she didn't end up beating me (due to a tangle with a shark), she did swim all the way across the Ocean Sea. And, on my Fourth Voyage, one of my youngest sailors succeeded in having sex with a thousand women. In a single week! Nothing is impossible if you focus all of your energies on a single goal. All you have to do is break the cycle of working and eating and sticking around with your wife or mistress and go discover what there is to discover. Before it's too late and there's nothing left to discover but the stars, about which I do not have any but astrological advice to share with you. Yet.

The secret is taking control of your destiny. And of everyone's around you. Convince them that your will is their command. Don't take no for an answer, my friend. Realize that Providence is on your side and that your destiny lies on the horizon. Vanquish guilt and justice and all those other silly virtues, and learn to fudge fudge fudge. Remember: what you get is over someone else's dead body. If everyone were to follow his dream to swim across the Ocean Sea, the shark population would grow so quickly you couldn't even wade anymore. A great opportunity to invent the underwater rifle, but not a happy prospect in the meantime.

If a lug like me can make it, so can you, my friend. You don't have to break any laws; you just have to make them. You don't have to kill anyone; you just have to give the appropriate orders. When you have absolute power, when you have others to do all your work, when you have stamped out everyone else's dreams, there is no risk; there is only discovery. I made a lot of mistakes, and I paid for them dearly. But I am near my death and I have a lot of money with the goldsmiths and I will be leaving all my rights in the Other World to my sons. I am a greater man than my father, and you can be greater than yours. All you have to do is believe your father was a bum, believe in God and in yourself, and believe that no one else matters at all.

AFTERLIFE

If the end of Columbus's story had been a quiet burial, there would be no *Columbus à la Mode*, or any of the hundreds of other books and essays about Columbus. But his life had hardly begun when he was buried, and that's probably the way he would have liked it.

I have decided to conclude my ulnography with a parody of a recent book that is one of the most popular, controversial, and bombastic in the long line of books and essays about Columbus. In this parody, Columbus defends himself by responding to the book in the author's style.

Conquest Is Paradise

à la Kirkpatrick Sale's *The Conquest of Paradise*

Kirkpatrick Sale recently wrote a book entitled *The Conquest of Paradise* (Alfred A. Knopf, 1990; Plume, 1991), in which he calls me just about every name in the book. I've been dead for 486 years, and I've kept my mouth shut as a progression of now dead, white males have made me the symbol of what meant most to them and meant little or nothing to me. I've been made an icon or epitome of the spirit of exploration, of the courageous individual overcoming adversity, of the free individual overcoming the tyranny of kings, of progress, of crossing new frontiers, of the good Catholic, of the pride of various nations and ethnic groups. What *I* cared most about was wealth and immortality.

But now I feel I have to take a stand. People all over

the world are infected with a bizarre frenzy of spitting on my tombs and monuments and taking my name in vain. True, this is certainly not all Sale's fault, and Sale's limitations, I hasten to say, are not his alone; they are those of his culture. But if I am to be roasted for being part of my culture, then it's only fair and fitting to put in my two doubloons about him and his.

It is fair to sum up Sale's study by calling it a high-handed accusation that my disputable discovery of the Other World (which I still cannot bear to call . . . well, you know) destroyed the paradisiacal ecosystem and way of life, not to mention the lives of its occupants (who were, by the way, not natives; they just got there first). While no court of law in the United States would convict me on the basis of Sale's evidence, I have to confess that I was a little caught up in the excitement of finding new lands, setting up the first colonies, and looking for gold and pearls. But I was no more excited and no more caught up than Sale himself was in con-demning my posterity, not to mention my posterior. Conquest is paradise, and the conquest of another's paradise is the most paradisiacal of all. What paradise is it that Sale has sought to conquer? Why, the paradise of heroic mythology, of course, and I happen to have been hailed as one of the greatest heroes in history.

Sale's prose fairly throbs with insensitivity to others' feelings, needs, and beliefs. Could it be that people have actually been nourished by the myths and fables he ac-cuses me of having created and by the myths and icons that have been piled upon my grave? Could it be that people need to have heroes who are courageous, adven-turous, virtuous, and brilliant, who go from rags to riches and who come from once-oppressed ethnic groups?

It is not hard for me to suppose that Sale saw clearly that people were living happily in a paradise of myths about me and my associates—such as Jesus, Santa Claus, and the Kennedys—and that it was a paradise ripe for conquest in this most conquistadorial of centuries. Continuing this supposition, it is fitting to argue that once Sale conquered this paradise, exploited and destroyed its major figures, and let the disease of disbelief do the rest, mankind's fablistic ecosystem would be changed beyond all recognition and, most likely, would be replaced with Sale's own icons and role models. As we might expect, the civilization of left intellectuals in the United States would thus be forced upon creatures who are so clearly beyond the pale of God's favor that they could rightfully be regarded as beasts ready to applaud Peter Pan as well as me. And as with all ideologies, including my own Christian beliefs, Sale's special new formula would be sold under the rubric of Truth.

It can fairly be stated that Sale's bosom holds little capacity for empathy with anyone anyone differing with him has admired, just as I felt little empathy with those I considered savages. This is not the author's fault—at least not directly; more likely, it has something to do with his upbringing, but I have a great deal of trouble understanding what Freud says, and he hasn't gotten anywhere psychoanalyzing me for the last fifty years (even God thinks I'm Jewish, so we're stuck in limbo together).

I think it is fair to say, as he says about mine, that Sale's is a civilization that has lost its bearings. But it is fitting to note that Sale himself writes as if not enough bearings have been lost. He'd throw away the compass as a dangerous piece of modern technology, and he'd toss away the North Star as just a bit too twinkly to be real. I, too, was looking for Paradise, and on my Third Voyage I thought I'd found it. But for me Paradise wasn't something real, at least not in the modern sense; it was something man couldn't return to before he had earned a Second Coming by being virtuous according to what we thought were virtues. I looked forward to returning to Paradise and, like Michelangelo's Adam, I reached my finger toward God; Sale looks back at the loss of Paradise and points his finger at me. I suppose I should take this as a compliment.

I was nothing but a greedy, guilt-ridden compulsive liar and megalomaniac who could not bear becoming a bum like my father—or appearing as one to the world—and I translated all my compulsions into discovering a whole new world, a discovery that the twentieth century has done everything it could to deny me. So I did nothing and I am to blame for everything. I was incompetent and yet I destroyed Paradise, enabling others to put up the parking lots. I was, it may be argued, the alpha as well as the omega, and so perhaps it is only fair to warn Sale not to mess with me, because I might very well be the Second Coming Himself and the world I discovered and left to mankind may be Paradise Itself, no matter how distasteful a garden it may seem to mere humans (God never did promise you a rose garden, and anyway, rose gardens have thorns, require a lot of care, and get devoured by Japanese beetles). However, as one would expect, Sale won't believe a word of my warning;

he'll say this is another one of my bizarre psychoses
that lie behind today's neuroses.

In all fairness to himself, though, maybe he'll think
twice before he takes my name in vain again.

HUMOR FROM CATBIRD PRESS

For Lawyers and Other Denizens of the Legal World

Trials and Tribulations: Appealing Legal Humor. Edited by Daniel R. White, author of *The Official Lawyer's Handbook.* A collection of the best in legal humor by humorists such as Twain, Benchley, and Perelman, as well as legal humorists such as Prosser, Arnold, and Mortimer. With lots of cartoons. A great gift. $19.95 cloth, 320 pp.

The Handbook of Law Firm Mismanagement. By Arnold B. Kanter. The misadventures of a mythical law firm, told via its memos and notes of committee meetings. "To the law firm experience what *M*A*S*H* was to the Korean conflict." —*Chicago Bar Assoc. Record.* Our bestseller. $12.95 paper, 192 pp.

For Travelers — Armchair and Otherwise

The Humorists' Guide Series. Edited by Robert Wechsler. Collections of stories, memoirs, descriptions, light verse, and cartoons all about traveling abroad. Thurber, Dickens, Buchwald, Blount, and all the rest. From irony to nonsense and back again, these volumes contain all the absurdities and delights of travel. "A first-rate gift for the traveler-to-be as well as for stay-at-homes." —*New York Times.* Each volume is $10.95 paper, 200 pp.

> In a Fog: The Humorists' Guide to **England**
> Savoir Rire: The Humorists' Guide to **France**
> When in Rome: The Humorists' Guide to **Italy**
> Here We Are: The Humorists' Guide to the **United States**
> All in the Same Boat: The Humorists' Guide to the **Ocean Cruise**

These books can be found or ordered at better bookstores everywhere, or they can be ordered directly from Catbird Press. Just send a check for the appropriate amount, plus $3.00 shipping no matter how many books you order, to Catbird Press, 44 North Sixth Avenue, Highland Park, NJ 08904. For information, call 908-572-0816.